A GARRISON

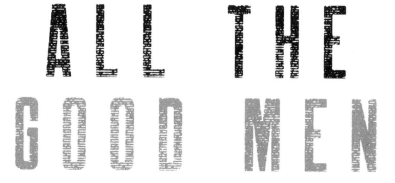

CRAIG N. HOOPER

Copyright © 2020 by Craig N. Hooper

All rights reserved.

ISBN 978-1-7333755-2-8

No part of this book may be reproduced in any form or by any electronic or mechanical means, including information storage and retrieval systems, without written permission from the author, except for the use of brief quotations in a book review.

Website: http://craignhooper.com

Email: craig@craignhooper.com

There are two important things in politics. The first is money, I can't remember the second.

— MARK HANNA

CHAPTER ONE

I SLID A Walther P99 handgun from under the driver's seat and thrust it toward the United States senator sitting to my right. The senator had been sipping a cup of joe from one of DC's finest establishments, Compass Coffee. When he saw the pistol coming at him, he sprayed a mouthful of coffee across the dashboard of the compact rental car.

"What the hell, Chase?" The senator batted the gun away, then wiped his chin with the back of his left hand.

I dangled the gun by his chest. "If you insist on going to this meeting alone, then you should at least take this. I know it's overkill, sir, but I'm super cautious with all my clients."

He huffed, his breath filling the tiny car's interior with a pleasant coffee aroma.

"Please, Senator." I placed the Walther on his lap.

He brushed the gun off his thigh dismissively. Senator Felton Byrd wasn't a stranger to firearms, and he certainly wasn't the scared type. The fact that I was sitting next to him right now and not the cops or feds proved the latter.

"You're paying me a lot, sir. Since you won't let me tag along on this meeting, I'd feel much better if you were carrying. Just as a precautionary measure."

Felton didn't pick up the gun or glance at it. We sat in near silence. The only sound was the car heater pumping hot air in a winless battle against the December cold.

He cleared his throat. "Listen, I appreciate your cautious nature, Chase, but like I said, Morse is going to clear everything up at this meeting and tell me what's going on. It's probably all a big misunderstanding—"

"A misunderstanding? Really, sir? Yesterday we confirmed the threats came from his computer." I jabbed my finger at the condominium complex we were parked in front of. "From the very condo you're about to enter—alone, I might add. If you hadn't told me Morse Cooper owns more guns than socks, that the man's a total gun nut, then I wouldn't be so insistent."

Felton held up both hands, signaling he understood my misgivings. He looked at the Walther for a moment, then out the passenger window.

Approximately a week ago, Felton Byrd received two death threats via email. Threats weren't that out of the ordinary for a prominent US senator like Felton. But these particular threats came from Felton's friend and fellow senator, Morse Cooper. Ironically, Cooper, one of the Wyoming senators, chaired the Senate Select Committee on Ethics, which Felton was also a member of. Morse was supposed to be the ethical gatekeeper for his ninety-nine colleagues.

Washington. Its hypocrisy never ceased to amaze me.

Felton turned toward me and swept up the Walther. "Fine, I'll take it to appease you, but I won't need it." He stuffed the Walther into the right pocket of his black Patagonia jacket.

"I take it you still know how to use that, sir?"

Felton looked away and sighed. His warm breath steamed against the passenger window's cold glass.

"Just checking," I said.

When Felton looked back, my eyes drifted to his nose, which I couldn't help. It was so long and thin I swear you could pick a lock with it. The joke, of course—which social media had a field day with—was that his last name was Byrd and he had a beak.

Felton opened the door and climbed out. A frigid East Coast breeze poured into the car. Being born and raised in Southern California, I never felt prepared enough for the cold. I zipped up my waxed trucker jacket as high as it would go. A beanie would've been appropriate to warm up my bald head, but I was in a rush this morning and left it at the hotel.

Before closing the door, Felton leaned in. "Sorry about the coffee. I'll bring some paper towels from Morse's condo and wipe up when I'm back."

I shook my head. "No need, it's a rental. And the coffee aroma masks the stale cigarette smell."

Felton nodded and pulled back his jacket sleeve to reveal a watch. "This will be a somewhat quick meeting. Morse and I need to be at the Capitol in forty-five minutes, so I'll be back here in twenty, maximum twenty-five. Obviously, we can't be late to this healthcare vote. Probably one of the bigger votes in the Senate's history."

"I'll drive you, of course."

"You can drop me off at my office and I'll take the Senate subway into the Capitol."

I furrowed my brow. "Senate subway? What do you mean? There's a subway just for senators?"

"Sure," Felton replied. "Two lines for the Senate side and one for the House of Representatives."

"You're kidding me, I hope."

Felton looked quizzically at me. "No, been around a hundred years. Ferries us around the heart of Washington."

I shook my head. "I'd rather be ignorant to the perks you guys have."

The senator smiled. "Keep the car warm for me."

As he turned, I called after him, "Be safe, sir."

He waved me off and didn't look back.

I watched Felton Byrd slip into the old building and out of sight. Seeing him wave me off like that got me thinking. Maybe I was being too protective. Felton certainly wasn't concerned about Morse after the two spoke yesterday and agreed to meet today. Drumming my fingers on the wheel, I thought about the threats.

Both emails from Senator Cooper, which came two days apart, were vague. Originally, we assumed Morse's email had been remotely hacked. Just yesterday, however, we verified the emails were sent from his laptop. They warned Felton not to screw up their long and productive relationship. The first email told Felton to drop it or die. The second one said pursue it and perish. Neither email elaborated on what to drop or what not to pursue, though. Apparently, Morse was going to explain everything and clear the air at this meeting.

Settling into the seat, I wondered if Morse had too much scotch those nights—which I'd heard he had a propensity for—and fired off the drunken death threats because Felton opposed him on the recent healthcare bill. Maybe Morse felt terrible about that and was about to apologize. Or perhaps this was a last-minute attempt to persuade Felton to vote with him today.

I rubbed my hands together in an effort to warm up. When Felton hired my buddy Slim's private security firm to investigate the threats he'd received, I finally felt a twinge of excitement for my recent career choice, which was subcontracting some security work for Slim's firm. The firm specialized in investigating members of Congress. When I accepted the Felton job, all I wanted was to uncover some deep-seated Washington corruption. That excitement faded throughout the week, however. Now I feared it would die a quick death if I found out this was all a silly drunken mistake.

Suffice to say, investigating members of the Washington elite had been a snooze fest the past year. Most of my clients were congressional folks who hired me to dig up dirt on themselves. They wanted to know what could be found out about their past so they could get out in front of it during their next re-election campaign.

Not exactly my dream career.

I shut off the rental car and decided to distract myself by getting coffee. I knew if I sat here for the next twenty minutes all I would do was ponder my questionable life choices. So I took two deep breaths and ventured into the cold, heading toward a Compass Coffee shop I knew was three blocks from the condo complex.

The line was five people deep. By the time I got my Americano and walked back, I expected Felton to be standing by the rental.

He wasn't there.

I fired up the rental and cranked the heater. Since I had two keys, I locked the doors and left the car running, then slipped into the condo's lobby to warm up. A rotund security guard sat behind a counter-height desk to the right of the elevators. He looked jovial enough, so I smiled and gave a courteous wave.

"Good day, sir," he said. "How can I help you?"

"Just waiting for a senator," I responded.

"Which one," he said, chuckling. "This complex is a who's-who of congressional delegates."

"Felton Byrd, the senator who came in about twenty minutes ago."

"Right, he's visiting Senator Cooper."

I nodded and turned my attention to the Americano in my right hand; I was never much for chit-chat. After five minutes of waiting and sipping and avoiding the security guard's stare, I pulled out my phone and called Felton to prod the man along.

The call went to voicemail after four rings. Not bothering to leave a message, I flipped the phone shut and walked to the security desk. I stuck out my hand.

"Garrison Chase. Nice to meet you"—I glanced at his nameplate—"Chuck."

"Likewise," the chubby guard said with a genuine smile. The heating vent for the room was directly above the security desk, so strands of the guard's wispy blond hair swirled around and distracted me.

I blinked and cleared my throat. "Listen, Chuck, do you have a way to buzz occupants of the building? Maybe an intercom system in each unit." I looked at my watch. "The senators are pushing it. They have an important vote in about twenty minutes they can't miss. And Senator Byrd isn't answering his cell."

"Sure thing, Mr. Chase." He glanced at his watch. "You're right, they really have to get a move on. I heard the vote's at ten this morning. I'll buzz Senator Cooper's place."

The buzz was louder than expected and reverberated through the small lobby. We waited in silence for a response.

After twenty seconds, the guard tried again.

"Maybe they're on their way down," I said, turning toward the elevator. However, the elevator numbers weren't lighting up on the panel above the doors. "Maybe they're in the stairwell." I walked to the stairwell door and opened it. After listening for a few seconds, I walked back to the security desk and shook my head.

"Try again," I said to Chuck.

He buzzed a third time, but no response came.

I looked at my watch and took a deep breath. Leaning over the counter, I said, "You have security cameras back there? Maybe they went out another exit. Did you see anything?"

The only thing behind the counter, however, was an intercom system and a laptop.

"Naw," Chuck said, "this is the only entrance and exit that people use." He thumbed over his shoulder. "There's a service stairwell at the other end of the building that leads out to an alley where our dumpsters are kept, but it's not used as an entrance."

"But it can be used as an exit?" I asked.

"I guess," Chuck said. "But that's not common. Plus, there's a silent alarm on the door that buzzes up here if it's opened without the code punched in. And it hasn't gone off."

"Hold tight," I told him. "I'm going to circle the building. Maybe the alarm is busted and they went out the back exit."

Before Chuck could respond, I hustled down the long corridor toward the back door. When I reached it, I pushed it open with two hands and stepped into a standard-looking alley. Glancing around, I spotted no people. To my right, the alley dead-ended into the back of some business. I walked quickly to my left until I reached the cross street.

As I rounded the corner to circle the building, I looked to my right. I noticed two people walking toward me and a cable man crossing the street and walking away. No sign of Felton or Morse, however. I continued around the next corner, expecting to see the senators standing out front, or at least Felton by the rental.

Nobody was there.

When I entered the lobby and saw Chuck sitting by himself, I ran my hand over my bald head. "No sign of them?"

He shook his head.

I listened in the stairwell again. No sounds. The elevator numbers were dark, too. I looked at Chuck. "I take it you have a master key for the condos?"

He hesitated to respond.

I glanced at my watch again. We were now a full seven minutes past the maximum time that Felton had laid out. Thinking about the death threats and the Walther P99, I was definitely feeling uneasy.

"Do you, Chuck?" The question came out a little too forcefully. I took a breath. "Please, it's important."

The guard eyed me, eventually asking for ID and a business card.

After studying my license and a business card Slim had made for me, he reluctantly nodded. "I do have a key."

"Let's go then," I said. "We have to get those two moving. What floor is he on?"

Chuck studied his watch. "They're gonna miss the vote, aren't they?"

"Not if we hustle, Chuck. What floor?"

He sighed. "Three. In condo 322."

"You take the service stairwell at the back," I said. "I'll take the front stairs. Don't want to miss them if they're on their way down. Bring that master key, just in case."

I waited until Chuck squeezed out of his chair, then I ducked into the stairwell and proceeded to the third floor by taking two stairs at a time.

There was no one on the third floor. There were three condos on each side of the hall. The walls were made of beautiful red brick and at least ten feet high. The floor was worn hand-scraped planks about eight inches wide. My footsteps echoed loudly against the wood as I hustled to the senator's condo, which was second down on the left.

I rapped on the door as soon as I reached his place.

Close to a minute later, after no response or sounds of movement inside, I used my palm and banged hard on the door. Waited another thirty seconds. To my right, I heard Chuck's shuffling footsteps.

When Chuck reached the door, I motioned at it. "You have to open it. Something's wrong. I know it. I feel it."

He held up both hands. "Whoa, whoa, slow down. I'm not going to just open up and barge into a senator's place."

"Listen, I'm a former FBI agent working for Felton Byrd. For security reasons I can't go into now, I need you to open that door."

He looked reluctant, so I put my boot on the door. "Either you open the door, or I kick it in. That's how serious I am, Chuck."

He eyed me. "You said you *were* an FBI agent?"

I nodded quickly and motioned at the lock.

"This is on you then," he said, reaching for his keys.

When the door opened, I let out a deep sigh. My hope was to see the men in the living room, or at least hear voices somewhere, but the condo was eerily quiet.

Way too quiet.

I turned to Chuck. "Do you know the layout of this place?"

"Sure, they're all pretty much the same. Living room and kitchen are in the front. Down the hall on the left is the master. On the right are two bedrooms with a Jack and Jill bathroom between them. I think the senator uses one of those bedrooms as an office."

"Stay here," I told him.

The first bedroom door on the right was open, so I rushed into the room, which was empty. Another door was located at the back-left side of the room.

While standing in front of what I assumed was the bathroom door, I said, "Senators? Felton. Morse. Anyone in there?" When I didn't get a response, I barged in.

Empty.

As I swept across the bathroom toward the far door, which opened into the other room, I stopped. The door into the second bedroom/office was ajar, by about an inch. Lights were on in the room and a solid beam of light flooded the dark bathroom. Overtop of my heavy breathing, I heard a dripping sound in the background.

It wasn't raining or snowing outside, however.

The hairs on the back of my neck stood to attention. Something was terribly wrong.

Instead of busting into the bedroom, I gingerly prodded the door open, which creaked on its semi-circular path until it touched against the wall with a dull thud.

Then I stepped into the room. And into a bloodbath.

CHAPTER TWO

I CLOSED MY eyes, then opened them to make sure I wasn't seeing things.

Before I could process the scene, I stepped back into the bathroom. Not because the scene freaked me out. As a former agent in the FBI's Violent Crimes Division, I'd seen my share of murders. Plus, prior to being an agent I was a government operative, so I'd delivered some lethal shots in my heyday. I'd seen what a bullet could do to a human head.

No, I stepped back into the bathroom because Chuck the security guard didn't follow orders. The man didn't stay put.

I cursed under my breath as I heard his steps shuffle down the hall. Obviously, I didn't know Chuck, so I couldn't predict how he'd handle a gruesome crime scene like the one in the senator's office. I didn't want him seeing the bodies and overreacting, not to mention potentially contaminating the crime scene.

So I backpedaled and exited the bathroom door into the main hallway just in time to intercept Chuck.

I stepped toward him and held out my hands, palms nearly touching his chest. "I found them, and it isn't good. Not at all."

He looked confused. "What do you mean? I don't hear them."

"Well, Chuck, that's because they're dead."

His eyes went wide and his diaphragm started pushing up his bulbous chest, which heaved in my face. While Chuck processed the information, I pulled out my phone to call the cops, but I didn't have a signal—probably because of the solid brick walls.

"You need to go downstairs and call the police," I said. "Wait for them in the lobby."

He stood still and blinked a few times, his ruddy cheeks fading to pasty white.

"Chuck, now, please."

"Both of them?" he said, swallowing. "Both are dead?"

I nodded, then repeated myself. "Call the police. Please."

He stepped toward the bedroom/office door.

"That's not wise," I said. "For the crime scene, and for your sake."

After two deep breaths, he said, "You're probably right." He glanced at his phone, then back to me. "Cell signals are spotty at best in this old building. Probably our number one complaint. I'll go downstairs."

I watched him retreat down the hall. I could tell by his pace that the man was relieved to be vacating the condo.

Once Chuck was out of sight, I stepped into the bathroom and moved toward the office door, stopping short of the threshold. One thought repeated itself: *This can't be happening. This can't be happening.*

Since I harbored denial, I leaned forward and peeked into the room to confirm what I saw earlier.

Sure enough, both senators were dead. No doubt about that.

Thoughts raced through my mind, so many I couldn't delineate one from another. Taking a deep breath, I tried to focus my mind. If I could clear my head, I could step into the room and accurately assess the scene.

Suddenly the Walther, with its distinctive green polymer frame, popped into my head. Was that the murder weapon? Did Morse threaten Felton in person this time and Felton used the Walther in defense?

The dripping sound pulled me from my questions.

Where was that coming from?

I entered the room, making sure not to step in or on anything. The first thing I saw was the lifeless body of Felton Byrd. He was in front of me, ten feet to my left and on the other side of Morse Cooper's desk.

I sighed while running my hand over my bald head.

Felton sat in an oversized brown leather chair with his head slumped forward. If it wasn't for the shredded hole on the left side of his jacket, you'd think the man had simply passed out—which wouldn't have been a stretch to believe since there was a bottle of scotch and two empty tumblers on the desk. Felton had unzipped his jacket but hadn't taken it off, probably because he hadn't planned on staying long.

After carefully side-stepping around the right side of the desk, I located the dripping sound.

On either side of Felton's hips were two small pools of blood, with more slowly spilling over the sides of the chair and dripping in alternating fashion. The drops splattered against the hardwood and gathered together into a large puddle at Felton's feet. From my angle, it looked like the bullet had struck directly through his heart. I imagined the exit wound was double the size on Felton's back. The blood obviously poured out of the wound and flowed down the man's spine, pooling where the chair back met the seat.

The puddle on the floor slowly moved my direction. I carefully side-stepped around the approaching blood until I was behind Felton's chair. Morse Cooper's partially headless body was now in my direct field of vision, obviously commanding my attention.

I blinked a few times. Even for a seasoned investigator like me, the carnage was hard to take in. Senator Cooper was behind the desk, seated in a similar brown leather chair as Felton's. His body was crammed against the left side of the chair, a result of the bullet that entered the right side of his head and exploded out the left. There was muzzle burn on his right temple, indicating the gun was pressed against his head when it went off. Almost certainly self-inflicted.

Most of the senator's left temple, forehead, cheek, and ear were gone. Blown into bits across the room. All the bloody carnage from the head shot was in the corner of the room where the hallway door opened into the office.

My emotions got the best of me. And it wasn't panic or sadness or a sickening feeling inside me. It was anger. Anger at not following my intuition. Anger at not insisting I attend the meeting with a client I was responsible for.

Looking at the bodies and bullet placement, it appeared this was a murder-suicide. One I could've prevented. One I should've prevented.

My fists clenched, then shook. To dissipate my anger, I released my balled-up fists and wiggled my fingers. But that didn't help. I kept questioning my actions—or inactions, really. Moments later, I realized I had limited time to assess the crime before the cops arrived, so I refocused on the dead men in the room.

Aside from the scotch and two tumblers, there was a white envelope and a letter opener on the desk. The envelope looked empty. The letter opener was askew on the desk and closest to Felton. Perhaps Felton lunged toward Morse with the letter opener, and Morse fired at Felton to stop him, then turned the gun on himself, realizing his life would most likely be over after sending his colleague death threats and then shooting him.

I got down on my knees and scanned the floor. It only took a few seconds to spot the gun. Not surprisingly, it was a little way under the desk in front of Morse's right foot.

And it wasn't the Walther P99. That must still be in Felton's jacket.

I went back around the right side of the desk, hopping over the blood that had snaked a path and stopped at the floor's molding along the wall. Crouching down behind the desk, I studied the unusual gun.

It was a Maxim 9, which was easy to determine since there was only one handgun in the world that looked like it. The Maxim came with a silencer built into the pistol. The gun looked boxy and futuristic, like something from the movie *Bladerunner*.

It was also an oddball choice for a gun. But then again, Felton told me that Morse Cooper was a gun nut. Maybe Morse kept it in his desk because he liked to show it off.

It didn't matter, anyway. It was clearly the murder-suicide weapon, so I moved on.

Standing, I looked at everything in the room except for the bodies. One thing I noted was how meticulous the office was. Nothing was out of place. No loose papers around, no files out, no books askew on the shelves. Which was why the envelope stood out to me. It felt important.

I studied the upside-down envelope, wanting nothing more than to turn it over and look inside and confirm it was empty. Of course, I didn't do that. I knew better than to tamper with a crime scene. Plus, for all I knew there was a home security camera recording everything. Which would be great if there was a camera in the room. Then we'd have a recording of the murder-suicide. Despite the death threats, the turn of events seemed surreal, so it would be nice to know exactly how things played out.

Before I could continue my inspection, the condo's buzzer went off. Then again. And again.

I made my way to the front door and pushed the intercom button. "Yeah."

"Cops are almost here," Chuck said. "I'll escort them up."

"Got it," I said. "Did you tell the police the victims were senators?"

"I did. Why?"

"Just curious," I said.

I opened the front door and walked to the kitchen, thinking along the way. Local police would contact the feds, so the FBI would be here shortly. They'd take over the investigation since the victims were federal employees. No doubt about that. And no doubt the feds would grill me about the Walther, which was actually registered to my buddy Slim. As a civilian, I couldn't bring a gun on my cross-country plane ride, so Slim lent me the Walther when I arrived on the East Coast. The cops and feds would also be pissed when they learned about the death threats and that no law enforcement agency had been informed.

That wasn't my decision, though. It was Felton's.

The senator was a rational, measured man, so he didn't overreact when the threats came through. Instead, he hired Slim's firm to figure out if the threats were credible before involving any agency and making a scene. Last thing he wanted to do was make a Senate squabble tabloid fodder, especially if the threats weren't serious or sent by Morse. Those were his exact words.

Of course, the threats ended up being serious. I banged my fist on the kitchen table.

For the next few minutes, I thought about the emails. *What was Felton to drop? What was he not supposed to pursue?*

My thoughts were interrupted by the stampede coming down the third-floor hall. Before long, a couple of DC cops, two crime scene workers, a plainclothes cop—most likely the lead detective—and Chuck were inside the senator's condo.

The detective was already heading down the bedroom hallway.

"Sir," I said, stopping his stride. "You should go in through the bathroom door, there's—"

"And you are?" he said.

"Garrison Chase. I found the bodies."

The detective glanced back at Chuck. The security guard nodded. Obviously, Chuck had told the detective about me.

"Why do I need to go in through the bathroom door, Mr. Chase?"

"On the inside of the main office door, there's quite a lot of"—I paused and thought about the appropriate words—"skull bits, along with blood and hair and stuff you shouldn't disturb until crime scene pictures have been taken."

"Noted," he said. "Thanks for the advice."

I wasn't sure if that comment was sarcastic or not.

"Stay put, Mr. Chase," the detective said. "I have some questions for you."

He turned before I could respond or nod.

"One other thing," I said. "Just to get it out in the open."

The detective reluctantly looked back.

"A Walther P99 is in Senator Byrd's right jacket pocket. I gave it to the senator. It's registered to my colleague."

His eyes swelled.

I quickly added, "But it wasn't fired at the scene, sir."

"And why did you give a firearm to Senator Byrd?" the detective asked.

"Long story, but the gist is I wanted Felton to be protected at this meeting."

He eyed me. "Okay. Now I have even more questions for you. Lots more."

"Fair enough," I said.

"Stay right here. And don't touch anything." He turned and proceeded down the hall.

The crime techs followed behind. The uniformed officers began a conversation with Chuck. I used the opportunity to text Slim. He needed to know about the shocking turn of events, so I pecked off a short text to his phone. Within minutes, he responded, telling me he was dropping everything and heading straight to the condo.

I sat on a kitchen chair and waited for the detective to return. Close to five minutes later, he was back. He pulled up a chair, scratching his head.

I furrowed my brow. "What's wrong?"

"You said the gun was in Senator Byrd's right jacket pocket. That's what you said."

I nodded. "Yeah, I watched him put it in there. Why? What's going on?"

"Well, Mr. Chase, there's no gun in Byrd's right jacket pocket, or his left. Or anywhere on the man, for that matter."

I quickly shot back, "No, it must be in that room. It must be. It has to be."

The detective shook his head. "There's only one gun in that room, and it isn't a Walther P99."

CHAPTER THREE

THE DETECTIVE PEPPERED me with questions. I didn't respond. I'd sunk back into the kitchen chair, my mind fixed on the Walther handgun and where it could be.

"Mr. Chase." The detective snapped his fingers.

I blinked and looked at him. He was probably in his mid-to-late-thirties, white, non-descript. So non-descript, in fact, I wouldn't be surprised if his name was John Smith. He had dark, close-cropped hair and smooth skin for his age, though his forehead currently sported two deep, well-defined creases.

He leaned forward. "I asked—"

I held up my hand. "The Walther must be in that room; it must be."

He sighed.

I kept at it. "How thoroughly did you check? I mean, you were only in the office for five minutes. You hadn't moved any of the bodies yet, had you? Maybe Felton's sitting on the Walther, or it's behind his back."

"Listen," he said. "We—"

"Detective, did you move Felton's body?"

"Well, no, not yet. We checked both pockets and inside his jacket. No gun."

I sat up. "Okay, good. It's probably underneath him or behind him then."

"Maybe," the detective said. "Listen, tell me why you gave the senator a gun and what's been going on."

"I will, but it's important we locate the gun. I mean, if the Walther isn't at the crime scene, that suggests a third party must've been in the room to take it. Right? Which changes the course of the investigation."

He rolled his eyes. "Let's not jump to any conclusions here."

"Check again. Let's locate the Walther, please, and ease my mind."

He eyed me. I was a stubborn sort, and I think he picked up on that. He eased out of the chair. "Fine. We'll move Senator Byrd if they're finished taking pictures."

Before I could say thanks, he turned and disappeared down the hallway.

About a minute later the feds arrived. In full force. A team of blue jackets swept into the condo, quickly getting the lay of the land and setting up shop on and around Morse Cooper's dining table. The Evidence Response Team, or ERT, immediately got to work. One of the team members rushed over and asked me some questions, then took my driver's license and handed it to an agent working behind a laptop.

I sat in the kitchen chair and watched the scene unfold. The FBI takeover was methodical, not chaotic or dramatic. It's a myth that the FBI doesn't work well with law enforcement. Most times the feds work just fine with local police, the Sheriff's office, and other law enforcement agencies. At this particular crime scene, the initial responders, which were the local cops, were fully aware the feds would take over. It was a given considering the victims were prominent politicians and federal employees.

After the initial wave of feds filtered in, two special agents—a man and woman—entered the condo. They breezed through the living room and down the hallway. Didn't glance in my direction. They were gone about ten minutes.

When they came back, the detective was right behind them. I tried to get his attention with a hand wave, but he was deep in conversation with the two agents. Eventually, all three turned and looked over at me.

Desperate to find out about the Walther, I held up my hands at the detective and shrugged.

He shook his head, telling me he didn't locate the gun.

What? I didn't have time to process the information, though, since the male agent quickly approached me. He turned a kitchen chair around and sat backward on it; didn't introduce himself or extend his hand for a courtesy shake.

"Former agent Garrison Chase," he said, looking at my ID and handing it back. I detected a slight Midwest accent. "Well I'll be damned," he continued. "Damned indeed."

That was all he said.

I prodded. "And you are?"

"Special Agent Skaggle. Tom Skaggle." I thought he was going to offer me his hand, but he smoothed out his flowing blond hair instead. The only thing the man did offer was a pompous smirk.

He thumbed over his shoulder, toward the crime scene. "Got yourself involved in one hell of a case again, didn't you? How do you keep doing that? Especially since you're not an agent anymore."

I stared into his beady eyes for a moment, not responding or reacting to his comments. My eyes drifted up to his orangey-brown forehead. It was a skin hue I hadn't seen before. The man looked like John Tesh but with thicker hair and considerably more time in a tanning bed.

Skaggle continued. "Would love to know what happened a year ago with the presidential election catastrophe you were involved in. Lots of speculation in the Bureau over why you left after that. Alas, we have more pressing concerns. Far more pressing. Am I right?"

I kept silent, wondering when I last heard someone use the word "alas."

"Detective Harmon says you gave Senator Byrd a gun before he came up here to meet Senator Cooper. And that now it's missing. Why? What's going on? Why are you involved with the senator?" He leaned forward and stared at me.

I couldn't tell his eye color because his slits were so small.

"Why don't you start at the beginning," he said. He motioned his partner over but didn't introduce her.

The woman flipped open a notepad in preparation to write down what I said. She was much easier on the eyes. A looker, to say the least. Dark, shoulder-length hair. Perfect, poreless light-brown skin. She barely wore any makeup, just a hint of pink gloss on her lips. She could've been Sofia Vergara's sister. I swear.

I kept my story tight, strictly facts. "Senator Byrd hired my colleague Hans Schlimmergaard, who goes by the nickname Slim. Slim owns a security firm here in the city, in which his main clientele are Washington power players. I occasionally work for him. The senator wanted Slim's firm to look into a situation."

Skaggle butted in. "So that's what you're doing now? You're a PI?"

I quickly shook my head. "I'm not. I subcontract some work for my colleague, who's also my friend."

Skaggle made a face. "Subcontract? Your security work involves investigation, surveillance, that kind of thing, doesn't it?"

I nodded. "Sure, but there's more to it than that."

"So you *are* a PI then." He scoffed.

"Actually, I'm not." For some reason, I hated being labeled a private investigator. Plus, I wasn't technically a PI anyway. I had no valid license, or any intention of getting one.

Skaggle threw his head back and gave a short laugh. "Not a PI. Okay, sure. You're a subcontracting investigator. Whatever. Talk about semantics."

I was about to respond, but the female agent stepped in. "Doesn't matter, gentlemen." She extended her hand toward me. "Agent Sanchez. Ramona Sanchez."

I took her hand but couldn't quite remember if I shook it. "Nice to meet you, Agent Sanchez."

She nodded and pulled her hand away. "You said the senator asked Slim's firm to look into a situation. What situation?"

I kept my eyes on her. "About a week ago Felton received two emails from Morse Cooper. One told him to drop it or die, the other said pursue it and perish. They were vague threats with no elaboration. From what I understand, the two had a falling out the past year, which was mainly due to this recent healthcare bill, but they also have a long history together. Morse, being a senior member of the Senate, took Felton under his wings and groomed him during Felton's first term as a senator. Morse even nominated Felton for a spot with him on the Senate Select Committee on Ethics. Anyway, according to Felton, the threats seemed way out of character for Morse. So he confronted his mentor right away. Morse was incredulous and immediately denied it. Then—"

"Wait a second," Skaggle jumped in. "Who knows all this?"

"Well, Slim and I do, of course. And now I guess you two know as well."

His blond brows lifted. "You didn't report this to anyone?"

"Listen, Felton Byrd is extremely level-headed. He's not a limelight guy, wants no attention or drama. He wanted to keep this on the down low, which is why he approached the firm. Felton assumed Morse's email had been hacked and some wacko was sending the death threats, so he didn't want the authorities to get involved and risk a media leak. I shadowed Felton around the city in case this wacko was actually serious, and Slim worked on confirming where the death threats actually originated from."

I paused.

Skaggle rolled his hand. "And did Slim?"

"He did. Yesterday his team confirmed the threats came from Morse's computer; the laptop in his office." I pointed down the hall. "I saw it on one of the shelves."

Skaggle whistled.

Agent Sanchez said, "How can they be so sure? Hackers can spoof IP addresses, make things appear to come from a certain address."

"Certainly, they can," I replied. "Listen, Slim doesn't do the work himself. He has some contractors—kids really—that he hires to do the work. We're talking young adults right out of MIT. They know how to spot a spoofer. His experts are one hundred percent confident the threats came directly from Morse's computer."

"Okay," Sanchez said, "so what did Felton do?"

"Confronted Morse again. And again, Morse denied it. But this time Morse wanted to meet and clear the air, said he would explain everything, so he set up this meeting with Felton."

Sanchez figured out the rest of the story. "Senator Byrd probably insisted on speaking with Morse alone, so you gave him the gun as a precaution."

I looked away. "Yup."

After a moment of self-deprecation, I looked back at Sanchez. "Felton convinced me everything was likely a miscommunication and that Morse was going to explain what was going on at this meeting. Obviously, I wasn't cautious enough."

Skaggle weighed in. "So, as of now, the gun you gave the senator is missing?"

"It is," I said.

"You sure he brought it to the meeting?" Skaggle asked.

"Ninety-nine percent positive. I watched him put it inside his jacket and walk into the building."

"We need to find it," Sanchez declared.

Skaggle stood. "We do, and we will. If the senator brought it to this meeting, then it's in this condo. Morse had some serious issues with Felton. This wasn't some misunderstanding, obviously. This was a confrontation meeting, and it went seriously south." He pointed down the hall. "That's one of the clearest murder-suicide scenes I've seen."

Agent Sanchez didn't respond. She turned and walked to the dining area. I could hear her telling other agents to scour the apartment for the gun.

Skaggle followed behind her, then turned and looked back at me. "The detective said it was a Walther P99."

I nodded. "With an army green polymer frame."

Minutes passed, and no one shouted out that they found the gun. I was pretty positive the Walther was somewhere in the office. Needless to say, when Skaggle came back and announced they'd performed a thorough check of the office and didn't find the gun, I was stunned. That turned to downright confusion when Sanchez informed us the Walther was nowhere to be found in the condo.

"You're positive," Skaggle said, eyeing me. "Positive Felton Byrd had the Walther on him."

"Yeah," I snapped at Skaggle. "I'm positive."

If I was being honest, though, some doubt crept in. I started to replay everything that had happened since Felton stuffed the gun in his jacket pocket. *Had he left it in the car without me noticing?*

"Maybe," Skaggle said, interrupting my thoughts, "Senator Byrd was nervous holding a handgun. Maybe he dumped it down a garbage chute because his nerves got the best of him. I think there's a chute out in the hallway, a few doors down."

I shook my head. "Highly doubt it. Felton was from Minnesota and a known hunter. He grew up around rifles and handguns. He was comfortable with them. And besides, he wouldn't dump the gun I gave him down a chute when he was supposed to reconnect with me in twenty minutes. That doesn't make sense. How would he explain that to me?"

Skaggle scratched his left temple. "Maybe he took the stairs up here and left it in the stairwell. Or left it in the elevator. Maybe he hid it in the elevator call box."

I shook my head but tried to stay positive. "Maybe, Agent Skaggle, maybe. By all means, be thorough and check."

As Skaggle left the condo with Sanchez, I settled back in the kitchen chair and replayed the conversation I'd had with Felton in the rental. The more I thought about it, the more I realized I must've missed something. I mean, Felton took the Walther to appease me. It wasn't like he was one hundred percent committed to taking the gun. He didn't feel it was at all necessary to bring a gun to the meeting. Maybe he slipped it out of his pocket and placed it between the seat and door without me seeing. Or maybe he eased it into the small, open storage compartment at the bottom of the passenger door.

I thought about that. I'd been momentarily distracted by his beak of a nose. Perhaps he used that opportunity to move the gun from his pocket, or maybe he discreetly dumped the Walther on the floorboard as he climbed out of the vehicle.

I left the condo and headed to the service stairwell. When I opened the door, I saw Agent Sanchez climbing the stairs.

She stopped and turned back. "Checking the entire stairwell. Hopefully I'll find the Walther. Where are you going?"

"Double-checking the rental car. I gave Byrd the gun while we were in there."

She nodded and kept climbing. I descended to the first floor and proceeded to the lobby. A number of cops and federal agents were milling about. Chuck was doing his best to manage the people in the small lobby area. Just as I weaved through the personnel and approached the elevator, the doors opened. Tom Skaggle stepped out.

I addressed him. "Anything?"

He shook his head. "Where are you going?"

"Double-checking something. Be right back."

"We have more to talk about," he said. "And we'll need to gather any evidence you and Slim have."

"Sure thing," I said, moving toward the lobby doors.

A blast of cold air hit my face as I stepped into winter wonderland. My breath instantly turned thick and cloudy. There were a number of reporters lurking around, but I didn't pay much attention to them. I stared straight ahead at my rental car.

Slim leaned against the front passenger quarter panel. Since he was a boxy monster of a man, just a fraction of his weight displaced the vehicle's front end. It looked like the wheel well was actually touching the top of the passenger tire. Even though it was near freezing out, he wore a T-shirt with no jacket.

He ran hot, to say the least.

Slim had wide eyes and a concerned look on his face. As I approached, he said, "This is nuts, Chase. Nuts. I can barely believe it." When he stood and straightened, the car groaned and popped up a few inches.

I nodded and didn't say anything until I was right in front of him. I looked around, then spoke softly. "And it may be worse than what I'd mentioned in the text."

"You're kidding," he said, stepping toward me.

I was a decent-sized man, about 6'3". Every time I got close to Slim, though, I felt tiny. Though he only had three inches on me, his body eclipsed mine. It was super thick and rectangular. A refrigerator had more curves than Slim.

"What's going on?" he asked.

"Gotta check one thing," I said, moving past him to unlock the passenger door.

Immediately my eyes darted down. No gun at the side of the seat by the floorboard. I looked to my right. The passenger door had a small storage compartment at the bottom, but the only thing in there was an old, shriveled air freshener shaped like a tree.

"What are you doing?" Slim asked. "What are you looking for? You know you left this thing running, right?"

I jammed my right hand under the seat, just in case Felton had somehow tucked the Walther underneath there. Nothing. Empty.

I turned and straightened and looked at my pal. Momentarily at a loss for words.

He prodded me. "Seriously, Chase, what's going on?"

I swallowed. "I don't think this was a murder-suicide, pal. Somebody else was in that office. And whoever it was murdered two United States senators."

CHAPTER FOUR

Eastern Montana
Fort Peck Lake

BAKER CUNNINGHAM'S CELLPHONE pinged, alerting him to the incoming text he'd been waiting for. He glanced at the screen. The text was a random string of letters, numbers, and symbols. In and of themselves, the string of letters and characters meant absolutely nothing. It simply alerted Baker to an email in his ProtonMail account.

He sat at his desk and opened his MacBook, then went through the security protocol for logging onto Proton. ProtonMail was a secure email system based in Switzerland. The company was far different from the typical cloud-based email services that similar companies offered. Proton's main datacenter was located under a thousand meters of granite rock in a heavily guarded bunker, one that could survive a nuclear attack. They stored nothing in the cloud. The company used end-to-end encryption and kept no IP logs whatsoever, so even they couldn't decrypt and read his email. No matter what.

Cunningham felt incredibly confident in their services. In fact, the only way you could hire him and secure his services was through Proton-Mail communication. Which not only protected himself, but also his clientele.

The email he'd been waiting for was there, but there was no text, just a video file. He clicked on it and began watching the video. It played within the email itself. Baker would've preferred to download it onto his computer, enlarge it, and increase the quality. But he wouldn't risk having the video on his personal computer. No traceability whatsoever.

That was his motto.

As a forty-eight-year-old, his eyesight wasn't like it used to be, so Baker squinted and watched the video. When it finished, he sat back and looked out his third-story office window. He took in the view of the southern portion of Fort Peck Lake and thought about what he'd just seen.

The video hadn't been what he expected. He stroked his goatee and kept thinking, eventually turning his attention to the video and playing it once more.

Beginning to end it was only ninety seconds. He wished it would've been shorter, like he'd been promised, but there was an unforeseen circumstance. And there were always unforeseen circumstances in situations like this. After a minute more of deliberation, he nodded and said to himself, "But it'll do. It'll do just fine."

Baker Cunningham clicked the forward button, typed in a seemingly random nonsensical email address, then sent the video to his client.

CHAPTER FIVE

WE SAT IN the rental car, thinking. Slim had somehow crammed his behemoth body into the passenger seat. With his knees touching the dashboard, he looked up at the roof and ran his fingers through his short, coarse red hair. The muffler burbled in the background while the heater strained to keep the temperature just warm enough so that we didn't see our breath. There was still a faint aroma of coffee in the vehicle.

Slim blinked and glanced over at me. "So you're pos—"

"I'm certain," I said, interrupting him. "He walked into that building with the Walther, Slim. Positive."

"You think maybe he dumped it somewhere before the meeting?"

"I don't. Feds and the locals scoured the office and the rest of his condo. Plus, they did a quick check of the elevator and stairwells. So far, it hasn't turned up."

Slim nodded, then a moment later said, "A gun doesn't just disappear like that."

"My thoughts exactly."

"I'm with you then," he said. "There must've been someone else at the meeting. Who, though? Did Felton mention there was a possibility someone else would be there?"

"Nope. It was just the two of them. Felton didn't even want me to attend. I also connected with the building's security guard. He didn't say anything about another party showing up."

"But you didn't ask him directly?"

"I didn't, but I'm pretty sure Chuck would've said something. I'll need to reconnect with him and ask. He may have a login or signup sheet for visitors at the security desk. If so, I should check that."

Slim straightened in his seat and held out his hands. "Just slow down, pal. This is your first case with me that's blown into something. And it's something huge, beyond huge. But you're reverting to your old ways, your law enforcement ways, and that's not how it works for you anymore."

"I get that, but—"

"No buts, pal. You're outside the law now. You can't investigate this. That's part of the rub with our job. We discover things like this and pass it off to the authorities. Case closed for us; we move on to the next client. Believe me, I'm with you and share your concern and wish things were different. I mean, it's my gun that's missing. And the Walther could've been the murder weapon. Right?"

I hadn't thought about that. He was right about the Walther, and about everything in general. Once the media got full wind of the story, it would blow up into the biggest news story of the year. They'd want answers, culprits, motives. And I wouldn't have any part in getting to the bottom of things. I blew out a breath and leaned back into the seat.

"We have a narrow window here," Slim continued. "Feds will want to know everything we know and take whatever evidence we have. And then they'll be done with us. We have to point them down the right path, give them good evidence, and provide some motive for why we think a third party was responsible. Then hope they do a good job following through."

I thought about the motive angle.

Slim interrupted my thoughts. "If somebody did kill the senators, then why? It likely has to do with the healthcare vote, doesn't it? There hasn't been a more controversial bill in the last decade that I can remember."

"Maybe," I said. "The problem is, Morse and Felton were on opposite sides of the vote. So, if some wacko wanted to set this all up to look like a murder-suicide, but their real motive was so the senators couldn't vote and influence the outcome, it doesn't make sense."

"Right. Their votes would simply negate each other. No sense in going to all that trouble."

I eyed Slim. "What about postponing the vote? Is that what might've happened this morning when the senators didn't show up? You know more about the Senate voting process than I do."

He shook his head. "Not sure if today's vote was a Voice Call vote or a Roll Call vote. Either way it doesn't matter since senators must be present to vote. There are rules around that, which sometimes allows absent senators to vote, but only if a senator knows ahead of time and has a valid reason for missing. They wouldn't have postponed the vote this morning. In fact, voting is over now, and the bill will be on the way to the president's desk if it passed."

I ran both hands over my head, thinking about other motives. "There was an empty envelope on Morse's desk, along with a letter opener, two tumblers, and a half empty bottle of scotch. There's something to that."

"What do you mean?"

"I mean, the office was immaculate, not a single piece of paper out of place, so the envelope stood out to me. It appeared to be the center of conversation between the men. Now I'm fully aware the whole scene may have been a setup, but that's my initial take. I think the envelope played a big role in whatever went down."

"Makes sense."

I continued. "An envelope implies a letter or document was inside. Let's assume whatever happened in that office had nothing to do with the healthcare vote. Both senators were on the Senate Ethics committee, so maybe a letter was sent to the committee accusing a senator of something nefarious."

Slim nodded. "You could be right. Maybe it was about one of their fellow Republican senators and they had a drink to commiserate about it."

"Sure," I said. "Or it could've been a senator on the other side involved in something bad, and they were drinking in celebration."

"Could be. Whichever the case, it must've been really good or really bad for them to have a drink at nine in the morning."

"Or maybe they're both raging alcoholics," I said.

"Maybe," Slim said, chuckling.

A moment of silence ensued. Then I said, "Motive is a problem here, Slim. There are too many potentials. We should focus on the third party. We need to find the person who was in the room. That's our best bet."

"You're probably right. But it's going to be the feds who track down the third party. Our best bet is to point them toward a suspect. What potential suspects do we have?"

Before I could think about that, somebody rapped on the driver's side window and startled me. Looking left, I was even more startled to see Tom Skaggle's orange face about a foot away. I reluctantly hit the window button. Cold air flooded in, instantly overwhelming the heater.

Skaggle leaned into the open window. "I'll need whatever evidence you gathered, gentlemen. And right away."

Neither of us responded.

He eyed us. "In other words, get to it, gents. Toot sweet." He tapped his hand on top of the door.

Slim stifled a laughed, probably because he hadn't heard anyone use that expression before. I know I hadn't. Not in many years, anyway.

My partner turned his mountainous frame to the side and pulled out his wallet. He handed Skaggle a business card. "Swing by my business address. We don't keep any sensitive information in the cloud, so it's not like we can forward you the emails."

Skaggle didn't say anything about having to retrieve the evidence himself. By the look on his face, however, you could tell he was miffed. He backed out of the window. "We'll be there shortly then." He pointed at us. "You gents be ready. No wasting our time. Capiche?"

I started rolling up the window. Skaggle had to quickly pull his finger away before I squashed it.

With the window up, Slim said, "Mr. Charming, isn't he? Is that a special agent tactic you learn in the FBI handbook? Straight to business and act like a prick."

"Not in the handbook, that's for sure. You got the Skaggle special; so did I earlier."

Slim smiled. "Think his orangey glow is courtesy of tanning lotion or a spray booth? I'm leaning toward the latter."

I laughed.

My buddy pointed ahead. "Double-time it to my work. We have to get out in front of this. I don't want Mr. Orange Face rolling in there demanding to confiscate our servers. If that happened, and word got out about it, business would be over for me." He stabbed his finger at me like Skaggle just did. "Capiche?"

I punched the accelerator and put Slim back in his seat.

While weaving through traffic, Slim spoke with his IT guy. He wanted his computer expert to pull off the email communication between the senators from their server and store it on a thumb drive.

We arrived at Slim's building and parked in the underground garage. Slim's security firm occupied the eighth floor. We were greeted by his computer expert and administrative coordinator when the elevator doors opened.

The two led us into the conference room. Slim dialogued with Becky, his admin person, for a few moments. I sat in one of the chairs and watched the IT guy set up the room's projector. The idea was to show Agents Skaggle and Sanchez the email communication on the big screen that hung on the wall at the end of the conference table. Then Slim would give them the thumb drive and hope they were satisfied.

Becky turned and addressed me. "Anything for you, Mr. Chase? We have just about any drink imaginable, and lots of different snacks."

"Just black coffee, Becky. Thanks."

By the time she came back with my coffee, the special agents were on their way up.

A minute later, Becky ushered them into the conference room, seating them across the table from Slim and me. Agent Sanchez was pleasant and smiling. Skaggle had a look on his face like he just whiffed a bad fart.

Slim introduced himself, mainly focusing his attention on Sanchez. "Would you like anything to drink, Agent Sanchez?"

She politely declined. He turned to Skaggle. "Anything for you, Agent? Becky can get you whatever you like. You look like an orange juice man?"

Skaggle dismissed Slim with a wave of his hand, which clearly bothered my buddy. Slim leaned forward. "What about a snack, Agent Skaggle? Feeling peckish? We have a broad range of treats, anything from pumpkin seeds to goldfish crackers."

It was just like Slim to make fun of the agent's orange hue.

Skaggle sighed. "Let's just get down to it. Tell us what you got."

Slim couldn't help himself, however. He leaned farther forward. "You sure? Like I said, we have a wide assortment of things. How about some Cheez-It crackers or Sunny Delight?"

I intervened by shifting my chair toward the screen and kicking Slim's right leg under the table.

My partner settled back and motioned to his IT guy, who clicked on the projector. Two emails appeared on the big screen. "These are the emails," Slim said, "that Felton Byrd received a week ago. They came two days apart." He paused and gave the agents time to read them.

I read them again, too. The first said:

Don't blow this, Felton. We have a long, healthy working relationship. Not to mention good friendship. Drop this or die. Your choice.

The second one said: *Don't ruin everything we've accomplished. Pursue this and perish. I mean it.*

Slim broke the silence after a few moments. "My chief computer man here, Sanjit, will explain how he traced the origin of the two emails."

While Sanjit launched into a rather lengthy explanation, I watched the two agents. Sanchez had pulled out her notepad and took the occasional note. She seemed to be tracking with the explanation. Skaggle, though, took no notes. And he didn't look at Sanjit. Not once. Instead, he squinted at the projector's screen with his mouth slightly open.

Around the eight-minute mark, Skaggle waved his hand at Sanjit, stopping the explanation. "Got it," he said. "The emails definitely came from Morse Cooper's laptop. That's clear." He turned to me. "Obviously there's not much we can gather from the email threats since they're so vague. What did the senator think about them? You spent time with him the past week. Surely he must've said something, gave you some type of theory."

"Well, Agent Skaggle," I said, "the assumption the first five days was that Morse's email had been hacked. When we traced the emails back to Morse's laptop, and confirmed the origin of the emails without a doubt, Felton was shocked and confused. He didn't try to postulate a theory to me, or to himself, as far as I know. He simply confronted Morse. Remember, the confirmation came just yesterday. And Felton was meeting with Morse this morning to get the answers. In that short intervening time, he offered no theories. According to Felton Byrd, he wasn't pursuing anything controversial that needed to be dropped. Certainly nothing that warranted a death threat."

Sanchez was busy taking notes. Skaggle subtly shook his head, like he was pissed at me for not pursuing it further, or because I had nothing more to offer. His judgment irked me. I was prepared to irritate him some more, perhaps suggest where the investigation should go next, but Sanchez intervened.

"Mr. Chase," she said, "tell us about the timeline from when you last saw the senator until the moment you discovered their bodies."

"Sure," I said, refocusing on her, which calmed me down. "By the way, did Senator Cooper have a security camera set up anywhere in his apartment?"

She shook her head. "Unfortunately, no."

"Too bad," I said. "So the senators' meeting was scheduled for 9:15 a.m. We arrived in front of the condo complex about five minutes before that. Since the Senate vote was at ten a.m., Felton told me he'd be back in twenty, twenty-five minutes tops. That gave him about twenty minutes to get to the Senate floor. At just before 9:15 a.m. I watched Felton enter Morse's building. About twenty minutes later, I entered the condo lobby since the senator wasn't back yet. I called him, but he didn't answer his cell. A few minutes after that I had the security guard buzz the senator's condo and got no response. We tried that twice more to no avail. So I circled the building, thinking maybe the senators went out a back exit. When they were still nowhere to be seen, I convinced the security guard to unlock Morse's condo. I entered the condo and discovered the bodies approximately ten minutes after the maximum time laid out by Felton. So, thirty-five minutes from when I saw him enter the complex, which would put discovery at approximately 9:50 a.m."

I paused to give Sanchez time to catch up and write down the relevant times.

"That means," I continued after a moment, "the third party, who's the killer in my opinion, and the person in possession of the Walther, took out the senators sometime between 9:25 and 9:40. That's a fifteen-minute window where the killer could've snuck out the service exit at the back of the building. Hopefully one of the buildings in the alley has a closed-caption feed of the area, or perhaps we could get some footage from the cross street of the perp coming out of the alley during that timeframe."

Skaggle shook his head at me. "You're not a law enforcement agent anymore, so let's get that out in the open and perhaps modify your inclusive use of 'we.'" He pointed at Sanchez then back to himself. "We are the 'we' here. We're in charge of the investigation."

I remained professional and nodded.

Sanchez seemed to be tracking with my theory. "Why those times? Why 9:25 and not 9:20?"

"Could be 9:20, Agent Sanchez, but that's pushing it. Felton got up to the third floor about 9:15 ish, and it appears the senators had time to take a shot of scotch and maybe discuss whatever letter or document was inside that envelope. So that's why I think 9:25 makes more sense. By the way, we have to find whatever was in that envelope. And if it's not in the office, that's more proof that a third party was present. Because that person must've taken the envelope's contents along with the Walther."

Skaggle huffed twice as I was speaking. Before he could pipe in, Sanchez spoke. "I agree on the timeline. 9:25, maybe even 9:30, is more likely for the killer to exit the building."

Slim said his first words in a while. "Or the killer never left the building, just snuck back to his or her condo. We have to keep that in mind as a possible theory. We have to canvass all the occupants of the building, talk to the ones who were home this morning."

I pointed at my partner and smiled. "*We* do, don't we."

Skaggle pushed back from the table. "All right, gents, enough. Again, we're in charge here and will be fielding this one without you two. For the last time, drop the 'we' language."

"Fair enough," Slim said. "We're just invested in this and want to see the truth come out."

"And I don't?" Skaggle snapped back.

"Not saying that," Slim responded. "Not at all. It's just your body language every time we mention a third party suggests you aren't open to that theory."

"Listen, I'm open to the facts, and I'm an Occam's razor guy. The simplest theory is often the truth. The fact is Morse Cooper sent Felton Byrd multiple death threats. Unequivocal. Then Byrd winds up with a bullet to the chest after confronting Cooper with what looks like a letter opener. Then Cooper panics, maybe thinks nobody will buy a self-defense theory since he was the one who sent the threats, so he offs himself. Sure, we have a missing gun and letter that is intriguing and poses some questions, but it's mainly speculative at this point. Remember, I don't have either in hand right now, do I? I'm going with what's tangible, with what's before me. Plus, gentlemen, it's early in the investigation. Before we came over here, Agent Sanchez sent a couple of agents to the basement garbage chute. We might find the Walther down there, which would end the speculation over a third party, wouldn't it?"

It would, but I didn't acknowledge it. Instead, I said, "I agree with you about the facts, Agent Skaggle. And ERT will have some facts soon. They'll do a gunshot residue analysis, I hope, on both senators. Ballistics is key, too. There's a possibility the bullets in Felton's chest and Morse's head aren't from the Maxim, which would then give the third-party theory credibility."

"Sure," Skaggle said, standing. "It certainly would. But it would also point to a really sloppy setup, too. Wouldn't it? Like the worst setup ever. So, I'm not holding out hope on that theory. Now"—he wiggled his fingers—"if I could get that thumb drive evidence, we'll be out of your hair. For good."

Slim handed it over. Skaggle headed to the door without so much as a goodbye.

Sanchez started to leave. I noticed she left her jacket on the chair. Just as I was about to say something about it, she made eye contact with me. Her eyes flicked to the jacket, back to me, then she left the conference room.

I picked up on the cue.

But Slim didn't. When he saw her jacket on the chair, he rushed over to it. I intercepted him before he could yell out to her, whispering, "She left it on purpose, pal. She'll be back momentarily to get it. Without Mr. Charming, that is."

Sure enough, less than five minutes later Agent Ramona Sanchez stepped off the elevator by herself. Slim and I had been waiting in the conference room for her.

She swept in and wasted no time. "Sorry, guys, he's the senior agent and a pompous ass. Like you couldn't tell. Anyway, I've learned how to manage him over time. Unfortunately, that means working behind his back." She smiled and grabbed her jacket from the chair.

"Listen," she continued. "I'm with you two. This situation with the senators is definitely not cut and dried. The missing gun and letter are beyond speculative in my opinion. Just wanted you both to know that. I'm heading back to the complex to canvass the neighbors and see if my team found the Walther in the basement. I'll have another team working on locating and securing outside camera footage. We'll also be scouring the office for the letter. And I'll check with the security guard to see what kind of visitor logs they keep. Figure out exactly who was in—and not in—that building this morning. Plus, I'll make sure ERT is super thorough with their reports on gunshot residue and ballistics."

Slim and I looked at each other, at a loss for words.

She held up one of Slim's business cards. "I'll call if we locate the Walther."

I nodded, then Slim and I followed her to the elevator like puppy dogs.

Before the elevator doors closed, she shot a look between us. "Oh, and gentlemen, next time you come across Agent Skaggle"—she paused and smiled—"offer him orange Fanta and some Cheetos." She winked. "That's more to his liking."

I heard her laughing even after the doors closed and the elevator descended.

CHAPTER SIX

THE CROWD ACROSS the street from the condominium complex had swelled throughout the morning. Once it topped fifty people, Hattie Lattimer felt confident enough to emerge from the shadows and blend in.

She stood at the back of the crowd. Every time someone engaged her in conversation, she'd give a polite but terse answer, then shift away. She wore gray yoga stretch pants and a black North Face winter jacket. She'd pulled the hood up, which covered her recently dyed hair. She wore polarized sunglasses that were slightly too big for her face. The woman looked like any other onlooker interested in what was happening across the street. With the hood and sunglasses, nobody could identify or recognize her. And Hattie wanted to keep it that way.

Conversations in the crowd speculated about what had happened at the congressional housing complex across the street. Somebody had said an ambulance showed up behind the building an hour ago and rushed two covered bodies away. Hattie didn't offer any speculation to her fellow onlookers. However, she had a sickening feeling that she knew exactly what was going on. Every five minutes she refreshed a news app on her phone, waiting for the story to break.

So far it hadn't.

She hoped her theory was wrong. In fact, she'd be elated to discover she was wrong. Hattie knew the condos housed many members of Congress, so she prayed one of the dead bodies wasn't Morse Cooper. All week she'd been following Morse in an attempt to get the senator alone. She'd been told he was the only person she could trust.

However, Morse Cooper was beyond busy with meetings. And she hadn't worked up enough courage to just stroll up to him on the street.

She checked her phone again. Still no update.

She blew out an exasperated breath, which turned to an icy cloud as soon as it left her lips. If Morse Cooper was dead, she'd have no one to trust.

Not a single person.

CHAPTER SEVEN

I'D SPENT THE afternoon and evening in my hotel room waiting and hoping for some news from Agent Sanchez.

I didn't get any.

News networks hadn't broken any details about the senators either. So far, the nation was in the dark. I also passed the time in my hotel room video chatting with my five-year-old son Simon. I heard all about his week, and also prepared him that I might not be home when I'd planned.

When I agreed to work for Slim a year ago, I promised Simon and my mother that I wouldn't be gone for more than a week at a time on assignment. I was dangerously close to violating that promise, something I hadn't done before.

After a restless night's sleep, I woke to an early morning text from Slim, telling me to get my butt to the firm's office. Sanchez had apparently communicated with him that morning. Slim, however, didn't provide any details in the text. I dug the sleep from my eyes, brushed my teeth, then headed over.

As soon as the elevator doors opened and I stepped onto the eighth floor, Becky handed me a steaming cup of black coffee. What a saint. I clutched the hot cup between my hands to warm my icy fingers. It was an even colder morning than yesterday, if possible.

Slim sat at the conference room table. He started in before I had a chance to take off my beanie and sit. "Ballistics worked overnight," he said. "If you can believe it."

"Not surprising," I replied. "Considering prominent senators are involved. Though I can't recall any ballistics team in my resident agency ever working throughout the night."

Slim kicked back in his chair. "Bullets in the senators are a direct match with the Maxim. And Sanchez said her team checked the basement, dumpsters, roof, all around the building, in every nook and cranny of the complex. No sign of the Walther."

I kicked back, too, putting my warm hands over my face.

"And," Slim continued, "which you certainly won't be pleased about, the Bureau is moving forward with the murder-suicide story."

I snapped forward in the chair. "You're kidding? They can't, Slim. They can't."

He shrugged. "They can, pal. And they are."

I held out my hands.

"Hey," he said. "You worked for the Bureau. You, if anybody, must know the incredible pressure they're facing to get the story out."

"Sure, but not the wrong story. The letter and Walther are still missing. They could be inside someone's unit. What did Sanchez say about those things?"

"Nothing, she didn't mention the letter or tell me about her canvassing efforts."

I stood. "I need to speak with her then. Did she leave us a business card? Or provide a call-back number?"

Slim shook his head. "I got the distinct impression that was the last communication she wanted between us. She was just being courteous, wanted to give us a heads-up. If it means anything, she did apologize."

I shrugged. Moments later, I paced the room while firing off a text to my girlfriend, Karla Dickerson, asking her to get Ramona Sanchez's direct number. Karla was an agent with FBI Los Angeles, so she'd be able to access numbers for Washington field office agents. I'd never asked her for info like this since leaving the Bureau, but she would know I had a good reason for needing it. I followed up the first text with another, telling Karla I'd explain everything later.

While waiting for the return text, Slim tried to calm me down. For the second time in as many days, he went over how the PI business worked. About how PI work wasn't about justice served, wasn't about wrongs made right, wasn't about perps being incarcerated. It was about gathering intel, giving it to the client, then moving on.

"Listen," Slim said. "I know this is hard, but it's the nature of the business. It'll take some time to get used to, but what else can you do? I mean, this morning the feds are going to tie this case up with a bow and hand it to the general public. The police and feds are going to move on, so we have to as well."

I shot him a look. "You're okay with potentially letting a killer, a murderer of two United States senators, get off?"

He pointed at me. "I'm not, Chase. If I had unlimited time and resources, I'd pursue something. But I don't. I have bills to pay and a business to attend to. In fact, I have a job for you, maybe starting in about a week. Gives you some time to go home and reconnect with the family."

"Hell no," I said.

Before I continued arguing with Slim, my cell buzzed. Karla had texted back with Sanchez's number, along with a smiley face emoji and a quick note that she looked forward to seeing me this weekend. I'd totally forgotten it was her weekend to drive north for a visit.

I clicked the number on the screen and let the phone dial for me. Just when I thought voicemail would pick up, the ringing stopped, and a voice answered.

"Sanchez here."

"Agent Sanchez, it's Garrison Chase."

"Impressive, Garrison. How'd you get my direct number? By the way, is it okay to call you Garrison?"

"Sure, most people use my last name, but Garrison is fine. Just don't call me Gary." I forced a laugh.

"Okay, Garrison, so seriously, how'd you get my number?"

"I kept the Rolodex from my days with the Bureau."

"Ha!" she said. "A Rolodex. Good one. Not even sure my father used one of those."

"Listen, I—"

"I know you must be upset," she interrupted. "And I'm sorry. I truly am. I've been trying to slow down the wheels of justice here. But I'm on my own. No surprise but Skaggle went with the murder-suicide theory. As soon as the ballistics report came through, and we found no evidence of the Walther in the building, he ran the theory to the top brass. He didn't even mention the Walther. He—"

"Wait! What? They don't know about the Walther?"

"No," she was quick to respond. "They do now, after I told them. It's just . . ."

"Just what, Agent Sanchez?"

"Can I be frank?"

"Sure. You can be Frank or Ramona. Whatever suits you." As soon as I said it, I cringed.

"Ouch," she said. "That's like a total dad joke. And a really bad one at that."

"I am a dad, actually, so hopefully you'll forgive me."

"Maybe," she said. "Listen, I don't know what happened a year ago. Why you left the Bureau, and whether it was on good or bad terms, but I'm guessing it was bad."

"Why do you say that?"

"Because when I mentioned your name, and that you were the one who gave Felton Byrd a handgun, I was dismissed from the room. About twenty minutes later they brought me back in and told me they were pursuing the murder-suicide theory. When I questioned them about it, they said the Walther wasn't the murder weapon and that you were an untrusted source, so they wouldn't pursue its apparent disappearance. That's all they said."

I pulled the cell away, so she didn't hear me sigh. When I heard her ask if I was still there, I put the phone back. "Yeah, I'm still here. I guess their reaction isn't too surprising. I had it coming."

"What happened?"

I didn't respond right away, thinking about my final case with the feds. I'd tampered with some crime scene evidence. It was an ethically questionable move. Of course, I felt I did the right thing in the end. However, the pencil pushing, by-the-book bureaucrats didn't exactly agree with me on that.

Sanchez broke the awkward silence between us. "Sorry, that was obviously super pushy of me, and really none of my business."

"No," I said. "It's a fair question, it's just a conversation for another day." I quickly changed subjects. "What about the letter? And did you learn anything from canvassing? Anyone home on the third floor and see anything? Anybody act suspicious when you questioned them? Plus, what about the GSR analysis? Anything there?"

"Not that it matters," she said, "since the Bureau is wrapping this thing up, but canvassing led nowhere. Since the complex is ninety percent Congress members, most occupants were in the Capitol. It's a busy time, not just because of the healthcare vote but because Congress is about to break for the winter recess, so the House is busy as well. Of the five floors, there were only three tenants home at 9:30. And all three saw or heard nothing. ERT worked overnight on ballistics, fingerprints, and GSR. No unusual prints in that office or condo. And residue was found on Cooper's hand but not Byrd's."

"Okay," I said. "What about video footage?"

"The complex itself has no internal or external cameras. And from what I learned that's deliberate."

"What do you mean?"

She paused, probably wondering if she should tell me. Seconds later, she decided to. "Listen, senators and House members don't want video evidence of their comings and goings. From what I gathered, that's the last thing they want. They don't want video of who they're fraternizing with and bringing back to their residence."

"Sneaky bastards," I said.

"Agreed. Anyway, we secured two feeds from nearby businesses. The footage is from different angles and shows that three people were on the cross street nearest to the alley opening. None of them looked suspicious."

"Any of them emerge from the alley?"

"Can't be positive from the footage and angles we have. There's a possibility that a cable worker did, but we can't be certain. It shows the man rounding a corner and heading toward the camera, but the camera is pretty far down the street. Since the alley and street on the front side of the condo are so close together, depth perception is hard to determine. You can't tell whether he's coming out of the alley and turning right or rounding the corner of the condo complex and turning right."

I blew out a breath. "Nothing at all then? No leads?"

"Not from canvassing and the video capture."

"So you did find something?"

"Nothing that's going to lead anywhere or overturn the feds' murder-suicide theory."

"What then? Did you find the letter?"

"Nope, no sign of a letter in the office or condo. But the envelope had something on the back."

"It did? I saw the back. It looked like a plain white envelope."

"Which it is. However, it contained a faint imprinted monogram in the same color. It's easy to feel, but a little hard to see."

"A monogram? What were the initials?"

"CM."

"CM?" I thought for a second. "Those are pretty common letters. Lots of names could start with those initials."

"Exactly."

"Any thoughts on who it could be?"

"I don't. Even if I did, I couldn't pursue it. Perhaps if we'd found whatever was inside the envelope, and it looked suspicious, maybe I could convince my superiors to let me look into it. But not now. Not when we're about to go public with the murder-suicide theory."

I squeezed the cell, then said a cordial goodbye and hung up.

Before I could look at Slim, he said, "What'd she say? I heard something about initials."

"Canvassing led nowhere," I replied. "And the contents of the envelope are missing, thus still a mystery. But they noticed the envelope had a lightly imprinted monogram on it with the initials CM."

Slim repeated the initials a few times.

I added, "They're not pursuing it anyway. Like you said, they're about to go public."

Slim repeated the initials one more time, then shrugged. "Sorry, pal, they're moving on, and so must we." He looked at his watch. "Don't you have a plane to catch this evening?"

I nodded. I'd booked a roundtrip ticket to DC, returning exactly one week later.

"You'll be home in time then," he said, "to keep your promise to your family."

"Slim, we gotta pursue this lead. Find out who CM is."

"No, we don't. We're under no obligation, in fact."

I ignored the comment. "One of your computer experts must have some type of software they can run the initials through, cross-check it with Capitol workers, lobbyists, et cetera. Or I'm sure they could write a quick computer code with a few distinct search strings. Right?"

He walked to the conference door. "Say hi to Simon for me."

"Come on, buddy," I said as he opened the door. "Just run the initials. There's evidence those senators were murdered, Slim. I mean, where's your gun? We can't just turn our backs. We can't."

He sighed. "You're too much." While he paced, he said, "Maybe I could get one of my employees on it. Maybe they'll find something. Maybe I'll . . ."

I encouraged him. "That's the Slim I know. Let's do it. Come on. Please."

He pointed at me. "I'll do it on one condition. Scratch that. Two conditions."

"Two?"

"Yes, two. First, you get on that plane this evening and go spend time with your family."

"Okay, easy. What's the second?"

"About a week from now, you're back here in DC. I need some help with a couple of backlogged cases. When you're back, I'll tell you if we came across anything with those initials."

Now it was my turn to pace the conference room. Flying to the East Coast was not something I wanted to do. Certainly not twice in a month.

My deal with Slim was to take any case I wanted west of the Mississippi. Felton's case was the first time I'd flown out east to do work.

After a moment of thinking, I reckoned I wouldn't get a better deal. But I wasn't going to give in that quickly.

"Fine," I said. "Agreed. I'll see my family and head back here in a week. But I want to hear right away if you get a hit with those initials. The very moment you find something. I'm not waiting a week."

Slim smiled. "Agreed."

CHAPTER EIGHT

HATTIE LATTIMER WHISKED through Penn Quarter, her jacket zipped all the way up to protect her face from the biting chill. She'd checked her phone five minutes ago and saw no news update. Now as she passed Penn Quarter Sports Tavern, she saw a multitude of television screens broadcasting a breaking news event.

She hustled inside the tavern, its warmth enveloping her within seconds. But she didn't pay attention to that. In fact, she didn't pull her hood back or unzip her jacket.

Hattie stood still, mesmerized by at least twenty TVs all simultaneously projecting the same visual. The tavern had just opened so there weren't many customers or workers inside. The few people inside were all riveted to the screens. Just like she was.

The FBI director and the DC police commissioner were on television talking about the shocking murder-suicide of two prominent Republican senators. Hattie heard Felton Byrd's name first, which brought a sense of relief. But that vanished the moment she heard the other senator's name: Morse Cooper.

She immediately looked around, expecting somebody to be looking at her, making that connection between her and the senator. But, of course, nobody paid her any attention.

Frozen in place, Hattie tried to concentrate on what was being said. She wanted to know the details of what had happened between the senators, but she couldn't focus on that. All she could think about was where to go from here. Who could she tell her story to? Who would listen? Worse, who would believe her?

Moments later, somebody touched her left shoulder.

She flinched and looked left.

The female bartender held up both hands. "Sorry, I called out to you a few times."

Hattie swallowed. "I'm out of it, sorry, just taken aback by the news."

"Right," she said, motioning toward the bar. "We all are. Come have a seat. The next round is on the house for everyone in here."

"Thanks," Hattie said, "but I can't stay."

She quickly made her way outside and walked two blocks to the northeast, toward the Judiciary Square Metro. As she rode the Red Line toward her stop, Hattie wondered if it was time to revisit the bank and try accessing the safe deposit box. Last time she tried, she noticed two men follow her into the bank, so she abandoned the effort. She figured if she would've accessed the box, she would've never stepped foot outside the bank again.

Maybe the men were gone. Maybe now was the time. Maybe it was worth the risk.

To find the truth.

CHAPTER NINE

THE FLIGHT FROM DC to Los Angeles took approximately five and a half hours. For the first hour of the flight, the cabin was awash in talk about the murder-suicide. Adding to the chatter was the statement made by the president just prior to boarding.

President Henrietta Valenzuela made a nationally televised statement from the oval office, preempting the evening news. Just about everybody in the Ronald Reagan Airport was glued to a TV screen watching it. Our flight boarded during the statement, so it was the first time I'd seen people not crowd and jockey for position in the boarding line.

Since I hated crowds and long lines, I boarded comfortably with only a handful of other passengers. I figured I'd watch a recording of the statement later. Based on the cabin chatter, I'd gathered that the Republican president made a big deal about the tragedy of losing such great Republican senators. Of course, not everybody agreed with that sentiment. Hence the chatter, which devolved quickly. I'd heard some insensitive whispers about how the country was one step closer to draining the swamp of white, old man politicians.

At any rate, since I was the one who found the bodies and had doubts that it was an actual murder-suicide, it felt weird listening to all the remarks and speculation and not weighing in on the matter. But I kept quiet, and to myself. My mind didn't stop, however. Not once during the flight did I come close to dozing off.

During the first half of the flight all I thought about were the initials CM. I figured the envelope on Morse's desk was most likely from a contemporary politician. But the only politicians I knew were the folks who'd hired me the past year, the president, and a few high-ranking executive level cabinet positions. And none of those people had the initials CM.

My mind drifted to ridiculous examples like Charles Manson, Cheech Marin, Claude Monet, and Cormic McCarthy. After two hours of thinking, the only remote political example I could come up with was a politician's wife, Cindy McCain. But her husband John had passed away in 2018.

I spent the second half of the flight thinking about the missing Walther P99. In my mind, there was no other explanation about its disappearance except a third-party involvement. Somebody else must've been in Morse Cooper's condo. And that person had to be involved in setting up the murder-suicide.

The question I kept coming back to was: Where did the killer go then? Did he or she slink back to a condo unit and wait for the heat to dissipate, or exit the building and get away scot-free?

Every time I closed my eyes during the flight, I felt like I was right back in DC at the murder scene. Instead of fighting it, I envisioned the events leading up to the gruesome discovery. Specifically, I focused on the moment I banged open the service door and stepped into the alley. From there, I replayed the moment when I came out of the alley, my body turning to the left and rounding the corner, but my eyes looking to the right.

Of the three people I saw, two were walking toward me. Obviously, then, they were unlikely suspects since they weren't leaving the alley. The cable man, however, was thirty to forty feet past the alleyway and crossing the street. He angled away from me and toward the only vehicle on the other side of the street. I envisioned what I could remember about him.

He held a black duffel bag in his left hand. He wasn't wearing a tool belt, so he couldn't have been coming from a job. And I remembered he walked toward the driver's door of a sedan. Not a cable truck.

He was a definite suspect.

What I needed to do was have Agent Sanchez find another video feed showing whether he came out of the alley. Because if he didn't, if cable guy came from the front of the condo and turned right onto the cross street, he couldn't have been the killer. Which meant the killer must've tucked away inside a condo unit. But if he came out of the alley, he could've been the killer. And he needed to be found and questioned.

When we touched down in Los Angeles, my travels weren't over. I waited forty-five minutes, then took the last connecting flight of the day to a Central California hipster town called San Luis Obispo or SLO. From there, I grabbed my car and drove home to Cayucos, a quaint beach town about thirty minutes northwest.

A year ago, when I left the FBI, I moved to Cayucos with Mom and Simon. My mother was a big fan of the town, vacationing here in her childhood. The place was near crime-free, oceanfront, and had a good elementary school. Perfect for raising a young, adventurous boy like Simon.

I brought Mom along for a few reasons: One, she was dear to me. Two, I needed help with taking care of my five-year-old son when I was on assignment. And three, we needed to pool our money so we could both afford the area.

Fortunately, we found a fixer-upper ranchette north of the small town. It needed a lot of work, but it had a peekaboo view of the Pacific and a few acres where chickens and my dog could roam free. I was sold. Plus, as a bonus, the place had a granny unit, which probably saved the relationship between Mom and me.

It also made it way less awkward when Karla came to visit.

When I arrived home, it was just past one in the morning. The place was peacefully quiet. Nothing to be heard in the background except crickets chirping and the subtle roar of the Pacific. My scaredy-cat German Shepherd named Ranger finally came out to greet me after realizing I wasn't an intruder. The dog was skittish from his tenure as a bomb-sniffer in Afghanistan, so I cut him some slack and refrained from calling him the worst guard dog ever. At least not to his face.

Before sleeping, I snuck into Simon's room and eased onto the edge of his bed. He still liked to sleep with a nightlight, so I was able to sit and watch him for a while. I never thought I'd be the creepy parent watching their kid sleep, but here I was.

In the morning, Mom, Simon, and I had a great time reconnecting. But when I dropped Simon off at Cayucos Elementary School, my mind immediately went back to the case. I dialed Ramona Sanchez before leaving the parking lot.

But she didn't pick up. I wondered if she was busy or simply screening my calls. Either way, it didn't stop me from leaving a long-winded message about my reservations concerning cable guy. I asked her to confirm via additional footage if he came out of the alley.

I did resist the urge to call Slim and bug him about the initials. Instead, I busied myself by cleaning up the ranch and doing laundry. Following that, I worked with my dog Ranger. My long-term plan for Ranger was to rehabilitate him somewhat back to normal. I'd gotten in touch with some experts in the canine field and developed a training regimen to hopefully alleviate his scaredy-catness. I worked on some drills with him for about an hour.

Since my son wasn't quite old enough for kindergarten, he attended transitional kindergarten, which was for five-year-old kids born between September and December. School for him only ran to noon, so I picked him up then and we spent the afternoon together. It was enjoyable, but my mind was elsewhere. Even Mom could tell. She asked me about it when Simon was excused from the dinner table that night. I told her my recent case was unresolved and itching at my mind.

Just after dinner, Slim called. I stepped outside and answered it.

"Whatcha got, pal?" I said. "Tell me it wasn't Charles Manson from the grave leaving a cryptic note for the senators."

"You're funny."

"Seriously, anything on the initials?"

"Not Charles," he said. "Charlie. Charlie Milliken. That's our best guess."

"Charlie Milliken," I repeated, scratching at my bald head. "Can't place the name or face, but it seems familiar."

"The senator from the East Coast who died about three months ago. Routine scan uncovered an inoperable brain tumor at age forty-five. Wife of twenty years, three teenage kids."

"Right, right," I said. "Remember the story, just not the name."

"You have to do better, partner. Washington power players like Charlie are our bread and butter. You have to remember senators' names, even the dead ones."

"Your job is to remember them and schmooze them. I'm just your subcontractor, buddy."

"And when are you going to get your PI license anyway?"

Not wanting to go down that road, I said, "If I remember correctly, Milliken didn't die from his brain tumor, right?"

Slim scoffed. "Man, you may not follow politics or care much for it, but you evaded that question as well as any seasoned politician I know."

"I'll take that as a compliment. Seriously, Slim, didn't Milliken die in a car crash?"

"He did. Doctors think he may have had a seizure and driven off a cliff into the sea while vacationing in Maine."

I stayed silent.

Slim huffed on the other end of the line. "Ah, geez, don't tell me your mind is already entertaining some conspiracy theory."

"Why?" I quickly replied. "Is yours?"

"No, no, it's not, actually."

"Why, then, is an envelope from a deceased senator on the desk of two murdered senators?"

"Any number of reasons."

"Give me one valid one," I said.

"I'll give you two," he quickly responded. "The first, and most obvious one, is that we're wrong. CM doesn't stand for Charlie Milliken. Like I said, that's our best guess since the only member of Congress with those initials is Charlie. It doesn't have to be from a politician, does it? Could be from a lobbyist or someone like that. I believe even you mentioned that earlier. Second, maybe the envelope and whatever was inside was from Charlie. Maybe Felton and Morse were simply having a drink in honor of their dead buddy. Reminiscing over an old letter he'd sent. I don't know."

"I said a valid one, Slim. Too many problems with that theory. For instance, where the hell did the letter go then? Which is also a problem with your first theory."

"Fine, what about you? Give me a good theory for why you think the envelope situation is suspicious."

I thought for a second. "How about Charlie's wife used her dead husband's stationery to send the chair of the Ethics Committee a letter. A letter in which she accuses somebody else in the Senate of being involved with her husband's death. That it wasn't a car accident but made to look like one. The perpetrator catches wind of the wife's accusation and letter. The perp shows up at the meeting, kills the men but makes it look like murder-suicide. Perhaps Felton pulls out the Walther right before the perp shoots him. Before leaving, the perp sets up the scene perfectly and takes the letter and handgun."

A moment of silence on the other end. Then Slim cleared his throat. "Wow, that's not bad, actually, not bad at all."

I was stunned, too. "I agree. That just came out of nowhere. It's a wild theory, but plausible, right?"

"Truth is often stranger than fiction," Slim said.

"What we need to do is contact the Milliken family and find out if that monogrammed envelope is indeed his. If so, question the wife about it. Had her husband sent Felton and/or Byrd a letter before his passing? Or maybe she recently did?"

"Again, slow down, Chase. We're not cops or feds."

"Granted, but we must do something, buddy. Otherwise, nobody will. Certainly not the cops or the feds. And that's not an acceptable outcome for me."

"I know, me neither."

"What do we do then? Between us, we have talent and resources. And I'm the talent and you're the money, just to be clear."

"Comedy's not your talent, that's for sure. Listen, I think Agent Sanchez is reasonable. We have to get her onboard. I'll help out with my considerable talents, maybe even resources, if we can get her to help."

"Deal," I said. "I'm calling her now."

But Agent Ramona Sanchez didn't answer again. I wondered if she'd ever call me back.

Fortunately, I didn't have to wait long to find out. By the time I went to the kitchen and poured two fingers of Bulleit bourbon and took the first sip while sitting on my front porch, my cell rang.

I didn't recognize the number, so I cautiously answered, "Yeah."

Silence on the other end, but not a hang-up.

"Who's this?" I said.

A moment later, somebody blew a faint breath into the phone. "It's Ramona Sanchez. I can't believe I'm calling you on a burner phone while parked in a Best Buy lot."

I wasn't sure how to respond to that, so I went cheesy. "You probably missed my dad jokes and are calling for another."

"Certainly not," she shot back. "Listen, Garrison, I probably shouldn't be calling you, certainly not from a career standpoint. If Skaggle or my superiors knew I was still looking into this and communicating with you, it wouldn't go well for me. That's why I bought a cheap pay-as-you-go phone from Best Buy. It's overkill, I know, but I really love my job. From a personal standpoint, though, I felt I had to call you."

"Why? What'd you find out?"

"After listening to your voicemail about the cable guy, I went back to the condo area. I canvassed some local businesses and found a better video feed, one that shows him clearly coming out of the alley at 9:32."

"I knew it!" I raised my fist in the air, then realized how silly that looked and lowered it. "Suspicious, right? I mean, smack within the timeframe of when the killer would've exited the building."

"I know," she said. "I know."

I continued. "He wasn't on a job. He didn't have tools with him or a work truck. Maybe he was heading to work. You know, kept his tools and truck there. And if that's the case, he must live in the condo complex. All the other buildings in that alley are businesses, no other residences there. And if he lives in the complex, we can easily find out."

I waited for a response from Sanchez. Finally, she said, "We could, you're right. It's just . . ."

"I get it. You need more evidence before you get involved. Is that where you're going?"

"I definitely need more before going up the chain. I'm willing to do it; I just need more."

"Got it. You need me then."

"I do. As a private investigator—sorry, subcontractor—you have certain freedoms and luxuries I don't have. Red tape and bureaucracy you don't have to worry about. But I also know it's a risk for you. I know—"

"Say no more, Agent Sanchez. I'm in."

"Really? I mean, if things go south for some reason..." She didn't finish the sentence.

So I did. "You and your colleagues won't have my back. No worries, I get it. I won't mention our conversation. I wouldn't expect the Bureau to have my back anyway."

I detected some relief. "Thanks," she said. "I really need your help."

"Do you have latitude to investigate something else? Something not directly related to the dead senators?"

"Maybe. Why? What do you have?"

"Slim believes the initials on the envelope stand for Charlie Milliken."

She responded a few seconds later. "Senator Milliken; I hadn't thought about him since he passed away. Why would an envelope from him be on Morse Cooper's desk?"

"Don't know, but we have to find out. Could you investigate his death without drawing attention? See if there's anything suspicious?"

"I think so." She paused. "Scratch that, I will. We both have to risk something."

"Great. I'll call you on this number when I'm back in DC. That work for you?"

"Perfect," she said.

Then I hung up and made plans to catch a murderer.

CHAPTER TEN

BAKER CUNNINGHAM STARED at his MacBook screen, blinking every few seconds.

Money had just reached his Swiss account. Though he knew it was coming, it was still hard to believe the amount. Especially for just one job, one job that sped up his retirement by five years. Easily.

Baker took a final glance at his account total, then logged off the banking website and shut down his computer with a giant smile.

Pushing back from the desk, he looked out over the lake. He'd grown up in various remote parts of the state. An avid fly fisherman and hunter, Baker Cunningham saw the second act of his life in a completely different environment. Dreams of warm tropical weather, scuba diving, and deep-sea fishing had been on his mind the last five years. He hadn't picked out his perfect retirement spot just yet, but he did know it would most likely be on one of the small Dutch Caribbean islands. Or maybe somewhere in the Indian Ocean.

Since his men were waiting for him, he pushed the thoughts from his mind and exited his office, excited to let his most trusted men know the mission was a success.

CHAPTER ELEVEN

I USED MY key to Karla's place to open her apartment door.

During my three-and-a-half-hour drive south, I'd texted Karla to let her know I'd stop by before hitting LAX. Since it was the middle of the night, as I creeped up her steps and approached her bedroom door, I said, "Don't shoot, Karla; it's just me."

She had her service piece drawn when I opened the door.

"You're that upset I had to cancel our weekend plans?" I said.

"Totally pissed," she said, smiling. A moment later, she used the gun to wave me over. "Get in here." She put the gun on the bedside table and pulled the comforter back.

I kicked off my shoes and slipped under the covers before turning toward her.

Karla Dickerson reminded me more of a cheerleading coach than a federal agent. She was a petite, fit woman who looked like a younger Meg Ryan. As she snuggled close, I smelled her short, stylish hair, which brought rosehips to mind. Karla's body was warm and soft and felt great next to mine.

"How long can you stay?" she asked.

I pulled her tight, then glanced at my watch. "Less than an hour. I need to be at LAX early to catch a standby flight."

"Bummer," she said. "I was really looking forward to this weekend, you know."

"Me too."

We didn't speak for the next few moments, just held each other. Everything they say about the difficulties of maintaining a long-distance relationship is true. Since Karla and I didn't see each other often, it was hard to deepen our connection. I knew for me to grow in the relationship I'd have to be in closer proximity and interact with her on a regular basis. Just didn't know how that was going to happen.

She broke the silence. "So who's this agent I gave you the number for? This Ramona Sanchez. And what's going on with you suddenly flying back to DC?"

I kissed her on the forehead, then settled back and told her everything. Which took the better part of the hour.

At the end of the story, Karla was eager to help out. "I could look into the video surveillance of the cable guy. I could do it discreetly on my end and not draw attention."

"That would be great," I said.

"I could get a plate number from the vehicle that the cable guy drove off in. Trace the number and see what I come up with."

"Perfect, thanks." I gave her Ramona Sanchez's burner phone number and told her to call Sanchez to get the most recent video footage. Then I reluctantly crawled out of bed and said, "It's that time. Sorry."

"Me too. Before you go, how're Simon and your mom doing? I know this will be the longest you've been away from them in a while."

"It is, but they'll manage. Mom actually encouraged me to fly back. She could tell my mind wouldn't be right until I solved this."

She nodded but didn't say anything else.

I motioned toward the door. "I have to go. Again, I'm sorry."

As I walked out, I heard her quietly say, "I'm sorry, too."

CHAPTER TWELVE

DURING THE CROSS-COUNTRY plane ride that morning, I thought a lot about the case, and a lot about my relationship with Karla. At some point soon, Karla and I needed to have the tough conversation about next steps. Whether we were going to take them, and if so, what they would look like.

By the time the plane landed and I made it out of the airport, my mind was off Karla and focused on the case. My goal was to get to Morse Cooper's condominium complex as quickly as possible, which was the reason I didn't stop to get a rental car but rode the Metro into the city instead.

I needed to ask Chuck the security guard some important questions. Assuming he worked the day shift, I thought he would be done in an hour or two, thus the hurry.

When the Metro hit my stop, I got off and hustled five city blocks to Morse's condo. When I opened the lobby doors, I was relieved to see Chuck behind the security desk. He looked shocked to see me.

"Mr. Chase, wow, didn't think I'd see you again. Man, it's been a crazy two days."

"I can imagine." I reached out and shook his hand. "You doing all right?"

He nodded. "Wanted to thank you for not letting me into that office. Word has it the scene was gruesome. I'm glad I don't have that visual on my conscience."

"No prob. Can we chat?" I motioned at the sitting area behind me. "I imagine you've fielded a ton of questions from the FBI. I have a few more to ask."

"Sure," he said, getting up from his chair.

I sat on one end of a sofa while Chuck took a chair across from me. I got right to business. "I didn't directly ask you this before, and I know the feds must've asked the same thing, but it was just Felton and Morse in the condo, right? Or did somebody else arrive before Felton?"

He smiled. "That good-looking female agent asked the same thing. Senator Cooper had no other visitors that morning."

"What about other members of Congress? Did anyone have a visitor?"

"Nope. Everyone was leaving the complex that morning."

I nodded. "It was a busy day in the Capitol. What about workers? Was any work being done on any condos? Painters, electricians, maybe a cable guy?"

He shook his head. "We didn't have anything scheduled that day."

"So, Felton Byrd and I were the only ones you saw that morning who didn't live in the complex?"

He nodded but looked skeptical. "What's going on? Where are you going with this?"

I thought for a moment. Agent Sanchez was right. There were certain freedoms I didn't have not being in law enforcement anymore. For instance, I didn't have to worry about commenting on an ongoing case.

"I'm not convinced it was a murder-suicide, Chuck. I think someone else was in that condo with the senators, and I'm trying to figure out who it was and how they got in there."

He deflated into the chair. "That's a turn I didn't see coming."

"I need your help. You saw the news; the feds are done with the case. And I think they're wrong. If those senators were murdered, we can't let the killer go free."

"Of course," he said. "But why do you think someone else was involved?"

I didn't want to go into the details about the missing gun and letter, so I decided to tell him about the cable guy. "Remember when I circled the building?"

He nodded.

"When I came out of the alley and turned left to circle back, I looked to my right to see if the senators were walking down the street. They weren't, of course, but there was this cable guy walking away from the alley and crossing the street. The good-looking agent, Sanchez, found some video footage proving he emerged from the alley. And it was within the tight timeframe for when the perp would've left the building."

Chuck ran his fingers through his wispy blond hair.

I asked him, "Are any of the tenants in this building cable workers?"

He quickly shook his head. "Not that I know of. And I basically know everybody. It's part of my job, too."

"Sure, sure it is. Technically, tenants could leave the building through the service exit into the alley, which you told me wasn't common and would set off a silent alarm. How do you avoid the alarm?"

"You need a code."

"Okay, so what tenants know the code?"

He didn't respond right away.

"Chuck," I prodded, "how many tenants know that code?"

He hesitated, his face turning a little red. Eventually, he shook his head. "None that I'm aware of."

Clearly, he was hiding something, so I kept pressing. "If the cable guy was involved in the senators' deaths, and he left this building through the alley, he must've known the code, right? And he must've got it from somebody who lives here."

Chuck swallowed. "Maybe he came from another building. There are other businesses that exit into the alley."

"There are, you're right. So what's the process for getting into this building through the service door? Obviously you need the code."

He nodded. "And the key."

"So to get into the building you need the key and code, but to leave you just need the code?"

He looked away. "Right."

"I take it you're going to tell me that no residents, as far as you know, have the key either?"

He thought for a second, his face getting even redder. Then he cleared his throat. "None that I know of."

"Positive?"

His lips started to form a "no" response, but he stopped himself before actually saying the word.

Instead of prodding him, I kept an inquisitive stare going. Chuck had some beads of sweat on his forehead. The longer I looked at him, the more stressed he got. And the more beads appeared.

"Just come clean, Chuck. It's clear you're hiding something."

He looked up at the ceiling, then back to me. "This job is more about maintaining privacy, Mr. Chase, than it is providing security. Members of Congress count on me to be discreet." He paused.

"I get it, Chuck, I certainly do. You have to put that aside, however. We're talking about a double homicide here, in which the killer could be roaming free."

He held up his hand. "I know, I know." He gestured me closer.

I leaned in.

He lowered his voice to a whisper. "There's a promiscuous senator. Likes to bring in the ladies, you know."

I nodded.

"Simple exchange between us one day: he gave me some money, a hefty sum in fact, and I gave him the code and my key for the service exit. He returned the key the same day. We've never talked about it since. Never."

"Obviously he made a copy. How often does he use it? And what's his name?"

"Thankfully, I have no idea how often he uses it. And that's the truth. It's so far down the corridor I can't hear any comings or goings. He doesn't trip the silent alarm since he knows the code. And there's not a single camera in the building or around it. The less I know, the better. I'm sorry, but there's no way I'm giving a name."

I held out both hands. "Really, Chuck?"

"Nope, no way."

"I have to investigate this, you do realize that, right? Wouldn't it be better for me to do it than the feds or cops? If it turns out to be nothing, this promiscuous senator will never know I was looking into the situation. But if the feds do the investigation . . ." I let that hang for a moment.

He looked away. After sighing twice, he said, "Fine then. It's Senator Aidan Agnew. He sneaks the ladies in and out."

"Okay, thanks. Anyone else I need to be aware of?"

He shook his head.

I pulled out a small notepad I kept in the inside pocket of my trucker jacket. Slid it across the desk. "Could you also write down the name and condo numbers of Morse Cooper's neighbors?"

He gave a "you're pushing it" look.

"Hey," I said. "Murder, coverup, conspiracy. That's what we're talking about here; I think that definitely warrants the information."

He reluctantly scribbled down a few names and condo numbers. After tucking the notepad away, I thanked Chuck and left the building, heading to the alley. The condominium complex took up one side of the alley, which dead-ended into the back of a restaurant. On the other side of the alley was the rear of three more businesses.

I walked around front and visited all four establishments. Told the workers inside I was part of the investigation into the senators' deaths. Since I only had one innocuous question, the employees didn't ask my name or who I worked for. Turned out two of the businesses didn't even have cable on their premises. The other two had it, but they didn't have any recent problems, so neither business had called for a worker.

Cable guy must've exited into the alley from Morse's complex.

While thinking about cable guy as a suspect, I ambled to the local Compass Coffee. Along the way, Karla texted. She'd connected with Ramona Sanchez earlier in the day. Her text stated a street address in Annapolis, Maryland. She followed that text up with: *Address of registered car owner.*

After getting an Americano from the shop, I proceeded to the nearest Metro station with a pep in my step. Not only had I confirmed that cable guy was a plausible suspect, but I'd also confirmed he had a plausible way into the building without being noticed. And now I had the man's address.

When I arrived at Slim's office, it was just before his firm closed. Slim was finishing up with a client, so Becky seated me in the conference room. After refreshing my coffee, she excused herself for the day. While waiting on my partner, I'd texted Sanchez and told her to call me back as soon as she could. She called a few minutes later, right as Slim walked into the conference room.

I placed the cell in the middle of the table and put Sanchez on speaker. Then I told them both what I'd learned. Midway through my story, Slim stood up and paced the room. Sanchez didn't interrupt or say a word.

"What do you think, Agent Sanchez?" I asked. "Is that enough to get your office involved?"

"Well . . ." she said, trailing off.

"Understood," I replied. "I know it's speculative and that you probably need something more concrete to go on."

"I'm hesitant. If we had video of the cable guy coming directly out of the complex, or of him using a key to get into the complex, or if we can link him directly to Senator Agnew, then I'd feel confident going to my superiors."

Before I could say something, Slim intervened. "No problem, Agent Sanchez. We'll go to Maryland early morning and scout out the address. See what we can find out about this cable guy. And I'll personally look into Agnew. I have considerable depth of knowledge when it comes to the one hundred senators."

A brief hesitation. "Tread lightly, gentlemen. Be careful."

Slim and I smiled at each other. Ramona Sanchez had no idea of the missions we'd been on in the past. This was simple reconnaissance for us, no big deal. Slim and I had been successful in our military careers, so we'd been recruited to work for a government black ops organization called The Activity. We were partners while on that covert team. Once I became a father, I left The Activity and took a federal agent position so I could be home to help raise my son. Slim wanted to focus on his family, too. When he left The Activity, he started the security firm. Now here we were: partners once again.

I asked Agent Sanchez, "Did you find out anything about the envelope and Charlie Milliken?"

"Not yet, but I'm meeting with his widow tomorrow morning."

"Great," I said. "Keep us in the loop."

"You as well," she said. "Call me as soon as you learn something."

When I hung up, Slim had an ear-to-ear grin. "What's that creepy look for?" I asked.

"I've got a great plan for the morning."

"You do, do you?"

"Absolutely. An old PI trick of mine. I think it will work perfect in this situation. And it involves you wearing brown shorts."

CHAPTER THIRTEEN

HATTIE USED TWO fingers on her iPhone screen to zoom in on the men. The sun had recently retreated behind the tall downtown buildings. Though the hotel window was a little dirty, she could see across the street much better now that the sun's reflection on the window was gone.

From her current location on the hotel's eighth floor she couldn't make out any facial details of the men, but she could tell they were preparing to drive away. The man in the passenger seat exited the dark blue sedan and threw out the trash the two had collected throughout the day in a nearby garbage can. Leaving at this point made sense since it was close to five in the afternoon and the bank was about to close.

No need to await my arrival anymore, Hattie thought.

Once their vehicle drove away at 5:01 p.m., she collapsed into the hotel room chair she'd pulled close to the window eight hours ago. By her calculation, Hattie figured the men had now spent at least seven business days parked out front of this particular bank awaiting her arrival. She figured it could've been a day or two longer since she didn't immediately visit the bank when she received the letter. The amount of time and money involved in this operation was beyond comprehension.

She took a shower to refocus and clear her mind. After toweling off and donning a warm, fluffy Hilton bathrobe, she lay back in the queen bed and stared at the ceiling, formulating a plan. Ten minutes later, she made up her mind: she'd visit the bank tomorrow. She had to. It was worth the risk to find out what had been left for her.

Yes, she could try to wait out the men in the car, but her assumption was that they wouldn't be going away anytime soon. She'd disguise herself as best she could and slip into the bank, hopefully undetected. She'd enter the building and immediately head to the women's bathroom on the right side of the lobby. She'd hang out there for a few minutes, then exit the bathroom and scan the bank for the men. If they followed her into the bank, she'd abort.

If not, game on.

CHAPTER FOURTEEN

Annapolis, Maryland

I WAS IN southeast Annapolis in a commercial part of town. I'd driven twice around the suspect's block. Just to get a feel for the area. There were a few mom-and-pop businesses in the vicinity, but most of the shops were boarded up.

That included the suspect's place.

The Annapolis address turned out to be a wholesale furniture store. I stayed at Slim's place last night and used his computer to check the address on Google Earth. I wasn't surprised, then, when I rolled into the neighborhood and saw it was a run-down, vacated part of the city near the docks.

Slim wasn't with me this morning. He had clients scheduled for eight and nine o'clock. He'd given me one of his cars and his Beretta PX4 Storm. Told me to be careful.

Honestly, I didn't feel that I needed to be careful—or needed a handgun, for that matter—since I assumed the boarded-up furniture warehouse was completely devoid of life, minus a few rats, of course.

After my third circle around the block, I parked two hundred feet down the street from the warehouse. While I basked in the heater's warm air, I tucked the Beretta into the back of my shorts and untucked my shirt to conceal it. When I exited the vehicle and began walking south to the furniture store, I tried not to focus on the frigid forty-degree weather. Instead, I laughed at how big the uniform was. I wondered how Slim secured such a large UPS outfit. The shorts hung well below my knees and the shirt easily shifted around as I walked.

Slim frequently used the outfit as a disguise when he needed to check out a house or business. I agreed that it was a good ruse. I could walk quickly around the building and peer into the windows and look like a legitimate UPS employee curious if anybody was home to sign for the package.

When I reached the store, I realized there weren't too many windows to actually peer into. I hustled from pane to pane, my cold breath clouding the frosty glass. A majority of the windows were boarded up; the few that weren't had been painted white. There were red letters in the windows spelling out words like "clearance," "closing for good," "everything must go."

Fortunately, a few of the windows had chipped paint, so I was able to look inside. No surprise, a ton of furniture appeared to fill the warehouse. I couldn't tell for sure it was furniture because every item had a dusty, cream-colored tarp lying over-top of it.

Stepping back from the windows, I surveyed the business. The place was huge, maybe forty or fifty thousand square feet, and it expanded around the corner. There were four large roll-up metal warehouse doors on this side of the street. People would've been able to amble in and out of the business to easily check out the goods without committing themselves too far into the warehouse. I imagined when all the doors were rolled up, light would've entered the place so it wouldn't look as scary and dingy as it did right now.

I hurried to the cross street and rounded the corner, stopping in front of two more roll-up doors. What caught my attention were the locks on the doors. They were padlocks, made from massive chunks of metal. The base of the padlock was twice as big as my balled-up fist. And they were clearly new. The metal doors themselves were faded and had rust spots in certain areas, so the locks stood out in stark contrast.

Continuing on, I stopped in front of a heavy wooden door at the far end of the business. My guess was the door opened into the office area, where customers would go to inquire about the furniture or settle their bill.

I pounded on the door. Not expecting anyone to answer, I walked back to the corner, blowing my breath into my hands to warm up. Halfway there, to my surprise, I heard a click, followed by the door opening. I hustled back to the open door.

But nobody was standing inside the doorway.

Had it opened on its own?

I peeked in, holding the UPS package out in front.

"Um, hello," I said. "UPS."

A male voice responded. "I didn't order no package. Not that I recall."

The voice came from straight ahead, but I couldn't see the man since it was fairly dark inside the warehouse. Once I stepped in, though, I saw a figure standing on the top third of a staircase directly in front of me, about fifty feet away.

The man said, "'Course I be drinking often and could be prone to making an impromptu online purchase. The misses used to say that about me. Certainly, she did."

To get a better look, I stepped farther into the office area. The warehouse wasn't warm, but it was at least fifty degrees, so I couldn't see my breath anymore. As I stepped toward the staircase, I heard a subtle whir to my left. I looked over and saw a camera tracking my movements.

"That's right, Mr. Package Delivery Man, I saw you peeking into my establishment and all." He made a tsk-tsk sound with his tongue against the roof of his mouth.

I cleared my throat. "Just doing my job, sir, trying to figure out if this is the right address."

Two steps later, I could see more details. From the man's outline, he appeared to be average height and weight. Could be the cable guy. His right hand rested on the landing to his right. His palm and fingers were between the wooden railing slats and out of view, so I wasn't sure if he was stabilizing himself or holding onto something.

The man said, "What address you looking for, son?"

I recited the wrong address.

He tsked again while waving his left hand across his body. "That's clear across the street, boy, maybe two or three doors down as well. You mighty far away."

I glanced at the package. "Didn't know I was that far off." I chuckled. "What's your name? And what address am I at anyway?"

"You can't be that bad at your job, son, can you? Mighty cold out there to be jacketless." The man kept still and didn't proceed down the steps. In fact, he didn't move a muscle.

"Let me see that package," he said.

He still didn't move, however, which was odd and put me on alert. I probably should've apologized and retreated. But I really wanted a look at his face.

Against my better judgment, I proceeded forward, angling slightly to my right because I wanted to glimpse his right hand to see if he was holding something. Like a weapon.

Before I reached the base of the stairs, I kept my head straight, but my eyes scanned left and right. That was when I spotted it, just a few feet to my right. The cable man uniform. The pants and shirt were draped over an office chair, which was partially tucked under a desk.

This was the guy.

When I reached the base of the stairs, he said, "Put the package on the steps, son."

I hesitated because the man stayed so rigid. He didn't move or point or even gesture. I still didn't have a solid view of his right hand since I was now too far underneath the landing.

But I could see more details. The man wore combat pants, along with a gray tank top and black boots. He looked to be around fifty or sixty years old. He had a strong, wiry upper body. Full-sleeve tattoos on both arms. His hair was curly, disheveled, and hung about shoulder-length. He reminded me of Jim Morrison from The Doors, but not a peaceful Jim. Far from it.

"Put it down, son," he said, pointing at the bottom steps with his left hand.

His calculating eyes stared me down. I'd seen that look before from hardened veterans. This guy was skeptical and on edge about my presence. I was ninety percent sure his right hand was on a weapon.

"Never mind," I said, glancing at the package again. "I'm way off on this delivery. Sorry for bothering you. I'll get out of your hair."

Before I stepped back, the man spoke in a fierce tone. "Son, let me see it. Put the package on the fourth step from the bottom. NOW."

I hesitated, not liking the situation one bit. The man wasn't budging or taking his hand away from the railing. I quickly formulated a plan.

"Sure enough," I replied. "Sounds like you really want to see it. The name and address are right there on the label." I leaned forward and pretended like I was going to put the package down. "Nothing special in the package either. It's pretty light. Probably just some papers or documents inside."

Just before I placed the package on the fourth step, I looked up. "Actually, why don't you see for yourself." I flung the box at the man, keeping all my attention on his right hand.

The man let the box hit his torso. After that, his left hand pounded against the wall. A button was there, one I hadn't noticed before. Suddenly the door behind me slammed shut.

Then the man moved his right hand. As soon as I saw a gun stock, I dove to my right.

A second later, wind from the buckshot blew past my feet, but no thunderous boom echoed through the warehouse. I scrambled to my feet and proceeded to safety around the back of the staircase, pulling out the Beretta PX4 Storm in the process.

I didn't hear any footsteps rushing down the steps either. In fact, it was deathly quiet. All I heard was my own breaths, which were clearly escalating.

I clicked off the safety and racked a round into the gun's chamber. The sound echoed throughout the large space.

"Definitely no delivery man," the man said. "Like I reckoned."

It sounded like he was at the top of the staircase, opposite me. I couldn't make a run for the door.

"What kinda delivery man carries?" he continued. "Sounded like a Beretta. Am I right, son?"

Geez, this guy was good, though I didn't acknowledge it aloud. Instead, I looked around, paying particular attention to the standalone staircase leading to the second floor. I could see the underside of the second story protruding a few feet out from the stairs. I cautiously stepped forward and glanced up. A railing circled the perimeter. The second story wasn't enclosed. It overlooked the warehouse floor.

Moments later, a shotgun protruded over the railing. It had a suppressor, a Salvo 12, attached to the end. I eased backward, wondering what the hell I'd gotten myself into.

Cable guy was serious business.

I controlled my breathing as I watched the man case the warehouse floor. He slowly moved the shotgun from left to right. I took my eyes from the gun and looked behind me, toward the closed door. I calculated the time and distance to make it there, ultimately deciding it was futile. Especially if the door had automatically locked. All the man would need to do is turn and take a few steps down the stairs, then fill my back with buckshot as I struggled with the door.

When I turned my attention back to the shotgun, the suppressor suddenly dove straight down, then angled in. Before I could react, a muted boom blew a hole in the concrete floor three feet in front of me.

Bits of concrete pelted my legs and chest, but otherwise I remained unscathed. Stepping back further, I aimed the Beretta at the railing above me and waited.

The man laughed. "I don't hear ya. Did I getcha, son?"

I heard the shotgun cock. The engaging click was the loudest sound I'd heard since the altercation started. When the shotgun appeared over the railing again, I immediately pulled the Beretta's trigger.

The sound from the Beretta was intense, so loud it covered up the clank of the shotgun as it dropped from the railing and smashed against the concrete floor. My first instinct was to run and grab it, but after three steps I stopped myself. Cable guy could have a handgun in the back of his waistband. And he'd waste me when I ran out to grab it.

"We know you killed the senators," I shouted. "Snuck out of the building in your cable man outfit." As I spoke, I stepped behind the chair with the uniform draped over it. The chair was on old caster wheels. While gingerly rolling it backward, I continued, "We have video evidence of you leaving the building."

"Hmm," he replied. "You're an imposter, son, an intruder, and now a liar. Not very becoming of you."

Once the chair was in position, I said, "We got you, old man. Of course, we don't know why you did it, but we got you."

"Lookedy-here," he said. "'Bout the only thing you got is yourself in a situation. If you know anything 'bout anything, you know I have an elevated position with views in all directions." He paused and racked a round into the chamber of whatever gun he now had on him. "Tactical advantage: me. Disadvantage: you. You're a dead man, son."

When he paused again, I put both hands on the back of the chair and pushed it as hard as I could. The chair wheeled in the opposite direction of the shotgun. As soon as it emerged from under the second floor, it exploded into pieces from whatever hand cannon the man used.

But I was already moving in the opposite direction toward the shotgun. I scooped it up without missing a step. There was a tall, covered piece of furniture just a few feet past the shotgun. I dove behind it just in time.

The tarped object splintered and crumpled from the onslaught of bullets. Within moments, the tarp shredded away, revealing an old grandfather clock. Pieces of the clock rained down on my back. But I was only focused on counting the shots, waiting for the pause in the action, waiting to make a move.

Bullets kept coming, however. After fifteen shots, I knew he was using a high-capacity magazine. More than likely, he had eighteen rounds in the magazine, so he was about to run out.

I grabbed the shotgun, which was already pre-cocked. Cable guy had fired two rounds already. Since most shotguns held three shells, I figured I only had one shot left.

When the man stopped firing, I rolled out from behind the clock. Getting to my knees, I quickly pointed and fired. And destroyed a portion of the second-story railing. About a six-foot-wide swath of broken wood was all that was left in the shot's wake. The buckshot, however, hit left of the man's position, so he didn't take a direct hit.

The man did scamper back, though. Perhaps I hit him in the leg; I wasn't sure. I cocked the gun but immediately felt an empty chamber, so I dropped it, whipped out the PX4, and fired off some cover shots as I scrambled forward, stopping at the base of the staircase.

Breathing heavily, I took a moment to regroup. While I did, I heard the man shuffling upstairs. I was safe by the staircase for the time being. Unfortunately, I couldn't move away from the stairs unless I risked putting myself in the man's line of fire.

I knew I'd have to hunker down and wait for his move.

And he only had two moves.

He'd either come charging down the stairs or drop over the railing where I'd blown a wide hole. And if he came over the railing, I'd put five holes in him before he hit the ground. So I doubted he'd be that dumb.

He'd come down the stairs, fully armed with guns ready to blaze. That was my best guess, and what I'd do. The safest place for me to be, then, would be on the back side of the stairs where I was now. But I had another idea, one less obvious.

I slowly eased my way to the east side of the stairs, which was drywalled from the ground to the underside of the second story. In contrast, the other side of the stairs had no wall, was open to the office, and had a spindled railing that followed the stairs' descent. There was no hiding there.

As I approached the edge of the wall where it met the base of the stairs, I heard the man slowly descending the steps. He whistled some tune, which I didn't pay attention to. I got prone to the floor, keeping my body tight to the wall and the PX4 stretched out in front of me. I planned to blow out his knee or foot at the exact moment he stepped around the edge of the wall looking for me.

He wouldn't expect me so tight and low to the wall.

Each step grew louder. The whistling did, too, but again I didn't focus on it. Instead, I counted his steps. I guessed the staircase was about fifteen steps or so. By the time the man hit the tenth step, the anticipation was too much. I held my breath.

Two steps later, the man stopped his descent. And his whistling.

Then I heard it: a slight whirring sound. The same sound I heard earlier with the office camera. But this whirring was farther off and barely noticeable. I glanced left and strained my eyes. Seconds later, I picked up the camera, which was mounted high on a wall about sixty feet away. The camera angled down and pointed right at me. The lens moved forward and back, trying to focus in on my position.

The man probably had his security cameras linked to his phone. And he could be looking at the screen right now, at my exact spot on the floor.

It was a stupid, awful mistake.

One that was about to cost me my life.

CHAPTER FIFTEEN

INSTEAD OF FIRING right away, he said, "Gotcha, son."

That gave me two seconds to roll, creating just enough space away from the wall. The shot blasted a gaping hole through the drywall. The bullet dug a softball-sized crater in the concrete floor, right where my head had been. The shot ricocheted into the warehouse.

With only seconds to spare, I scrambled to my feet and dove for cover behind the desk to my right, the one where the chair had been.

The man pumped the desk full of lead as I skidded behind it. The desk splintered and cracked but stopped the bullets from penetrating my body. When he paused on the trigger, I spun around, leaned to my right, and fired off two shots in his general direction.

The shots weren't meant to hit him. They acted as cover fire as I backpedaled to a new position. The only thing I had going for me was all the tarped pieces of furniture in the warehouse, which enabled me to retreat deeper into the warehouse while providing cover.

As I moved from piece to piece, keeping my body crouched as low as it could go, the furniture took a beating from the barrage of bullets, which came in rapid succession and followed my every movement.

Bullets hissed and plunked into wood or ricocheted off metal in seemingly endless fashion. The shots were suppressed, zipping around me in near silent mode. The loudest sounds came from a few ricochets that broke the warehouse windows, and two that rattled off the metal roll-up doors.

Every time I thought there'd be a break in the firestorm, bullets kept whizzing overhead.

Where was he getting all the firepower?

By the time I reached the corner farthest from where I believed the man to be, I stopped retreating and took a cover-fire position, kneeling beside a tarped couch. There was a large piece of furniture eight feet in front of me that protected my position and took the brunt of the man's fire. I guessed it was an entertainment center, but it disintegrated into pieces so quickly it was hard to tell.

With the PX4 outstretched, I peeked around what was left of the entertainment center and watched the man. He worked the perimeter of the warehouse, closest to the roll-up doors, moving furniture to furniture from north to south. The man stopped at random pieces of furniture and fired a full magazine my direction, then dumped the weapon and moved on. I quickly realized he'd stashed weapons throughout the warehouse. Twice I watched him reach under a tarp and pull out a new gun, then unload it at me.

So I played his game. I fired a few shots in his direction. Since I was on the opposite side of the warehouse, the east side, I worked south to north, stopping at each piece of furniture I encountered and pulling off the tarp, searching for his weapons stash. Every four to five seconds I fired off a shot toward the southwest corner of the warehouse.

When I pulled the third tarp away, I was shocked to find an M16 rifle on a recliner. What surprised me more was the grenade launcher fitted to the rifle. It appeared to be the M203 launcher, one I'd used before. That particular launcher held a variety of different rounds for special purposes.

As bullets hissed by my left ear, I dove on the ground for cover. After the onslaught stopped, I popped up and fired whatever was in the launcher toward the southwest corner.

It hissed from the barrel and left a smoky trail. There was no explosion on impact, which told me it wasn't a grenade in the launcher.

Seconds later, thick smoke filled the corner and I heard the man coughing. I'd fired a CS round at him, tear gas that cops used for riot control. When the man emerged from the white cloud, I fired the M16 rifle. The selector had been set to a short blast, so three rounds exploded from the barrel.

And at least one round hit his lower leg. The man spun and fell behind a piece of furniture. When he emerged, he was scrambling on his belly. I pulled the trigger and, unfortunately, missed him to the right with the three-round burst.

He disappeared behind another tarped piece, then about fifteen seconds later popped up wearing a gas mask.

I switched the M16 to full auto and blasted a swath of bullets his direction. The rounds tracked slightly overhead. Before I had a chance to realign—to my surprise—the man limped straight back into the billowing gas cloud. I fired into the haze, unsure if I'd gotten another piece of him.

Moments later, the CS round, which was still pouring gas, hurtled toward me. It landed over my head. I fell to my knees, gagging. The gas scorched my throat and burned like acid in my eyes.

After a coughing and blinking fit, I knew I had to move. *But which direction?* Ahead would put me directly into the gas. Behind would expose me to the man.

My momentary hesitation cost me. The gas overwhelmed my lungs, causing me to drop from my knees to my stomach, clutching at my chest. With my eyes closed, I buried my face in my shirt sleeve, desperately trying to find some relief.

As I lay prone, I coughed and sputtered into my shirt. Suddenly I felt a massive kick to the side. I doubled over and curled up, holding my aching side. I blinked a few times until my burning vision cleared, just enough to see the masked man standing over me. Wispy white clouds of smoke obscured his entire body. All I could see was a floating head wearing a black gas mask.

Then I saw the sole of a boot coming at me.

That was the last thing I remembered.

CHAPTER SIXTEEN

I WOKE TO incredible discomfort. And the discomfort wasn't from my hands being shackled behind my back and wrapped around a railing spindle. It was from the aftereffects of the CS gas and the boot to the face.

Worse than my throbbing nose and splitting headache were my burning eyes. I blinked, squeezed them shut, opened them wide. Nothing seemed to help. Eventually, I closed them and slumped my head, staying that way for who knows how long.

I fell asleep or passed out or some combination of the two. When a bucket of water splashed onto my face, I came to. The water also helped clear the lingering effects of the gas from my eyes. After some rapid blinking, I finally was able to see again. Unfortunately, I was staring into the face of my captor.

"You look like garbage, son."

I felt even worse.

"Not that it matters," he continued. "You'll be dead soon. In fact …" He stuck a crooked pointer finger in my face. "You should be dead by now, but I reckoned I better talk with you first and figure out just what you think you know."

The man squatted on his haunches and leaned in. With his shaggy, long hair he'd looked like an older Jim Morrison. Up close was a different story. He reminded me more of Keith Richards. The man had a gaunt, haggard-looking face. His complexion was sallow and pockmarked. What drew my eye were his cheeks. They were incredibly sunken, so deep they'd make a super model jealous.

"So tell me, son," he said. "Who else knows you're here? And what's this about some video of me leaving an alley. What kind of shenanigans do you think I was up to?"

I swallowed, then smiled. "Alley, I never said alley. I said we have video evidence of you leaving the building in your cable man outfit. Nothing about an alley."

He responded with a toothy grin. "You think you're smart. So smart, don't you, son?"

I didn't respond.

"Tell me what you know—or think you know—and who you told it to."

I scoffed. "Why would I talk? You just told me I'm a dead man."

"Reckoned you'd say that." He stood and gingerly stepped back. I'd shot him in his left calf; he'd crudely tied a tourniquet just above the wound.

By his right foot was a large battery with a wand attached to it via some wires. He skidded the unit toward me until it touched my feet, then grabbed the collar of my shirt. Two tugs later, the UPS shirt ripped clear down the middle, exposing my bare chest.

He reached back and grabbed the wand. Unfortunately, I knew exactly what the device was. The bronze tip and insulated handle gave it away.

"Know what this is, son?"

"I have an idea."

"Maybe a little jolt will change your mind. Human body is a surprisingly good conductor of electricity. 'Course this truck battery isn't strong enough to stop your heart and kill you. But it's certainly gonna smart. Like a real bugger."

I maintained eye contact and didn't flinch.

He eyed me, eventually dropping the wand and resting it on my left thigh. "I'll give you a second to think about that, son, before using it. Maybe a moment of reflection will help you make the right decision."

I didn't spend a second thinking about how much pain the wand would inflict. Instead, I studied my surroundings while he limped backward. We were on the second level of the furniture warehouse, which was open on three sides. I was affixed to the wooden railing that circled the perimeter. The area was sparsely furnished. To my right was a futon bed. A footlocker sat at the end of the bed. To my left was a makeshift kitchen. A few pots, coffee maker, microwave, and a hotplate sat on a piece of plywood. The wood had been cut in half and propped up by milk crates on either end. A real janky-looking kitchen counter. Clearly, the man lived up here.

In between his bed and the kitchen was a large metal desk with a rolling chair. Cable guy was currently seated on the chair. On the desk itself was an array of monitors, along with two computer towers. I counted eight screens. Each monitor was hooked up to cameras inside and outside the building. It looked like there were three outside feeds: one camera above the office door, the other two cameras focused on the different sides of the building. There were five indoor cameras. Every square inch of the warehouse, both inside and out, was covered by a live video feed.

While the man studied the live feeds, he spoke with his back to me. "Your Beretta made quite the racket. Fortunately, this is a pretty unpopulated part of town. Doesn't look like there are any prying eyes on my place." He glanced at his military watch. "You were out for an hour, so it's safe to assume nobody heard the commotion. Otherwise, they'd already be snooping around here."

He turned to look at me. "Nobody's coming, son. That's the point. Let's not draw this out and make it painful for you. Tell me what you know."

"I know you made a mistake," I said. "That's what I know. And it was a huge mistake."

He wheeled himself over on the chair, pushing with his right foot. He studied my expression as he covered the twenty feet separating us.

I kept my face blank as he approached.

When he got within three feet of my face, he narrowed his eyes and smiled. "You know jack squat, son. Nada." He snickered and leaned back. "Maybe you have footage of me leaving the building. So what if you do? What does that prove?"

"Walther P99." That was all I said.

He stared at me while maintaining a good poker face.

Eventually, I broke the silence. "With an army green polymer handle. You took it with you, old man. Why would you do that? You realize that was a huge mistake, right? It proves a third party was present in the office."

Though his face betrayed no emotion, the fact that he had no quick comeback told me I'd caught him off guard.

I kept at it. "You should've left it at the scene. Why didn't you do that?"

He didn't respond.

"If you would've left it at the scene," I continued, "we wouldn't have thought twice about things. Never would've entertained a third-party involvement."

He narrowed his brows and said one word: "We?"

I nodded. "We."

He let out a long sigh, looked up toward the high ceiling, and ran his fingers through his wavy hair. "The feds made an official statement. I watched the press conference."

"But we found a credible third party on surveillance video leaving the building at the time of the murders. And that was after the statement was made."

He eased from his chair and limped the length of the floor. He paced from where I'd busted open the railing with the shotgun to the far corner of the room where his futon bed was positioned. Along the way, he muttered, "I was careful. So careful."

While he paced, I glanced at the camera monitors because I saw movement. There was a woman on one of the outside cameras peering into a warehouse window. I was ninety percent sure it was Ramona Sanchez. I strained my eyes to see better, but then quickly stopped when the man looked over. I had to keep all his attention on me, so he wouldn't turn back toward the monitors.

So I baited him. "You weren't careful enough, I guess, were you? You were sloppy; in fact, awfully sloppy."

He steamed toward me. "I wasn't sloppy; I was prepared, careful. It was your Walther, wasn't it? Felton Byrd never carried a sidearm with him. That's what my research told me." He jabbed his crooked finger at me. "You gave it to him."

Before I had a chance to respond, he jabbed the wand into my right pectoral muscle. The current raged through me; immediately my limbs ceased, and my jaw clenched. Following that, my whole body shook and vibrated on the floorboards. My neck tightened during the shaking, which craned my head skyward.

As I writhed in pain, staring at the ceiling, I prayed for it to end. And it did, eventually.

When the man pulled the wand away, he shouted at me, "Who's the 'we?' Who else knows about the Walther? Who?"

I was too spent to respond.

So he jabbed me again.

After another agonizing round of shaking, the current stopped. This time the man didn't say anything. Instead, he waited for me to recover enough so I could respond.

After a minute, he spoke. "I said, who else knows about the Walther?"

"The feds," I said, coughing. "That's the 'we'; the FBI knows all about the Walther."

"You're a fed?" He furrowed his brow. "What other feds know? I want names."

Not a chance I would give names, so I kept it broad and lied. "Everyone; the entire local field office in Washington knows."

"The WFO knows about me?"

I nodded. "Everyone there does." Which was obviously far from the truth since I didn't even know this guy's name.

He looked away for a moment, deep in thought. His right knee bounced with nerves or frustration or a combination of the two. Suddenly I realized he may freak out about the info I just provided.

Maybe he'd snap and do something rash because he thought the feds were on their way.

I interrupted his thinking. "One of the cameras outside the congressional complex picked up your movements, saw you crossing the street and getting into a car. I traced the plates to this address. On Google Earth, however, it seemed clear this was a non-operational business and not your living quarters. So I first wanted to swing by and poke around and see if it was a legitimate lead. Which it obviously was."

He turned back. I could see the tension in his body had abated somewhat.

"You're on your own then?" he asked. "That what you're saying?"

"For now," I replied. I didn't want him thinking the cavalry was about to storm in, but I also didn't want him getting too comfortable and thinking he had ample time to continue torturing me.

"What does that mean?"

"I mean, when I don't show up to work, people will get suspicious and look into my whereabouts. And I certainly didn't keep this address a secret. There's a sticky note with your address right on my desk."

He looked away again. I took the opportunity to squint in the direction of the security monitors. The woman I'd seen was definitely Ramona Sanchez. She was currently standing in front of the office door. She had her hand raised like she was about to knock.

I held my breath.

She did the smart thing and refrained from knocking. She stepped back from the door and whipped out her cellphone. I figured she was either calling me or calling for backup. Earlier, when she peered into one of the windows, I imagined she saw the remnants of a gunfight, so I hoped she was calling in backup.

Regardless, I had to buy time. "Listen," I said, "you're obviously going to dispose of me. Eventually the feds will track you here. It might not be this morning, or this afternoon, maybe not even tonight, but by tomorrow morning they'll be here. For sure. And you're a smart, prepared, careful man. I already know that, so I imagine you have an exit plan. Probably booby-trapped this place to burn, am I right?"

I didn't wait to see if he'd answer, just continued talking. "So why don't you tell me what went down in Cooper's office. Why take the Walther with you? And who hired you to take out the senators? Why not tell me since I'm a dead man? You're going to burn this place and destroy all the evidence, anyway. Including me."

He scoffed. "You think I'm gonna say a word to you? Just how much of that electricity went to your head, son?"

"You tell me what went down in the office and who hired you, and I'll tell you exactly what the feds know. That could come in mighty handy for you. Enable you to get out in front of things. What do you say?"

"I say I'm gonna shake the info outta you. How about that?"

"Listen, you hunted down a Salvo 12 to suppress the shotgun blast. The weapon I found on the armchair was an M203 grenade launcher attached to an M16. It fired a CS round in your direction. And that wand in your hand is a picana wand, or technically speaking, a picana electrica. It's been used mainly in Argentina and a few other South American countries. Laymen and civilians aren't privy to that type of weapons and torture info, and you know it. I ain't giving up jack, old man, no matter how many times you juice me. And neither would you if the roles were reversed."

He eyed me, taking a moment to think. Eventually, he looked at his watch and sighed. "Fine then, what the hell, you're a dead man soon, anyway. I'll show you the video from inside the senator's office. Not a chance I'll tell you who I work for, so don't even push it. Not even worth your breath to ask. In return, you tell me how much the feds know."

I knew I wouldn't get a better deal from him, but I pretended like I was mulling it over. What concerned me was the video. He'd have to go get it, which would potentially turn his attention back to his computer and the monitors.

The man tapped his watch face. "Time's ticking. Take it or leave it."

Perhaps he'd have to uncuff me and take me over to his computer to watch the video. If that was the case, it would provide me with an opportunity, a fighting chance at least, to take him down. "Fine, I agree."

"I'll go first," he offered. "That way if you suddenly clam up, I'll get the chance to see what this picana can really do to a human body. See what you're really made of, soldier."

He turned toward the desk.

My eyes widened as I strained forward and looked at the monitors. Moments later, I masked a sigh of relief. Ramona Sanchez was not on any of the screens. I guessed she'd called in backup and was waiting for them to arrive while sitting in her car. At least that was what I hoped had happened.

The man paid little attention to the monitors. He grabbed a laptop from the top right-hand drawer, then used a key to open the drawer below it. Pulling out a flash drive, he limped back and took a seat on the chair. He stuck in the flash drive, queued it up, then spun the computer around so I could see it.

"Here you go," he said. "Hope you're not squeamish."

The recording flickered on. I immediately recognized the senator's office. The camera was in the back-left corner of the room; I assumed it was hidden on one of the bookshelves in that corner. You could clearly see Morse Cooper, his desk, the entire wall behind him, including the bathroom door. In the forefront, you could see the back of Felton's chair and the top of the senator's head. The men were discussing something. I didn't know what since there was no sound. From the look on Cooper's face, whatever they were discussing was serious. Cooper had already poured the bourbon shots. He had a letter in his hand, gestured to it, then put it on the desk and slid it toward Felton Byrd.

Suddenly the bathroom door jammed open. A man stood in the doorframe with the Maxim 9 clutched in his right hand. His left hand held a black duffel bag. The man had pantyhose stretched over his face. Though the mask obscured his features, it was clear he was the man sitting in front of me. You could easily tell because of the wiry frame and bushy long hair protruding from the bottom of the makeshift mask.

As cable guy brought the Maxim into firing position, I noticed movement from Felton. No doubt he was extracting the Walther from his pocket.

Sure enough, a second later I saw Felton's arm and the Walther extend from the chair. Though I couldn't hear them, I could tell shots were fired almost simultaneously. The man in the doorway flinched but didn't drop, telling me Felton's shot had missed.

Felton, on the other hand, took a direct hit. His head slumped forward and disappeared from the camera's view. The Walther dropped straight to the ground on the right side of the chair.

Morse Cooper, in total shock, had taken a standing position in front of his chair and placed both hands over his mouth.

The assassin wasted no time. He ordered Cooper to sit, then quickly pinned Cooper's right hand against his shoulder. No doubt so that gunshot residue would cover Cooper's hand.

Before the senator knew what was happening, the killer pressed the gun against his temple and pulled the trigger. He didn't spend a second looking at the carnage. Instead, he stood by the right side of Cooper's chair and held the Maxim out, eyeballing where head level on Cooper had been. Then he dropped the gun on the ground and side-stepped his way past the desk.

Next, he turned his attention to the bathroom door. Seconds later, he found what he was looking for: the slug. Felton's shot had lodged into the left side of the doorframe. The man pulled a knife from his pocket and dug out the round, then stepped back and looked at the hole. Clearly, he didn't like what he saw, so he stepped forward and used the tip of the knife to splinter the wood around the hole. Then he peeled away a strip of wood so it didn't look anything like a bullet hole.

No wonder ERT didn't find it.

Satisfied, he turned his attention to Felton Byrd, in particular the Walther that was on the ground to the right of the chair. He looked at it for a few seconds, then bent down and picked it up. While at Felton's right side, he pulled out what looked to be a wet wipe and thoroughly scrubbed Felton's right hand.

He knew GSR was like talcum powder and could be wiped away.

Next, he placed the duffel bag on the corner of the desk and pulled out the cable uniform, along with a towel. The man used the towel to wipe a small amount of blood from his neck, as well as dab some of Cooper's blood that had covered his shirt. Then the assassin put on the uniform, covering up his bloody shirt.

He placed the Walther in the duffel bag and swept up the letter on the desk. Then he picked up the envelope, quickly eyed it, and put it back down. He slid the letter opener across the desk until it was closest to Felton Byrd's side.

After stepping back, he took in the scene for a moment, then proceeded to the bookshelf. There were a few seconds of fumbling as the man pulled the camera from its hidden spot. Seconds later, instant darkness filled the screen as the feed cut out.

Before I had a chance to process the video, the man started talking. "Every detail was planned, every single thing. In minutiae. I'd broken into that office a week earlier. Set up the camera and grabbed Cooper's Maxim. Then hacked into the senator's laptop and sent the death threats to Byrd. I waited—"

"Where?" I asked. "Where'd you wait?"

"I holed up in that building a total of nine days. Nine days, just waiting for Felton Byrd to come. Sources told me the two discussed issues quite frequently in that office. He would surely come ask his pal about the threats; that's what I was told. Which, in the end, was true. I just didn't know I'd have to wait a whole week."

"Holed up where?" I asked again.

"What threw me the most, however, wasn't the waiting, it was the Walther. That damn Walther surprised me." He shook his head.

I tried a different question. "Did you send the death threats to fit the narrative of a murder-suicide, or did you send them to ensure the two men got together?"

"Both," he replied. "Didn't want the murder-suicide to come from seemingly nowhere, so we fabricated a serious spat between the two. Since we knew they were good friends, we knew Byrd would confront Cooper over the threats. We knew they often met at Cooper's to discuss serious issues."

"We?" I said.

He responded with a toothy grin. "Already told you too much, son. Not a chance you'll get that outta me."

"Can you at least tell me why? Why go to these lengths?"

He laughed. "They knew something. Or at least Cooper knew something, and we assumed he told Byrd. But don't even ask what. We've chatted enough, and I honestly don't know. Have no clue what it's all about."

I sort of believed him. I tried one more question. "The Walther, why didn't you just leave it at the scene?"

He thought for a moment. "It didn't fit the narrative. We planned for it to look like a murder-suicide. Senator Byrd confronts Cooper over the death threats. They meet to hash it out, but things get heated. Byrd reaches for the letter opener and comes at Cooper, so Cooper takes him down. Distraught over killing his buddy, and not sure people would believe it was in self-defense, especially since Byrd came at him with only a dull letter opener, he takes his own life. I think having two guns at the scene makes it less likely to believe Cooper would've taken his own life in that situation. Right? Plus, Felton's shot was nowhere near Cooper's body. It was a good ten feet to the right of Cooper's office chair."

I nodded; he was probably right.

"Of course," he continued, "I definitely would've left it if I knew it wasn't his and that someone had given it to him, and that people would be looking for it." He paused.

Wanting to keep him talking, I said, "You couldn't have known. You were holed up in the complex for days. You couldn't have known that Senator Byrd hired me to investigate and protect him after the threats came through, and that I gave the senator a sidearm just prior to the meeting."

He didn't respond to my comments.

"So where did you hole up? Who put you up in that building?"

The man opened his mouth to speak, but he never got a chance to say a word. Because a huge boom echoed from below and interrupted our conversation.

We both glanced at the camera monitors. All three outdoor camera feeds showed the presence of armed men. At first, I thought they were SWAT, but then I realized Ramona had called in the big guns. It was HRTU, a hostage rescue team unit from the Bureau. Probably ten to twelve of them in riot gear, maybe more.

Another loud bang rocked the building.

My eyes flicked to the camera feed above the office door. Two men held a battering ram and were smashing it against the heavy wooden door.

The man didn't freak out like I thought he would. He turned back and simply grinned. "It's gonna boom a lot louder in a second. My advice: curl up and get as small as you can."

CHAPTER SEVENTEEN

UNFORTUNATELY, I COULDN'T curl up.

Not a chance. My hands were cuffed behind my back and wrapped around one of the railing spindles. I brought my knees up as far as I could instead. Just as I buried my face into my knees, my head snapped back from the explosion. It bounced hard off the spindle behind me.

I saw stars for maybe a minute or so. When my vision cleared, I saw the cable guy standing at the base of the footlocker. He'd laid out some weapons, along with a bunch of ammunition. Everything was on the floor to the left of the locker. He'd just finished donning a helmet and was currently clipping two hand grenades to his vest.

The man was beyond prepared.

Strapped around his back was a Colt Commando, an assault rifle similar to an M16, but with a shorter barrel and designed for close-quarters combat. Exactly what the man was preparing for with the HRTU below.

As the man swept some extra ammunition off the floor, he started turning my direction. I hung my head and pretended to still be knocked out.

Either the man was going to rush by and return later to kill me, or he was about to bury a round into my head. And I couldn't do anything about it.

His footsteps approached, then stopped. He felt close, real close. I didn't know if he was debating what to do, or if he was checking out the wound on the back of my head. But I didn't dwell on it. Simon popped to mind instead. I pictured my son's beautiful smiling face.

If I was about to die, I wanted Simon to be the last person I remembered.

A few tense seconds later, I heard footsteps shuffling away. When he started descending the stairs, I let out a sigh of relief and opened my eyes. Just as I did, a burst of gunfire echoed from below. The shots came from the Commando rifle. I could tell because the shorter barrel suppressed the rounds, which gave the assault rifle a distinctive sound.

I got to my feet, shimmying my hands upward as I stood. Then I leaned forward and looked at the monitors. Cable guy had obviously booby-trapped the office door with explosives. There was a massive hole in the wall where the door used to be. An HRT member suddenly appeared in the doorway, then just as suddenly dropped. I heard the short burst from the Commando a fraction of a second after seeing the man drop.

My eyes flashed to the inside cameras. I scanned each one to see if I could get a bead on cable guy's position. I couldn't. He was hidden somewhere, likely casing the opening in the wall, willing another unit member to come in. No way they would, however, not after witnessing their man go down like that.

Turning my attention to the railing, I heaved and yanked my arms upward in an attempt to break through the railing cap and free my cuffed hands. The cap was solid and sturdy, however, so I concentrated on the vertical spindle and kicked backward. After three solid boots, I heard the wood splinter. My adrenalin spiked at the sound.

I pounded the spindle with the sole of my boot, dead center where the wood was the weakest. The kicks were drowned out by the gunfire below. Cable guy and HRT were exchanging fire in short, concentrated bursts.

On the fifth kick, the spindle gave way, splitting in the middle. Immediately I crouched and slid my hands down until they were free.

Wasting no time, I ran to the desk. The laptop was to the left of the computer towers. Since my hands were still cuffed behind my back, I turned around and grabbed the edge of the laptop. I spun it until I felt the flash drive, then pulled out the drive and dropped it into my back pocket.

A huge *boom* erupted from the first floor, right underneath me. I glanced at the monitors. HRT had lobbed a flash grenade into the warehouse through the open wall. A smoke bomb immediately followed. I found cable guy on one of the screens. The team's actions didn't faze him. He was the picture of calm, kneeling in a cover-fire position with the Commando extended. He'd set up exactly where I'd been: beside the tarped couch in the southeast corner.

I watched him unleash a flurry of rounds into the spreading smoke, daring anybody to enter his facility. When he paused on the trigger, I heard a saw in the background. One of the outdoor cameras showed two HRT members buzzing through one of the massive locks on the roll-up doors.

I willed them to stop. If cable guy had booby-trapped the office door, surely he'd done the same with the roll-up doors. In fact, that was probably why he'd put such heavy-duty locks on the doors in the first place.

How do I warn them?

Just as I moved toward the footlocker to see what weapons were in there, I stopped. The desk's bottom drawer was still open. Cable guy hadn't closed and locked it. At the back of the drawer was a gun: Slim's Walther P99.

I used my foot and pulled out the drawer until it fell onto the floor, then I flipped it upside down. The Walther spilled out, but unfortunately, nothing else did. I'd hoped to find the handcuff key or maybe the letter from Cooper's office.

Moving toward the desk, I turned backward and opened the top drawer. After rooting around, I found nothing of interest, so I got down onto my butt beside the overturned drawer and picked up the Walther.

Holding a gun behind my back was, of course, useless, but I wasn't about to leave the Walther behind.

When I stood, I heard a beep from the computer towers. My eyes flashed to the screens. On each monitor was a timer in the top right-hand corner counting down from thirty. I blinked a few times in shock, unsure if the timer was for the warehouse to blow or for the computers to self-destruct.

I quickly peeked behind the two hard drive towers and saw the crude setup. Two red detonating wires extended from each tower. Both wire ends were attached to a piece of C4 plastic explosive, which was formed in the shape and thickness of a pencil, about three to four inches long.

Being a novice to explosives, I didn't even consider pulling out a wire and trying to defuse the small bomb. Instead, I hightailed it to the staircase, but I stopped before descending. Smoke billowed up the staircase, and I heard the staccato of gunfire from somewhere behind the thick white cloud.

Not a chance I was going down the stairs and into a direct path of bullets.

I hurried to the blown-out part of the railing, cursing my predicament. If my hands weren't cuffed behind me, I could easily hang drop the ten feet to the warehouse floor. Now I supposed I had to launch myself off the second floor from a sitting position.

I glanced back at the monitors.

Ten seconds.

Nine.

The C4 wouldn't cause huge amounts of damage, but it would blow up the desk, towers, and monitors, and send a ton of debris flying my direction. I had to get away from the blast. As I turned back, the number seven flashed on the screens.

I sat and scurried my butt to the floor's edge. My feet dangled two feet closer to the ground. Now I had an approximately eight-foot drop. I may or may not bust a leg.

I counted in my head: five seconds.

The worst part of the drop was having my hands behind me. I couldn't brace any part of the fall with them.

Four seconds.

I sucked in a nervous breath and teetered on the edge, but didn't launch myself off.

Was this my best move?

With two seconds on the timer, I said screw it and inched off the ledge, prepared for pain.

The ground came quicker than I imagined. I hit the floor at about the exact moment the monitors and desk blew into shrapnel. During my quick midair flight, I'd rotated a little to my left. Though my legs hit first, they immediately buckled. Most of my weight landed on my right shoulder.

On impact, I tried to roll out from the fall and mitigate the damage, but it didn't work. Instead, I writhed on the floor in excruciating pain. It felt like I'd tried to stop a train with my shoulder.

The gunfire started right after the noise from the explosion died. The sound of whizzing bullets pulled me from the pain and got me moving.

I looked around, located the Walther, then scooted on my knees and picked it up with my left hand. With the gun behind my back, I bent over and ran behind the shattered grandfather clock.

The fight had turned from short, concentrated bursts of fire to a full-out assault by both parties. From my current position, I couldn't physically see cable guy, but I could tell his gunfire was still coming from the southeast corner. The HRT guys hadn't breached the roll-up doors yet, which was a good thing. Hopefully they realized it might be a death trap.

As I contemplated my options, I knew I had to stop cable guy. Though HRT was highly trained and outnumbered him, the man was talented and prepared to fight to his death. He currently possessed two grenades, which meant imminent death for any unit members who got close to him. And for all I knew he'd hidden a flamethrower or bazooka under one of the tarps, which would easily wipe out the entire unit.

I kept low and worked toward his position, moving from furniture piece to furniture piece. What I wanted to do was crawl on my belly and stay hidden, but I quickly learned you can't crawl with your hands behind your back. Fortunately, there was so much noise and chaos, neither party saw nor heard me moving.

When I got close to cable man's position, I angled toward the inside warehouse wall. I worked my way along the perimeter until I was directly behind him. The only thing I had going for me was surprise. I had to sneak up on him without being spotted. If I was spotted anywhere in his periphery, he'd simply shift my direction and mow me down.

Once I was about fifteen feet away, I stayed put and watched cable guy. It looked like he was nearly out of ammunition for the Commando. However, he had another handgun and assault rifle lying on the floor to his right.

When HRT's current assault stopped, cable guy fed the last of his ammunition into the Commando and unleashed the weapon toward the northwest corner. Since the man was hell-bent on firing at HRT, he never stood a chance at seeing me.

The sole of my left boot connected in the middle of his back, so square and hard that I actually felt his spine bend inward. The Commando flew from his hands and skidded to a stop ten feet away. He collapsed onto his chest, but quickly rolled to his back. He saw me stepping toward him and reached for a grenade on his chest, but I'd been preparing for my next move.

His chin met the top, flat part of my right boot with incredible velocity. I teed him up as if I were kicking an NFL punt. Since he wasn't a particularly heavy man, his whole body lifted an inch off the ground and collapsed back. He immediately rolled on his left side and groaned in pain. No doubt I broke his jaw in a few places. Moments later, he stopped moving.

But HRT didn't.

They rushed toward me. When I saw them coming, I shouted, "Sanchez! I'm with Agent Sanchez. I'm the hostage!"

In return, all I heard was heated commands to put my hands up.

"Hands are cuffed!" I yelled back. "I CAN'T PUT THEM UP. I CAN'T!"

Fortunately, I'd provided enough info to stop them from dropping me. Unfortunately, they were still screaming at me to put my hands up. I wanted to drop the gun and turn to show them my cuffed hands, but I didn't dare move. Not a single muscle. I didn't even want to blink, for that matter.

As calmly as I could, I said, "Get Agent Sanchez. Please."

Sharp commands turned from "Hands up" to "Don't move." Which, of course, I wasn't even considering. I heard team members relay calls to get Sanchez. It took her probably twenty or thirty seconds to enter the warehouse, but it felt like twenty or thirty minutes.

As soon as she saw me, she shouted at the team, "He's with me. He's friendly. Ease up, he's not a target."

Sanchez stopped and looked at cable guy, still immobile on his left side. "He took out the target, obviously."

"Agent Sanchez," I said. "I have the Walther behind my back. My hands are cuffed. I don't want to move or drop the gun."

She nodded and told an HRT member to assist me. One of the men hurried over and took the Walther from my hands. He helped me into a sitting position, then worked on my cuffs, informing me he had a universal key.

Sanchez and another HRT member approached cable guy.

"Careful," I told them. "He has two grenades clipped to the front of his vest."

"I see one," Sanchez said. "But not the other."

The man with her said, "Probably under his left side."

I was so busy watching the two I hadn't noticed that my hands were free. I rolled my shoulders and flexed my fingers as I thanked the HRT member.

He held out the Walther. "Agent Sanchez, what do you want me to do with this?"

"Set it down and wait for ERT," she said. "It's evidence, so it needs to be bagged and tagged."

The man nodded and put it on the ground to my right.

Sanchez and the other HRT guy prepared to roll cable guy onto his back. While they got into position, I noticed cable guy's right foot shift, just a fraction. At least I think I saw it move.

As they began rolling him onto his back, cable guy's eyes flickered open, distracting the HRT guy and Sanchez for a second. But not me.

When his chest came into view, I noticed that his left pointer finger was hooked around the grenade's pull ring. Just as a smile spread across his face, I snatched the Walther off the floor and fired.

And pinned his left hand to his chest with a dead center shot, square in the back of his hand. Unfortunately, the bullet also blasted a hole in his heart, instantly killing him.

Sanchez looked back at me with huge eyes. The HRT guy realized what had happened and quickly secured the grenade, unclipping it from the vest.

There was silence in the warehouse for a few seconds as everyone else realized they just escaped being blown to bits. I dropped the Walther to my right and put my hands over my face.

Moments later, Sanchez was at my side. She put her hand on my shoulder. "You had to put him down, Chase. It's okay, you had to."

I looked at her. "Oh, I know. I'm not upset I had to shoot; I'm pissed he's dead."

"No worries," she said, shaking her head. "All in self-defense. We all witnessed it."

I tapped her hand, which was still on my shoulder. "You don't understand. Dead men can't talk, Agent Sanchez. And that guy"—I pointed at his body—"really needed to talk. He had plenty more information in his head. Information we desperately needed."

"Right," she said, nodding. "He really did, didn't he?"

CHAPTER EIGHTEEN

BAKER CUNNINGHAM CLOSED his office door and eyed the two men sitting in the chairs opposite his desk. "Gentlemen, what I'm about to tell you stays between the three of us."

Neither man broke their gaze. They nodded in unison.

To Baker, these men weren't soldiers he trusted to carry out the group's mission; that wasn't why they'd been recruited. They were recruited for their skills and expertise in combat; they were two of the original six men who'd been chosen and paid well to protect the organization, along with Baker Cunningham's personal interests.

Taking a seat, the leader continued. "I'm shocked to just learn of an important mission failure. The ramifications are huge. Beyond huge, actually. I can't stress that enough. We're all in jeopardy, especially myself."

He paused to see if either man had something to say. They didn't.

"The feds," Baker said, "will eventually make a connection and investigate our organization, so it's critical to keep them off our trail. And it must happen fast."

"How can we help?" the man to Baker's left asked.

"I have a plan," Baker said, "but it's best you two have no clue about it. Plausible deniability protects you both. Your mission is to protect this compound. For the actual plan itself, I'll hire outside assistance: people outside our state and the organization. Your job is to stay here and guard what we've built. Don't let the government come here and take what's not theirs."

Baker slid a piece of paper toward them with the names of the other soldier recruits in the organization.

"Everyone else," he continued, "is home for the holidays." Baker pointed at the man on his left. "I want you to deliver that message to the men. Normally I would, but it's safest if I get out of the country as fast as I can. I'm out as soon as we're done here."

He motioned at a duffel bag. "Anyone asks, whether it's our men or the cops or the feds, all you two know is that I'm away and you have no idea where."

Both men nodded.

"So you know, my plan is brash and bold and borderline treasonous. But I think it's the only way to get out of this mess. Only way to confuse the feds and ensure they don't come calling."

He leaned forward. "It's the only way, gentlemen, to potentially keep us all out of jail."

CHAPTER NINETEEN

SLIM AND I were at his house, which was just outside the city on a few acres of beautiful wooded land. He had a man cave at the back corner of his property. Half the building housed a small workout facility, along with some of his boy toys. The other half was his office. Currently we were in the office, sitting across from each other at a small table sipping some mediocre bourbon and decompressing from the day.

After I was released from the WFO, Slim drove me to Maryland to get his car. Along the way, I'd filled him in on everything that went down at the furniture warehouse.

Slim poured another two fingers of bourbon into our tumblers. "Just what the doctor ordered," he said.

"Not sure the doc would like me mixing bourbon with the cocktail of painkillers he gave me," I said. "But what the hell."

Just then, my cell rang.

"Who's that?" Slim asked.

"Agent Sanchez," I said, looking at the screen and scratching my scalp. I answered it and spoke with her for a brief moment.

"What was that about?" Slim asked after I hung up.

"She's out front of your house."

"You gave her my address?"

I shook my head. "Though I told her I was staying here tonight. Obviously, she tracked us down."

He pointed at me. "Good thing she's attractive. Normally wouldn't be too pleased to have an FBI agent knocking on my door." He left and returned with Ramona Sanchez less than five minutes later.

When she entered the office, she motioned at my outfit. "You still haven't changed, Garrison?"

"Tell me about it," I said. "Been cold all day, though the jacket you lent helped, so thanks. I've been a little busy and couldn't change."

Which was an understatement. My morning was spent at the hospital getting my shoulder attended to—which was now in a sling—and my head stitched up. My afternoon consisted of six straight hours at the WFO going over everything that had happened with cable guy. I can't tell you how many times I'd watched the now infamous video of Cooper and Byrd's murder with various federal agents.

"Plus," I said, "Slim thinks I look great in brown, so I didn't want to rush into a new outfit before he had a chance to see me."

With one hand, I eased off the blue FBI jacket that Sanchez had given me earlier in the day. While handing it to her, I displayed my legs for Slim's amusement. "And he's always had a thing for my legs."

He laughed. "Listen, your legs are your best feature. It certainly isn't your face. Looks like it's getting more swollen and bruised by the hour. Didn't know that was possible." He gestured at my exposed chest. "Can you at least cover up?"

Since cable guy had torn the UPS shirt, I couldn't button it up.

"This isn't Hawaii," he continued. "And you're far from Magnum, PI, pal."

"Slim's right," Sanchez said, handing back the windbreaker and looking away.

I laughed and covered up with the jacket.

Agent Sanchez took a chair from Slim's desk and brought it to our small table. "I was restless at the office and went out for a drive to clear my head. Figured I'd bring you two up to speed. Good news or bad news first?"

"Bad news," Slim and I said in unison. We clinked tumblers.

She gestured at me. "I wanted to bring you onboard in official capacity, as a sort of outside consultant. Or to borrow your term: a subcontractor." She smiled, then glanced at Slim. "I wouldn't say it's routine, but it's not that unusual for the Bureau to hire an outside expert. Since Garrison's been involved from the beginning, and a seasoned investigator, I figured he could help. Not to mention he knows more than anyone about Sherman Adams—"

I interrupted. "Sherman Adams?"

"Sherman Adams," she repeated. "That's his name. Our cable guy who offed the senators."

I nodded. "Let me guess, the WFO wanted nothing to do with me."

"That's for sure," Slim added. "Bet they used some lame excuse like they couldn't hire you because of the Anti-Pinkerton Act." He laughed.

Since I didn't get the joke, he addressed my confused look. "It's an old 1893 law that limits the federal government's ability to hire private investigators and mercenaries."

"No," Sanchez replied. "They didn't use a lame excuse like that. They were clear they wanted no part in hiring him. And, for the record, no federal agency follows that act any longer. Anyway, here's the good news: Agent Skaggle drew serious ire from the bigwigs for repeatedly insisting the Walther wasn't a viable lead, which, in retrospect, made them look pretty stupid. They pulled him off the case. No way were they going to reward him the investigation."

"Nice," I said. "Did they give it to you? If they did, they're smarter than I give them credit for."

She threw back her head. "Hell no. I'm on the team, of course, but the Bureau established a massive task force, which is being led from headquarters."

"Right," I said. "Makes sense."

She leaned forward and looked at me. "I think headquarters is making a huge mistake by not consulting your services. I don't know you well, Garrison, but I have a hunch you're not going to let this go, so we might as well work together and share insights."

Slim responded before I could. "He lets nothing go; he still mentions the ten bucks I owe him from some Thai takeout we had twenty years ago. Your hunch is dead on, Agent Sanchez."

"Figured that," she said before I could respond. "Anyway, I may need you both, in fact, so I'd like to keep our lines of communication open. If you guys are okay with that arrangement as unofficial consultants."

I stared. "Your bosses aren't going to like that."

She shrugged. "Maybe not. Easier to ask for forgiveness than permission. Right?"

Though I appreciated her maverick attitude, I knew there was more to it than that.

After a moment of holding my stare, she said, "Fine, I'll come clean. You two are knowledgeable, skilled, and have a vested interest in this case. You may provide me with some valuable information and leads. Which could catch the killer or killers. And could ultimately help my career. There, I said it. I just think—"

I held up my hand. "No need to say more. I appreciate your honesty and ambition. And I get it. I can only imagine how hard it is for a female agent in that federal boys club."

She nodded. "Appreciated. To be even more clear, this is off the books and unofficial, so I can't pay much." She paused. "Okay, nothing, in fact."

"Forget money," I said. "I'd love to help you out. Nothing would give me greater pleasure than nailing whoever hired Sherman Adams, and if that helps your career, even better."

"Forget money?"

Sanchez and I looked at Slim.

He shrugged. "Don't like the sound of those two words together. Never have. They shouldn't go together."

I glared at him.

He kicked back in his chair. "I guess my firm is due for some probono work, even if it is to help out the feds."

"Tell me about Sherman Adams," I said. "What'd you guys find out?"

"See for yourself." She reached into the brown leather valise she'd brought with her, extracted a file, then slid it across the table.

I opened the file and read the cover sheet. Pushing back in the chair, I filled Slim in on a few details. "Sherman was a thirty-year vet. Recruited out of the Army's 75th Ranger Regiment for a Delta Force position. Left Delta about five years ago."

He whistled.

"Makes sense he's Delta," I said. "The man had considerable skill."

"And considerable firepower," Sanchez added. "Read the bottom of the cover sheet, something interesting there."

I read it. "OTH discharge. Wow, that is something."

"OTH," Slim repeated. "Really?"

I nodded, then looked at Sanchez. "Were you able to find out anything concerning that?"

She shook her head. "You know how that goes."

I did. OTH stood for "other than honorable" discharge from the military. The United States Army wouldn't be forthcoming about what that exactly meant. Whatever he did wouldn't necessarily have been criminal, so there wouldn't be a public record of charges. Bottom line, though: an OTH discharge wasn't good. More than likely Sherman Adams lost some or all of his retirement benefits from that type of dismissal from the United States Armed Forces.

Slim was thinking along the same lines. "Could he have been acting alone on this then? As a result of the discharge? Maybe an unhinged revenge plan against the government for losing his benefits?"

Sanchez was quick to respond. "Highly doubt it. From the limited information we've accumulated so far concerning Mr. Adams, we're almost positive he was hired by an outside group."

"Plus," I said, "he specifically told me not to ask about his employer, to not even waste my breath asking. It was clear from our conversation that he wasn't working alone. He repeatedly used the word 'we.'" I turned to Sanchez. "What'd you learn that's not in this file?"

"Since his retirement he's been associated with at least four different political groups. And we're talking radical groups, from both sides of the aisles. Doesn't look like he has a political philosophy he's committed to."

"Because he's a hired gun," Slim said.

I added, "A bipartisan hitman, if you will."

Sanchez laughed. "Good one."

I kept at it. "He likely despises the government. A man who will do anything for the highest bidder. Any timeline associated with his various group involvement? Like who hired him last?"

"Not one hundred percent positive," she responded, "but it appears his most recent association was with a radical paramilitary left-wing group out of eastern Montana."

I furrowed my brow. "Like an Antifa militia?"

She nodded. "Exactly."

"Makes sense," Slim said. "At least broadly speaking since the senators were both super conservative Republicans. Understandable targets for a radical left-wing group, I suppose."

I ran my hand over my bald head. "It's a huge step up for any radical group, right? I mean, we're talking double homicide of prominent senators."

"Agreed," Sanchez said. "Totally agreed, in fact. But remember, this was supposed to look like an internal squabble that led to a murder-suicide. So it wasn't planned to be a showy, hate-the-right-wing-government revenge plot. Wasn't supposed to be a statement killing."

"You're right," I said. "Instead, it was devious and nefarious and underhanded. I wonder if this paramilitary group had a specific beef with the senators and wanted them out of the picture, so they hired Adams directly. Or was this group approached by someone else who had a beef with the senators? That person or persons hired the group to take out the senators. They chose Sherman Adams because he was on their payroll and had the skill to get the job done."

"Good point," Slim said. "Do these murders stop with the group, or is the group just the middleman?"

For the next ten minutes we debated that theory. When we started getting off track and going down rabbit trails, I tried to steer the conversation back.

"Let's go back to the basics," I said. "Let's start with what we know for sure. And what we don't know. Like at a very basic level we know the senators were murdered, but we don't know why."

Sanchez had been pacing. She took a seat and continued the conversation. "The senators must've been onto something big, had some important piece of info to warrant their murders. Of course, we don't know what they knew."

"It was probably just Cooper who knew something," I said.

"Why do you say that?" Sanchez asked.

"Felton Byrd seemed to have no idea why the death threats were sent or what Cooper was going to say at their meeting. I think Cooper planned on bringing Felton into the loop. And I think the people responsible for their murders assumed Cooper had told Byrd already."

"You're probably right," she said. "At any rate, whatever Cooper knew got them both killed."

At this point, Slim was behind his desk testing out markers on a small whiteboard. He was always a visual learner, so it didn't surprise me when he drew two different colored columns on the whiteboard. The left column he labeled, "What we know," the right he labeled, "What we don't know." Then he filled in the points Sanchez and I had made.

Following that, he filled in some information of his own.

He pointed at the board. "We know Sherman Adams was the hired killer. What we don't know is whether this radical group wanted the senators dead, or whether another party did."

"What about Charlie Milliken?" I asked. "Was he involved in this? In particular, the missing letter that he penned. It would seem so, right? Otherwise, Adams wouldn't have taken the note with him." Suddenly I remembered Agent Sanchez had planned on visiting Milliken's widow.

I looked at her. "Did you speak with his widow this morning?"

She nodded. "I did, her name's Gloria. We had coffee at her place this morning. She confirmed the envelope was from her husband. And a few other interesting things as well."

I leaned forward. "Like what?"

She waited until Slim took a seat. "That the letter was sent from Charlie after his death."

"After?" I said. "Really?"

She nodded. "Apparently in his will there was an odd stipulation that stated if he died suddenly, as a result of anything other than natural causes due to his disease, then the letter was to be delivered immediately to Cooper."

"Does she have any idea what was in the letter?"

"Nope," Sanchez said. "She's in the dark about the contents."

"What else did she say?"

"That there was some serious controversy over delivering the letter."

"How so?" I said.

She put her arms on the table. "The executor of the will was Charlie's brother, not his wife. Which made sense since his brother's a lawyer. Anyway, Gloria and her brother-in-law didn't see eye to eye on the letter. She didn't think the letter should be delivered, citing her husband's death was a seizure at the wheel and therefore a natural result of the disease. The brother didn't agree, and he wanted to honor his brother's dying wish and have the letter sent. I could tell Gloria was super upset about it all."

"Obviously the brother won the argument," Slim said. "Probably should follow up with him and see what he knows."

Sanchez nodded in agreement.

"Did either of them contemplate opening the letter?" I asked. "Considering the odd stipulation in the will, it seems super important and worth the privacy violation. It could cast doubt on Charlie having a seizure at the wheel."

"Maybe," Sanchez said. "But Gloria said the lawyer brother is a stickler, a real by-the-book kind of guy. Wouldn't have even considered it; that's my understanding. Gloria has been anxious about the letter, wondering if anything would come of it. I was the first person to mention anything about it to her since it was delivered."

We sat in silence, processing the new information.

Slim walked to the whiteboard. "Cooper had enemies, serious ones. He knew some important information, obviously." In the left column he put, "Letter is important," and in the right column, "Unsure of contents."

I looked at Sanchez. "Your team needs to scour the furniture warehouse for that letter."

"They're already on it. I'll follow up with them soon."

"Good," Slim said. He tapped the whiteboard. "What else are we sure of? What else do we know?"

"Sherman Adams's whereabouts," I said. "Twice he told me he was in the building for over a week, waiting for the two senators to meet."

"Whose place did he stay at?" Slim asked. "That's important."

"It is," Sanchez acknowledged. "Probably the most imminent question we need an answer to. The task force is working on it. Before I came over here, they'd already informed the occupants of Cooper's complex that they'd be by in the morning to re-question everyone."

I thought about Aidan Agnew. We'd discussed him at Slim's office during the speaker call, but I hadn't followed up on him with Slim. "What about Senator Agnew? He could definitely be involved. Maybe he let Adams into the complex or even gave him a place to stay. Any leads there?"

"Still working on it," Slim said. "Nothing to report quite yet."

"Okay," I said, "I have some other names for you to look into." I pulled out my notepad and tore off the top sheet. "All the names of the third-floor occupants in Cooper's complex."

"How'd you get that info?" Sanchez asked.

"From the security guard. I coaxed him to give up the names."

"You're something else." She glanced at her watch. "I hate to say it, but it's time for me to head back. Told a few members of the team I'd be back within an hour or so and would bring some good coffee."

I couldn't resist. "You do need some career help. Getting coffee, wow, that's like junior agent stuff."

She slugged me on the shoulder. "Funny."

"What do you want us to work on?" I asked her. "Maybe something the task force isn't going to look into right away. Slim and I need to work in the shadows, obviously."

She paced for a moment, thinking.

"I'll keep working on Agnew," Slim said, "and look into these neighbors. I have lots of information you can't find in an FBI database."

"Perfect," she said. "I'll connect with Charlie's brother in the morning.

Double-check the story and find out if he knows anything else. How about we meet tomorrow night and share our discoveries?"

"Sure thing," Slim said.

"What's your plan?" Sanchez asked me. "Help out Slim?"

"No, I want to swing by Cooper's complex and ask the security guard if he remembers Sherman Adams."

Sanchez nodded and walked to the door. Before opening it, she turned back and pointed at Slim. "Your best theory as to what's happening. Let's hear it."

"Politics is my game," he said, "so I'll stay in my lane on this one. I think it's far too coincidental that the senators were murdered right before an important and historic vote. I think this has to do with the healthcare vote."

"But they were—"

Slim held up his hand, interrupting me. "Understood they were on separate sides of the vote. Just hear me out. Maybe Cooper had dirt on Felton, something serious. Maybe dead Charlie Milliken passed along the info to Cooper; I don't know. At any rate, perhaps Cooper was prepared to use the intel against Felton if he didn't vote along party lines, and he waited until the very last second to essentially blackmail Felton. I mean, this was a tight vote in the Senate, as tight as they get. One vote ended up being the difference, and it fell in favor of the Democrats."

I stood. "You think somebody on the left found out about Cooper's planned blackmail, understood what this meant for the vote, and approached a radical left-wing militia to take out the senators? To ensure their victory with the vote."

"Yes," Slim said. "Given what I know right now, that's my best theory."

"Interesting," Sanchez said. "Which is why they would've planned for it to look like a murder-suicide."

Silence for a few moments. "A decent theory," I said.

Sanchez looked at me. "What's your best theory?"

"To me, the letter is key. The fact that Sherman Adams took the note means something big was written in that letter. I think Charlie's death was not an accident or a result of his illness. He was murdered. And I think Cooper found that out, and he was preparing to let Felton in on that secret. Of course, whoever was responsible for Charlie's death discovered Cooper knew about the murder and assumed his buddy Felton did as well. So this person or persons hired Sherman Adams, either directly or perhaps indirectly through this militia group, to ultimately silence the senators."

After a few moments, Slim said, "Not a bad theory as well."

Sanchez smiled. "You two are a good team. See, I'm glad I came here."

Before she left the office, I called out, "Not so fast, Agent Sanchez. You need to bring a theory to the table yourself. No stealing our ideas." I winked.

"Fair enough," she said. "I think this all revolves around the radical left-wing group. I don't think they're the middleman in this case. Perhaps the staunch conservative Charlie Milliken was investigating the group because he'd discovered something really bad, maybe something to do with their involvement with a Democratic senator or senators. The group murdered him, but made it look accidental. Except Charlie's brother didn't think it was an accident, so he followed Charlie's wishes and sent the letter. And the letter revealed info about the group and whatever they'd been up to. It makes sense since Cooper was one of the recipients and he's the head of the Ethics Committee, which Byrd is part of as well. The corrupt senator or senators—who are involved with this radical Antifa-type group—then figure the Ethics Committee will open an investigation, which will expose the corruption, so they approach the group to handle it. They tell this group if they don't kill Cooper and Byrd, then they'll go down as well. In response, the group sends Sherman Adams to deal with it."

Slim nodded. "Right, to silence Cooper and Byrd through a murder-suicide plot."

"Could be something along those lines," I said. "The group may not be a middleman in all this."

"Absolutely," Slim concurred. "That's three decent theories."

Sanchez walked back to the door. "We'll reconvene tomorrow, and hopefully be able to narrow them down."

After Sanchez left, Slim turned to me. "I'm dying to check my files, see if I have anything on Cooper's neighbors. I think I'll swing by my office tonight and grab them. Won't be able to sleep if I don't. And if I have anything on these Congress members, pal, it could be juicy. Maybe we'll break this case before the night is up."

CHAPTER TWENTY

BAKER CUNNINGHAM SHUT off the car and opened his laptop. He'd parked in the lot closest to the airport so he could pick up a Wi-Fi signal from the Departures terminal. Once the MacBook powered up and connected to Wi-Fi, he logged onto ProtonMail. Earlier he'd sent an email to some unsavory associates on the East Coast, outlining what he needed from them.

But he hadn't mentioned how much he'd pay for the job.

Which was intentional. Baker didn't want to throw out a lowball number and have the men not respond. And he didn't want to highball the job and lose a bunch of money. So he asked them to name a price to get the job done.

Once onto his email account, he paused before clicking on the reply from the associates. *Here goes nothing,* he thought.

Baker clicked the email and immediately searched for numbers. He held his breath when he saw the digits, in particular the zeros. It was definitely on the higher end of what he'd imagined. If he agreed to pay that price, he'd lose almost everything he'd recently gained.

Drumming his fingers on the wheel, Baker figured he could survive five, maybe ten years outside of America on his current savings.

But if I do this, there's a chance I could maybe return one day.

He hit reply on the email, then typed that he agreed to the terms. He also said he'd wire the money in a few hours. Since he was currently late for his flight, he'd wire the money during his layover at LAX.

He reached over the seat and grabbed his only luggage: a medium-sized duffel bag. Inside were a few different outfits, his mask, snorkel, and fins, and ninety-five hundred in cash. Which was just under the legal amount that you could carry internationally.

Before closing the laptop, his finger hovered over the mouse pad. The cursor was on the email's SEND button, but Baker couldn't bring himself to click it.

Questions filtered through his mind: *Was this wise? Would this work? Was it worth it?*

But in the end, he figured what the hell. Since he was off to a beautiful country with no extradition treaty, he thought he might as well give it a shot. He had nothing to lose.

With a shaky finger, he clicked the SEND button.

CHAPTER TWENTY-ONE

HATTIE LATTIMER STABBED the remote's power off button.

Double homicide? You're kidding me?

The FBI director made the retracted statement about the senators' murder-suicide on national TV. He informed the nation that new evidence came to light proving the senators were murdered, and that the perpetrator was killed during the apprehension attempt.

Shocked at the late-night breaking news, Hattie collapsed onto the hotel bed and stared at the ceiling. It was bad enough when she thought Cooper had committed suicide, worse now that she knew the senator was murdered.

Deaths were snowballing. From the beginning, Hattie suspected Charlie didn't die from a seizure at the wheel, but she had no way of knowing for sure. Now that these two senators were dead, both murdered, Hattie felt confident that Charlie was murdered as well.

Three murdered United States senators.

She switched off the table lamp, tucked herself under the covers, and curled up. Even though she'd been on the run and in hiding since receiving the letter from Charlie, the threat on her life was even more palpable. Whoever was behind the senators' murders surely wouldn't think twice about ending her life.

No way would she get a restful night's sleep. Tomorrow was a huge day. Getting into the safe deposit box was even more critical. And now even more dangerous. Maybe the men camping out in front of the bank weren't there to stop her from accessing the box. Maybe they were simply waiting to kill her.

She tossed and turned for hours, trying to calm her mind and find some semblance of sleep. A few hours before dawn, sleep finally came. Before drifting off, her thoughts turned more ominous. They weren't, however, about how and where the men would kill her. They were about whether there were any good men left to help her.

With Cooper murdered, was there anyone she could trust?

CHAPTER TWENTY-TWO

WE DIDN'T BREAK the case last night. Far from it.

I plunged the French press, then poured myself a cup of black coffee and tiptoed into Slim's living room before settling onto the couch and taking my first sip of liquid gold. It was five in the morning and everyone else was still asleep. Slim and I had talked and strategized until nearly two a.m.

There was a chance I got two or three hours of sleep, but it wasn't close to being deep or refreshing. Finding good sleep when working a case was always a challenge, which went back to my days as a government operative and continued with my time as a federal agent in the Violent Crimes and Cyber Crimes divisions. Now, apparently, it also plagued my role as a subcontractor.

About halfway through my coffee, my mind started firing on all cylinders. I replayed what I learned from Slim about Cooper's neighbors. There were six condos on each floor of the complex, so Cooper had five neighbors. Naturally, Sherman Adams could've stayed in a condo on another floor, but we wanted to start with his five closest neighbors. Plus, they were the only names we had other than Senator Agnew.

Of the five neighbors, three were in the House of Representatives and two were in the Senate. Unfortunately, Slim didn't have much juicy gossip stored in his files on them. Only one of the neighbors was a person of interest: a senator from Utah, a man by the name of Bobby Blanton.

Blanton was interesting because he was one of three independent senators. The other two always caucused with their respective parties, but Senator Bobbly Blanton had allegiance to neither party. Sometimes he caucused with the Democrats, sometimes the Republicans. Kind of a blow-to-and-fro type guy. At any rate, it made him an important vote in the Senate.

And Bobby Blanton made sure everyone knew that.

Since Slim's pet theory over why Cooper and Byrd were murdered revolved around the healthcare vote, he had good reason to believe Blanton might be involved somehow. And that suspicion gained more traction when Slim checked the voting record and confirmed that Blanton had voted in favor of the healthcare bill. There was a possibility that Blanton might've housed Sherman Adams. At the very least, he was a decent suspect.

I planned to visit Cooper's complex after finishing my coffee. I wanted to ask Chuck about Sherman Adams, and if Bobby Blanton might've had a key and code to the service entrance, too.

While enjoying my coffee, I thought about the other neighbors on Cooper's floor. The other senator was a Republican power player, the president pro tempore of the Senate, a man by the name of Edwin Keating. He was third in the presidential succession line and well respected by both parties. However, according to Slim, Edwin hadn't lived in the complex for at least three years. The senator still owned the unit, but he rented it to his niece who attended George Washington University. Apparently, three college girls lived there.

The remaining three neighbors were a congresswoman from California, a congressman from Oregon, and a congressman from Florida. Slim knew of them, but he didn't have any evidence or reason to believe they'd be involved in the murders, though he wanted to double-check. He planned on clearing his afternoon and following up on the congresspeople.

After finishing my coffee, I pulled on a jacket and beanie and left Slim's house. I took Slim's car again, which was a five-year-old aqua green Lincoln Continental. Slim told me he bought the Continental solely for the legroom. When pressed about the horrific color, he said he got the vehicle at a bargain basement discount. The salesperson told Slim that nobody wanted to drive around in a car that looked like an immense green apple Jolly Rancher candy.

I fired up the green beast and headed to Cooper's complex. My hope was to catch Chuck before the feds arrived. As I drove, I thought about the task force. Sanchez said they'd return in the morning to recanvass the occupants. I imagined the task force spent most of the night outlining a game plan. They'd split up into sub-teams and pursue different leads this morning. My best guess was a sub-team would roll in at about eight. Looking at my watch, I saw I'd be there fifteen minutes before six; plenty of time to hopefully catch Chuck before the feds showed up.

When I arrived in Cooper's neighborhood, I drove around the block a few times, trying to see if there was an ideal spot to park and watch the complex. There wasn't. And even if there were, I was in this ridiculously large and vibrant sedan, which screamed attention, so I didn't want to park too close. I ended up parking the sedan three blocks away, well out of view of the complex.

Not wanting to hang out in front of the building and look suspicious, I chose to sit in a diner catty-corner to the condominium complex. That way I could keep an eye on the front of the building and await Chuck's arrival.

About halfway through a cup of terrible coffee, I saw Chuck walking toward the complex. I happily left the cup behind and exited the diner.

While waiting for the light at the cross street, I watched Chuck enter the building. At the same time, I witnessed something else: a man emerging from the alley and walking to his right. Since his back was to me, I couldn't make out a face, but the fact that he was hustling out of the alley intrigued me. The man was dressed well, sporting a navy blue peacoat and gray dress slacks. More than likely he was from the condo complex and not one of the other businesses with a back door into the alley.

What was this person doing leaving out a back exit so early in the morning?

I stopped on the other side of the street and wondered what to do.

Since Sanchez said that the occupants had been informed about the feds' arrival this morning, I found it suspicious this man was leaving the building, so I abandoned my plan to question Chuck and double-timed it after him.

When I got within half a block, I slowed down and matched his pace. Confronting him wasn't best. What would I even say to him? Plus, I'd be memorable with my busted face and shoulder sling, so I decided on following him to his location and gathering as much info as I could. If he hopped into a car, I could walk by as it warmed up and catch a glimpse of his face and note the license plate.

While following him, I zipped my jacket up all the way and pulled down my beanie as low as it'd go, just in case the man turned around and spotted me. I didn't want him getting a good look at my face.

We took a circuitous route for about a mile and a half, ending up in the heart of the US Capitol. A few times I caught a decent profile look when he turned a corner, but I was questionable as to whether I could ID him from a straight-on picture. My hope was for him to enter a coffee shop or breakfast place so I could follow him in and order something. But we were in the middle of government-ville, so there were no such businesses around.

He kept a quick pace until he reached an important-looking government building. A security guard opened the door as the man climbed the steps. The guard didn't address him by name, but he did say, "Good morning, Senator."

I walked by the entrance, glancing at a sign on the building. The man had entered the Russell Senate Office Building. Was he Senator Blanton, Senator Agnew, or another senator?

Unfortunately, I didn't have internet capabilities on my flip phone, so I couldn't check Google for pictures. I found a bench just down from the building and quickly called Slim to see if he would recognize the man from my limited description, but the call went to voicemail.

As I sat on the bench, my mind focused on Aidan Agnew. Last night Slim had also brought me up to speed on what he knew about the senator. He'd confirmed that Agnew was known in a relatively small circle for his promiscuity.

On the surface, however, Senator Aidan Agnew appeared to be a devout Mormon with a charming, beautiful blonde wife and seven children under the age of fifteen. In reality, he spent too many extra months living at his DC condo without his family. Even when Congress took breaks, the senator always stayed an extra few days or weeks.

Since Agnew's term was coming to an end in the next election cycle, about six months ago Slim was hired by a competitor for that particular Senate seat. It took Slim's team less than two weeks to obtain damning photograph evidence of Agnew with four different women. All brunettes, by the way. Two of the women were on staff for the senator. However, Slim assured me the photographs clearly showed they weren't attending a staff meeting.

I waited on the bench, hoping to see the senator leave the building. But I gave up after an hour and walked back to the complex, arriving there just before nine.

It didn't appear that the feds were there yet, which surprised me. I thought about running in and asking Chuck about it, but I figured the feds would arrive at any moment, and I didn't want them questioning me about why I was in the lobby. So I went back to the diner, avoided the coffee, and ordered eggs benedict. I figured I'd wait and see what transpired.

At just past ten, in the distance I spotted the same well-dressed senator, now headed back to the complex. I trapped a twenty-dollar bill under my plate and quickly left the restaurant.

Once I crossed the street, I hung out just past the corner of the condominium complex with my back against the wall. I didn't know if the man would go down the alley and enter the building through the service door, or if he'd use the front door. I kind of hoped he'd use the alley door, which would confirm he had a key. However, I wouldn't get a solid look at his face if he turned down the alley.

When he didn't turn, I slowly ambled to my left and around the corner. I stopped about ten feet from the front entrance. Keeping my head down, I pretended that I was looking at my phone.

Just as the senator approached, I looked up. And made direct eye contact with him. He scowled at me for a moment, then hustled inside the complex. With his face fresh in my memory, I called Slim to get an ID.

But moments later the door to the condo complex opened and Chuck hurried out.

When he saw me, he stopped in his tracks. "Mr. Chase? What are you doing? The senator just told me there was some beat-up, suspicious-looking character out here."

I ended the call before Slim or voicemail could pick up. "Sorry, that was obviously me."

"What are you doing out here? And what happened to your face and arm?"

I pointed at the door. "Who was that? Senator Blanton? Agnew? Or someone else?"

He didn't respond right away.

I leaned in. "Chuck, I saw him leaving early this morning from the alley."

He looked left and right, then back to me and whispered, "Okay, that was Senator Agnew, but let's not chat out here."

"The feds are coming," I said. "In fact, they should've been here hours ago. I don't really want to be in the lobby when they arrive."

He shot me an inquisitive look. "I highly doubt they're coming."

I returned the look. "Why? They must've told you they're coming this morning."

"You obviously haven't been near a television or on the internet."

I shook my head.

Chuck's eyes went wide. "Definitely talk inside, then, not out here."

When he sensed my hesitation, he added, "Mr. Chase, I doubt the FBI will be coming anytime soon. They're probably overwhelmed and way too distracted right now."

"What's going on, Chuck?"

"Inside," he said, moving toward the door and opening it for me. "You need to be seated for what I'm about to tell you."

CHAPTER TWENTY-THREE

HATTIE LOOKED AT her driver's license picture, then glanced at herself in the bathroom mirror.

She had to get her makeup, and her overall look, just right.

Earlier she'd called the bank to confirm she'd need to show her driver's license to access the security box in her name, so she couldn't look too different from the picture. But she couldn't look too similar either, otherwise the men in the vehicle would easily spot her entering the bank.

She adjusted her wig, which was of premium quality and comprised of long, curly, reddish-brown hair. And her hair's natural color was dirty blonde. Her plan was to wear the wig into the bank. Once inside, she'd take it off and freshen up in the bathroom, then peek out the door to see if the men had followed her.

Satisfied with her look, and the plan, Hattie went to the window. As usual, the two men were in the car in front of the bank. She had the afternoon to kill, figuring it would be best to enter the bank around four p.m. Her rationale was the men would hopefully be tired of watching people all day. Perhaps they'd let their guard down in their final hour of surveillance.

Hattie sat in the chair, which was positioned directly in front of the window. She settled in and began watching her watchers.

CHAPTER TWENTY-FOUR

I DIDN'T TAKE a seat. At least not right away.

My cell momentarily distracted me. Slim was calling me back, but I ignored the call because I wanted to hear from Chuck. So I pocketed the cell and came around the back of the security desk. Chuck played a news feed on his laptop. He thought that would be better than having to explain the sordid mess to me.

When the news story ended, I staggered to the small sitting area and collapsed onto the couch. Another male senator had been murdered, and a female senator had been abducted. Though the female senator was currently listed as missing, no doubt her body would turn up soon. I looked at Chuck, who was seated behind the desk, running his fingers through his wispy hair. "They don't live here, do they?"

He shook his head.

"Both Democrats, right, that's what the news said?"

"Yeah, it's crazy, somebody's actually picking off senators. Two by two it seems. First Republicans, now Democrats."

"Right," I said. "A bipartisan killer."

He chuckled. "Good one, Mr. Chase."

That was the last thing we said to each other for a while. Not sure how long I sat there looking up at the ceiling. What snapped me out of it was my phone buzzing.

Slim's text read: *If you haven't heard, get to a television. One dead senator, one missing. Both dems. Both members of the ethics committee. Get here when you can.*

I returned to my daze after learning they were on the same committee as Cooper and Byrd. Unbelievable. The fricking Senate Committee on Ethics. Four of the six members were now dead. Obviously, something big was going on, but this new development blew my mind.

I looked at Chuck. He'd been hopping between different newscasts. He'd turned up the volume on the laptop, probably so I could hear, but I hadn't been paying attention.

"What else are they saying about a connection between Cooper, Byrd, and the other senators?"

"One news report claims they all served on the same Senate Committee. And get this: it's a committee on ethics. Can you believe that?"

I stayed silent for a few moments, thinking. Eventually, I shook off the thoughts and reminded myself of why I was here. "Chuck, how good's your memory?"

"Pretty sharp, I guess. Why, Mr. Chase?"

"Can you remember back a little less than two weeks ago?"

"Sure," he said.

"Any new guest arrive in that time period? A man planning an extended stay, nine days to be exact." I described Sherman Adams as best I could.

Chuck shook his head. "Probably would remember somebody like him. And I don't remember any visitor showing up here with luggage or the sort."

"Right. What about a worker who looks like the man I described? He might've worn a hat."

Chuck tapped his fingers on the security desk. "Not that I recall. 'Course someone could've come in late during the other guard's shift." He held up his left pointer finger. "But we keep a visitor log. Maybe Jim logged somebody."

After crosschecking dates for a minute or so, Chuck looked up. "Jim didn't log anything unusual." He turned back to the log. "Around that time frame we had a few grandchildren visit. And two women. No men were logged, and no workers either."

I steered the conversation to a new topic. "Outside you asked how I got this messed-up face and arm. It was from Cooper and Byrd's murderer. I tracked the man down in Maryland and confronted him. When I was—"

"Really?" he interjected. "You caught him? You did?"

"I did. And before I shot him, he told me he'd been holed up here nine days waiting for the senators to meet."

"Wow, nine days?"

"Yup. So if you have no log of the man coming into the building, he must've come in through the alley entrance."

I paused while Chuck sighed. He knew where I was going.

"I want to know—"

"Say no more," he interrupted. "I get it. You think Senator Agnew may be involved." Chuck looked around, then whispered, "Maybe he let the killer in through the back door, right?"

"That's a definite possibility. Just wondering if there are any other possibilities."

He quickly shook his head. "I promise, no. He was the only one."

"What about Jim, the other guard? Think he gave out a key and code to somebody, too?"

"Doubt it, but you never know. I mean, I did, so he may have as well."

I made a mental note to follow up with the other security guard. Just as I was about to continue questioning Chuck, my phone alerted me to another text.

This one was from Ramona Sanchez's burner phone. It read: *get somewhere private and call me.*

I excused myself and stepped outside. I figured I'd go to the alley and make the call. By chance, maybe I'd catch someone else using the back door.

She picked up on the first ring. "You heard?"

"I did. Must be chaos there."

"That's a serious understatement. Listen, I've only got a minute or two. All task force members are being shifted around as we speak. Priority is the missing senator, obviously, followed by the death of the other senator. In short, I'm being pulled off what I'm working on and I need your help."

"Anything you need, Agent Sanchez. Fire away."

"Before I do, no more Agent Sanchez. All right? I mean, you saved my life, so please call me Ramona."

I smiled to myself. "Okay, Ramona, tell me how I can help."

"That's better. So I spoke with Charlie Milliken's brother this morning on the phone. Asked all about the letter, which actually turned out to be letters."

"Letters? Like with an s?"

"Yes, apparently there were two letters. One sent to Cooper and the other to a woman named Hattie Lattimer. The brother had no idea of either letter's contents. Two interesting things I learned: After Hattie received the letter, she went into hiding. She's off the grid."

"Definitely interesting. What's the second thing?"

"Since Gloria didn't mention the other letter to me, I figured she didn't know about it. But when I asked the brother if Gloria knew about the second letter, he said of course she did."

"Why'd she withhold that information?"

"Exactly my question, so I called her and asked. Basically, Gloria said Hattie and Charlie went to grade school and then prep school together. She said Charlie had been acting awfully strange in recent months, like maybe he'd been hiding something. She suspects Hattie and Charlie were having an affair."

"She was probably too embarrassed to bring it up then."

"Right. And she probably didn't think it was relevant anyway."

I thought about it for a moment, then asked, "Okay, so what kind of help do you need from me?"

"Before I got yanked off this, I'd made some calls and pulled some quick info on Hattie Lattimer: banking, credit card, phone records, stuff like that. Like I said, she's off the grid. No sign of her at her apartment or work for the past three months. No use of credit cards or her cell either.

She pulled out fifteen grand before leaving town, which means she's probably living off cash right now. Her last cell call, three months ago, was to her mom in Baltimore. Older cell records show she's pretty consistent with calling her mom once a week."

"Baltimore's not far from DC. You want me to pay her mom a visit, I assume?"

"I'd love that. There's no way I'm going to convince my superiors to let me chase this lead with the letters. Not in the next day or two anyway."

"Understood. Text me the address."

"Will do. Hattie's mom is Mildred. She lives in south Baltimore, so it will probably take an hour and a half."

"I'm on it. With Mildred, how do you want me to approach my involvement? Can I say I'm working with the feds on this?"

"Absolutely. If this gets back to the task force, I'll take full responsibility for sending you. We'll keep our plan and meet up tonight. I'll fill you in on everything, and you can update me about your developments."

"Think you can get away tonight?"

"I'll make it happen."

She hung up before I could say goodbye. Moments later, she texted me the address in Baltimore. I formulated a quick plan, then hustled back to the Lincoln.

I didn't drive straight to Baltimore. Instead, I swung by Slim's office and filled him in on the latest. Then I went into his filing cabinet and grabbed a prop: a fake badge. Slim told me you could get anything on Amazon these days, including decent replicas of law enforcement badges. He was right.

The replica I'd chosen looked pretty similar to my previous standard-issue FBI badge. Most people wouldn't have thought twice about its authenticity. I wasn't too concerned about impersonating an officer. I reckoned Mildred Lattimer was concerned about her daughter—that is, if she didn't know her whereabouts—so I guessed she'd be happy to see an officer inquiring about Hattie. I doubted she'd ask to see a badge.

Turned out I was right. When Mildred opened the door and heard I was working with law enforcement to find Hattie, she ushered me into the house without a second guess.

"Have a seat anywhere you like," she said. "Coffee or tea?"

"Black coffee is perfect. Thanks."

"Anything, anything at all, dear. Anything for the man who's going to find my precious Hattie."

She whisked away before I had a chance to respond, the faint smell of a classy perfume trailing behind her. I was in a fancy sitting room with a couple of ornate chairs and a sofa fit for the Queen of England. Though I imagined the Lattimer family didn't call it a sofa. That would be too unsophisticated for them. I imagined they referred to it as a davenport or a chesterfield.

Scattered about the room were various family photos. While waiting on Mildred and the coffee, I glanced at them. Hattie had an identical twin sister. There were lots of family pictures from when the girls were younger but no recent photos of the four. In fact, there was only one recent photo. It was of Hattie and her mom, or I guess it could've been Hattie's sister. At any rate, I took a seat on the davenport and wondered what had happened to the family.

Mildred interrupted my thoughts, handing me a steaming cup of coffee. "Here you go, dear."

I took the mug, which had a coat of arms on it, probably their family crest. Mildred sat in one of the chairs to my left. I wouldn't necessarily say she was attractive, but she was well put-together. She wore a silky red pantsuit that harkened to the old Hollywood movie star days. You could tell she was from money, but she didn't carry herself in an upper-class snobby way. At least I'd seen no signs of that yet.

I sipped the coffee and gave a nod of approval.

"Been worried sick about Hattie. You know, Mr. Chase, I—"

"Mr. Chase is my father," I said, smiling. "Just Chase is fine or Garrison if you prefer."

"Garrison, I haven't heard from Hattie in months. You know, she usually calls me at least once a week."

"Do you have any idea where she could be? Why she's disappeared? Anything at all, Mrs. Lattimer?"

"Mrs. Lattimer." She politely waved her hand. "That's my ex-husband's dead mother. Heavens no, not Lattimer, dear. Hattie kept her father's last name, but I use my maiden name now: Ranklin. Please, though, just call me Mildred."

"Mildred, anything you can tell me about Hattie would be great."

She sipped her tea, slowly and delicately, eyeing me over the dainty cup. "Garrison," she said, putting the cup on its saucer. "I must ask, what's your exact involvement in this? Why is law enforcement looking for Hattie? What's going on?"

"All fair questions," I said. "To cut to the chase, your daughter's name came up in our investigation of Senator Charlie Milliken. Charlie's—"

"God rest his soul," she interrupted, making the sign of the cross. "Charlie and Hattie were school chums, but I'm sure you already know that."

"I heard. It's my understanding that Charlie left a letter for Hattie, one that was delivered to her after Charlie's death, which is unusual. We believe there could be something in the letter that suggests Charlie didn't die by accident. As soon as your daughter received that letter, she disappeared. We'd love to find her and ask her what was in the letter and figure out what's going on."

"That's a lot to digest, Garrison." She sipped on her tea for a few moments. "It's odd, especially since I have no idea what the letter is about, and Hattie always keeps me in the loop on things. But she didn't mention a thing about Charlie or this letter when I saw her last."

"Did she tell you anything? I know she called you right before disappearing."

"She actually came for a visit, called beforehand to let me know she was coming."

"Oh, I didn't realize that."

"Yes, she spent a Wednesday with me a few months ago. At the end of the day she informed me I wouldn't hear from her for a while. Of course, I pressed her about what was going on, but she remained aloof and said she needed to get away and clear her head, and for me not to worry."

"Did that strike you as strange?"

"Yes and no. At first, it didn't. You have to understand that Hattie was never the same after losing her sister twenty-five years ago."

"I didn't know that. I'm so sorry, Mildred."

She nodded. "We lost Hattie's sister in a terrible accident. None of us have been the same since, especially Hattie. Identical twins share an unearthly bond. It's deep and hard to explain. Something only other twins know about and experience. For Hattie, losing her sister was like losing part of her. She's drifted through the second half of her life, hasn't held down a career. This must be her fourth time leaving a job and disappearing for a while. Except this time, it's a little different."

She paused. I waited for her to resume, but instead she fidgeted in her seat. I sensed she wanted to tell me something but wasn't quite sure if she should.

I prodded, gingerly. "Can't imagine how tough it's been for your family, Mildred. Why was this time a little different?"

She sipped her tea and kept eyeing me over the cup. About twenty seconds later, she pulled the cup away. She put it down, along with the saucer, on the small coffee table between us.

"It's different," she said after a deep breath, "because Hattie hasn't traveled far. She's nearby, right under my nose, but my daughter hasn't reached out to me. That's so uncharacteristic of her."

"So you know where she is then?"

"Maybe."

I looked confused, so Mildred explained. "I got a call from one of my credit card companies a day or two ago. It was a card I hadn't used in a year or more. Since it hadn't been active for quite some time, the company said they were performing due diligence concerning the recent charge. They wanted to check in with me to make sure it wasn't suspicious activity."

I nodded.

She continued. "The charge was from the DoubleTree hotel in downtown DC. She's less than two hours away, Garrison, and I haven't heard a peep from her in months."

"She couldn't use cash at a nice hotel like that. Are you sure it's

Hattie, though? Maybe someone else stole the card, or maybe someone stole your online profile?"

"Dear, I'm seventy-five years old and have never used a credit card online. That particular card is buried deep in my wallet. Plus, my purse doesn't leave my sight. When Hattie was here a few months ago, I remember her asking for some mints. I told her to get them from my purse. She knew I wouldn't miss that card. It's so unlike her; I'm worried to death. I wanted to give her a little space and see if she reached out and swung by for a visit. I was going to head over to the hotel in a day or two if I hadn't heard from her by then."

"So she's never done something like this before, taken money or a credit card from you?"

"Heavens, no. As I'm sure you can see, money has never been wanting in this family. The fact that she took the card worries me. Why would she do that? She has her own line of credit. I'm hard-pressed to believe she's maxed out her line."

Hattie may have depleted her cash since she'd been on the run for three months. And if she wanted to continue living off the grid, she wouldn't use her own credit card for fear of being traced. But I didn't let Mildred in on my suspicions.

"I'll find her," I said, putting my coffee cup on the table and standing. "And I'll let you know as soon as I do. She's going to be just fine, Mildred."

She stood and walked over, hooked her left arm around my right arm, then patted my forearm. "God bless you, dear. You're one of the good ones."

I left Baltimore and drove directly to the DoubleTree hotel in downtown DC.

CHAPTER TWENTY-FIVE

HATTIE ENTERED THE bank's bathroom, located to the right of the main doors. Since nobody was inside, she stood in front of the mirror and peeled off the wig.

Stuffing the wig in her oversized purse, she quickly adjusted her matted hair and proceeded to the door. After cracking it and seeing that neither stalker had rushed onto the main floor, she strode confidently from the bathroom.

The bank was a newer setup, so there weren't tellers behind a tall centralized desk. This particular bank had desks scattered all around the floor. Each desk had a computer with a young man or woman behind the terminal and two comfortable chairs in front.

Since there were nameplates on the desks but no titles, Hattie figured anyone behind a desk was approachable. Only the offices on the perimeter had titles etched into their glass doors.

Hattie slipped into a seat and informed the young woman named Jamie that she needed access to her security box. The woman was pleasant and all smiles. After quickly checking Hattie's ID, she whisked away to one of the outside offices.

Hattie shifted her chair slightly so she could see Jamie, along with the main entrance doors. Fortunately, the men didn't enter the bank while Jamie was gone.

Two minutes later, she returned and said, "Sit tight. Just spoke with our head manager and he'll be right with you. You'll need his key, along with yours, to open the box."

That was the end of the chitchat as she returned to typing on her keyboard. After about five minutes of waiting, Hattie addressed Jamie. "Apparently he's a busy man."

She stopped typing and grinned. "He is. Much to do."

Hattie turned her attention away from the main doors and watched the manager Jamie had approached. He'd just hung up the phone. Instead of leaving his office, however, he simply sat there. After a minute of watching the man do nothing, Hattie decided to go speak with him.

But just as she stepped toward the office, she saw one of her stalkers rush into the bank and head toward the same manager.

She plunked back into the seat, trying to mask the creeping panic.

Jamie stopped typing. "Ms. Lattimer, I am sorry. I'm sure it won't be more than a few minutes. Can I get you something to drink?"

Hattie took a deep breath and turned to her. "I'm sorry, I can't wait any longer." She swept up her purse and bolted for the main doors.

CHAPTER TWENTY-SIX

I ARRIVED AT the DoubleTree just after four. The hotel lobby was large and welcoming. To the left of the main doors was the check-in counter. To the right was a sitting area with various chairs, tables, and sofas. Since nobody currently occupied that area, I didn't want to wait for Hattie there and stick out like a sore thumb. People already stopped and gave me a double take, which I couldn't blame them for since my arm was in a sling and I had deepening dark circles around my eyes. Plus, I had five large stitches in the back of my head with no hair to mask them.

I tried my best to blend in at the lobby bar, which was comfortably full due to happy hour. The bar was situated directly in front of the main entrance, and the entire front was glass. I sat facing the main doors and worked on a tasty East Coast Hazy IPA while talking to Mom on my cell.

After updating Mom as best I could, I asked her, "Can you put Simon on?"

"Sure, dear." Moments later I heard, "Hey, Dad."

"Hey, buddy. Man, I miss you."

"When are you coming home? I miss you, too."

"Soon, pal. How's school?"

For the next two minutes I listened to him excitedly tell me about his past few days. I knew there'd be a time when I'd ask him what he did at school and he'd respond with "nothing," so I wanted to cherish this time.

After more chatting and telling him I loved him, I hung up and dialed Karla's number.

She picked up on the fourth ring. "Who's this?"

"Funny," I said.

"Seriously, I don't recognize this number."

Oh, boy. "Sorry, Karla, been busy here. Should've called sooner." I paused. "Wait, it's only been a day or two, right?"

She laughed. "Kidding, Chase. Boy, you're tense. It must be crazy there. Tell me what's been going on."

I returned the laugh. "I am tense. Give me a second, I need a swig of beer to loosen up." After taking a sip, I launched into the details of the previous twenty-four hours. Midway through my story, I watched a woman rush into the lobby. At first, she appeared to be in a hurry. Nothing that out of the ordinary. But when she shot a nervous glance over her shoulder, I knew something was wrong. Following that, I got a solid look at her face when she raced by the bar.

It was Hattie Lattimer. At least I was eighty percent sure it was Hattie. I wasn't positive because this particular woman wore a ton of makeup. And Hattie didn't wear makeup in any of the pictures I'd studied at Mildred's; she seemed partial to the natural look.

"Chase," Karla said into the receiver. "Are you still there? Do we have a bad connection or something?"

The woman veered to her right, away from the elevators and toward the stairwell doors. As I watched her, I caught something in my periphery. Glancing back at the main doors, I saw two men come in quickly, slow themselves as they passed the lobby desk, then pick up the pace as they rushed by the bar. They followed Hattie through the stairwell doors.

"Chase!" Karla said again.

"Sorry, Karla, gotta go. Will call you back soon."

I hung up, abandoned my beer, and went after the two men. When I opened the doors, I was immediately struck by loud, echoing sounds. Above me was a footrace in the stairwell as the men chased Hattie down.

I bolted up the steps three at a time. I tore off the sling and dropped it in the stairwell so I could pump my arms and climb faster. The adrenaline masked the pain of my aching shoulder.

On the third floor I rounded a set of steps and smashed into the back of a man. He fell forward, extending his hands onto a step and bracing himself from falling.

When he straightened and turned back, I snapped, "What are you doing? Why are you chasing that woman?"

We were face to face on the stairwell landing. The man was out of shape and struggling to breathe. He held out a finger and slowly reached into his jacket pocket. "Cops," he managed to say. "My badge." He pulled out a folded leather wallet and flipped it open. "She's wanted for questioning." He snapped the wallet shut, but not before I got a quick look at it.

"Let me see that badge," I said.

The man hesitated, eventually complying and handing it over.

After another glance, I confirmed my suspicion. "You know, you can buy anything on Amazon these days." As a confused look came over him, I flicked the badge in his face.

Capitalizing on the surprise, I grabbed the top of the man's hair with my good arm and slammed his head straight down, where it met my knee as it exploded upward. The opposing forces created a monstrous impact of flesh and bone.

The man's nose splintered against my thigh, and I swear a few of his teeth cracked off on my kneecap. He dropped on all fours and moaned in pain. I continued his pain by helping him down the next flight of steps with a boot to the rear. As he tumbled down, I continued upward, running as fast as I could toward the commotion above me.

After another four flights of steps, I stopped. Just above me on the next landing was Hattie and the other man. He had his left arm crimped around her neck. The gun in his right hand was pressed into her back. At least he was trying to keep it pressed there.

Hattie flailed and kicked and arched her back, yelling and screaming. Any second I expected the man to pull the trigger and silence her. The scene was chaotic and intense.

Figuring a gunshot would ring out any second, I didn't wait until reaching the top step to make my move. On the third step from the top, I leaped forward and aimed my body at the man's back foot.

I slid across the landing and bowled him over, sweeping under his leg and toppling him onto his back. Hattie landed on top of the man and rolled off to the right. As he sat up, clearly stunned by my presence, I got to my knees, pivoted my body to the right, then brought my left fist around and threw the hardest punch I'd ever thrown with my left hand.

I flattened him. Two sickening smacks echoed in the stairwell. One from my fist hitting his face, and the other from his head hitting concrete. I hit him so flush on his right cheek that my hand didn't even hurt from the blow. It felt like I extended my fist right through his face. If I'd have connected with his temple, I may have killed him.

Hattie had swept up the man's gun and gotten to her feet. She was pointing the gun at me, backing up and yelling that she'd shoot.

She didn't, though. Instead, she turned and hightailed it through the eighth-floor door.

Yelling after her that I was on her side didn't work, so I followed her through the door and watched her sprint down the corridor. Eventually, she entered a room at the end of the hall on the right. I didn't go after her. Instead, I waited to the right of the open door, ready to clobber any man who rushed through it.

Nobody did, however.

I peeked into the stairwell and heard voices. It sounded like the two men were retreating to the lobby. I wanted to go after them, but I couldn't afford to lose Hattie, so I hustled down the hall to the room I saw her enter.

When I reached the door, I wanted to pound on it and demand she open up. Then demand she answer all my questions.

But I didn't do that. I took a deep breath and knocked, then stepped back from the door since I knew she'd be watching me through the peephole.

"Hattie," I said. "I'm here to help, not hurt."

I put both arms in the air, which was a struggle with my ailing right shoulder. I spun and used my left hand to pull up my shirt when my back was to the peephole.

"And I'm not armed, Hattie. I just want to help."

CHAPTER TWENTY-SEVEN

HATTIE PRESSED HER left eye to the peephole glass and tried to control her breathing. The man on the other side of the door breathed hard, too. Clutched and shaking in her right hand was the gun she'd taken from the man in the stairwell.

He kept pleading that he was here to help. But Hattie knew people who insisted they wanted to help typically meant the opposite.

Her thoughts flipped. *But he did take down the man in the stairwell, and presumably the other man as well.*

"Please, Hattie," he said from behind the door. "My name's Garrison Chase. I just want to ask a few questions. Your mom's worried about you, too. In fact, I just met with her."

She tensed while listening. When he referred to her as Mildred and said he was just in south Baltimore, Hattie raced to dial Mom's number from the hotel phone.

Sitting on the bed waiting for someone to pick up felt like an eternity. She feared Mom wouldn't answer. *Worse, what if the police answered the call?*

"Hello?"

As soon as Hattie heard her mom's voice, she hung up and breathed a sigh of relief. While the man continued talking in the hallway, Hattie grabbed her small, wheeled luggage and mindlessly packed her few belongings. The whole time she kept wondering about him.

Garrison Chase wasn't armed. He hadn't pounded on the door or tried to break it down. Or killed her mother, for that matter. And since the men from the bank hadn't made an appearance on the eighth floor, he definitely scared them off and potentially saved her life.

After another moment of contemplation, she decided she'd open the door and hear him out if he was still waiting. She wheeled her luggage into the hallway and left it by the door, then unlatched the deadbolt. With a deep breath, she held out the pistol in her right hand and opened the door with her left.

He didn't barge in, which was probably due to the gun leveled at his chest. Garrison Chase simply stood and smiled. Hattie couldn't tell if it was genuine or rehearsed. But she didn't focus on that; she was too focused on his beat-up appearance.

What happened to him?

"Hattie," he said. "Put down the gun. I'm not these men." He thumbed over his shoulder toward the stairwell. "Not with them, not like them, nothing of the sort. I'm not even sure why they're after you. Maybe it has to do with the letter."

She tried to hide her surprise. *He knows about the letter. How?*

He rambled a bit, but Hattie wasn't listening as her mind processed the new information. *If he knows about the letter, then he's probably here to silence me. Like everybody else.*

Hattie tightened her finger on the trigger, on the verge of shooting the man in the doorway and running for her life.

As he stepped over the threshold, she jabbed the gun at him. "Stop!"

He did, then held up both hands.

She eyed him, eventually motioning at his face. "What happened?"

"Confronted Senator Morse Cooper's killer. He did a number on me, but I got the upper hand in the end." He gave another disarming smile, then motioned to his right arm. "My shoulder is actually hurting the most. I ripped off the sling so I could run up the stairs faster. To help you."

The man used his left hand to ease his right arm into a more comfortable position.

Hattie decided she wouldn't shoot him, but she also didn't trust him and his story. So while he was momentarily distracted, she wound up with her right foot and kicked the man square in the nuts, connecting hard between his legs with the point of her shoes. She'd never kicked a person like that before. It was so devastatingly hard, she heard and felt her big toe break.

Immediately the man crumpled to his knees, then fell forward and lay motionless. The kick had knocked the wind out of him, so he fought to suck in a breath. He couldn't yell or even moan in pain yet.

Hattie bent down and whispered in his ear, "I'm sorry if you truly are here to help. Really, I am. I don't trust anyone, especially men. Please, Garrison Chase, just leave me alone."

Since he'd fallen in the doorway, Hattie wheeled the luggage over his body. She took quick looks in either direction to make sure the coast was clear, then promptly limped away.

CHAPTER TWENTY-EIGHT

I WRITHED AND moaned and cursed, probably for the better part of three minutes. The sharp pain in my groin eventually turned to a deep, throbbing ache. Eventually, I managed to get to my feet and stagger toward the window. Everything in me wanted to chase after Hattie Lattimer, but I was having a hard time just standing.

I hung onto the drapes and watched the street. My hope was to catch the direction Hattie fled. So far, I hadn't seen her. When two more minutes ticked by, I knew I'd missed her. She either exited onto another street or I was too late to the window.

Instead of going after her, I paced the room and walked off the pain. When I felt somewhat back to normal, I did the next best thing: I studied the hotel room for clues.

Since the room was tidy and void of trash, I knew Hattie Lattimer was neat and meticulous. There was only one thing in the entire hotel room that was out of place: the chair by the window. It'd been turned one hundred and eighty degrees and pulled tight to the glass. Hattie Lattimer sat in the chair and stared out. Obviously.

At what, though?

I took a seat and scanned what was immediately in view. There was a bank, a coffee shop, a dry cleaner store, and a mini mart. Nothing unusual or noteworthy.

Beside the chair was a small table. Two items were on it: a lamp and a hotel notepad. Written on the pad was a local number. I went to the phone and dialed the number.

Three rings later, a female voice picked up. "Far East Bank. How can I direct your call?"

I hung up and went back to the window, confirming that the bank in view was a Far East Bank. Why was she watching a bank? Was she at the bank prior to rushing into the hotel lobby? Sitting back into the chair, I thought about those questions for a solid five minutes.

In the end, I had no theory. And there was no point in continuing to speculate until we had more information. Information like who worked at this particular branch, whether Hattie had an account there, and if she had any association with one of its employees. Either Ramona or Slim could hopefully dig up that info.

I left the hotel room and took the stairs down, picking up my sling along the way. Before entering the lobby, I cracked open the door to see what sort of activity was happening. For all I knew, Hattie might've called the police or hotel security and alerted them to my presence. I doubted the two men in the stairwell would've called the cops. If anything, they would've regrouped for a second run at Hattie or called in some additional goons for backup. Or perhaps somebody had been higher up in the stairwell and heard all the commotion. Maybe they alerted hotel security.

However, the coast looked clear, so I strode through the lobby and tried my best to walk normally. My man parts were still aching, so each step was painful. Once outside, I looked around to see if I could spot the men spying on the hotel from a distance or watching from a vehicle.

No sign of them, though.

I texted Slim and told him I was headed to his firm. By the time I got there, he'd texted back to say he'd be there around six p.m. He also gave me the code for the elevator since he wasn't sure if anyone would still be at the office.

I punched in the code, which enabled the elevator to stop at Slim's floor. Becky wasn't there to greet me. After a quick check of the offices, which confirmed nobody was there, I visited the kitchen. The freezer contained a ton of fruit, probably for smoothies. No doubt Becky made a good one. Grabbing a bag of frozen blueberries, I went to the conference room and sat in a chair, nestling the frozen goodness underneath my sensitive parts.

Replaying my encounter with Hattie, I realized things took a turn when I mentioned the letter. She'd tried to hide it, but I'd seen her eyes widen a little. Then, of course, she kicked me like she was gunning for a sixty-yard field goal.

All these things somehow related to the newest and most shocking development: the murder and abduction of two Democratic senators on the Ethics Committee. It seemed clear that the Ethics Committee was investigating—or about to investigate—something big. Something huge, in fact, since it now involved murder *and* kidnapping.

But what were they investigating? Felton Byrd gave no indication they were onto something huge. Perhaps he didn't know yet. Maybe only Cooper was privy to that information since he chaired the committee. Or maybe Felton did know, and he simply was forbidden to even mention any case they were investigating.

I knew Slim, with all his political knowledge, would have some insights on the Ethics Committee and could provide some answers, so I stopped myself from theorizing. Instead, I called Karla back, but she didn't answer. I left an apologetic voicemail, then grabbed the laptop in the room and searched the internet for stories about the recent senatorial murder and abduction.

After twenty minutes of perusing news feeds, I had a solid understanding of what had transpired. The male senator was named Logan Mills. The woman was Rachel Fornetti. Rachel had a rental house in the Georgetown Park area. The last communication from her cell came from that house. It was a text to one of her aides around 11:30 last night. When Rachel didn't show up at her office for an eight a.m. meeting, that same aide drove to the house. Rachel, of course, wasn't there, but there were signs of a forced entry. Neighbors hadn't heard a thing. Since Rachel was single and didn't live with anyone, there were no witnesses. The whole thing looked like a dead end.

Logan Mills, on the other hand, was an entirely different and more dramatic story. He rented a condo in the expensive Berkeley suburb of DC. Mills was married, but his wife was back in his home state of Arkansas. One of his sons, however, unexpectedly showed up yesterday morning at the condo. The son attended University of Maryland. He said he needed to get away to study for fall semester finals, so he showed up at his father's place for a few days of quiet studying.

About three a.m. the son heard some commotion in the house. Thinking it was just his father up for a late-night snack, he didn't investigate until he heard his dad shout. The kid ran into his dad's bedroom and interrupted two masked men subduing the senator. Apparently, the son barging in shocked the intruders. They both lunged toward him. His father used the opportunity to sweep up his cell and run into the attached bathroom.

He never made it.

One of the intruders planted a 9mm round into the senator's back, and the son watched his father bleed out on the bathroom floor while the intruders tied him up and then fled the scene. Since the intruders wore masks, they probably decided they didn't need to kill the son as well.

Poor kid. I couldn't imagine the horror of seeing your pops die in front of you like that. To clear my mind, I went back to the kitchen and made a cup of coffee. By the time I returned to the conference room and had repositioned the frozen berries, I heard the ding of the elevator.

I didn't get up for Slim when he entered the conference room. Being the astute man he was, my buddy noticed something unusual about how I was sitting.

"What's going on?" he said, giving me the once-over. "Wait, what are you sitting on?"

I didn't try to hide it. "Frozen blueberries. My boys met a foot this afternoon, and it wasn't a pleasant meeting."

He laughed so hard he had to sit. Finally, after about a minute, he said, "I'm sorry, pal, I know how sensitive the jewels are. It's just, you're such a mess. I mean, your arm, your face. And you know those stitches on your head look like Frankenstein stitches. Now you have elephantiasis of the scrotum. This is too much."

"I'm glad I can be your comic relief."

He held up both hands. "I'm sorry, I'm sorry. Let me make it up to you. I think you need this."

Slim left the room, still laughing. He returned a minute later carrying a bottle of bourbon and two highball glasses.

My eyes got big. "Is that Pappy Van Winkle? I take it back; you can laugh at me as much as you want."

"Hold your horses," he said, pouring two fingers in each glass. "It's good stuff, the best I own, but it isn't twenty- or thirty-year-old Pappy's." He handed me the bottle for inspection. "It's Old Rip Van Winkle."

"Not bad. The ten-year-old stuff. We can stay friends, I suppose."

While we sipped the delicious bourbon, Slim grilled me about what had happened. I filled him in on the additional letter from Charlie Milliken to Hattie Lattimer, visiting Hattie's mom, the stairwell takedown, and the unpleasant meeting of Hattie's foot.

"This Hattie," he said, "sounds like one heck of a woman. Can't believe she got one up on you."

"She surprised me, for sure. It's not common that somebody pointing a gun at you ends up using their foot. I couldn't have blocked her kick with this bum shoulder anyway."

"So you didn't even slow down the kick? A direct hit, huh?"

I nodded. "Listen, enough about my parts and plight. Fill me in on your thoughts about the murdered senator and the abduction. I don't know much about the Ethics Committee. It's not something you hear about very often."

"Right, it isn't. It's actually a select committee in the Senate. It's different than other committees since it's comprised of six members and they're equally divided, three Dems and three Republicans. The majority party, however, always chairs the committee. That was Cooper, as you know. The Vice Chair is always a member of the minority party, and that position is currently held by Rachel Fornetti."

"Wow, I didn't know that."

"Yup, this whole thing is nuts." He gestured at my privates. "Sorry, bad choice of words."

I didn't respond.

He continued. "Obviously, the Ethics Committee had something on their docket, some epic case of conspiracy they were investigating, or one that was next up in their queue. I'm sure the feds are grilling the other two members of the committee as we speak."

"And giving them around-the-clock protection," I added.

"For sure."

Just then, my cell buzzed. Ramona sent a text saying she was on the ground floor and needed to be let in.

"Ramona's here," I told Slim.

He stood. "Ramona? You're on a first name basis now. Wow. And I see you're on a texting basis, too. Does Karla know?"

I tried to slug him on the shoulder as he exited the conference room.

A minute later, the two entered the room together.

"Looks like I'm a little late to the party." Ramona gestured at the bourbon. "And you're double-fisting, Garrison. Coffee and bourbon. Nice combination. I like it."

She took a seat across from me. I'd straightened up in the chair and pulled it close to the table to hide the frozen berries.

"Coffee or bourbon?" Slim asked. "Or both?"

"Coffee would be great," she said.

"I'll get you some," Slim said. "But don't start without me."

"I'll fill her in about Hattie while you're gone."

Which I did. The only part I didn't elaborate on was how Hattie got away.

Slim came back with the coffee in hand and a new bag of frozen berries; raspberries this time. He held up the bag. "Need a refresher?"

"Thanks, pal," I said. "Thanks a lot." I swapped out the bags and was about to explain to Ramona.

She held out her hands. "I can sorta read between the lines here."

I steered the conversation elsewhere. "What's the latest with the dead and abducted senators? Any leads?"

"Unfortunately," she said, "nothing solid. What we know is that both jobs were highly professional. Without a doubt. These guys knew exactly what they were doing. Although it seems clear they messed up with Senator Mills. The son being home changed that job."

"How so?" I asked. "Aside from surprising them, of course."

"We believe they meant to abduct the senator, like they did with Rachel. The son said the intruders were trying to subdue their dad when he barged in. If they were there to kill him, they would've snuck in and quietly killed him. Or at least shot him right away when he started making noise."

"So they meant to abduct both senators," I said. "What were they going to do with them?"

Slim offered a thought. "Take them somewhere else and kill them and hide their bodies so law enforcement spent all their time searching for them. Or perhaps they planned to take them to a location and try to extract information, see what they truly knew about whatever the committee was investigating."

Ramona nodded. "It's likely one of those theories."

"What about the son?" I said. "I know the intruders wore masks, but did he provide any more information about them?"

"He said they were average height and weight with neutral accents. Nothing distinctive he could remember."

"What about the other two members of the committee? I'm sure you picked those two up as soon as you learned of the connection."

"We did," she said. "They're in protective custody for the foreseeable future, but neither senator said their current caseload would warrant this type of action or reaction."

I eased back in the chair and looked at the ceiling. "It's all connected. I feel it. It goes back months, to Hattie and the letter. The two senators you have in protection probably hadn't been brought in the loop just yet. Whoever is behind this likely didn't know if the whole committee knew or not. Slim's latter theory is probably correct; they were abducted with the intention of being grilled for intel. The senator being murdered was collateral damage for the son's sudden appearance. This likely means Rachel Fornetti won't survive either. Are you on the team to find her?"

She shook her head. "I made a pitch to my superiors, said this goes back to Cooper and the letter from Charlie Milliken, and that I'd be more useful following up on that lead."

I shot forward in the chair. "What about the Cooper letter? Did the task force find it at the furniture warehouse?"

She shook her head. "They believe it may have been in the desk, which was blown to bits as you know. They found fragments of various paper documents strewn about. They're going through all the fragments to see what they can piece together, but it will take time and doesn't look too promising."

"We need to catch a break," Slim said, pouring himself another finger of bourbon.

I waved him off when he went to pour me another round.

"Run me through the connections you see with Hattie," Ramona said. "Why are you so convinced about her involvement?"

"Well," I said, "Logan Mills and Rachel Fornetti are connected to Cooper and Byrd via the Ethics Committee. And Cooper and Byrd are linked to Charlie Milliken via the letter. Now we know there are actually two letters. And the other letter connects Charlie and Hattie, who have a long history together. These two letters don't have to be identical, or even related for that matter. You could hold a theory like Charlie's widow; what's her name, by the way?"

"Gloria," Ramona said.

"Right, Gloria suspects her husband and Hattie were having an affair. In Gloria's mind, then, the letter to Hattie was likely a love letter or something similar."

"But if that were the case," Slim interjected, "Hattie wouldn't have gone into hiding."

"Or been chased by those two men," I added. "There was something important in Charlie's letter to Hattie, so I think our best bet is to focus on her. The entire WFO and everyone in the Hoover Building, along with the local PD and Sheriff's office, are hunting these men who killed and abducted the senators. Hopefully they catch them and unravel the case. While they're doing that"—I looked at Ramona—"we might as well investigate Hattie and the letter. We need to find her, convince her to talk, and hopefully unravel that particular thread."

"I agree," she said. "Where do you think she is?"

"Great question, I have no idea. I do know something interesting, something I haven't told either of you yet." I paused to finish my coffee. "I don't know what it means, but it's something. At Hattie's hotel room, I noticed she turned one of the chairs around and was watching the bank across the street. I assumed it was the bank because she'd scribbled their phone number on a notepad."

"What bank?" Slim asked.

"Far East Bank," I replied.

"Far East?" Ramona said. "They've been all over the news the past few months."

"What for?" I asked.

Ramona explained. "Duke Tweed is trying to buy the Far East Bank. But Tweed recently bought another smaller bank, so the acquisition is being blocked by the government for further investigation. All Tweed's acquisitions and mergers are highly scrutinized after the whole oil fiasco."

"Understandable," I said.

Ramona nodded and took a sip of coffee. Meanwhile, Slim stood and paced the other end of the conference room.

I thought about Duke Tweed, who just about everybody in America had heard of. He came from a long line of wealthy oil barons. We're talking stupidly wealthy people. Tweed had inherited and taken a controlling interest in his family's private company at the relatively young age of thirty-five. The Tweed parent company owned many oil companies in their portfolio. So many, they actually commanded a sizeable portion of domestic oil production, along with a decent-sized piece of the foreign production pie. Unbeknownst to most people, including members of his own board, Tweed started secretly selling off some of his family's oil companies. When he'd sold enough that it became common knowledge, he formally admitted he was taking the parent company in an entirely different direction. He said he no longer wanted to be part of the fossil fuel problem; he wanted to be part of the solution. Eventually, he divested all his family's interest in oil and embraced new, innovative sources of energy production. In particular, wind and solar. What people didn't know was Tweed had allegedly curbed production of oil at his own companies while he was simultaneously trying to sell them off, thus raising demand. When oil prices soared, Duke Tweed sold every last oil company in their portfolio for a huge profit.

Naturally, many groups were irate with the scheme. But the man was so rich he had an army of lawyers to explain how everything he'd done was above board. Most people didn't buy it. Unfortunately, the government didn't prosecute because they couldn't prove beyond a reasonable doubt that he'd been manipulating supply and demand. In the end, Duke Tweed became one of the wealthiest men in America, and by far the largest Democratic political donor the country had ever seen.

I'd noticed Slim was still pacing with his head down. He hadn't said a word since I mentioned the Far East Bank. "What gives, buddy? What's going through that big head of yours?"

He stopped and looked up. "Not sure if this is simply coincidence or not. You guys know I have intel on senators, and I know quite a bit about Charlie Milliken. He and Duke Tweed were the best of friends. Charlie was likely the only Republican that Duke publicly respected. The two grew up together. They—"

"Really?" I interrupted. "That's crazy. Hattie went to grade and prep school with Charlie, so I imagine she knows Tweed as well."

"Maybe," Slim said. "Probably, in fact."

"Another connection," Ramona said, running her fingers through her hair. That was when I noticed just how luxurious her hair was.

I stared for a moment, then refocused. "You guys think maybe Tweed is up to his old ways? Wants to pull off some scheme like he did with the oil industry?"

Slim joined us at the table. "A scheme like what exactly?"

I shrugged. "Like buying up banks to somehow manipulate the supply and demand of money. Or maybe interest rates or bonds or something like that. I don't know if you can do that type of thing by owning banks. I think I failed my microeconomics course in college."

"You probably did," Slim said with a smile, "since you're talking more about macroeconomic stuff. You fail that class, too?"

Ramona intervened before I could respond to his jab. "It could be both, you guys. And for the record, I got A's in both courses." She winked. "Micro focuses on individual markets whereas macro looks at the economy as a whole. We'd have to ask an expert, but I don't think buying up banks could affect the money supply."

"You're probably right," I said. "That's all controlled by the federal reserve. It's just Tweed's history makes me suspicious."

"And it should," Ramona said.

Slim added, "Anything's a possibility with Duke Tweed. That man is always angling, and the angle typically points back to him."

I nodded. "And the lining of his pockets. What if Tweed is trying to influence the federal reserve somehow? If the reserve controls the supply of money and, of course, sets interest rates, then if Tweed has an inside man at the federal reserve, couldn't he profit heavily from owning banks?"

Suddenly Slim slapped the table, startling me.

"Wait a second," he said. "Wait a second. Agnew, isn't Agnew . . ." His voice trailed off as he grabbed the laptop in front of me and spun it around.

"What's going on, pal?" I asked.

He held up his finger. "Give me a sec."

About a minute later, Slim exclaimed, "I knew it. I knew it." He spun the laptop around so Ramona and I could see it. "We all know Aidan Agnew is a suspect since he has a key and code for the back door. Look at this." Slim pointed at the screen.

The website on the screen belonged to the government.

"This is the website for the Banking, Housing, and Urban Affairs Senate Committee," he continued, clicking on a link. "And one of their subcommittees is the Economic Policy Committee. Look at their responsibilities." He pointed at some text on the screen.

Ramona and I leaned forward. On the left side of the screen was a jurisdiction list, citing the committee's responsibilities, which included monetary policy, functions of the federal reserve, control over currency and commodity prices. Before I could continue reading, Ramona pointed at the right side of the screen.

"And look who's on the committee."

I followed her finger and saw Aidan Agnew's name listed as one of the majority members. I took a moment to process that.

Slim was on the edge of his seat, snapping looks between us, waiting for somebody to say something.

"Let's assume," I said, "which isn't a stretch, by the way, that Tweed is up to something underhanded with his recent interest in buying banks. He approaches and probably pays off Agnew so he can have an inside man on this important committee. Charlie Milliken somehow catches a whiff of what's happening, but he's hesitant to turn on his best friend. However, he knows the stakes and the corruption, so he sets up the letter delivery in case he bites it. The letter naturally goes to Cooper since he's the chair of the Ethics Committee, and the letter reveals the scheme or hints at Tweed and Senator Agnew's involvement. Tweed and Agnew subsequently find out about the letter and approach this militia group to take care of the problem before it becomes public."

Ramona gestured in my direction. "And you throw a huge wrench into their plan by tracking down and confronting the man the group hired to do the deed."

Slim nodded along. "Tweed and Agnew had no idea if the minority members of the Ethics Committee knew anything, so they planned the abduction to find out what they knew, or to simply kill them and hide their bodies."

"If all this is true," Ramona said, "how does Hattie fit into this?"

I offered a simple solution. "Charlie was having an affair with her. Perhaps he told her everything in the letter he sent, which put her on the Tweed hitlist."

"You're probably right," Slim said.

"Charlie's wife, Gloria," Ramona said, "seemed convinced her husband had something going on with Hattie. Gloria said he was in a dark place the months leading up to his death. Something weighed heavily on his mind, but he wouldn't share it with her no matter how much she pressed."

"Because," I said, "it wasn't just the Tweed scheme on his mind. The affair and guilt were eating away at him, too."

"The puzzle pieces are falling into place," Slim said, standing. "Where do we go from here?"

Ramona stood and put on her jacket. "To Cooper's complex. We can surprise and confront Senator Aidan Agnew. I don't care that it's late. We're going now. And you gentlemen are coming with me."

CHAPTER TWENTY-NINE

BAKER CUNNINGHAM LOGGED nearly eighteen hours in the sky. During the long flight between LAX and Singapore, he tried to push everything from his mind and get some sleep. To help in that endeavor, he didn't check the news or his email during the flight. Still, he only found an hour of sleep at most.

So when he exited the plane on his layover in Singapore, the sights and sounds and smells of the vibrant airport snapped him out of his funk. What really perked him up, however, was seeing a bank of television screens covering the murder of another United States senator: Logan Mills.

Murder? What the hell happened?

Baker didn't watch the footage or read the ticker at the bottom of the television screen. Instead, he immediately searched for a coffee shop. When he found one, he grabbed a steaming cup of coffee and opened his laptop.

While checking the American newsfeeds, his cell buzzed, alerting him to an email in his ProtonMail account. He wondered if that email was his former employer demanding some or all of the money back, or if it was his East Coast associates explaining their mistake.

It was neither, however.

As he read and re-read the email, he couldn't help but smile at his good fortune. Moments ago, his world was crumbling. Now he found himself in an incredible position. A position where he could play men off each other. Something he was extremely skilled at.

If he played this just right, he could possibly reverse all the damage of the previous failed missions. And maybe put himself in a far greater economic position than before.

CHAPTER THIRTY

SLIM, RAMONA, AND I walked into Cooper's complex just after eleven p.m.

Jim, the guard I hadn't met—or even seen before—sat behind the security desk. Slim and I stayed by the elevator as Ramona approached the desk and flipped open her FBI badge. She got straight to business, asking the guard for Senator Agnew's condo number and telling him the visit was related to the current murder and abduction of United States senators.

"406," the guard said without hesitation. "Don't know if he's there, though, haven't seen him tonight."

Ramona nodded while I pushed the elevator button. I figured Chuck and this particular guard never had a clue when Agnew was in or out. While Ramona and I loaded into the open elevator, Slim walked up to the security guard. The plan was to have him hang back and grill the guard to see if he'd ever given out the back-door code and key to anyone.

We exited the elevator, quickly realizing that condo 406 was at the opposite end of the fourth floor, right by the back staircase. As we walked, our shoes clomping against the old wooden floors, I asked a question that had been nagging me. "Are you going to get in trouble for bringing Slim and me along on this?"

She waved her hand. "Highly doubt it. The WFO is stretched so thin on this case—cases, I should say—they're letting me lead the inquiry here at the complex. Two-thirds of our agents are either investigating Mills' death or trying to locate Fornetti. The other third is processing the warehouse crime scene and looking into the left-wing militia and Sherman Adams connection."

"So you're in charge of this endeavor?"

"I am," she said.

"Good for you." I stopped at Agnew's door. Motioning toward the stairwell, I whispered, "Right by the stairwell. This guy can easily slip in and out of this place without anybody seeing. Along with his ladies."

"And his hired killer," Ramona said.

"Touché," I replied.

Ramona gave a terse knock and held out her badge. Then knocked again. And again. Neither of us heard a peep from inside the condo.

"Guess the security guard was correct," Ramona said. "Nobody's home."

"Or he's dead."

Ramona put her hands on her hips. "You think?"

"Probably not, but you never know."

"We'll come back in the morning. Grill Agnew and knock on a bunch of other doors, too."

We took the back staircase down one level, then walked along Cooper's floor, stopping in front of his door.

"We should recanvass this floor. Describe Sherman Adams to Cooper's neighbors. See if anyone saw him or had an encounter with him."

Ramona added, "Or see if they act suspicious when we mention him."

"Right." I pointed down the hall. "On either side of Cooper's condos are congressmen, one from Florida and the other Oregon. Down that end is a congresswoman from California."

Turning one hundred and eighty degrees, I pointed at the door in front of me. "This is Senator Blanton's place, and by the staircase is Senator Keating's place, which apparently he rents out to a bunch of Georgetown students, one of whom is his niece."

Before Ramona could ask how I knew all this, I said, "Intel courtesy of Slim. It's his business to know members of Congress."

We walked back to the staircase. "I want to get a closer look at the back door," she said.

When we reached the rear exit, Ramona gave the system a good once-over, then looked at me. "We should check to see if the alarm actually works."

"We should," I said, pushing the door open. "And if it does, we should time the guard's response."

"Is it a silent alarm?" she asked. "Otherwise, it's broken."

"It's silent; it buzzes behind the security desk if it's opened without the code punched in. On the outside, you need the code to deactivate the silent alarm and the key to open the door."

After a moment, we shut the door and returned to the hallway, meeting up with Jim about halfway back. He'd done a decent job hustling to the service door.

"Just us," I said. "We wanted to make sure the alarm was working properly."

He seemed relieved, nodding quickly and then returning to the front desk.

When I approached the lobby and saw Slim sitting on the couch, he immediately shook his head. Ramona spoke with the guard and informed him we'd be back in the morning, and to take down any names of occupants who left the complex before we got there.

After we piled into Ramona's car, I addressed Slim. "So nothing, huh? I take it you pressed him pretty hard."

"I did. He's a docile man. He would've admitted to giving out a key or code. My take: he knows nothing and did nothing. What about you guys? The fact that you were back so quickly tells me you got nowhere."

"Agnew wasn't home," Ramona said.

"What's our next move then?" Slim asked.

While Ramona offered some thoughts, I tuned out because a vehicle across the street and about a hundred feet to the north commanded my attention. I'd seen it earlier on our drive from Slim's office. The fact that it had parked down the street wasn't the suspicious part; it was the fact that I could see somebody sitting in the driver's seat looking our direction.

I waited and watched the car while listening to tidbits of Ramona's plan. After about five minutes, I heard Ramona say she had to get back to her field office.

Slim, in the passenger seat, turned toward me. "What do you think, pal? Good plan?"

I'd only heard bits and pieces of the plan but knew the basics: Ramona and I were meeting back here at eight a.m. while Slim planned to use his considerable resources to try and locate Hattie.

"Sounds good," I said, opening the back door. "Something may be off about that car down the street." Slim immediately looked at where I was pointing.

"It's worth a look," I continued. "You guys go on ahead. I'll get myself back to Slim's office."

He turned back. "Want me to join and help out?"

"Heck no. I'm already a sight for sore eyes. And you're about as inconspicuous as the sun. I'm—"

"Wait," he said. "Is that a fat joke, buddy?"

I stepped out and shut the door without responding.

As the car drove off, I headed back into the condominium complex.

CHAPTER THIRTY-ONE

HATTIE GLANCED AT her watch, then back to the complex.

Where'd he go? He's been gone over ten minutes.

While she strained to see the front door, her fingers tapped her right knee. All sorts of questions ran through her mind. Unfortunately, there were too many questions and not nearly enough answers. Hattie knew she couldn't keep going it alone.

Was this the guy to trust, though?

Not taking her eyes off the door, Hattie turned the ignition over, then cranked up the heater. Within moments, however, the car felt stuffy, so she cracked the window. The whole time she kept her face pressed to the driver's side window.

Without warning, the passenger door suddenly swung open. A cold blast of air rushed in. And so did a man.

"Evening, Hattie," Garrison Chase said.

Panicking, Hattie reached for the gun in her right jacket pocket.

Garrison grabbed her wrist as the gun came out. It was a solid grasp, not one meant to hurt her, just strong enough to control the situation.

He reached with his right hand toward the gun.

Hattie screeched as he easily wrestled it away. Before she could open her door, he clicked the locks.

"I'm not here to hurt you, Hattie."

She didn't respond. Instead, she smushed her body against the door and pushed the unlock button.

He said the same thing twice more as they exchanged button pushing.

Finally, he reached toward her with his left hand. The gun was in his right.

"Don't touch me," she said. "Get out. Please, just get out. Now!"

He stopped reaching and held his palm flat toward her. "Easy, easy. To prove I'm not here to harm you, take the gun back. I'll even keep it loaded and click the safety off. You know you had it on, right? I just need you to be calm, Hattie. All I want is to talk."

Garrison Chase eased the gun toward her, carefully placing it on her right thigh.

"Guns," he said, "as I'm sure you're aware, exert control and power. And that's an incredibly powerful gun, Hattie. It's a Springfield XD pistol. You now hold the power, so just hear me out for a few minutes. At any point if you feel threatened, point that gun at me and tell me to leave. I'll go. Without argument. I promise."

Hattie eyed him, studying his bright green eyes. Eventually, she nodded. "Okay," she said. "As long as you're answering questions, not me. Aside from your name, I don't know you, don't trust you, don't know why or how much you're involved."

He held the stare while giving a subtle nod, then spoke calmly. "That's fair, totally fine by me. I understand." He paused.

Silence filled the vehicle. He seemed to be waiting for something.

"A piece of advice," he said. "Before we move on."

Hattie furrowed her brow.

He suddenly swept the pistol off her knee and gently pointed it at her. It happened so quickly she had no time to react.

Her eyes went wide.

Just as quickly as he'd grabbed the gun, though, he gave it back, twirling it around and thrusting it toward her.

"It's all about trust, Hattie," he said. "Take the Springfield, just don't leave it between us. Hold it in your left hand, as far away from me as possible."

Hattie swallowed and followed orders.

"Good," he said. "Now ask me anything you want."

CHAPTER THIRTY-TWO

I WATCHED HATTIE'S left hand tremble.

I knew I'd put her on edge by sneaking up and jumping into her vehicle. But even with her pointing a Springfield XD pistol at me, she was still skeptical and scared. More so than I would've thought.

She squinted at me. "What's your connection with Senator Cooper?"

I stuck to the truth. "The big man you just saw with me, the man the size of a dump truck, owns a security firm here in the city. Investigates members of Congress, primarily. I do some work for him. My latest assignment was Felton Byrd. He'd received some death threats from Cooper and hired us to find out if they were legitimate. Which turned out they sort of were. Anyway, I'm trying to figure out why the senators were murdered in that complex." I pointed toward Cooper's place. "And just what the hell's going on since another senator was murdered and a fourth abducted."

"You're not police or a fed or someone official in law enforcement?"

"Correct," I said. "I'm not a cop or a fed."

"You're a PI working on this then? A private investigator? That's what you're saying?"

Ah, geez. I didn't want to go down that road, but I did. "No, no, I'm not a PI. The big man is, but not me. I subcontract some work for him. I'm not a licensed PI."

She looked confused, which was somewhat understandable.

"What are you then?" she asked. "Enlighten me. Because right now, for all I know you're a hitman working for some organization and trying to get rid of me."

I pointed at her left hand. "Hopefully the fact that I handed you a loaded gun, twice as you'll recall, buys me some credibility. And Hattie, I'm truly giving you a technical definition of what I do. My buddy needs help on certain investigations, so he hires me out as a third party. As a—"

"Subcontractor," she said, interrupting me and rolling her eyes. "I heard you."

I didn't want to tell her about my past. She could be super hesitant to reveal information to someone formerly in law enforcement. But I felt I had to clarify.

"I used to be a federal agent with the FBI, once upon a time working in the Cyber Crimes division, though most of my time was spent with Violent Crimes. Because of my former skills, I'm basically a hired consultant."

She mulled that over for a bit, shooting eye daggers my direction. Finally, she spoke. "If you're investigating all this, how'd the investigation turn toward me? Why are you on to me and tracking me to a hotel? You mentioned a letter before I uh . . . kicked you."

She paused. It felt like she was about to apologize for spearing my boy parts, but then she moved on. "If there was a letter, how would you possibly know about it? Especially if you're not in law enforcement. Where are you getting this information?"

"Fair enough. Listen, I'm involved in this and kept in the loop by the feds because I found the senators' bodies. That's the truth." I gestured toward Cooper's complex again. "On Cooper's desk was an empty envelope, which we later found out came from Charlie Milliken. Gloria Milliken confirmed it. We also discovered that two letters were sent after Charlie's death, which is strange in and of itself. One was sent to you and the other to Cooper. We don't know the contents of either letter, though. No clue, in fact."

I paused. Upon mentioning another letter, Hattie looked surprised but didn't say anything.

"My mother," she said, breaking the silence. "How's she doing?"

"Worried about you."

"I take it she discovered her missing credit card and told you. That's how you tracked me to the hotel?"

I nodded. She looked disappointed. So I offered, "It was a decent plan, Hattie, using an older credit card of hers like that, especially since she has a different last name than you. No need to beat yourself up over it. That was a nice hotel, so you needed to pay with a credit card. You couldn't use cash like you've been doing. And you had to be at that particular hotel since it was just across the street from the bank you were watching."

Her eyes widened.

Shoot. I may have blown it.

"I don't need your approval," she snapped. "I certainly don't need you commenting on my decisions or trying to make me feel better. You know a lot, Garrison Chase, perhaps too much for my comfort."

I felt like our conversation was about to end, so I went for it. I had to ask.

"What was in the letter, Hattie? What did Charlie say?"

She narrowed her eyes.

"Hattie, I have to know. The country has to know. Three senators have been murdered, four if you include Charlie in that count, and one is still missing. You could be holding the clue to unravel whatever's going on. Please, tell me."

She opened her mouth, just a fraction, then quickly closed it.

I wasn't above groveling. "Please, Hattie. Earlier, when you rolled the luggage over me, remember that? You told me you didn't trust anyone, especially men. That women you saw"—I gestured toward the condos—"the one who got into the driver's seat, she's a federal investigator working on this. Tell her what you know. We're meeting back here tomorrow at eight a.m." I pointed at one of the coffee shops I'd visited. "Meet us there, in public, plenty of people will be around. We'll have some coffee and chat, nothing formal, just a conversation."

Again, her lips parted, but this time she spoke. "You know too much. Far too much." Her left hand came forward, jabbing the pistol at me. "You promised, didn't you?" She jabbed the gun again. "You need to leave. Now."

I hesitated, but only for a moment.

As I stood on the curb and watched Hattie drive away, I hoped she was testing me to see if I was a man of my word. I prayed she wasn't driving off, never to be seen again. If so, that would be the second major mistake I made in this case.

And one I'd have a hard time living with.

CHAPTER THIRTY-THREE

"IT'S TWENTY PAST eight," Ramona said. "What's the call? Still wait?"

I held up a finger. "How about one more cup of coffee? Then we can start canvassing."

"I don't think my stomach can take another cup of this stuff."

"Pretty bad, isn't it? The stuff two doors down is even worse. In my opinion, this is the only time it's acceptable to use cream and sugar."

I grabbed our cups and took them to the self-serve coffee area. There were six different pump-top thermoses. I chose the lesser of six evils and brought the cups back to the table, along with a small dish of French vanilla creamer.

The coffee shop was cramped and bustling with activity and noise. We sat at the only booth in the restaurant, which was by a large window at the front of the store. As I opened my mini creamer cups, I refrained from glancing out the window for signs of Hattie.

Honestly, I had no clue if she'd show up. Considering the time, I guess I'd blown it with her yesterday. I probably should've hauled her to the WFO and let federal agents take a crack at her.

I stirred the creamer in my cup a little too aggressively.

Ramona noticed. "We'll find her, Garrison. If Slim doesn't track her down, I'll get somebody in my office to work on it." She reached across and patted my hand.

Before I could respond, the bell above the coffee shop door tinkled.

A gust of cold air swept in, followed by Hattie Lattimer. For a moment, I stopped stirring and stared. Ramona shifted in the booth to see what I was looking at.

I snapped out of it and smiled at Hattie, then waved her over.

Ramona did as well. When Hattie didn't move, Ramona scooted out of the booth and asked her, "What can I get you? Coffee, tea, a muffin. Maybe a donut?"

Hattie eyed us and didn't say a word. She was about to bail, or at least she was seriously considering it.

"Please, Hattie." I gave her my best soft eyes look, not sure if it appeared genuine or forced.

A moment later, she walked to our table. I noticed a slight limp in her step.

Hattie unzipped her jacket and pulled back the hood, but kept on her white beanie. "Nothing for me, thanks." She slipped into the booth opposite me. Ramona took a seat on my side.

"I'm Agent Sanchez, but please call me Ramona."

Hattie nodded but didn't make eye contact. Her eyes flicked from patron to patron. It was clear to me she'd been on the run, clear she'd been looking over her shoulder for far too long. Her demeanor was a combination of tiredness and worry, evident by the way she slumped in the booth.

Eventually, her eyes flicked back and met mine. "I don't know if I should be doing this." She pulled her hands away from the table. I could see her arms moving under it, so I assumed she was wringing her hands.

"I'm a naturally skeptical person," Hattie said. "Even more so considering everything that's happened to me in the past few months." She narrowed her eyes at Ramona. "Since Mr. Chase has such a colorful, public past, I was able to learn a few things about him on the internet last night. But not you, Agent Sanchez, you're more of a mystery. Tell me your position in the government and the division you work with. Most importantly, I want to know what you'll do with any information I give you."

Ramona nodded. "Sure, no problem."

While Ramona began the conversation, I studied Hattie. Last month, on Karla's last visit, we'd finished watching the television series, *House of Cards*. Hattie reminded me of the lead actress, Robin Wright. Partly because they shared the same delicate, unassuming features, and because of their age—which I assumed was around fifty. But the real similarity between the two was the large divot at the base of Hattie's neck, the spot between her clavicles. It wasn't as big and round as Robin's, but it stood out and drew the eye's attention. For all I knew, though, Hattie could have dark, curly hair, and when she took off her beanie, she could look nothing like Robin Wright.

Hattie looked at me. "Mr. Chase here says he's working on this case as a consultant or contractor or some sort of outside investigator. He's certainly nuanced about his exact title. I just want to know if it's true or not." Her eyes flicked to Ramona.

"It is," Ramona said. "He's been involved from the beginning since Senator Byrd hired his friend's firm. And the FBI has continued working with him since he found the bodies and confronted the senators' killer. Not to mention he's a former agent himself. Speaking of the beginning, can you start there, Hattie? Tell us about your relationship with Charlie, and whether or not he sent you a letter."

Hattie took a deep breath, then pulled her hands from under the table. She reached inside her jacket and extracted an envelope. She placed it on the table, but she didn't slide it toward us. Instead, she shifted forward in the booth, trapping her palms over the letter. Her fingers interlocked while her thumbs fidgeted together.

The letter. It exists. It's intact!

Just as I started to gesture toward it, Ramona flicked my thigh under the table, signaling me to relax.

She was right. I needed to.

Hattie swallowed. "Yes, he sent me a letter as you can see. Sending me a letter was surprising enough, let alone that it came posthumously. Charlie and I had known each other for quite some time, from grade school all the way through college. However, we rarely connected post-college. About a month before his death, he contacted me and said he wanted to catch up, which we did. But it was an awkward meeting since I could tell Charlie's intention wasn't just to catch up. When I pressed him about what was really going on, he apologized and said he had stuff going on in his life. Too much stuff, he said; complicated life stuff that consumed him on a daily basis. Apparently, he just wanted to reminisce with me about the past, to think about a time when life was simpler and more carefree."

"You didn't buy that, though," I said.

Hattie shook her head.

Ramona leaned forward. "But the letter gave you a clue as to what was going on, right?"

Hattie winced. "Sort of, but not really."

"What?" I said. "Why wouldn't it?"

"Read for yourself." With a slightly trembling hand, she opened the envelope and slid the letter forward.

Heart thumping, I took it, unfolded the thick white paper, and placed it between Ramona and me so we could read it at the same time.

Hattie,

If you're reading this, it means I'm dead. It means there's suspicion surrounding my demise. It means the men I've aligned myself with are more selfish, cunning, and ruthless than I wanted to believe. I'm naïve. Naïve to believe I could've lived a normal life, naïve to think I could've put everything behind me, naïve to think my life would be spared.

More important than my naivety, though, is my contrition. I'm sorry, Hattie. So sorry that it's gotten to this point. Sorry that I wasn't man enough to make things right. Deeply sorry I couldn't tell you in person.

My strength was being a people-pleaser, going with the flow, not ruffling feathers, and avoiding confrontation as much as possible. Ultimately, it was also my downfall. There are brave men out there, Hattie. Men willing to fight for what's right, fight for what's good and noble and true. Painful as it is to admit, I'm not one of those men, though I wanted to be. When I received my diagnosis—which everyone knew was a death sentence—I thought perhaps I could finally be one of those men. Perhaps I could step up and be the man I always believed I could be.

I was wrong.

Cowardice and selfishness ran deeper in my being than I knew. I couldn't bring myself to tell you the truth in person. I couldn't imagine saying those words in front of you. Even now, as I pen this letter, I simply cannot write the words. It's fear that's dug its tentacles deep within my soul. Fear of what you'll think of me, of what my family will, of how history will view me.

It's fear of man I could not conquer. I'm ashamed to say: It conquered me.

You're a stronger, braver, and better person, Hattie. You always have been. You'll make things right; I know you will. The deep regret of my life is that I wasn't able to do it myself. I know you'll probably never forgive me. And I want you to know, I accept that. I understand.

I've left a safe deposit box in your name at the main Washington, DC branch of the Far East Bank. The key to the box is in the envelope. The contents of the box, which is an 8mm video, will explain everything. The only man I trust to help is Morse Cooper. I've sent him a letter, too. Take every precaution you can. Be safe.

Charlie

I read the letter again. I think Ramona did as well since she sat there without saying a word.

After the second read-through, I looked up. "What's this all about, Hattie? What's Charlie referring to? And what was on the video?"

Ramona looked up when I asked the questions, but Hattie didn't respond. Instead, she looked around and fidgeted with her hands. Finally, she looked back and sighed. "I don't know. And I'm sorry about that. I'm not sure what Charlie's letter is about. I haven't been able to access the security box yet, so I haven't seen the video."

Ramona and I both leaned forward at the same time.

"Wait, what?" I said. "Why haven't you accessed the box?"

"There have been men watching the bank around the clock. I've tried to wait them out, but every day they keep showing up." She looked at me. "The day we met I made an attempt to access the box. I disguised myself and slipped into the bank without being noticed. But once I requested access to the box, the men rushed in. I freaked and rushed out.

I'm convinced they were tipped off by one of the managers. Those men would've taken the video, then perhaps killed or kidnapped me. I'm sure of it."

I nodded. No doubt she was right. "You did the smart thing, Hattie. Surely, though, you must have some idea what Charlie was referring to in the letter. I know it was cryptic, but something must jump out to you. Right?"

She hesitated. I didn't know if that was due to embarrassment for not having a clue about what was going on, or if she was simply holding back on us.

Instead of answering my question, she said, "I don't want to speculate; I hope you both understand. I need your help to access that box. If you help, you can be there when I open it; we can view the video and learn together. I need you guys, and you need me." She paused.

Ramona wasted no time, standing and saying, "It's a deal, but we go now. The bank just opened. We'll sweep in first thing and catch them unprepared. In fact, we can't afford to wait. For all we know, they could be watching you this instant. Maybe they know you're speaking with me, so we need to surprise them."

I shimmied out of the booth and stood beside Ramona.

"It'll be perfectly fine, Hattie," I said. "You'll be safe with us. We'll access that box and finally get some solid answers. And figure out just what the hell's going on."

CHAPTER THIRTY-FOUR

"I DON'T SEE their car," Hattie said as we approached the bank's front door.

"Doesn't matter," I said. "We stick to the plan and move fast."

I opened the door for the women. Ramona walked in first, followed by Hattie. I took the rear and walked backward to keep an eye out for Hattie's assailants.

In single file—flanking Hattie—we marched toward one of the offices on the bank's perimeter. The only spoken words were Hattie directing Ramona where to go.

Ramona didn't stop and knock on the manager's door. Instead, she whisked open the door and rushed inside. Her badge was already out. Hattie followed Ramona into the office. I stayed outside so I could keep an eye on the bank, not just for the assailants but also for signs of anybody reaching for a phone or acting suspiciously.

As I surveyed the bank floor, I could hear Ramona berating the manager in a sharp tone. She demanded immediate access to the safe deposit box and informed him that any objections or stalling would lead to an obstruction of justice charge.

When she finished, I could hear the bank manager's worried tone.

"Absolutely, right away," he said. "I'll call the floor manager. He'll escort Ms. Lattimer straight to her security box."

Since our plan was to make sure the manager didn't call anyone, I shot a look over my shoulder into the office.

Ramona saw me looking and held up her hand, signaling that it was okay.

And it was. She stood a few feet in front of the manager while he made the call, close enough to hear every word. Plus, she'd subtly placed her right hand on her hip. That pulled back her blue suit jacket, which revealed her Bureau-issued Glock 17M.

And the bank manager's eyes were glued to the gun. I watched his Adam's apple bob up and down. Twice.

The conversation was short and effective. Within moments, I watched a heavyset man waddle across the bank as fast as he could. By the time he reached me, a sheen of sweat had glistened across his forehead. He introduced himself as Mr. Wisenberg.

While Hattie and I followed Wisenberg to the security box area, Ramona hung back and grilled the other manager. She wanted to know who he'd called when Hattie made her initial appearance at the bank.

The security box area was, as you'd suspect, nothing unusual. The room was probably twenty feet by twenty feet. Along all four walls were brass box plates stretching from three feet off the floor all the way to about seven feet high. There was a large, rectangular table in the middle of the room.

I stayed by the room's entrance, shooting looks into the bank every so often. I also watched the floor manager and Hattie. They put keys into the box, then simultaneously turned them. Wisenberg eased the box from the wall. The box itself was deeper and longer than you'd expect.

He placed it on the table and waddled away, giving Hattie her privacy. It took everything in me not to rush over and examine the box's contents, but I refrained and gave Hattie some space. I wondered whether there was more than just an 8mm video in the box. I also wondered how we would play the video. The Video8 style camcorder was in production around the late '80s, early '90s. Where would we find one of those?

I shook off the questions and turned my attention to Hattie. She stood over the box with a confused look on her face.

She blinked a few times, then looked at me with wide eyes.

"What?" I said. "What is it?"

She shoved the box, turning away in disgust. "See for yourself."

I hustled over. About five feet away I could already see why she was disgusted.

The box was empty.

CHAPTER THIRTY-FIVE

MY CONVERSATION WITH Wisenberg had turned heated. So loud that Ramona must've heard our exchange from across the bank.

She rushed into the security box room. "What's going on?"

I motioned toward the box on the table. "Empty. Nothing in there. No video, nothing."

Her shoulders sagged.

Looking at Wisenberg, who was clearly flummoxed, I said, "I find everything here highly suspect, sir." I glanced at Hattie. "Two men staked out this bank for how long?"

"Over a week," she said. "Maybe as much as two."

I held out my hands, palms open. "Then it appears one of your managers called these same men when Ms. Lattimer came in to access her box. They chased her across the street to the hotel. I witnessed it, eventually intercepting the men myself. And one of them had a gun. Now we finally gain access to the box and it's empty. Suspicious, Wisenberg. Highly."

"With all due respect," he said, "I don't know anything about the men you're referring to. And this security box, well, I hope you're not suggesting that we had anything to do with its lack of contents. That's clearly against the law. The law only allows us to open a box without the owner in the rarest of situations. And Ms. Lattimer's situation clearly isn't one of those. It's entirely plausible that nothing was placed in the box in the first place. It's plausible that the paperwork was completed, payment made, keys issued, but no contents were actually placed in the box."

I was about to let Wisenberg have it, but Ramona stepped in. "What sort of record keeping do you have with these boxes? Do you keep a log of the contents or log every time someone accesses the box?"

He wiped the sweat off his brow. "Regarding the contents of the box, it's wise for the box's owner to keep a record of what's in there. Quite often I advise owners to take a picture of the contents. As a bank, however, we have no idea of contents. Not a clue. And no obligation to know, for that matter. Regarding record keeping of visits, certain states require access logs, but our state doesn't."

Ramona put her hands on her hips. "What you're saying then is you have no idea what or if anything was ever in the box. To boot, you have no clue who's accessed it."

Sweat had already re-beaded on his forehead. "Basically," he said, clearing his throat. "That's basically correct."

I pulled Ramona aside, figuring we wouldn't get anywhere with this guy.

"What did your man say?"

She shook her head. "Feigned ignorance mostly. Said there was a flag in the system attached to Hattie Lattimer's account. He assumed it was some vital paperwork Hattie hadn't completed, and that he was to call up the chain whenever she checked in at the bank."

"You buy that?"

"Not really. I don't think he knows what's really going on, but I do think he's aware it isn't a paperwork issue." She thumbed over her shoulder at Wisenberg, who was in a conversation with Hattie. "He called someone above that guy, apparently the general manager of the bank. And just our luck, that manager isn't in."

"Of course not," I said. "But I'm sure they'll find out about our visit right away."

"Yup, which will give the manager time to think up some story and report back to whoever is behind this."

"Which could be Duke Tweed. It's too coincidental that he's also trying to buy this bank. Right?"

She nodded and gestured toward Hattie, who was still speaking with Wisenberg. "We need to ask her about Tweed, for sure."

Like a true administrator, Wisenberg was concerned with paperwork. Moments earlier, an aide had entered and handed him some form. Currently he was explaining to Hattie the importance of filling out the paperwork regarding the missing contents. As if that would go anywhere. I could tell Hattie wasn't buying it either. She was bent over the table quickly filling out the form and not really paying attention to his jabbering.

I looked at Ramona. "What if those men who chased Hattie are waiting outside? We didn't spot anything unusual, but it's not like we did a thorough surveillance check. Plus, there could be new men on the job, with a new vehicle."

"There could be," she said. "You're right."

"On my walk across the bank I noticed stairs in the far-right corner, which obviously ascend to a second floor. No doubt the bank has some offices up there, and some will overlook the street. What if you and Hattie leave here and go in opposite directions? I'll get Wisenberg to escort me to a street side office on the second floor. Then I'll have an elevated position and can see if anyone follows either of you."

She thought about that. "I like it. It's worth a shot."

"Good. You guys walk a few blocks in either direction, then turn west and proceed a street over. We'll meet up in the middle, one block west from here."

"It's a plan." Ramona walked toward Wisenberg and pulled him aside. Told him that the FBI would open an inquiry as to what went down at the bank. Then she berated him again, but not for long. By the time she'd finished, Hattie had the paperwork in hand and gave it to him.

Ramona told Wisenberg they were leaving but would be in touch.

As Ramona walked by, I whispered for her to stall until I gained second-floor access. As I followed the group out, I grabbed the manager by the arm and steered him toward the stairs. At the base of the stairs, I politely explained my request. He looked confused but didn't challenge me.

While the ladies headed toward the bathroom, I climbed the stairs with Wisenberg. About halfway up, I figured I may need to carry the man to the top. But he made it without collapsing or major incident.

He proceeded to the closest office with a window, huffing along the way. Since the office was empty, he opened the door and waved me in, then started to leave.

"Not so fast," I said. "Stay here with me."

He looked mildly peeved. "Is that really necessary? I'm a busy man, and this gives you some privacy to watch whatever you're watching, or whomever."

I smiled. "Not wise business practice to leave somebody alone in another person's office. Is it, Mr. Wisenberg?" Of course, the real reason I didn't want him to leave pertained to him getting on the horn and alerting his boss.

He didn't respond to my question. Instead, he lumbered over to the window. "Fine then. What are we looking for?"

I didn't respond, simply pointed to the empty desk chair, which he reluctantly squeezed himself into.

Just as I turned my attention to the street, I saw Hattie and Ramona peel out. Hattie veered north while Ramona went south. Hattie definitely hurt her foot when she speared me. The longer she walked, the more noticeable her limp.

My eyes scanned the street, looking at vehicles, pedestrians, even customers leaving shops. After five minutes of street scanning, I concluded that nothing unusual happened. Nobody, not even a vehicle, suddenly changed their course of direction and hustled after either woman.

For good measure, I waited and scanned an additional two minutes, then said goodbye to Mr. Wisenberg. I was out of the bank before he'd descended one flight of stairs.

Ramona was already at the meet-up spot, but Hattie wasn't. She didn't look at me as I approached. Her eyes were glued down the street, looking in the direction Hattie would be coming from.

"Nobody followed us I take it?" she said.

"Nope. I witnessed nothing unusual. Where's Hattie? Is she taking her time? Or did she get confused and go east? Maybe she went two streets west instead of one."

Ramona turned. "I was pretty clear that it was one street over to the west. I even pointed in this direction while going over the plan with her."

"Have we been ditched?"

I didn't wait for Ramona to respond. Instead, I kicked the nearby curb. "Boy, if she ditched us, I'm a fool."

"Me too," Ramona replied. "It never occurred to me she'd ditch us. Maybe now that there's no video, Hattie's done with everything. Maybe she sees it as a dead end and doesn't want to pursue it. We helped her gain access, so now she doesn't need us."

"Maybe," I said. "Listen, let's not jump to conclusions about her ditching us. Why don't you wait here, and I'll go east to make sure she didn't get mixed up and is waiting for us there."

I was off before Ramona finished nodding. I was also back about fifteen minutes later with no sign of Hattie. As I approached Ramona, I could tell by her dejected posture that Hattie hadn't turned up.

"We didn't get her cell number," she said. "We have no idea where she's even staying."

"It was a pretty stupid and rushed plan."

Ramona shrugged. "It could've worked, though. I mean, if the men were watching. Hopefully they weren't way down the street and picked her up."

"Highly doubt it. I could see pretty clearly about two blocks north and south. Nobody suddenly changed direction or crossed the street. And if they were any farther than that, then they couldn't see the front of the bank."

"You're probably right."

"You know what's really stupid of me? I should've taken the gun from Hattie yesterday. She picked up a Springfield XD pistol from one of her pursuers after I tackled him in the hotel stairwell. Your office could tell us the registered owner, if it's registered, that is. At the very least forensics could dust for fingerprints. That way maybe we'd get an ID on one of the assailants."

"No point in rehashing mistakes. Let's regroup and talk about everything later. I'd like to recanvass Cooper's complex, but I used my time this morning with Hattie. I have to report back to the office. Plus, I'm anxious to learn about any latest developments."

"Me too."

"If I can get away, maybe we'll canvass the complex around dinner. That way more people will be home."

I nodded. "We have to confront Agnew, and soon."

"Agreed, I'll see what I can do. I'll text you around six, let you know either way. What are you going to do?"

"Find Hattie. And when I do, I'm going to handcuff her to me. Can I borrow your cuffs?"

CHAPTER THIRTY-SIX

I DROVE TO Maryland, connecting with Karla along the way and updating her on the latest developments. I also checked in with Mom and Simon, telling them I'd be home soon. Mom called me out on what soon meant; she was good that way.

Once in Maryland, I staked out Hattie's mother's house. Since Hattie had asked about her mom, I thought there was a chance she'd check in with her. I knew if I stayed in DC, I'd be tempted to bang on Aidan Agnew's door and confront him. And if I knocked on his door, there was a possibility he'd ask to see a badge, which would force me to impersonate a federal agent. Which could be really bad for Ramona if she tried to take responsibility for my actions.

And she seemed to be that type of quality woman.

So I played it safe in Maryland. The only problem: no sign of Hattie. At about four o'clock I knew I had to get back on the road in case Ramona was ready to meet up at Cooper's complex around six.

Before I left, however, I felt obligated—as a parent—to knock on Mildred's door. She was a mother and deserved to know that her daughter was alive and in good health. Mildred, of course, had a ton of questions for me and insisted I come in for another cup of coffee.

I politely fought her off and kept things vague about Hattie. Told her I didn't know too much about Hattie's situation, which was partly true, and assured her that she was safe. I certainly didn't go into details about the men who were after her.

When I hit the outskirts of DC, Ramona texted and asked if we could meet at Cooper's. She said there was an interesting development: one of the neighbors had come forward and wanted to talk. That piqued my interest enough to floor the car through the city and arrive at the complex in record time.

We showed up at the same time, meeting in front of the complex so we could discuss the latest development. She didn't want to speak about it in the lobby and have the security guard overhear.

I leaned against the wall, about the same spot where I'd crossed paths with Agnew. "So what's the story with the neighbor? Was it Agnew trying to get out in front of things?"

"Nope," she said. "Edwin Keating called the WFO, said he had information he needed to share. His call was routed to me since I'm heading up that part of the investigation. Unfortunately, I missed the senator's call. But he left a message for me to meet him here at his condo."

"I thought he didn't live here. That his niece and some roommates did."

"Right, that's what you told me. I don't know. He didn't explain anything in the voicemail, just asked to meet."

I nodded. "What time?"

She glanced at her watch. "Six-fifteen, which is about now."

On our way up the elevator, I tried to manage my expectations. I didn't want to entertain any theories about what Keating was about to reveal. And I certainly didn't want to get too excited about catching a break in the case. So far, I'd been disappointed every time I got my hopes up. Ramona must've been thinking along the same lines since we didn't talk about it on the ride up or the walk to Keating's condo.

Before Ramona knocked on his door, I asked, "How do you want me to handle this? Probably best if I stay quiet, right?"

"Probably," she replied. "But don't hesitate to say anything if something jumps out at you, or if you think I'm missing an important line of questioning."

"Will do," I said.

Thirty seconds after she knocked, Ramona turned to me. "Odd, right? Did I not knock loud enough?"

"You did. But let me make sure." I pounded three times. When nobody answered, I put my ear to the door. "Pretty quiet in there. You're right, this is weird. The meeting was at six-fifteen, wasn't it?"

"Let me double-check." She pulled out her phone and listened to the voicemail. "Definitely six-fifteen. He's probably just running late."

To pass the time, I leaned against the wall and asked about Edwin Keating. "Think maybe Keating saw something the day the senators were murdered? I mean, his condo is in prime position, being on the same floor and right by the stairwell."

"Maybe. If he did, makes me wonder why he waited a couple of days to call."

"Me too. Maybe it wasn't him. Maybe the college girls saw something, and the niece relayed it to her uncle. Once Keating heard about it, he called your FO."

"Again, maybe."

We stayed silent for a bit, both realizing that we could go back and forth with a bunch of maybes.

Eventually, I broke the silence. "What's the latest with the task force? Any developments?"

Ramona leaned against the wall opposite me.

"No sign of Fornetti. No body turned up. No leads. No ransom note. Nothing. It's a complete mystery what happened to her and where she is. The task force is focused on Sherman Adams, naturally, since he's the only suspect we have, though he's dead."

"Have they deepened the connection with him and the left-wing militia group?"

"Actually, they haven't. Their focus has changed."

I furrowed my brow. "To what?"

"Another militia group. Adams's most recent travel was a flight to

Bismarck, North Dakota, which happened a few weeks back. At first, it seemed clear that he flew there because it's fairly close to the militia's base in eastern Montana. Like I told you earlier, though, the man had ties to other militias. Which makes sense since he was basically a gun for hire. A bipartisan killer, as you said."

"Bipartisan hitman were my actual words." I smiled.

She carried on. "Anyway, one of the other militias was a right-wing organization near the border in northern Minnesota, and that base is actually closer to Bismarck than the Montana one."

"I get it. Since the recent murder and abduction were both Democratic senators, it doesn't make sense to them to go after the left-wing group in Montana."

"Right. All their focus is on this northern Minnesota group. It's their best guess as to Rachel Fornetti's location, if she's still alive. As we speak, they're redirecting drones to get visuals on the compound near the border. Once they get intel and a solid plan, a raid will happen."

I nodded while glancing at my watch. "Why don't I check in with the security guard downstairs? See what he knows concerning the whereabouts of the senator or the Georgetown girls. Maybe you stay here in case he comes up this back stairwell?"

"Sure," she said.

Jim was behind the security desk looking at something on his laptop. "Quick question," I said as I approached the desk. "Edwin Keating was supposed to meet us at his condo about fifteen or twenty minutes ago. Any idea where he is? Not sure if he called the front desk here to let you know he's running late."

He shook his head. "I haven't heard from him. In fact, I haven't heard from Senator Keating in like nine months, maybe closer to a year. You do know he doesn't live in that condo, though he does own it?"

"Right. Apparently some Georgetown students live there, one of whom is his niece."

"Yup," he said. "Except the three aren't living there this semester."

"The condo's empty?"

"Sure is. Those three girls are studying abroad for fall semester. Italy, I believe."

"Thanks, that's interesting. Very interesting." I slowly made my way back to the third floor, thinking about the empty condo. I must've had a puzzled look on my face because Ramona addressed it.

"What's going on?" she said. "You look confused. What did he say?"

"That he hadn't heard from Keating in maybe a year, and that the Georgetown students are all in Italy studying abroad. Been gone all semester."

"Okay," she said. "The condo's empty. What am I missing? That doesn't sound that odd."

"You're right; it's just that I suddenly remembered Sherman Adams's choice of words. He told me, I think twice, that he'd holed up in this complex. 'Holed up' were the exact words he used. I hadn't really thought about that until the guard told me this condo was empty. 'Holed up' almost refers to hiding. Doesn't it?"

Ramona thought about it. "It does. Holed up makes me think that he was in a condo he wasn't supposed to be in." She thumbed at the door. "Like this one."

"Exactly. If he was staying with somebody in one of these condos, would he have used those words?"

We both thought about that for a few moments.

Ramona spoke first. "Probably not, but there's a chance he would. From his perspective, maybe he was living with somebody during those nine days, but he didn't want to leave the condo at all for fear of being spotted by others, so he felt holed up."

"Could be, you're right. It might've just been a figure of speech because he felt cooped up."

We continued debating the merits of that theory for another five minutes.

At quarter to seven, I asked the obvious question. "How much longer do you want to wait? Do you have a call-back number for him?"

She shook her head. "It was unlisted. I'd like to keep waiting, but I have a feeling we've been given the brush-off."

"So do I. Why don't you leave the guard your business card? He can give it to Keating if and when he shows up. That way Keating can contact you directly."

"Sounds good," she said.

"Since Slim's office isn't far, we can decompress there, check in with Slim, then shoot back here if Keating calls."

"Perfect. Before we do that, let's pop upstairs and see if Agnew is home."

Unfortunately, Senator Agnew was still not in. On our way out we asked the guard when he last saw Agnew. He told us it was before the murders, then he whispered that he was most likely staying with one of his lady friends. Apparently, both security guards knew about Agnew's propensity for the ladies.

Once we arrived at the agency and filled Slim in on the day's developments, the three of us were surprised to hear the buzzer go off. Slim hustled over and pressed the intercom button.

I was floored to hear Hattie Lattimer asking to be let in.

It was silent in the conference room as we waited for her to arrive. The first thing she said upon entering was, "I'm sorry. I had to get away to clear my head. All my decisions the past few months have been weighty. Not to be dramatic, but they've been life-or-death decisions. I needed the afternoon to decide how to proceed, especially after learning the video was stolen. Or maybe Charlie Milliken was such a coward that he changed his mind at the last second and decided not to share the video. Maybe he chickened out and didn't put it in the safe deposit box."

"Probably the former," I said. "I think someone high up in the bank stole it. Paid off by a third party who desperately needed that video. Either Wisenberg or Wisenberg's boss."

"Maybe," Ramona said. "But then why would they place men outside the bank if there was nothing in the box? If they'd stolen it already?"

"The men out front," Slim said, "could've been there for Hattie and not the video. We have to consider that. Maybe it wasn't about them getting the contents of the box, since nothing was actually in there, it was about getting to Hattie."

"Okay," I said, looking at Hattie. "If that's the case, then why would those men want you dead?"

Hattie had a grim look on her face. "I don't know; I'm sorry. I wish I could be of more help."

A thought popped into my mind. "I bet they knew about Charlie's letter to Hattie, but they didn't know what Charlie said in the letter. They would've assumed that Charlie mentioned something about what was going on, however. They probably didn't know Charlie was such a coward and couldn't admit to what he'd done or been a part of, even in a posthumous letter."

Ramona nodded. "Right. Maybe they'd already secured the video, but they needed to tie up the loose end with Hattie because they assumed she knew things from the letter."

I looked at Hattie, who still seemed worried. "It's too coincidental, Hattie, that Duke Tweed is trying to buy that very bank and he was best friends with Charlie. Tweed must be the third party behind all this. My guess is that Tweed and Charlie were up to something, which got out of hand. And Charlie Milliken got cold feet or a conscience, especially since he knew death was knocking, but he didn't have the backbone to confront a powerful man like Tweed. What's your connection and relationship with Duke Tweed? Surely you know him."

At this point, Hattie had turned pale. "I do," she said. "But . . ."

Ramona eyed me from across the table. She gave me a look that said to slow down, to give Hattie some time.

So I did.

Slim picked up where I left off, though. "Could be that Tweed and Charlie were in cahoots about the bank thing. Tweed was getting help from Charlie about how to get the government to sign off on him buying these banks. Perhaps Charlie brought Agnew into the picture. Maybe it was Charlie's suggestion to get somebody on the payroll who sits on the Economic Policy Committee, somebody like Agnew. In the end, Charlie gets his diagnosis, which makes him re-evaluate his life decisions. But he can't bring himself to do anything about it."

Ramona pointed at Slim. "That makes sense, especially after reading the letter to Hattie. Charlie only wanted to bring down Tweed if he went too far."

"Like if he killed him," I said. "That's why Charlie had the stipulation in his will to only send the letter if his death was suspicious. I bet Charlie confronted Tweed, maybe told him to stop pursuing the banks and trying to manipulate currency or interest rates or whatever they were trying to do. Or maybe Charlie simply said he was going to pull out of the whole affair, wanted nothing more to do with it, and Tweed got upset over that. Which made Charlie extremely nervous."

"Agnew must be involved in all this," Slim said. "There needs to be a reason why Charlie would send a letter to the Senate Ethics Committee. Charlie's letter to Cooper probably exposed the scheme and pointed to Senator Agnew as the inside man in the government."

Ramona stood. "Yup. Tweed and Agnew then took extreme measures to cover everything up. Agnew, of course, gave Sherman Adams access to the building. Perhaps Adams broke into Keating's empty condo and patiently waited for Cooper and Byrd to meet so he could stage the murder-suicide. Tweed and Agnew eventually went after the other two members of the committee because they were unsure if those members knew anything."

When she paused, I jumped in. "I like where we're going with this, but there are two problems in my mind. One, murder and kidnapping and staging suicide are extreme measures. And for what? Sounds like Tweed and Agnew were planning some sort of financial manipulation for their own benefit, but they hadn't actually done anything so far. Are we saying it's a huge cover-up for an attempted criminal activity? That seems a little extreme.

"Second, and a bigger problem, at least for me, is the letter to Hattie." I glanced at her. She immediately looked down. "How does the letter to Hattie make sense in terms of her involvement with some banking conspiracy? Why would Charlie send a letter and video to her about that? Unless, of course, we're saying that the letter to Hattie is about something entirely different. Are we? But then that doesn't make sense because Charlie specifically referred to Cooper in Hattie's letter. Which assumes the letters are related."

With her head down, Hattie began shaking it. "Stop, stop. Everyone stop. Please, just stop. Please!"

We did. Then we waited.

Finally, Hattie looked up. "I don't think this has anything to do with a banking conspiracy. Nothing, nothing at all."

She looked around the room, her eyes meeting each one of ours.

"I'm sorry," she said.

I noticed her eyes were now glistening.

"Really sorry," she continued. "So far, I . . . I haven't been entirely truthful."

CHAPTER THIRTY-SEVEN

WE WAITED FOR her to continue, but she didn't speak for some time. It felt like minutes but was probably closer to thirty seconds.

Eventually, she began. "I wanted to see that video so badly to confirm what Charlie was talking about in his letter. But it was gone, stolen, maybe never put there, or whatever the case. Either way, I panicked when the video wasn't there because I didn't get the confirmation I needed. That's why I ran. Had to clear my head and figure out the next steps."

"It's okay, Hattie," Ramona said. "Like we said, it makes sense. We totally understand."

"Now there's mention of Duke Tweed," Hattie continued. "And that he owned or was trying to own this Far East Bank, which feels like a form of confirmation."

She paused and looked at me. "To answer your earlier question, yes, I know Duke Tweed. And it's true that Duke and Charlie were best friends, from as far back as I can remember. We all grew up in the same area. To be honest, I was good friends with Charlie but never liked Duke. He manipulated and used Charlie; that's what I saw in their relationship from as early as I can remember."

She looked off.

After a moment, I prodded her. "So you don't think this has to do with a financial conspiracy. What do you think it's about then?"

Hattie opened her mouth, then closed it. Tears welled and were about to roll down her cheeks. She blinked a few times and cleared her throat.

"My sister," she said. "I think this has to do with my sister."

My mind immediately returned to the pictures of her twin in her mom's house. I said, "Your mom told me your sister died in an accident." I was about to say something else, but I watched the first tears roll, so I held back.

"That's what we were told happened," she said, dabbing at the tear in her right eye with her pinky finger. She looked at Ramona and Slim. "She was my twin; she died years ago. We were as close as any sisters could ever be. Everything you've heard about the mysterious connection between twins is true. When I lost her, I lost part of me. That's not just an expression or hyperbole; it's existentially true. I mean it. Twenty-five years later, I'm still not the same. I'm not whole; a legitimate part of me is missing."

While she dabbed at a new tear, I asked, "What do you mean you were told she died in an accident? Was it a suspicious accident?"

"I mean, for the past two and a half decades, it wasn't suspicious; my family thought it was a terrible accident. But now, now I think that's just what we were told."

Ramona pulled a chair beside Hattie and put a hand on her shoulder. "What's the story you were told? If you're up for telling it, that is."

After a deep breath, Hattie launched into it. "Hallie, that's my sister's name, and I went everywhere together. We grew up in a very affluent part of New York. We were rarely seen apart. A lot of our friends had vacation places on Long Island in Nassau County, in the swanky, rich town of Sands Point. Every year Duke Tweed hosted a number of summer parties at his parents' place since they were never home. The same week Duke held his end of the summer bash, I came down with a terrible case of bronchitis. I was sick as a dog and in no shape to attend. Hallie said there was no way she was going either. But I knew she really wanted to go, so I encouraged her to do so."

Tears really flowed down her cheeks now. Slim excused himself for a moment while Hattie started shaking her head. "I encouraged her. I can't believe it. I actually encouraged her to go."

Slim returned quickly with some tissues. Hattie took two and sobbed into them, apologizing to us after a minute of crying.

Ramona reassured her. "No need to apologize. Take your time. I can't imagine how painful this is."

With a fresh tissue, she blotted her eyes and continued. "Hallie went without me, which I was fine with. Really too sick to care about anything that particular day. I was glad she was going to the party and not staying at home to worry about me. Didn't see the point of her watching me sleep. Anyway, from what I understand about the party, it was huge; at least a couple hundred people attended. And it was sinful. I mean, alcohol, drugs, sex, all that. The story goes that Hallie got pretty drunk. Witnesses remember seeing her around midnight stumbling and slurring, which, of course, was nothing out of the ordinary since everybody else was in the same shape, too. The difference, though, was that everybody else made it home that night, one way or the other.

"Honestly, and this isn't an exaggeration, I remember waking in the middle of the night and feeling incredibly anxious, like something bad had happened." She took a deep breath. "Which it did, of course. They found her body at the base of the cliffs. Massive trauma to the head and body as she apparently stumbled off the cliffs and dropped one hundred feet to the sea. Blood alcohol level was still well above the legal limit, according to the coroner's report, even though the test was taken hours after the fall."

Hattie paused. Nobody said a word. It felt like all the oxygen had been sucked from the room.

I felt awful for Hattie, losing her twin like that, right during the peak of their lives.

"I should've been there for her," Hattie said, staring straight down at the table. "She was always the slightly wilder one. We sort of balanced each other out that way. She loosened me up, but I kept her in line. I would've been right by her side during that party, would've told her to scale back the drinking once I saw her stumbling and slurring. I . . . I can't believe I encouraged her to go. Especially without me." She put her hands over her face.

Ramona took her hand off Hattie's shoulder and patted her back in a comforting way.

I wanted to tell Hattie it would be fine. That she couldn't have known what would happen. That she couldn't blame herself or be responsible in any way. You know, all those comforting clichés. But I knew Hattie realized all those things, and that she'd probably heard them a thousand times before. Plus, silence felt like the best approach here, so I followed my intuition and stayed quiet.

Probably a minute later, after wiping some tears with a fresh tissue, Hattie looked up. Her gaze fell on Ramona. "Maybe what happened to my sister wasn't an accident. Maybe that's what this is about. I don't know." She shook her head. "I just can't think of anything else that would warrant a letter like that from Charlie. And now as I replay the conversations I had with Charlie all those years ago, especially right after Hallie's supposed accident, maybe I had it all wrong."

When she didn't elaborate, I asked, "Had what wrong?"

She took a deep breath. "My take on Charlie. He was so incredibly sorry about Hallie. He took it worse than anyone else did at that party. And he was very supportive of me, for weeks and months after the accident, always checking in on me." Hattie flicked her eyes between the three of us. "But maybe it was all out of guilt?"

"Maybe," I said. "Definitely could be guilt. Maybe it wasn't an accident and Charlie was involved or knew something. After all, it was at Duke Tweed's house, so Tweed was obviously involved, too."

Hattie nodded.

I kept at it, reasoning in the process. "The fact that Charlie left you, or was supposed to leave you, an 8mm tape to explain everything is interesting. Camcorders from around the time of Hallie's death used 8mm video, so whatever Charlie was referring to in his letter would've been from the '90s most likely."

Hattie's eyes hardened. "Somebody could've been taping the party and the video caught something happening to Hallie. Maybe Charlie knew what happened." She jabbed the end of her pointer finger on the table. "All these years, all these years, he's been racked by guilt because he's a coward and couldn't come clean."

I could see the anger rising in Hattie, but I could literally feel it, too. Which was contagious. I pushed back from my chair and started pacing. "Maybe somebody was blackmailing Charlie and Tweed or threatening to expose whatever happened. Perhaps Charlie and Tweed disagreed over how to handle the situation. In the letter to Hattie, it seems Charlie was at least trying to come clean, especially since he was recently given a death sentence."

Ramona joined in. "And Tweed would have nothing of it. He caught wind that Charlie wanted to come clean about it to Hattie, maybe also to the Ethics Committee. So he used his considerable resources to put a stop to all of it. Maybe he was trying to buy the Far East Bank to gain access to the safe deposit box where the video was. When that got blocked, perhaps he bought off the general manager. And also bought off Aidan Agnew to let the hitman into the complex."

"What do you think?" I said, looking at Slim.

"I think Duke Tweed has enough money to buy off anybody, so anything's possible. We need to speak with him. That's what I think."

"We do," I said. "But how?" I looked at Ramona. "We only have theories and maybes at this point. It would be tough to bring in the feds, right? Especially when we have no concrete proof of Tweed's involvement."

She nodded. "Not sure what I would say to the task force about Tweed, at least at this juncture."

Slim waved his hand. "Forget the feds. We don't have time for that. Plus, who knows how many contacts Tweed has in the Bureau, anyway. We need to speak with the man ourselves."

"Sorry, Ramona," I said. "But I agree with Slim."

She held up her hands. "No offense; I get it."

"Somebody like Tweed is not easily accessible," I said. "And that's a problem."

"I know him," Hattie said. "I can get access to him."

"But if he is involved in all this," I said, "which certainly seems to be the case, then he may not want to speak with you. He may intentionally avoid you if you reach out."

Hattie leaned forward. "What if I tell him we need to talk about my sister Hallie? Maybe that'll rattle him. Couldn't I wear a wire? Hopefully get him to say something incriminating."

"Very risky," I said. "If our theory is true, Duke Tweed will do anything to silence you."

"Sure, I agree," Hattie said. "But you're missing two important things. First, there's no way I'd meet Duke Tweed on his own turf or in private. Has to be somewhere public, which means you two guys will be somewhere close by to protect me." She looked at Slim. "I hope you don't take this the wrong way, but I'm pretty sure you could dive on a hand grenade and suffer only mild abrasions." She smiled.

I did as well.

Hattie eyed Slim. "You can protect little old me. Quite easily, am I right?"

Slim eyed her back, trying to suppress a grin. "So what's the second important thing we're missing?"

"I'd do anything," she said, "absolutely anything, to get justice for my sister."

CHAPTER THIRTY-EIGHT

HATTIE LATTIMER HAD a great memory. She recalled details about Duke Tweed from over two decades ago. Because of her great recall, we devised a solid plan we believed would draw him out.

While putting the final touches on our plan, Ramona's phone rang. She said she didn't recognize the number. For some reason I made a bad joke that perhaps it was an ex-boyfriend or ex-husband calling. Not sure what was going through my mind to make that stupid remark.

At any rate, Ramona blushed at the comment and stepped out of the room to answer the call. When she returned less than thirty seconds later, she addressed me.

"That was far more interesting than an old flame calling. It was Jim from Cooper's complex. Apparently, Edwin Keating came in about ten minutes ago. He went straight up the stairs. The guard called after him, even mentioned our visit, but Keating didn't say anything or come back to ask. The guard thought we should know."

"That is very interesting," I said. "We should visit the senator right away."

"Absolutely," she replied.

I looked at Slim and Hattie. "You guys head to Slim's without me. I'll have Ramona drop me off after our visit with the senator."

Slim nodded. "Freda will put some sheets on the living room couch for you."

Earlier, during our planning phase, I'd pulled Slim away for a sidebar so Hattie couldn't hear. We both agreed to never let her out of our sight. It took some convincing, but we finally had her agree to stay in Slim's guestroom this evening.

When Ramona and I arrived at the condominium complex, we barely communicated with the security guard. She thanked him for the heads-up call. I was already halfway up the first flight of stairs by the time Ramona entered the stairwell. She did, however, beat me to Keating's door.

"FBI," she said while knocking. "Open up, Senator Keating."

Immediately we heard movement. Before the door had fully swung open, we heard the senator apologize.

"So sorry," he said again, waving us into the condo. "I got held up at another meeting, and by the time I got back here I felt it was too late to call. Considering the stakes involved, I really should've excused myself from the meeting and called. My apologies."

Ramona didn't acknowledge the apology. Instead, she flipped open her badge and introduced herself, then referred to me as her colleague.

We stood in a tight hallway. Edwin was directly in front of us, but he didn't let us pass through or invite us into the living room, which was immediately behind him. The situation was a little awkward, compounded by the fact that Senator Keating fidgeted from side to side and spoke quickly.

"My plan was to call in the morning," he continued. "To set up another meeting. I really was going to. Honest to goodness, Agent Sanchez. But I'm actually glad you're here. Really glad, in fact. The more I think about this, this is good. You guys need to look around this place, see what you see. Maybe you ought to call in a crime scene investigation unit. I don't know, though; that's your call, obviously."

"Whoa, Senator," Ramona said, stepping forward. "Just slow down. Let us know what's going on."

Her voice was soothing, which the senator responded to.

"Sure, sure," he said, running his fingers through his hair and backing up. "Of course. You're right."

While he took a breath, I studied the senator. The man appeared to be somewhere between forty and fifty. He had salt-and-pepper hair on the sides of his head, but a full mop of jet-black hair on top. Not one sign of gray hair on his crown, which made me wonder if the man colored it. The striking contrast between the tops and sides struck me as too unnatural. But who knows? As a bald man, I was hardly a hair expert.

"Okay, okay," he said, backing up into the living room. "I'd invite you both to sit but I don't want to disturb anything."

"Senator," Ramona said. "We're fine with standing. Start at the beginning. Let us know why your condominium may be a crime scene."

"Sure, sure." He looked down, his eyes flicking left to right as he debated where to start.

I said my first words. "Before you start, Senator, is there a body maybe we should know about, or blood or something suspicious like that? Just want to know what we're dealing with here."

He whipped his head up. "Heavens no. Referring to this unit as a crime scene was a misnomer. I'm sorry. There's a chance somebody who recently stayed here may have been involved in a crime." He swallowed, then gestured in the direction of Cooper's condo. "A pretty big crime, if you know what I mean."

Ramona and I couldn't help but glance at each other.

"But I'm really not sure of anything," Keating continued. "Not sure at all." He put his hand on the couch, then immediately looked at Ramona. "Wait, I'm sorry, I shouldn't touch that. Right?"

"It's fine," Ramona said, stepping forward. She put her hand on his right shoulder. "Who, Senator? Who do you think stayed here?"

"Well, I don't know who. Or if anybody really stayed here. A couple of weeks ago, I was asked if somebody could stay here, though."

I stepped forward. "By whom, sir?"

The senator took a deep breath. "Duke. It was Duke Tweed."

This time when Ramona and I looked at each other we held the gaze.

Ramona looked away first. "Senator, what's your connection with Mr. Tweed?"

"We're acquaintances," Keating replied. "That's how I'd characterize our relationship. We first met years ago when we were young, like thirteen or fourteen. His parents had a vacation place on Long Island and so did mine. I grew up in Massachusetts and spent my summers on the island. That was when Duke and I hung out. You may or may not know this but quite a few of Duke's friends went into politics. I did as well, obviously. Being a Republican, however, I eventually clashed pretty hard with Duke and we grew apart. That's why I say we're acquaintances now. I think Duke only had the capacity to befriend one conservative."

"I assume you mean Charlie Milliken?" I said.

Keating nodded.

"Was it odd then," Ramona said, "when Duke reached out for a favor? Considering you two clashed pretty hard."

"No," Keating was quick to respond. "It wasn't. Not at all. I spent six summers with Duke and his gang of school friends, so I befriended some of his mates. One of Duke's pals, who went to prep school with him, was Dan Rosenhip. Dan and I had a long friendship. We eventually went into business together, though I was a silent partner. Dan and Duke were always close, probably because they both had high business acumen. Anyway, when Dan died about eighteen months ago, Duke and I reconnected at the funeral. And we connected a few times after that, so it wasn't a surprise to hear from him. And it was an innocuous favor anyway."

"When he reached out," I said, "what did Tweed specifically ask for?"

"He had a friend in DC who needed a place to stay near the Capitol for a few nights. It was short notice, so most of the swanky hotels were booked. No big deal if I couldn't accommodate his friend, that was what he said. Tweed simply remembered that my niece was studying abroad and wondered if it was a possibility."

"Okay," Ramona said. "Since you said earlier you didn't know whether anyone stayed here, what happened?"

Keating shrugged. "Duke never followed up. He was supposed to reconnect with me for some details, like when exactly his friend would be in town, but he never did. I just assumed his friend didn't need a place anymore or that Duke put him up somewhere else."

"Got it," I said. "So what changed to make you think someone may have stayed here?"

"And been involved in the double homicide down the hall," Ramona added.

Keating rubbed his temples. "What I learned at lunch today changed everything. I mean, everything. Suddenly potential pieces started falling into place. I rushed back here just after noon because I thought maybe somebody had stayed here and was involved in the incident down the hall. The place, however, looked immaculate, just how the girls had left it. But . . ." He paused.

Ramona prodded. "But what, Senator?"

He reached inside his suit jacket pocket and pulled out a shiny silver piece of foil. It was about an inch and a half tall by four or five inches wide. "But I found this. It was wedged between the wall and the garbage can. When I moved the can, it fluttered to the baseboard and caught my attention. I think it's . . . Well, what do you think it is?" He handed it to Ramona, who studied it for a moment before handing it to me.

I immediately knew what it was. "It's the top of an MRE pouch. I've seen plenty of these in my days."

For clarity, Ramona looked at me. "Meals Ready to Eat?"

"Yup," I replied.

"I did a tour in the Gulf War," the senator said, "so I'm quite familiar with them as well. Why would there be an MRE pouch in this condo? It's not like my niece or her roommates would use dehydrated military meals. But from what I understand the man who murdered Byrd and Cooper was an ex-military guy."

Sherman Adams stayed here. And Duke Tweed put him up.

Ramona was likely deep in thought about Sherman Adams, too, since she didn't say anything right away.

So I did. "How would this man stay here, sir, since you didn't give Tweed a key? And from what we understand, the man responsible for the murders down the hall came in through the service exit, which also needs a key, not to mention a code."

"Really," Keating said. "The feds think he came in through the service entrance?"

"We do," Ramona said.

"Well that explains it then. Totally explains it."

I said, "Explains what, Senator?"

"Duke Tweed lived in this complex about five years ago. From what I understand, he was the one who wanted the security measures for the back exit. In fact, I'm pretty sure he paid for the system since the owner of the building wouldn't."

Again, Ramona and I looked at each other. Not only were the pieces falling into place for the senator, they were for us as well.

I kept up the questions. "What did you learn earlier, Senator, that caused you to suddenly rush over to check your condo?"

"Right," he said, giving a deep sigh. "Can we at least sit for this part? Maybe at the kitchen table."

"Sure," Ramona said. "By all means."

Once seated, Keating reached into his jacket pocket but held his hand there. "I just found this." He pulled his hand out a little way, then stopped himself. "Correction, I actually found this months ago, but I never did anything with it until today." He paused.

"And why was that?" I asked.

"Because I couldn't find anything to play it on. Do you know how hard it is to find something like that?"

With a shaky hand—and to our shock—he pulled out an 8mm video tape and slid it across the table.

CHAPTER THIRTY-NINE

RAMONA AND I sat silent, stunned at the sudden appearance of an old 8mm video tape.

I felt her looking at me, but I didn't take my eyes off the tape.

Senator Keating broke the awkward silence. "Maybe I should just play this for you two. Instead of trying to explain everything."

He waited for a response.

"That would be good," I said, prying my eyes off the tape. "You have something here to play it on?"

"Actually," he said, "I do. I brought it from work." He stood and walked toward the television in the living room. "Part of the reason I didn't see the video earlier was because I needed to locate the proper camcorder and then find the hook-ups to play it back on a modern TV. But today, one of my aides brought me the proper connector and I finally got a chance to view it. And . . ." He stopped. "Well, you'll understand in a second. You'll understand why I called the feds right away."

While the senator hooked up the camcorder to his TV, Ramona shifted in her chair to gain a better view. "You said you had this for months, Senator. Can you give us some context of where you got the tape? Who gave it to you, et cetera?"

"Sure, sure. I'll give you the context, then you can watch the content."

Once he finished hooking everything up, he stood in front of the TV. "So, like I said, my business partner, Dan Rosenhip, died in a tragic heli-skiing accident eighteen months back. Dan had a bunch of our company documents in his home office. It took his wife some time, but she eventually boxed everything up and sent it to me. I've been slowly going through everything in the past six months. About two months ago, I came across this lock box about the size of a phone book, but there was no key for it, and the lock was quite substantial. Dan's wife didn't have the key either. In fact, she figured I had it and that the lock box was company property."

"Was it?" I asked.

"Nope," he said. "It wasn't. Never saw it before. I eventually went to a locksmith to have it opened. The tape was the only thing inside. I knew it was old, probably from high school or college days, so I wasn't in a rush to watch it since it worried me a little."

"Why's that?" Ramona asked.

"Honestly, since it was locked up, I figured it was probably a sex tape or something along those lines. And I didn't want to watch something like that. Especially since Dan married his high school sweetheart just out of college. If it was a tape of him cheating on his wife, that would be awkward. And if it was a tape of Dan and his wife having sex, that would be awkward, too, since I know her really well." He looked at us to see if we had a response or any follow-up questions.

Since we didn't, he continued. "Anyway, that's the basic context, the backstory, if you will. On to the content, I guess. I can explain some things after you watch the tape."

Keating turned and pressed play.

The quality, of course, was nothing like a present-day recording. The video was far from high definition. Even though the lighting was poor and the video grainy, you could still tell what was going on.

Ramona and I got up from our chairs and walked closer to the TV for a better look.

The camcorder was held about shoulder height, and the person holding it walked toward a closed door. To the right of the screen was somebody's shoulder moving alongside the cameraman. The voices on tape giggled. Drunken young man giggles, however, and not higher-pitched female giggles.

One of them said, "She's in here, and she's been totally wild tonight, like I've never seen her before. I think he gave her something."

"Like what?" the other voice said.

"It's something new that accelerates drinking. Check it out." A hand came onto the screen and turned the doorknob.

The door opened to reveal a basic-looking bedroom. But I didn't focus on the room's details since there was a woman on the bed in the middle of the room.

And she wasn't moving.

"Geez," one of the young men said, walking toward the bed with his back to the camera. "Looks like she passed out already. He probably gave her too much."

As he turned to check on the girl, the camera picked up his profile. Duke Tweed. It was definitely a younger Duke Tweed.

"What a downer," the man holding the camera said. The video zoomed in on the girl. As soon as the lens picked up her face and focused in, I immediately recognized her as Hallie Lattimer. She looked identical to the pictures I'd seen at her mother's house.

The voice behind the camera said, "Man, her sister's finally not with her, so he gets his chance. And now it's blown. He's gonna be pissed."

Off camera you could hear a sliding door open. A new voice said, "Pissed about what?"

Nobody answered the question, however, because Duke Tweed suddenly shouted, "No, no, no, no, no. She's not breathing, guys. She's not breathing." The camera focused on Tweed bending over Hallie's body with his ear turned to her mouth. His right hand searched for a pulse on her neck. "I can't feel a breath or pulse. I can't!"

"No way," the new voice said. "You're lying."

"I'm not." Tweed's response was swift and high-pitched. "Totally not. I think she's dead. She's dead." His tone was grave, not something you could easily fake.

"You better be lying," the new voice said. "You better be."

The camera starting swinging toward the voice off camera.

You could hear Duke yell in the background, "Shut that thing off! Shut it off."

Just as the camera was about to pick up the person who'd entered the bedroom, a hand reached out and knocked the camera back.

"Turn it off!" Duke screamed. "Destroy the tape. Destroy it, Charlie!"

Ramona and I looked at each other as soon as we heard the name.

When we glanced back to the TV, the video was all over the place as the new person tried to wrestle the camcorder out of Charlie's grasp.

You could hear Charlie yelling, "Let go. Just let go. I'll handle it. I'll destroy it. Help him. Do CPR or something."

When the wrestling subsided, the camera ended up on a desk or dresser. The lens pointed mainly toward the bedroom wall and focused in on the detailed beadboard. The far righthand side of the screen picked up the bottom of the bed, but nothing else, just a voice. We could hear Charlie repeating himself. "This can't be happening. It can't be happening. This can't be happening."

Tweed shouted, "Shut it down. Now! Turn that damn thing off. And get over here."

Suddenly a much younger Charlie Milliken appeared in front of the camera. There was terror in his eyes and nerves in his voice as his hands reached toward the camera.

"Turning it off now," Charlie shouted. But he was panicking, and his hands shook, so he struggled to find the button to shut it off. "Where's that stupid button?" he screeched. "Where is it?"

"Idiot," a voice said. "It's on the back, not the front."

In the background, we heard Tweed say, "Destroy it."

"I will," Charlie snapped back. "I said I will!"

"No," a stern voice responded. "I will. I'll destroy it."

Right before the video went black, we heard Tweed's voice. "Definitely not breathing. No breath at all. She's dead. You killed her."

CHAPTER FORTY

WE WATCHED THE video a second time. Then I went back to the kitchen and collapsed into the chair.

Ramona followed suit and joined me at the table.

After a couple of deep breaths, I looked at her but couldn't say anything.

She mouthed, "Poor Hattie."

I nodded. My first thoughts and feelings revolved around Hattie, too. Soon she'd find out the truth. Not only that her sister had been killed, but that some of her supposed friends covered it up to protect themselves. She'd be crushed, pissed, depressed, violent. All sorts of things like that. I couldn't imagine the emotions she'd go through.

Senator Keating came over to the table. He slid the 8mm tape in front of Ramona.

"For the record," he said. "I want that to be the last time I ever watch it." He shuddered. "Tape is all yours, Agent Sanchez, and anything else you need. You need the lock box, I got it. It's at my office. Anything you need, you let me know. I have considerable resources and I'd be happy to help your investigation in any way. This is awful."

Ramona nodded.

I looked at Keating. "So the third man, whose face we don't see, is your business partner, obviously?"

He reluctantly nodded. "I hate to say it, and reveal his secret, but considering what he did, I don't mind now." The senator sighed. "Dan, Duke, and Charlie were good friends and as thick as thieves. During my teens, I joined their posse in the summers and hung out with them nearly every day. Dan loved his wife, who was his girlfriend at the time of the video. He knew without a doubt he was going to marry her one day. But he told me, Duke, and Charlie that he had a thing for Hallie. He'd have loved to have been with her, even just kiss her, you know. All he wanted was one fling with her before he got hitched for life. He told us that in confidence, a month or so before the party. At the party, I imagine he was stupidly drunk and saw perhaps his last opportunity before going off to college. So, it doesn't surprise me what he tried to do. But . . ."

When he didn't finish, Ramona asked, "But what, Senator?"

He cleared his throat. "But the cover-up is shocking. For Dan and these men to hide their crime by dumping Hallie off a cliff. Obviously, that's what we're assuming here. And then claiming ignorance and covering it up for more than two decades. Unbelievable. I mean, I worked with Dan all these years he harbored this horrible secret. Never saw a more honest man, never worked with or for anyone so ethical." He shook his head.

"Maybe Dan was overcome with guilt," Ramona offered. "And his guilt led him to overcompensate, ethically speaking, in other areas of his life. Like with his business, for instance."

I shrugged. "Honestly, the cover-up doesn't surprise me at all. I don't know these men like you do, Senator, but I'm familiar with the type. Dan, Duke, and Charlie were intelligent men from an affluent background. Young men on the verge of starting college, with their entire lives in front of them. Dan was clearly smart enough to see the life-altering ramifications of his actions. And Duke, since it was his party at his house, could also see how his life and reputation would change, too. I mean, I can envision their conversation. No doubt Duke Tweed or maybe Dan proposes the falling-off-the-cliff idea. Their reasoning being Hallie is dead anyway, why ruin their lives as well."

Ramona nodded along. "Duke was likely the master manipulator, and he could easily control somebody weak like Charlie. All the three had to do was take the secret to their grave." She shook her head. "How awful."

"The letter," I said, "proves Charlie cracked in the end."

"Right," Ramona replied. "But only because he was given a medical death sentence. And he really only wanted to reveal the secret if Duke turned on him. Pathetic."

I looked at her. "So how does it play out? Charlie tells Tweed he can't live with the secret anymore. Not surprising, then, when Tweed freaks out and tells Charlie he can't do that. Then Tweed later learns that Charlie has written a letter to Hattie about her sister, and maybe even to the Senate Ethics Committee, so he hires people to solve his problems."

"Sounds about right," Ramona said.

"Since Dan had the video, how does Charlie get it? For that matter, did Charlie ever have it since it wasn't at the bank?"

Ramona furrowed her brow.

I continued reasoning out loud. "On the video, Dan says he's going to take the tape and destroy it. He takes it, but he clearly doesn't destroy it."

Ramona pointed at me. "Later, though, he probably realized it would be good to have a tape with Duke and Charlie on it, to have leverage on them. He watched it back and saw that his face and name never made it on the video, so he didn't destroy it just in case either Duke or Charlie turned on him."

I nodded. "Exactly. That proves why Dan wouldn't destroy the tape, but it doesn't prove how Charlie gets it." I thought for a moment. "What if eighteen months ago it was Dan who grew a conscience? Perhaps he couldn't live with the secret any longer, so he made a couple of copies and sent them to Duke and Charlie and told them he needed to come clean."

"A possibility," Ramona said. "I like that idea. Maybe Duke loses it over Dan's attempt to come clean and kills Dan, then Duke follows that up by killing Charlie when Charlie announces his desire to tell the truth."

I looked at Keating. "Was Dan's death suspicious or controversial at all?"

"Honestly, no. He was backcountry heli-skiing when he died. An avalanche happened unexpectantly, which killed Dan and one other in his group of five. Duke Tweed is a powerful man, guys, but causing an avalanche is a stretch."

We didn't say anything for a few moments. My mind worked overtime. Eventually, I broke the silence. "My guess is that something happened to Dan that caused him to make copies of the tape and send them to his pals, or former pals I should say. When Dan unexpectedly dies, perhaps Charlie is concerned that Tweed may have had something to do with it, but, of course, he couldn't know for sure. That's why Charlie was paranoid and sent the letter posthumously."

Ramona bobbled her head side to side. "That's gotta be it, or at least close to what happened. It makes sense and hangs together. But the only problem is the letter—"

I finished her sentence. "To Cooper and the Ethics Committee. That's a problem for me, too. Why would Charlie feel the need to come clean about the cover-up of Hallie's death to fellow senators? Especially since the other two men involved weren't senators, weren't even government workers."

"It's odd," Ramona said. "A problem."

Keating spoke up. "Not for me. Now, I know I'm not an investigator here, but I'm a senator and I do know more than both of you about Duke Tweed. And what he's capable of. I can't even fathom how many connections Duke has with other senators. He's donated to my re-election campaign before, if you can believe it. I'm not even on the same side as him, and he's the most partisan man I know. He donated to my campaign because we saw eye to eye on one small policy issue that related to corporate taxation. It was Tweed's subtle way to remind me to keep fighting to push the legislation through. Think about how many illegal, closed-door, backwater deals Duke Tweed must have with other members of Congress."

"So what exactly are you saying?" I said.

"I'm saying if your theory is that Charlie Milliken wanted to come clean, but only in the event he thinks Duke has killed him, then it makes perfect sense for Charlie to send a letter to Cooper and the Ethics Committee. You two are probably thinking that the letter has to be the same, or about the same matter, as the letter he sent to Hattie, but it doesn't."

"Sure," I said. "You're right. The letter to Hattie was about Charlie coming clean for his part in her sister's death. But the letter to the Ethics Committee was about revenge. It was about Charlie revealing Tweed's devious dealings with certain senators; bringing down his buddy, but also revealing the government corruption. The pay-to-play situations that are all too common in Congress."

"It was ultimate payback for Charlie," Ramona said. "Makes sense. That's why he only wanted the letter to be sent if he died suspiciously."

I nodded. "If Charlie figured he got murdered, then he was bringing his murderer down with him."

Ramona tapped the table. "Tweed caught wind of everything and wasted no expense to silence Hattie, Cooper, and Byrd, and the other senators on the Ethics Committee who might've read Charlie's letter."

Ramona and I relaxed in our respective kitchen chairs.

Senator Keating leaned forward. "So where do you guys go from here then?"

Ramona answered before I could, taking the words right out of my mouth.

"Easy," she said. "We confront Tweed. We get a team together and bring down that murdering, manipulating sonofabitch. And we get justice for Hattie's sister."

CHAPTER FORTY-ONE

ONCE HATTIE AND I were issued FBI visitor badges, a young agent from Ramona's field office escorted us to her private office. The agent left us alone in the room, telling us Agent Sanchez would be with us momentarily.

"Are you sure you want to do this?" I asked Hattie as we took seats across from Ramona's desk.

"I'm sure," she said.

Though her voice was strong and her face fierce, I could tell she was scared. Her fidgeting thumbs gave her away, though she tried to hide them by putting her hands between her thighs.

We sat in silence until Ramona came in about a minute later.

"Okay, Hattie," she said. "I set up the video in another room. I'm so sorry it's come to this, but rest assured, we'll get closure and justice. We will. I promise."

Hattie nodded while looking straight ahead.

Ramona made wide eyes at me, mouthing that we needed to talk.

I turned to Hattie. "Would you like me to come with you to watch the video?" I crossed my fingers, hoping that she'd say no.

"I'd rather be alone, if that's all right."

"Totally understandable," I quickly replied.

Ramona took Hattie out of the office, returning a few minutes later.

"I feel awful for her," she said, taking a seat behind her desk. "So awful."

"I know. I hope we made the right decision letting her watch it. I have to be honest, I'm pretty glad she chose to watch the video herself. But I hope it wasn't a cop-out on our behalf."

"No, I don't think so. We owed it to her to at least give her the opportunity to watch it. Besides, I'd want to watch the video if I were in her shoes. And I'd want to do it alone."

Ramona sank back in the chair. The woman still looked striking, even though I could tell by her slightly puffy eyes and smudged makeup that she'd been up most of the night.

"You must be exhausted," I said. "I guess you didn't get any sleep."

"It's been quite a night."

"You mouthed that we needed to talk. What's the latest?"

"It's Tweed. He's nowhere to be found."

I shifted forward. "What?"

She looked at her watch. "It's ten a.m. now, so it's been three hours of the task force calling and searching and trying to find the man. All we know is that he hasn't been seen for about twenty-six hours."

"You're kidding?"

"I wish I was. Wife, business partners, personal assistant, nobody has seen him since yesterday morning. His private jet's been grounded the whole time. We've checked all the local airports for signs of him checking in for a flight. No sign of him. He's either disappeared or dead."

"What do you think?"

"Definitely disappeared. He probably caught wind that everything was unraveling, so he took off. With the amount of money he has, he likely bought a different ID and passport and is traveling on that. Or he's taken one of the twenty vehicles he owns and is in who knows what state by now."

"Could be either," I said. "What's the task force think about everything?"

"They're relieved to understand a motive in all this, and to have a suspect to pursue, but they're still focused on Minnesota and the missing senator. They're getting ready to deploy most of their resources to the compound this afternoon."

"Are you going with them?"

"Nope. I made a fuss about the Montana group, that we shouldn't forget about them. My suggestion was to divide our resources and hit both places at once. But the brass didn't buy it. They want me to hang back and take the lead with Tweed and Montana, see if I can find a direct connection with him and this left-wing militia. If things are a bust in Minnesota, then Montana is next on the list. But that might not be until tomorrow afternoon."

"And too late," I added.

"I know, that's my concern, especially if Tweed has caught wind of us securing the video."

"Considering what he's done so far, he'll have no problem finishing off another senator and fleeing the country."

"If he hasn't already."

We spent the next ten minutes talking about where to go from here. Ramona was given some resources to help establish the connection between Tweed, Sherman Adams, and the militia. She had a few different agents looking at Tweed's charitable donations, recent travel itinerary, phone records from the past thirty days, and any sort of connection with the leader of the militia, a man named Baker Cunningham.

"Do you think," I said, "it's also worth having Hattie try to contact Tweed? In case your team comes up with nothing. At least we'll have that in the works."

"Actually, that's probably a good idea."

I ran my hand over my bald head. "Could Hattie contacting him tip him off, you think?"

"I'm with you," she replied. "But now that we know he's likely in hiding, we have to assume he knows, so we're not tipping him off to anything. And if he does respond to Hattie, then we at least have confirmation he's alive. Plus, we can trace the call. Maybe he even does something stupid like agrees to meet or sends some more men after Hattie. And we can intercept those men and hopefully get intel."

"Agreed," I said. "I think that's our best course of action." After discussing some details for a few minutes, I looked at my watch. "She's been gone awhile, hasn't she? The video is pretty short."

Ramona called one of her agents, who poked his head into her office less than a minute later.

"Agent Sanchez," he said. "Um, she's just sitting there replaying the tape."

"Okay," Ramona said, "understood. I'll handle it." She looked at me. "Come on, let's go. She's going to need some encouragement."

I followed Ramona to the conference room. Hattie's back was to us as we entered the room. She didn't turn around or acknowledge our presence.

Ramona calmly walked over and stopped the playback.

Suddenly Hattie turned toward me. She had swollen eyes, red cheeks, and a heaving chest. "They're unbelievable cowards. Pure filth." She held out her hands. "What's wrong with these men? Are there any good ones left? Any at all?"

As she shook her head, the question hung in the air for a few silent moments.

Then Hattie's eyes flicked to Ramona. "Tell me where, Agent Sanchez?" Tears streaked down her cheeks. "Where are all the good men? Where?"

Hattie buried her face in her hands. I felt overwhelmed with emotion, too, primarily disgust. I was outraged at these selfish, deplorable examples of the male species. I wanted justice, and retribution. Badly.

While Hattie dropped her head to the table and sobbed into her forearms, Ramona and I stayed silent. We wanted to let her get it all out. I couldn't speak for Ramona, but those moments in the room listening to her sob strengthened my resolve against Duke Tweed. The man, without a doubt, had to pay. At any cost. I'd do anything to find him.

My fists shook underneath the table as I continued thinking. I knew nailing Tweed wouldn't bring Hattie's sister back, but at least the three men involved would be dead. Or at least Tweed would serve some serious prison time over his involvement and murderous cover-up.

Hattie, of course, was with me. After sobbing for a few minutes, she looked up, fire in her eyes. "Two of the three are dead. Duke is next. I want to try contacting him. Still need me to?"

Ramona nodded. "That's probably a good idea. So far, Tweed hasn't been located or responded to us. Maybe you can draw him out if he's still around."

She dabbed both eyes with her sleeve. "I have an old number for him, but I'll also reach out to some mutual friends to see if they have a newer cell number."

"Perfect," Ramona said. "And Hattie, if he does respond, we'll take it from there. We're not going to risk having you actually meet him."

Hattie narrowed her eyes. "Nope, no way. I'll do it. I wouldn't want to risk him not approaching. Or sending his men if he smells a setup. Besides, though he may be the only man on earth I trust, I believe Garrison can protect me. He took down the two men chasing me with relative ease. Plus, I'll have to insist he brings his hulking friend along, of course. There's a measure of comfort having him there as well." She touched my arm. "No offense."

I winked. "None taken."

Just then, an agent poked his head in. "We have some updates, boss. Important ones."

As Ramona left the room, I smiled at him calling her "boss."

"Shut up," she whispered to me as she walked by.

When Ramona was gone, I told Hattie I was going to step out and update Slim on our plan. She told me she'd try the number she had for Duke.

"You sure?" I asked her. "It's okay if you take some time to process everything. Even an hour or two."

"Chase, I appreciate your concern. But not a day has gone by in twenty-five years that I haven't thought about my sister. I'll have plenty of time to process everything once I know Duke Tweed is rotting in prison and held accountable."

I nodded and left the room.

By the time I updated Slim and returned to the conference room, Ramona was already there with Hattie.

"Get a hold of Tweed?" I asked.

Hattie shook her head. "But I left a message that we needed to talk about Hallie; that should rattle him."

"I got something," Ramona said.

"What's that?" I replied.

"A connection between Baker Cunningham and Duke Tweed. Two good connections, in fact."

"Two? Great. Fill me in."

"Cunningham is on the board for some far-left, radical super PAC political charity based out of Montana. Their chief donor is none other than Duke Tweed. My team has also been trying to track down Baker Cunningham. Turns out he left the country not long ago. Took a flight to LA, then on to the Maldives. Apparently, Baker goes there two to three times a year. The man is quite the diver, from what I understand. Anyway, Baker's last trip to the Maldives six months ago coincides with the last time Duke Tweed left the country and had his passport scanned."

I scooted forward in my chair. "And where did Tweed go?"

"The Maldives. The exact same seven-day time frame."

"You're kidding? Same flights?"

Ramona shook her head. "No, Tweed flew from the East Coast and Baker the west."

"Still," I said, "too coincidental."

"Exactly," Ramona said. "As of now, Tweed hasn't left the country on his passport or checked in at any airport. He's either still in the country, or he used a fake passport and is long gone. But I think he could be lying low at Cunningham's place in Montana. Maybe he even took off yesterday morning in a vehicle to Montana. He could be there by now."

"Could be," I said. "And he could have the kidnapped senator with him. They could be holding her hostage at their compound. You need to get HRT there right away. Like this afternoon."

"I know. I'll work on my superiors."

I blew out a breath. As a former agent, I knew it'd be challenging for Ramona to get clearance and resources from her superiors to send a team to Montana with such short notice.

"I know what you're thinking," she said to me. "We're going today. No matter what."

I liked her determination, her throw-caution-to-the-wind attitude. She reminded me of a younger version of myself.

"If they won't authorize a quick HRT mission," she said, pointing at me, "we're going it alone. And you and Slim will be my wingmen."

I liked the sound of that. A lot.

CHAPTER FORTY-TWO

"YOU'RE CLEAR, GENTLEMEN," the airport security guard said. "Once you're finished loading any luggage"—he pointed to the right—"park over there."

Slim thanked the guard and punched the Lincoln's accelerator. He glanced at me. "Never got to drive on an airport tarmac before."

"Me neither," I said.

He steered the vehicle toward the waiting plane, Edwin Keating's company Phenom 300 jet. "I think I'll back up close to the rear luggage compartment. Don't want any prying eyes to see us loading our cargo."

I thought for a moment. "We should check with Ramona first, see if she's all right with us bringing our own arsenal."

"Sure," he said, putting the car in reverse. "But this is all off the record, Chase, so I bet she won't mind."

I shrugged since he was probably right. When Ramona's proposal to raid the Montana site got rejected by her superiors, it was my idea to reach out to Keating. I remembered the senator said he'd do anything to help. And I also made a broad assumption that rich men like Keating most likely had their own plane, or at the very least access to one.

Turned out I was right.

Ramona came down the short staircase attached to the side of the jet.

As she walked over, Slim popped the trunk and then lifted the false bottom of the trunk floor.

I gestured at the cadre of equipment in the spot where the spare tire should be. "All right for us to bring some firepower?"

"What the hell," she said. "I guess. I have no idea yet what we're walking into, so the more the merrier. But I'm really hoping we don't put a bullet into anyone. Wishful thinking, but that's my hope. Can you at least put the gear in something?"

Slim nodded and pulled out a large canvas duffel bag, then loaded two custom rifle toolboxes, zip ties, duct tape, binoculars, a medical kit, and two IEDs into the bag. Ramona and I waited for him to park the car, then we boarded the plane together.

There were fourteen seats in the jet's cabin and plenty of room for the three of us. All the seats were cream-colored and made of soft, buttery leather. The whole cabin was a warm gray tone. Polished mahogany wood accents were everywhere.

There was an area with a marbled table and four seats positioned around it. Ramona already had some files on the table along with her laptop and a leather valise. She pulled out a plastic bag with Slim's Walther P99. "I didn't know you guys were going to bring that kind of firepower, so I brought this along." She handed the Walther to me.

I eyed her. "Not needed in evidence?"

"Probably, but I'll return it after our mission here."

As we took seats around the table, the captain emerged from the cockpit.

"Welcome aboard," he said. "Sorry about the limited flight crew. Since it was such short notice, it's just me today."

"Not a problem, Captain," Ramona said. "We're going to stay pretty busy for the flight. What's the time in the air?"

He looked at his watch. "It's just the three of you with limited luggage, so I can push it. Since the senator tells me you're in a hurry, I think we can achieve a three-hour flight plan. I'll get us underway." As he turned back to the cockpit, he gestured at a minibar. "Help yourself. Fresh coffee, water, juice, beer, and wine. And a few snacks."

"Appreciate it, Captain," I said. Then I looked at Ramona, who was busy powering up her laptop. "How's Hattie? Did she hear anything from Tweed?"

"Not a word. She's doing the best she can. She's hunkered down in my office, which is the safest place she can be. If Tweed does call, and stays on the line long enough, we have a tracer hooked up to her phone."

I nodded. "I highly doubt we'll hear from him, though. My guess is he's tying up loose ends and preparing to flee the country. I bet he has villas in various countries all over the world."

"For our sake," Ramona said, "let's hope he's in Montana tying up those loose ends."

Slim, who was on the other side of table since he needed a seat and a half to himself, asked Ramona, "What's the latest on the Minnesota operation?"

"It's in motion as we speak. Haven't had a recent update. But here's the good news." She gestured at her phone and laptop. "I'll get text updates from a member on the Minnesota team to my phone. And I'll get intel on the Montana site to my laptop during the flight."

Before I could ask a question, she explained, "The Montana raid wasn't a flat-out rejection. It's been greenlit for tomorrow morning if Minnesota turns up empty. Basically, it's okay for my team to perform due diligence in the meantime. Three team members are back at the office doing reconnaissance on Montana." She grabbed the two folders on the table. "So far, this is what they've gathered on the compound. Soon they'll send some sat images."

She slid the two folders across the table. I picked up one, Slim the other.

Before I read the file, I eyed Ramona. "Where do your team members think you are? Did you tell them about this trip?"

"Absolutely not. I told them I had some leads to pursue and would be gone most of the day. This is so far off the record I don't think there's a term for it."

I wanted to ask some questions, make sure she was positive this was the best course of action for her, but she blasted on.

"Fortunately, a satellite just recently passed over the middle of the country. So we'll get some time-lapsed feeds of the site, along with the surrounding area. We'll see exactly what was there just a few hours ago. By the time we land, we should have a good understanding of the area and a solid plan for infiltration. We'll also have word on Minnesota and whether we even need to visit the site."

Slim and I stayed silent as we perused the contents of the files. There wasn't a ton of information, but enough to get a feel for what we were up against.

Cunningham's property was lakeside, occupying about twenty acres in total. Most of the acreage was lakefront. There were four buildings on the land. One was clearly Baker's house, which was more like an estate, really, while the other three buildings could be just about anything. Those buildings were various sizes and had few windows. Plenty on Cunningham's house, however. Most of the large windows faced the water.

We definitely couldn't approach via the water. They'd see us coming a mile away. And since only one road led into the property, it was clear we'd have to approach from there.

That was the only thing we agreed on, however. At least for the next two and a half hours. When the satellite images came through from the WFO in the final thirty minutes of the flight, we got a definitive idea of how many guards were on the property and finally agreed on a basic plan.

On our descent into Glasgow, the nearest city to Fort Peck Lake with a car rental place, Ramona's cell buzzed on the table. We'd been waiting on word about the Minnesota operation.

"Well, guys," Ramona said, picking up her phone, "I'll guess we'll find out if our mission's a go. Or if we're refueling and heading back." Seconds later, she looked up from her phone. "It's a go for us. Minnesota was a failure. Nothing there."

Slim and I nodded, then buckled our seatbelts to prepare for landing. Honestly, I wasn't sure how I felt about Minnesota being a bust. I was partly elated to know I didn't come all this way for nothing. I was also excited to be on a mission with Slim again; it truly felt like the old days. Most of our operations were off the books and unsanctioned, so that part didn't bother me.

What bothered me was being a father. I needed to come home

unharmed so I could raise my son. On previous black ops missions, my mind was singularly focused on achieving the mission. I had an invincible attitude about things. Right now, not so much.

Questions nagged at the back of my mind as we landed and taxied. Would being a father cause me to hesitate in any way? And if so, would hesitation cost us our lives? My thoughts weren't all negative, however. I thought that perhaps being a father would provide a measure of caution. Perhaps I wouldn't act in haste and make a bad decision because I had more to live for.

I didn't know, and I didn't get more time to think about it since Ramona interrupted my thoughts. "I feel confident in our plan," she said, unbuckling her seatbelt. "Feel confident in you two. No matter what happens, I have both your backs."

"Just five guys," Slim said, waving his hand. "We got this."

"Five that we know of from the satellite images," Ramona corrected. "Who knows how many are inside the buildings or the house. How are you feeling about this, Garrison?"

I shrugged. "We'll draw them out, try to get the men near the water, then make an assessment from there." I eyed her. "You need to be at the rendezvous point in case we need to bail."

"Exfiltration is key," Slim added.

"I'll be there," she said. "My part is easy. I know this is wishful thinking, but if we can avoid any bodies, that would be helpful. I already have to run some serious damage control on this mission. But if we rescue Fornetti and bring down Tweed, well . . . "

She looked away and didn't finish that sentence. A moment later, she looked back. "Guys, just don't kill anyone, okay?"

I thought about Sherman Adams. If the five men currently guarding the compound were anything like him, we'd have a tough time avoiding any bodies.

"Yes, ma'am," I said. "You're the boss."

CHAPTER FORTY-THREE

SOMETHING ON THE video of her sister's death gnawed away at Hattie. Sitting in Ramona Sanchez's office, she racked her mind, desperately trying to remember details about Duke Tweed's house.

In the end, she couldn't remember clearly. And she couldn't calm her mind. There was only one thing she knew for sure: she had to investigate herself.

But she couldn't just leave the office. Though the agents at the WFO weren't keeping Hattie in the office against her will, they were keeping an awfully close eye on her. Last time she went to the bathroom they escorted her there.

This time, however, maybe it would be different.

Hattie left Ramona's office. The agent in the closest cubicle immediately looked up.

"Just heading to the ladies' room again."

The agent nodded and, fortunately, didn't feel the need to escort Hattie this time.

Hattie wound her way through the cubicles and breezed past the bathroom door. Her foot ached as she tried not to limp and draw attention. She wanted nothing more than to glance back to see if she was being followed or watched. But she didn't want to look suspicious, so she strode confidently and purposefully toward the nearest exit. Just as she eased the exit door shut, she peeked through the closing gap.

Nobody appeared to be running after her.

Perfect, she thought. She knew she'd have to get out of the building fast, figuring she had close to ten minutes before somebody went looking for her.

But that was just about the time she needed to exit the building and get on the road.

CHAPTER FORTY-FOUR

I WALKED DOWN the dusty, private dirt road with a red gas can in my right hand and my eyes focused straight ahead. My breath left a cold, hazy cloud behind me as I hustled toward my destination. I kept the quick pace because I wanted to stay warm, and because I wanted to look like a man who had run out of gas and needed help.

Any second I expected to see the green Ford pickup barreling toward me. From what we'd gathered on the satellite images, three men guarded the four buildings on the property. Another two men drove the pickup around the perimeter of Cunningham's land. We didn't know for sure, but we thought they drove the main road about once an hour. According to my watch, the truck was due anytime.

Slim flanked my right side, tracking my steps and staying in the shadows. There was a decent tree line on the east side of the road that hopefully camouflaged his movements. One of the big things we fought about was who would walk with the can and who would provide cover. Slim assured me that even though he was a rotund man, he could adequately stay undetected. I didn't quite believe him, but the man was an excellent shot, so I felt all right with the plan if things went south.

About a minute later, I saw a dusty cloud stirring ahead, then the green truck emerged. The guards drove quicker than I thought they would. As they got closer, I put on the biggest smile I could. I even waved at them and pointed at the can, hopefully easing their suspicion.

The truck skidded to a stop and cut its engine. The smaller, lighter man on the passenger side hopped out quickly. He was in camo pants, boots, and a thick hunting jacket. The bulkier driver just sat there and glared at me. The sun was behind the vehicle, so I couldn't see their facial features clearly.

"Whoa, mister," the man said. "You're on private land here. Can't you read? Didn't you see the signs?"

I kept up the smile. "Totally did, I'm just in a jam. My girl is back with the vehicle and we ran out of gas on the main road. That highway is pretty barren, so no cars drove by." I reached into my pocket.

Which caused the man to immediately reach into his. When I saw the hilt of a gun, I stopped moving.

"Sorry," I quickly said. "Was just going to show you my cell and that I had no bars to call AAA. I just need a few gallons to get back to Fort Peck." I waved the can. "Just a few gallons. Hope it's not a bother."

The driver still didn't budge. Like a statue, he sat there assessing the situation. Slim and I hadn't anticipated that. We'd figured they would've both exited the vehicle, then Slim could've snuck in behind them.

The man eyed me up and down silently. All I heard was the ticking of the Ford's engine. For what seemed like an eternity.

"You know what," I finally said, "if it is a bother, I'll head back and wait for a passing car. Sorry about the hassle."

As I turned, he said, "We'll drive ya, pal. Check out this missus of yours, and your story. You can siphon some of our gas if it checks out. We don't much like strangers coming onto our land unannounced."

For some reason I said, "Much obliged."

The man waved me into the front passenger seat while he took the backseat. Before I climbed in, he exposed his gun hilt again, a clear sign there was zero trust between us.

The driver fired up the Ford. Didn't glance over once, didn't say a single word. He was a solid man, probably a few inches over six feet and pushing three hundred, easily. He wasn't quite as big as Slim, but he was in the ballpark.

The driver wore Carhartt pants and a similar hunting jacket. Even though I looked in his direction, I didn't pay attention to his features. My focus was on the tree line to see if I could spot Slim.

I couldn't. At this point, we were improvising. Which wasn't that surprising or unusual. Rarely did quick makeshift plans like the one we'd developed on the plane work out as intended. My guess was that Slim would proceed forward and let Ramona and me deal with these two men. Slim would call Ramona and give her the heads up that I was coming in the truck.

"My lady is on the main road," I said as the truck got up to speed. "About a hundred feet to the north of this road."

Neither man said a word. The heater in the truck wasn't on, so the only sounds were our cold breaths, which pushed out in alternating fashion and left a thick cloud in the truck's cab. When we neared the entrance to the compound, I prayed the rental was still there. I hoped Ramona hadn't driven to the exfiltration site just yet.

Fortunately, the car was parked right where we'd left it. Ramona was seated on the driver's side. The driver of the pickup stopped quite a way back from the rental. I didn't immediately hop out because I wanted to give Ramona time to assess the situation through the rearview mirror.

"That's a fairly new car," the man behind me said. "How do you run out of gas in that thing? Must be all sorts of bells and whistles that go off when the gas is low."

"Absolutely right," I said. "I'm so cheap I opted to return the rental empty. You know how that goes. I thought I could get back to Glasgow, but boy was I wrong." I looked at the man behind me and laughed.

He didn't return the laugh.

So I looked at the driver and laughed.

He turned and looked at me, his face blank.

The guy behind me said, "So the rental company provides gas cans these days, is that a new thing I'm unaware of? Or do you always travel around with a brand-new gas can at your ready?"

I knew I was had, but I kept up the charade anyway. "My sin is thriftiness. You got me. I'm so cheap I bought a can the last time we filled up in Glasgow. Guess I should've put gas in it too, am I right? Can't tell you how many times I've run out of gas. Doesn't pay to be cheap, I guess. You'd figure I'd—"

"Shut up," the driver snapped. "Just shut up." He turned to his buddy. "Stay here with him."

The driver left and cautiously approached the rental. Trusting that Ramona could take care of herself, I turned toward the man behind me. "Your pal doesn't seem to believe me." The headrest blocked my view, so I brought both hands up and pushed the button on the side of the headrest, lowering it so I could see his face. "What do you think his problem is?"

The man frowned. "Mister, what the hell are you doing here? Seriously."

I paused, but not because I was thinking about what to say. I was looking to see if he had his right hand in his pocket where the gun was located. Fortunately, it wasn't, but it was on his lap and close by.

My left hand was still on the seat rest, right by the belt, which gave me an idea. I glanced back and confirmed the other man was far enough away to not hear anything. "Seriously, I'm just wondering about your pal and why he's so unfriendly." I jammed my right thumb over my shoulder toward the rental.

As the man followed my thumb with his eyes, I suddenly lunged forward with the seatbelt in my left hand. Extending it to get some slack, I used my right hand to grab lower on the belt and quickly loop it around the back of the man's neck.

Then I pulled as hard as I could toward me. Being such a small man, his upper body slammed forward. His forehead plowed into the back of the headrest. Using both hands on the seatbelt strap, I yanked it toward me, crushing his face into the headrest and hopefully smothering him until he passed out. Since the belt's pressure was around the back of his neck and not his trachea, I couldn't actually choke him.

He gagged and sputtered and tried to yell, but he couldn't. Unfortunately, he didn't pass out either. Instead, he fought back, arching his back just enough to turn his head. With his head to the side, he could now breathe and stay conscious.

I figured I could at least hold him in that position, so I grabbed some extra slack from the top of the seatbelt and looped it around his head again. That extra loop secured his head against the headrest without me holding onto the belt.

But the man had taken a few good breaths, so his wind was back. Enough so to think straight and remember he had a gun in his pocket. I shifted to my right just in time. Two deafening pops exploded inside the cab. Glancing down, I saw a cantaloupe-sized hole through the middle of the passenger seat.

Instinctively I jammed my left arm through the hole. A sharp metal wire protruded into the hole, and the back of my forearm raked against it. The instant pain told me I'd cut it badly, but my adrenaline was so high I didn't stop. I immediately grabbed hold of the man's wrist and snapped it ninety degrees until I heard the gun drop.

With a death grip on his wrist, I pulled backward with his forearm, grinding it against the sharp wire as I pulled his arm through the seatback. He sputtered and yelled and spat at me over the seat. When his forearm appeared on my side, I saw that his jacket had been torn wide open by the wire. He had a deep gash from the back of his wrist to his elbow. The angry wound poured blood.

I held his arm on my side of the seat, pulling it toward me and pinning his shoulder against the back of the seat. With my right hand, I latched onto the seatbelt strap and yanked hard, trying to tighten the loop around the man's neck. It tightened some, but not nearly enough to knock him out. As it slowly tightened, the man used his left hand to try and free his head.

To distract him, I stopped tightening the belt and threw four punches over the seat, connecting twice with his nose. In return, he threw two punches with his left hand and connected with my head. But the punches were weak and flailing and I could tell he was losing steam. I decided to latch back onto the belt and hold him in place.

And wait him out.

While I did, I looked at our arms. We were both losing blood, but he was losing it at a far greater pace. About forty-five seconds later, I felt his body give, just a little. Fifteen more seconds and most of the tension from his side of the seat abated. As soon as I felt his body go limp, I let go of the seatbelt and his wrist and turned to check on Ramona.

I breathed a sigh of relief to see her walking toward the truck. The big man was in front of her, his face still blank. She pointed her Glock at his back. When she was close enough to the windshield to make eye contact, she said, "You okay in there? Everything good?"

With the adrenaline subsiding, I suddenly felt weak from blood loss. I did manage to nod, though.

"Can you roll down the driver's side window?" she asked. "I'll lean him in, and you can cuff him to the wheel."

I struggled to my left and pushed the window button, then slumped forward in the driver's seat. My vision was spotty at best as Ramona tossed her handcuffs onto my lap. I couldn't pick them up. Ramona was too focused on the big man to realize I was losing consciousness.

Eventually, however, I heard her gasp and ask repeatedly if I was okay. When she leaned into the vehicle and got a solid look at the soaked sleeve of my jacket, she gasped again.

My vision slowly grew worse, from spotty to moments of temporary blackness. Every so often the blackness would dissipate, which enabled me to see for a few seconds. What initially caught my attention was Ramona's concerned look. Then something else did.

The top two buttons of her white blouse were undone. It was very apparent as she leaned into the truck and attended to my forearm.

She must've used her wily, womanly ways to distract the big man and get the upper hand.

I think I fainted with a smile on my face.

CHAPTER FORTY-FIVE

DUKE TWEED'S NEIGHBORHOOD looked nearly identical to how it did twenty-five years ago. Hattie could remember driving on this very street, searching for a parking spot. During one of Duke's summer parties, there were typically fifty to a hundred cars lining either side of the street.

There was no party this evening, however. In fact, there were no signs of life at Duke's house, which was exactly what Hattie had hoped for.

She checked her watch, then the sky. Though it was only five-thirty in the afternoon, it was almost dark since it was mid-December. Soon she'd head over to Duke's and gain access to the backyard. She wouldn't try and break in to the house since the Tweeds likely had a security system. She only wanted to get a look at the main floor of the three-story house. Something on the video didn't add up, and refreshing her memory of the Tweed estate would be helpful.

Approximately six minutes later, headlights lit up her car from behind. Hattie ducked low in the seat so her head wouldn't be visible above the headrest. She stared at the sideview mirror, watching the vehicle approach.

As it got closer, she could tell it was a large SUV, a Chevy Suburban.

Since it didn't turn off into any driveway, Hattie positioned herself as low in the seat as she could while maintaining a view out the driver's side window.

The SUV flashed past. Hattie glimpsed a driver and passenger but no more than that. When she looked forward, the red brake lights lit up the windshield. She stayed low in the seat and watched.

The Suburban backed into the driveway of Tweed's neighbor. It sat there idling for a second, then the large driver climbed out and proceeded toward the front door. The car kept running while the passenger remained still. All Hattie could see was the man in the passenger seat's bright gray hair. His shoulders and head looked familiar to Hattie, but at this distance, and in low ambient light, she couldn't be sure.

And if it was Duke, why would he be in the neighbor's driveway? The man was supposed to be far away, like in Montana or Minnesota.

Lights around the front door must've been on a sensor because they flicked on as the driver approached. Hattie turned her attention to the broad-shouldered man. She didn't recognize him. The man stood in front of the door with some keys. She watched him try three different keys, finally opening the door on the fourth try. He disappeared inside, but only for a moment. He suddenly reappeared right after the garage door started opening.

Hattie watched the man climb into the SUV and back it into the four-car garage. The other two vehicles already inside hadn't been backed in.

Something fishy was going on.

When the garage closed, Hattie thought about her next steps. Duke's place and the neighbor's house were both expansive properties, and it appeared their backyards blended together. Hattie vaguely recalled that there was no fence between them. But again, she couldn't be sure.

She'd have to find out.

Hattie pulled out her phone and sent a quick text to Chase, letting him know where she was and what she was doing. Then she opened the car door and headed to Duke's. Halfway across the street, she stopped and went back to the car.

She opened the passenger door, followed by the glovebox.

She pulled out the Springfield XD pistol she'd taken from the man in the stairwell and tucked it inside her jacket.

CHAPTER FORTY-SIX

I GASPED AND bolted upright.

"Wow," I heard Ramona say, "that stuff works immediately."

My eyes watered and I coughed a few times.

Slim laughed. "Sure does. That was fun for me. You okay, pal?"

I snorted and tried to blow the ammonium carbonate from my nose. Right away I knew Slim had given me smelling salts.

I felt Ramona's hand tap my thigh. "Seriously, you okay, Garrison?"

I looked around, realizing I'd been lying on the open tailgate of the truck. My left arm had been bandaged up quite nicely. It appeared Slim used a battle dressing to cover the wounds.

"He'll be fine," Slim responded for me. "He didn't lose much blood, not like the other guy anyway. Chase always was a little sensitive around blood." He slapped me on the back. "A few deep scrapes, no biggie."

I swallowed and blinked a few times, which made me feel a little better. "How's the other guy?"

"Well," Slim said, "turned out tragic, unfortunately. I only had one of those Carlisle Model Army field dressings in my kit. After much debate between the two of us, we decided to use it on you." He smirked.

"So the other guy didn't make it?" I said.

Ramona shook her head. "He's dead in the backseat. Too much blood loss."

I winced. "Sorry."

"Don't be," she was quick to reply. "I heard the shots, and it looked like a crazy situation in the truck's cab. You'll have to tell us about it later."

I noticed she'd buttoned her shirt. "You as well. Would love to hear how you got the upper hand on the big man. How long have I been out?"

Slim looked at his watch. "Not long, about fifteen minutes."

"Okay," I said, getting off the tailgate and testing out my legs. They were wobbly, but I figured they'd recover in a few minutes. "We gotta keep the plan moving forward. Fifteen minutes is five minutes too long. The others might start wondering where these two are."

Slim nodded. "That's what Ramona and I have been talking about while you were having your little siesta."

Before I could respond, she said, "The plan is to Trojan Horse this truck. Or at least you two will. I'll stick with the original plan and take the rental to the ex-fil site."

Suddenly the truck started rocking side to side. That was when I noticed the big man. He was handcuffed to the steering wheel, but his body was still outside the vehicle. Like a bull, he stamped his feet out of frustration, which swayed the truck side to side. He was still a man of few words. All he could manage were some low-level grunts.

"What's the plan for him?" I asked.

"I'll take care of it," Slim said. "Been waiting for you to stop hogging the tailgate."

Slim climbed into the truck on the passenger side. Ramona turned away as Slim wrapped his forearms around the man's head and starting squeezing. About twenty seconds later, after the truck stopped bouncing and the gasps ceased, Slim stepped out and addressed Ramona. "Don't worry, he's unconscious, not dead. You have keys for the cuffs?"

I watched Slim return to the truck and uncuff the man. As soon as the cuffs came off, the man's upper body slumped over the door frame. Then Slim displayed his raw power. He pivoted the nearly three-hundred-pound man toward him. As he kneeled, the man's body fell forward and draped over his right shoulder. Slim, with zero hesitation or struggle, stood from a squatted position and carried the man like a fireman would.

Ramona and I cleared out of the way as Slim dumped the body onto the tailgate, then he hopped in the truck and dragged the man's body all the way inside the bed.

"You should take off his jacket and wear it," I said to Slim.

He agreed. After taking off his jacket, Slim handcuffed the man's hands behind his back and used a rope in the truck bed to secure him to an eyelet welded on the inside of the truck's frame. He finished by throwing an old tarp over the body.

When he climbed down from the truck bed, I asked if he needed help.

"Funny man," Slim replied.

"You drive," I said, "since you're similar in size to the driver. From a distance, you could be mistaken for him. I'll hang out in the backseat."

"With the dead guy?" Ramona said.

"No," I responded. "I have an idea for him." I looked at Slim. "Help me get his body into the front seat."

Once we had the dead guy in position, I strapped the seatbelt across his chest. Unfortunately, the man's head slumped forward. While I debated how to remedy the situation, Ramona watched from the passenger side with a curious look. I recalled wrapping the seatbelt around the man's head earlier, which gave me an idea.

I pulled up the dead man's jacket and started taking off his belt.

"Uh . . ." Ramona said. "What are you doing? That's a little weird."

With the belt free, I looped it around the man's neck and cinched it behind the headrest, which held up his head nicely. "Not weird," I said, "it's perfect. If we're going to Trojan Horse this truck, we need to do it right. The other men likely have binoculars. If they take a peek at the truck when we drive in, both men should be in the front seat. We shouldn't tip them off that something is out of the ordinary. I'm way bigger than this guy and would stand out in the front seat." I zipped up the man's hunting jacket, which hid most of the belt around his neck. "And with Slim in the other bulky hunting jacket, they shouldn't look twice at the vehicle."

"I like it," Slim said. "I'll be able to drive right up to one of the buildings and dump you off without drawing suspicion."

"Exactly," I replied.

We wasted no time, each hopping into the truck in our respective positions. We were headed back to the compound before Ramona had climbed into the rental.

As we bombed down the dusty road, Slim looked over the seat at me. "Okay, quick review, pal. You lost some blood, so I want to make sure you're thinking straight and aren't forgetting anything. What did we name our plan?"

"Double-D."

"And what does it stand for?"

"Double diversion. Me first, then you."

Slim nodded and looked ahead. "We're almost at the entrance. Stay down."

I kept low on the floorboards so no body part could be seen through the passenger windows. Slim smoothly navigated the truck. He didn't push the engine or take any fast turns. It was important to not draw attention to the vehicle.

As I stared at the footwell in front of me, my mind wandered. The satellite images had revealed only five guards on the property, two of whom were no longer part of the equation. However, we had no idea the number of men inside the buildings. Could be none or could be thirty, a sizeable difference.

"All right, Chase, we're nearing the northwest building. None of the images we saw had men near this building." I felt the truck slow to a stop. "Hold tight for a moment. Doesn't look like anybody is around but let's make sure."

I remained still for close to a minute.

"Okay, buddy, we're clear." Slim handed me an IED over the seat as I sat up.

It was technically an RCIED, a remote-controlled improvised explosive device. The mini bomb was about the size and look of a track and field discus. Slim's cell had been wired to trigger both this particular explosive and the one he planned to use on Cunningham's boat.

"We only have two of these," he said. "So we can't screw this up. I'll wait for your signal."

"10-4," I said.

He gave me the Walther P99, then said, "And don't forget this baby." He held up a short-barreled assault rifle. It was a LaRue Tactical PredatOBR.

"I can't believe you have two of these things," I said. "Man, they're super expensive, aren't they?"

"They are. His and hers model. Our twentieth wedding anniversary gift to each other. The wifey loves to go to the range with me."

I took the rifle and looked it over. The convenient thing about the PredatOBR was that it could be broken down into parts and stored in a custom toolbox. A person could walk around with the box and nobody would have a clue you were carrying an assault rifle. Slim had spent some time on the plane ride assembling the two short-barreled carbines.

They were beautiful, accurate, and pricey.

With the rifle in tow, along with the IED, I exited the vehicle and snuck along the building, heading toward the southeast corner where the only door was located. Fortunately, there were no windows on the building, so I didn't have to worry about being spotted if anyone was inside.

As I moved around the building, I didn't hear any sounds from inside. Most likely this particular structure was a storage facility. Since it was the farthest building from the entrance, and because no men were guarding it, at least according to the satellite images, I couldn't imagine it being anything else.

When I reached the door, I placed the IED in position: at the bottom of the door directly beside the lower hinge. Then I retreated back the path I'd come. After reaching the spot where Slim had dropped me off, I scanned the area for a minute to confirm there were no eyes on me, then I hustled to a small grove of trees fifty feet away. There was a low spot in the middle of the thicket where I could remain hidden.

Once in position, I texted Slim that I was ready to go.

He texted back: *nearly there*. A minute later, he followed that up with: *here goes nothing*.

The explosion was thunderous, echoing loudly throughout the vast, empty land. I didn't see the explosion itself, but I certainly felt it. By the sheer power that vibrated my body, I knew without a doubt that the door had blown clear off the building. Most likely the corner of the building was gone, too.

As I sighted the rifle, I wondered if any men would evacuate.

But nobody did.

While waiting and watching, I kept Slim up to date via text. This first diversion was to draw everyone this direction, which hopefully left Slim alone at the waterfront to do his thing. Without the first diversion, Slim couldn't get to the waterfront unnoticed since it was broad daylight and the area was too exposed.

Less than a minute later, I saw the first sign of life. One man raced toward the building, the assault rifle slung around his neck bouncing at his side. Behind that man, two more suddenly materialized, running just as fast. When they got closer, I could see they all carried the same rifle, which appeared to be a Heckler & Koch German-made assault weapon. If another ten or twenty guys came running with similar firepower, Slim and I were in trouble.

Fortunately, they didn't. Only three men rushed toward the explosion.

I listened to them shout at each other and scramble around inside and outside the building. At one point, all three had congregated on the side that faced my direction. From my low, hidden position, I could've easily taken out all three with a quick pull of the trigger. However, this wasn't a kill mission; it was hopefully a rescue mission.

I shot a text to Slim, telling him the timing was perfect since I sensed the three men were about to expand their search away from the building. And I didn't want them coming near the tree grove and forcing me to shoot. I'd already killed one man too many.

Within ten seconds, another huge explosion rocked the property. Following that, a bigger explosion happened, which surprised me since we only had two IEDs. Moments later, however, I realized the second explosion was likely the gas tanks from Cunningham's boat igniting.

Thankfully, all three men immediately turned tail and ran toward the explosion.

Once they were out of sight, I raced around the building and entered it through the massive hole in the southeast corner. It was a storage building, mainly for non-perishable staples. The building had large Costco-style shelves on all four walls. Rice, water, and canned goods lined the shelves. No other rooms, no interior walls, no signs of any people. Certainly no Duke Tweed or Senator Fornetti.

Before leaving, I texted Slim to ask how he was faring. He didn't respond, and I understood why when I started hearing gunfire. As I left the storage building, I ran to an open area where I could see the lakefront. Though it was still a distance away, I could tell things were going according to plan.

We'd drawn the three men—thankfully I couldn't see any others—to the water. Even better, the men were near the end of the dock, the spot where the rapidly sinking boat used to be moored. Slim was somewhere off to my right. He'd laid down some ground fire from his hidden position. The men were sitting ducks on the dock, and they knew it. I could hear terrified shouts between them as they figured out what to do.

Every few seconds, Slim plunked rounds in the water and lodged some bullets into the wooden dock posts that surrounded them. The men were pinned down and had nowhere to go. Their only option was to swim for it, which was just fine with Slim and me.

Feeling confident Slim had the situation under control, I proceeded to the next building. That structure had a huge roll-up door on the east side. Once indoors, I could see this was clearly a garage for Cunningham's toys. A few vehicles were inside: one car and two SUVs. While searching for Tweed and the senator, I used my Kershaw folding knife to stab twelve tires on the three vehicles.

In the garage, there was only one walled room. I swiftly kicked in the door and jabbed the LaRue Tactical rifle into the open space, my finger tight around the trigger.

Empty. No signs of life or hidden rooms anywhere.

Frustrated, I vacated the building and hustled to the next one, which turned out to be a workout facility for the militia members. It was an extensive gym, including a small indoor basketball court, but nobody was inside.

On my way to the house, I studied the dock area. Bullets hissed back and forth. The three men were smarter than I would've imagined. All three had hopped into the frigid water about mid-dock, where the water level was waist-high. Underneath the elevated dock was an extensive network of wood pilings holding it up. The men slowly moved from post to post, inching closer to shore.

The two men in the rear were focused on Slim's location. Every few seconds they popped off shots in that direction. The lone man in front had recovered a huge piece of fiberglass from the blown-up boat. Since that particular piece floated, he pushed it in front of him, effectively providing a shield. Slim was being conservative with his shots to preserve his ammunition. That thought provoked me to move. I had to scour the house quickly for Tweed and Fornetti before returning to help Slim.

I entered the main house through a rear sliding door, then closed my eyes and listened for sounds. After thirty seconds, the only sound I heard was the humming of the fridge, which was off to my left in an expansive kitchen.

Moving room to room, I focused on no details. All I wanted was to find a human, preferably a bound but unharmed United States senator. My second choice would be a hiding Duke Tweed. Both would be ideal.

But on the main level of the house, I found nobody. And no signs of life or human activity. There were no red embers in the fireplace or warm coffee pot in the kitchen. The master bedroom was also on the main level and the bed was meticulously made. The shower and jacuzzi tub were bone-dry.

By the time I made it to the second story, I was stomping from room to room. I didn't try to sneak around and hide my frustration. The stupid house, all five thousand square feet of it, turned out to be a bust. The property was a total bust. In fact, the trip itself was completely useless. There was zero evidence of the abducted senator or a hiding Duke Tweed at this location.

Honestly, as I retreated to the main level, I felt like burning the place down. Maybe then, if Duke Tweed was indeed hiding somewhere inside, he'd come running out in a fit of terror.

I glanced at the fireplace when I got back to the first floor. I didn't seriously entertain the idea of burning down the house, just daydreamed about it for a moment. What pulled me from my spiraling thoughts was the lack of gunfire.

One wall of the living room was floor-to-ceiling windows. The windows faced east and displayed a majestic view of Fort Peck Lake. But I didn't focus on the view. My attention was drawn to the beach where Slim fended off the three guards.

Immediately I left the house through the rear sliding door. I worked around the estate in the opposite direction from the beach, then rounded the northeast corner and approached the men from behind. Their Heckler & Koch guns were lying on the beach. My guess was everybody, including Slim, had run out of bullets.

I didn't run, but I did keep a quick pace, leveling the LaRue on my right shoulder and taking aim at the men as I hurried forward. Slim was surprisingly still light on his feet, just like he was in our operative days. I watched him deliver a few head-snapping punches and a roundhouse kick to a man's side. The three finally got smart and stopped approaching him one on one. Two men flanked Slim while the other stayed in front. They slowly approached him like a pack of wild hyenas.

With their backs mostly to me, I remained unnoticed. I hesitated on pulling the trigger and taking the men out, especially now that I knew the mission had failed. I considered winging them, maybe planting a bullet in their calves. But then we'd have to attend to them and make sure they didn't bleed out and die.

I decided against firing. At least directly at the men. Instead, I broke into a sprint and fired the gun in the air, startling all three. As they ducked and covered their heads, I threw the gun a safe distance away and focused my attention on the man in the middle.

When he recovered and turned toward the gunfire, I launched into the air, extending my right leg straight out in front in a flying judo kick move. My boot connected squarely with his chest. I felt at least one rib snap from the impact. Heard it, too.

The man flew backward toward Slim. My buddy had already been moving forward, so Slim brought his meaty forearm up and clotheslined the man from behind. Honestly, I'd never seen a body stop moving and flip the opposite direction so fast. The man spun forward and flopped face first into the sand.

During the melee, one of the men had gotten behind Slim and was about to attack. While running forward, I yelled at my buddy, "Move!"

The man in the sand tried to lift his head, but I stepped on the back of his skull and used it like a launching pad to dive forward. Slim dodged left while I flew past him and slammed into his attacker. My head sank deep into the man's belly. A sucking gasp could be heard, and a six-inch-long knife dropped into the sand to my left. I had no idea he was about to stab my pal.

Since I ended up on top of the attacker, I straddled him and fed a flurry of punches to his face. When the man went limp, I pulled my punches and turned to help Slim.

The guard Slim had clotheslined was back on his feet, spitting mad and trying to brush sand off his face. The other guard had picked up a substantial-sized stick and was approaching Slim. He made a practice swing with the four-foot-long branch.

I tried but unfortunately didn't reach Slim in time. Sand man lunged toward Slim and threw a haymaker punch, which Slim easily blocked with his left forearm. But the other guard lunged at the same time, from the other side, connecting with a ferocious swing to Slim's right solar plexus.

Shockingly, Slim didn't drop or even stumble when the branch smacked his side. I was pretty sure he didn't yelp or make a sound, either.

I made it to the guard holding the stick just as he brought it back. Grabbing it by the thicker end, I easily yanked it away. Then I slammed it forward, driving the thinner end of the stick into the man's neck. It penetrated the soft spot between the clavicles, which immediately began spurting blood. He gagged and toppled backward onto the sand, but he sat up quickly, clutching and clawing at his throat and desperately searching for some air.

My heel slammed into his mouth and broke some teeth, which certainly didn't help him find the air he needed. He never got back up.

When I turned back, I witnessed Slim punching the other guard in the face like he was hitting a speed bag. The guard I'd straddled and punched had gotten to his feet and was taking a few deep breaths. I slid in behind Slim until we were back to back.

"Let's finish these guys off," Slim said.

On that cue, we both lunged forward and threw a punch, then quickly retreated until our backs touched again. I'd connected with a decent blow to the man's lower jaw. Since his mouth drooped like he was in a vegetative state, I must've dislocated it from his upper jaw.

Which completely pissed him off. I could see the fury in his eyes. He suddenly lowered his upper body and tried to ram me. But I brought my right knee up in time, which took the brunt of the blow and blocked him from knocking the wind out of me.

I brought my fists together and raised my arms, then clobbered him between the shoulder blades. A dull thump could be heard as the man dropped to his knees and wheezed.

Slim suddenly shouted, "Move, Chase!"

I sidestepped as Slim heaved his man toward mine. He'd picked him up by the back of the belt and bowled him into my man. They cracked heads in a sickening collision. Both writhed in pain, holding the sides of their heads and moaning.

By the time I turned back, Slim had deadlifted the unconscious guard over his head. What an ox. Though the man wasn't big, maybe a hundred and seventy pounds at most, it was still impressive to watch Slim hold him straight-armed over his head and throw him on top of his pals.

Slim casually looked at me. "Time to go. Follow me."

My right knee ached from the impact with the guard's head, so I limped after him, grabbing the LaRue on my way. The truck was parked on the south side of the estate. When I got there, Slim asked, "Are we picking up anyone else?"

I shook my head. "No sign of Tweed or the senator."

He banged the truck's quarter panel, then motioned at the lump in the truck bed. "Cut the rope and get in. We have to get the hell out of Dodge."

I pulled out my knife and sawed the rope free from the eyelet. After that, I opened the back door and unlooped the belt from the headrest, then returned to the front seat and dumped the dead guy onto the driveway. The truck was revving and Slim was itching to go.

"Seatbelt," he said.

As soon as it clicked in place, Slim dropped the truck into drive and stomped on the gas. The big man in the back slid toward the tailgate. Unfortunately, he was so big and heavy, he didn't slide far enough, so Slim eased the truck to a stop. Then he punched it again. This time, the body dropped out of the bed and we roared toward the ex-fil site.

We didn't speak for the first minute. Slim pushed the engine and squealed around a few turns. Finally, he looked at me. "Well, that was a bust."

I looked straight out the front window and spoke through gritted teeth. "A total bust."

CHAPTER FORTY-SEVEN

STANDING POOLSIDE IN Duke's backyard brought back vivid memories for Hattie. She could visualize her friends and sister milling around the pool, laughing, discussing boys, talking about which ones looked hot at the party and which ones they hoped to date. All those wonderful and carefree conversations they used to have, in this very spot.

As the cold chilled her body and the memories faded, Hattie found herself staring at a desolate backyard. The grass was brown and cold and ready for a blanket of snow. The pool had been drained and covered for the winter, and there wasn't a single person in sight. Or a single light on inside the estate.

Keeping a safe distance from the house, Hattie limped the length of the property. As suspected, there were no sliding doors on the main floor. Entrance into the house came via a beautiful set of French doors that opened into the living room. Another door on the far side of the property opened into the garage. Those were the only points of entry into the rear of the property on the ground floor.

No sliding doors at the Tweed estate, not on the ground floor or any other floor.

Thinking about that 8mm video, she knew Dan Rosenhip entered the bedroom through a sliding door. Though she didn't see Dan in the frame, she saw part of the slider when Charlie had swung the camera toward him. And she heard the telltale sound of a sliding door when he entered the room.

It didn't happen here, Hattie thought. *I knew it. Maybe next door?*

She moved quickly across the property. There was no hedge or fence between the properties as she'd thought. However, there was a shallow indentation between the lot lines. The depression was filled with landscaping boulders of various sizes. Before she weaved through the rocks, Hattie looked to her left, in the direction of the cliffs. The highest point, the spot where Hallie was thrown off—not fell—stood directly between the two properties.

Hallie was all she could think about as she moved through the rocks and approached the neighbor's house. She could see a light on in the middle of the ground floor, but no other lights were visible.

Fifty feet from the living room was a large maple tree. Though it was barren of leaves, it had a solid trunk that concealed Hattie's approach. Once behind the tree, she peeked around the trunk and looked through the large windows into the living room.

And saw the top of a man's head facing away from her on a chair beside the couch.

A door opening startled her. The large driver emerged from what looked to be a door leading to the backyard from the garage. He had a fat roll of carpet over his shoulder. Hattie immediately suspected a body was rolled up inside. That was confirmed when the man opened a sliding door to the right of the living room and Hattie glimpsed a hand protruding from one end of the roll.

Once inside the house, the man laid the carpet down so he could slide the door closed. Apparently, the person inside had been rolled up with their hands stretched out in front of them, likely to make the carpet slimmer and more cylindrical.

Just as the man picked up the carpet, Hattie saw the hand twitch.

Her focus, however, was on that sliding door.

As soon as the man left the room, she cautiously approached the sliding door and stopped in front of it. After a deep breath, she eased the door back on its slider, just enough to fit her slim body through the opening. Once inside, she just as carefully closed the slider. In the background she could hear talking and commotion, but Hattie paid no attention to it for the moment.

The room commanded her attention.

Though it had been converted to an office, Hattie knew this was the room. *The room.* The sliding door was identical, along with the size of the room. But it was the beadboard on the wall that confirmed it for Hattie. It still had the distinctive pattern that had been picked up on the video.

Her diaphragm heaved as she continued looking around, her mind wandering even more than her eyes.

They'd drugged her, lured her here. Away from the party. Away from people. Away from prying eyes. Dan wanted his way with her in this very room. Maybe the others did, too. Was that their plan?

Loud conversation from the living room stopped her thoughts. It seemed another party had joined the conversation. The office door was open a fraction, not enough for Hattie to see into the living room but enough for her to hear. She sidestepped along the wall, stopping behind the door. She pulled out her phone and began recording the conversation, which had turned heated. One of the men was clearly Duke Tweed; she'd recognize that voice anywhere. The new voice was familiar, too, but she couldn't quite place it.

As she stood tucked behind the door, her shaking hand holding the phone, Hattie's anger swelled as she listened to the men. Within a few minutes, she couldn't take it anymore. She tucked her phone into her front pocket, then extracted the pistol from inside her jacket and held it with two hands, like she'd practiced at the gun range. She took a deep breath and used the barrel to poke open the door, just as one of the men told the other to shut the hell up.

As she stepped into the doorway with the gun fully extended, her eyes widened when she saw the other man, a man she hadn't expected.

She jabbed the gun in their direction. "Both of you shut the hell up," she said.

The men turned. For a millisecond Hattie hesitated, unsure which man to shoot first.

"For Hallie," she said.

She shifted her aim to the right and pulled the trigger.

CHAPTER FORTY-EIGHT

A SOMBER MOOD in the jet's cabin was the understatement of the year. As the plane taxied to the runway, Ramona, Slim, and I sat in our respective positions around the marble table and didn't speak a word.

Though I'd be facing heat for my involvement, Ramona was really in for it. I hoped she'd just be fired, not fired *and* prosecuted. I turned to her. "Sure this is the right thing? We can call in the locals and wait for them, explain everything here in Montana."

She shook her head. "I'm already toast. If we stay here, I'll be sequestered for hours or days explaining everything, then I'll have to do it all over again in Washington. Nope, not going to do that. When we land, I'll bypass the WFO and go straight to headquarters. March right into the J. Edgar Hoover building and come clean. Get in front of this as quickly as I can. Mea culpa is the right thing to do, and probably my best bet. Maybe, just maybe, they won't charge me with anything."

I had nothing to say to that.

While the plane readied for takeoff, Ramona's cell buzzed. She quickly glanced at it, then threw her hands in the air. "Even better," she said sarcastically. "Just great. Wonderful."

"What?" I asked.

She sighed. "Apparently Hattie left the WFO without saying a word, snuck out a while ago, I guess. Nobody knows where she went."

How could they have let her out of sight? I wanted to grill Ramona about it, but I knew she had no idea how it happened. Plus, that would be rubbing salt into her wounds. I stayed positive. "She'll get back in touch. She wants this as badly as us, more so actually. I bet she needed to step out and clear her head, like she did the other day."

Ramona didn't respond.

Once we were at cruising altitude, I got up and made a pot of coffee. I needed to busy myself so I wouldn't focus on Hattie's disappearance or the fact that we were in trouble. Our investigation and involvement in bringing justice for Hallie Lattimer looked bleak. We had no current leads or a direction to pursue. And by the time we landed, I was in for a ton of questioning by my former employer. I wanted to bring up my role in the death of Cunningham's man with Ramona, make sure we were both on board with an appropriate defense, but I figured I'd wait an hour or two for her mind to settle, then approach the subject.

I never got the chance.

As we neared the end of the relatively silent flight, Ramona received a number of text messages, all in a row. The constant beeping reminded me that I'd powered down my phone before Operation Double-D began.

While Ramona paced and fired some return texts, I turned on my cell. A few seconds later, Ramona walked over to the table and put the phone in the middle.

"Read these texts and get up to speed. This is crazy, gentlemen." She spun and hustled to the cockpit.

Slim called after her, "What are you doing?"

"Speaking with the captain. We need to divert this plane right away."

"To where?" I asked as Ramona continued walking.

"Long Island," she shouted over her shoulder. "Read, gentlemen, read."

So I did, grabbing the phone before Slim and quickly reading the string of texts. It didn't take long to get the gist of the story. As I read, my phone beeped and alerted me to a text.

But I didn't check it because Slim motioned at Ramona's cell. "What's up? What's going on? Give me the quick story."

"Apparently Duke Tweed isn't in hiding or trying to leave the country. He was abducted."

"Abducted?"

"Yeah, but he got free. He left Ramona a voicemail not long ago, then followed up with the WFO looking for her. Explained everything to one of Ramona's colleagues. Apparently, he witnessed a crime and is still at the scene. Tweed asked for Ramona and a team to get there right away."

"To Long Island?"

I nodded. "Yup. There's an address here in Sands Point, which I'm assuming is his summer place."

"What kind of crime scene?"

"Didn't say."

Ramona suddenly swept out of the cockpit. Before she said a word, I felt the plane bank and take a more northerly path.

"We're close to New York. We'll be at JFK in no time, even beat the ERT there, I imagine." There was a sparkle of hope in her eyes. "We just might be able to salvage this, guys."

"Hopefully," I said. "Do you know any more details? Like who abducted Duke Tweed and why?"

"I don't." She gestured at her cell. "I can get texts and emails because we have Wi-Fi aboard but calls or voicemails won't come through until we land. Maybe Tweed explains more in his voicemail."

The captain came over the intercom system to inform us we would soon begin our descent into JFK, so I took the opportunity to read my text.

"No," I said, reading it. "No, no, no. Ah, Hattie. What are you doing?"

"What?" Ramona asked. "What is it?"

I read the text again, then looked up. "Hattie texted a while ago to tell me she drove to Sands Point. Said she wanted to investigate Duke's house."

Slim pounded on the table. "Not good, not at all."

Nobody said it out loud, but we all thought the same thing: that she must be part of the crime scene at Duke's place.

"Let's not jump to any conclusions," Ramona said. "Hattie could be just fine. Let's just get there as fast as we can."

As soon as we touched down, Ramona's cell beeped.

While she listened to the voicemail, I called Hattie's cell, but it went straight to voicemail. I didn't leave a message. Instead, I texted her asking if she was okay.

To get my mind off Hattie, I turned to Ramona. "What'd Tweed say in the voicemail?"

"That he wants the feds there right away. No details about the crime, said he didn't want to say anything over the phone."

"That's it?"

She rolled her eyes. "He wants us to bring a US attorney, too."

I shook my head. "Geez, this guy."

"What?" Slim said. "What do you think that means?"

"It means," Ramona says, "he's looking to cut a deal of some sort."

Nothing surprised me about that request. I pressed on. "Nothing else on the voicemail?"

"He gave his address and then hung up." Ramona grabbed her phone. "I guarantee an Uber is the quickest vehicle we can get; probably a few are waiting outside the Arrivals terminal. I'm requesting one right now."

"Get an Uber XL," Slim said. "If one's available."

Ramona looked up at Slim. "If none of this works out, and I'm fired for insubordination, I'll need a job." She smiled, the first time in a few hours. "How about it? The three of us make a good team, don't we?"

"My wife wouldn't allow it," Slim quickly replied. "No way. As head of HR, she'll shut that down right away."

She put her hands on her hips. "And why's that?"

"Cuz you're far too attractive, Agent Sanchez."

CHAPTER FORTY-NINE

THE FORTY-MINUTE DRIVE from JFK to Sands Point was silent and fairly awkward. I'd never driven to a crime scene in an Uber before. The driver had tried to make small talk at the beginning of the ride, but the three of us didn't engage with him for very long.

I sensed the others wanted to talk about things, but we couldn't because of the driver, so we retreated into our own thoughts. My thoughts revolved around Hattie. I can't tell you how many times I pictured her dead body somewhere in Tweed's house. Probably every five minutes I glanced at my phone, willing Hattie to text back that she was fine.

When the driver announced we were close to our destination, I snapped out of my trance. Since nobody had been to Duke's before, the driver slowed down at every few houses to read the numbers.

"Should be a few houses up here on the left," he said.

He drove a few more houses, then slowed down. "Nope, next house."

I was in the backseat on the driver's side, so I glanced at the mailbox we'd just passed. "Wait, are you sure? Pull over. That mailbox back there had the Tweed name on it."

The driver eased on the brakes and stopped, then looked at his phone.

"I'm sure," he said. "The address you gave me is the next house on the left."

I looked at Ramona. "Did you give him the right address?"

Before Ramona could respond, Slim, who was in the front seat, pointed at the next house. "I think that's our address. There are two men on the porch. And is that . . . is that Tweed?"

The colonial-style porch was large and well lit. Indeed, there were two men outside on the porch: one was Tweed and the other was a well-dressed man in his forties I guessed was Tweed's lawyer. I strained my eyes. "I think so," I said, reaching for my belt. "He probably owns that house, too."

Ramona placed her hand on mine. "Hold up, don't go charging up there just yet." She addressed the driver. "We'll get out right here."

Once she thanked him, and Slim had unloaded his duffel bag, we huddled on the side of the road. I spoke first since I was itching to confront Tweed.

"How do you want to handle this?" I asked Ramona.

"I want to look at the crime scene first. Just you and me, nobody else." She glanced at Slim. "All right if you wait with the men on the porch?"

"Would be happy to."

She continued. "I'd rather not hear a word from Duke Tweed about what happened until we first assess the scene."

I thought about it. "You're right, that's probably smart."

As I broke the huddle, Ramona held me back. "Obviously you know your way around crime scenes; just let me do the touching, if something needs to be touched."

I nodded and took off toward the house. As I approached, Duke Tweed stood and took a step toward us. I'd never seen the man in person, but I had seen him on news shows and a few documentaries. Surprisingly, he looked just like he did on television. Tweed's defining feature was his eyes. If you looked long enough, you realized his dark brown eyes were sunken too deep and slightly too close together. Tweed also had some fresh injuries on that badger face of his, but I didn't ask about them, and some abrasions on his wrists.

I couldn't help but engage with him. "What kind of crime scene? Your voicemail was vague at best, Tweed. Is there a body inside?"

He swallowed. "There is." When he started to speak again, I held up my hand.

Ramona was close behind me. "I'm Agent Sanchez, Mr. Tweed, and these are two of my colleagues. We'll check the scene first, then come back and get your statement. Sit and make yourself comfortable."

He sat down and put up his hands. "Since everything went down, I didn't touch anything, Agent Sanchez, or move the body. I called you, then waited for my lawyer here on the front porch."

I stepped aside and let Ramona open the door.

"Where's the body?" I asked Tweed.

"Living room," he said.

As soon as the door closed, I rushed toward the large open area in front of me, my heart beating fast. When I reached the threshold of the living room, I stopped. There was a body ten feet away with its back toward me.

I breathed a sigh of relief. It was a man. A large pool of blood radiated around him in a ten-foot circle. The black-and-gray hair on the back of his head looked familiar. I was pretty sure it was Aidan Agnew since I'd trailed behind the man for a mile or so, and the victim looked to be of similar size.

"So glad it's not Hattie," Ramona said, placing her hand on my shoulder.

I turned and nodded. "Looks like Senator Agnew."

Ramona took a wide swath around the body, then looked up and blinked a few times. "That's surprising."

"What?"

She cleared her throat. "You're wrong, it's not Agnew."

"Really?"

I hustled around the body, stopping as soon as I saw his face. Stunned, I couldn't talk for a few seconds. Finally, I managed, "Edwin Keating. What on earth?" I looked at Ramona. She had a perplexed look similar to mine. "What's going on?"

"No idea," she said.

We stared at the dead senator for a few moments.

Ramona spoke first. "We'll get answers soon enough, I suppose. Let's take in the scene and compare what we see."

I nodded and studied the body, focusing on Keating's position and placement. Then I looked around at every detail within a ten-foot radius. Eventually, I walked around the living room in an ever-widening path. My only stop was at a doorway to an office. And it wasn't the busted door or doorframe that caught my attention and made me stop, it was the gun leaning against the baseboard to the right of the door: a Springfield XD.

I ran my hands over my bald head when I saw it.

Ramona had been on the other side of the room. When she heard my deep sigh, she hustled over.

Stepping into the office, I immediately recognized the beadboard on the wall. This was the room where Hallie Lattimer was killed. A path of blood had dripped its way to the sliding door. I waited for Ramona to enter the office, then motioned for her to open the door, which she did.

After noting the trail of blood leading outside, we silently retreated to the living room.

"So," Ramona said, "what'd you see?"

"A lot." I pointed at a side table beside the couch. "This is Edwin Keating's house. Mail on that side table has his name on it. Which makes sense. Keating told us he had—or his parents had, I guess I should say—a place in Sands Point and that's how he knew Tweed. He just failed to mention that his summer home was right next door to Tweed's."

I gestured at the dead senator. "Obviously he took a center chest shot and likely died right away. Clearly it appears the shot came from the office doorway. What you couldn't know, though, is that the gun on the ground was the one Hattie took from the man in the stairwell when she and I first met. As far as I know, it was last in her possession."

Ramona's eyes went wide, but she didn't say anything.

I carried on with my assessment. "You do know that Hattie texted me and said she was coming here to investigate because something bothered her on that video. You probably saw it right away, too. That room is clearly where her sister died."

"Right," Ramona said. "That beadboard on the wall is distinctive. Keep going."

"It is," I said. "And, of course, Hattie would've noticed that right away. She must've come in through the sliding door." I gestured at the rope on the floor beside a kitchen chair. "Obviously Tweed's face had taken a beating, but did you notice his wrists?"

She nodded.

"His wrists were red, bloody, and raw," I said. "Since he claims he was abducted, he was probably sitting on that chair tied up. Hattie sneaks in, overhears their conversation. Somehow Keating is involved in all this, so Hattie steps into the doorway and mows him down. Then maybe Tweed yanks himself free from his bindings after Hattie runs for it. Which all seems somewhat straightforward, at least from what we know and what we see here. The problem is the blood and the doorframe."

"How so?" she asked.

I pointed at the frame. "There's a slug on the left side. Where'd that come from? Couldn't have been Tweed since he was tied up. Maybe there's a gun under Keating's body, and he managed to pop off a shot or two at Hattie before he bit it. One shot hit her, which explains the blood, not to mention her taking off. But if there's no gun under Keating, then it suggests someone else was here."

"My assessment exactly," she said.

"Wanna move the body?" I asked. "Just a little."

Ramona thought about it. "Nope. New York field office will be here any second. Let's wait for them and ERT to do their thing. Since our initial assessments of this scene are nearly identical, let's chat with Tweed and see what he has to say. Between the two of us, we'll sniff out any BS quickly."

"Let's do it. I'll get Slim to scour outside and look for Hattie. Follow the blood trail."

We left the living room together. On our way to the front door, just as we passed the large staircase to the upper floors, we heard a loud bang. Not a gunshot bang, but a dull bang like something had fallen onto the floor. Or maybe somebody.

"Could be Hattie," I said, running up the stairs.

The second floor was huge. At the top of the stairs, we split up to check rooms, yelling out to each other when we cleared one. As I finished searching my wing of the second floor and headed back toward Ramona, I heard her yell, "Locked door. Over here, Garrison."

When I reached the door, we flanked it for a moment and took a breath. Ramona motioned for me to kick it in. The door was an older, solid wood door of sturdy construction, so it took three powerful kicks to smash it open.

A huge king-sized bed was in the middle of the room. On the floor to my left, I saw some woman's hair. Ramona was already heading toward the body.

When I saw the woman curled up on the floor, bound and gagged, my heart stopped for a moment. But it wasn't Hattie. In fact, I didn't recognize the woman.

Ramona did, however. "Rachel," she said, immediately pulling off the gag. The woman's eyes didn't open, though she moaned a little, telling us she was alive.

"Senator Fornetti," Ramona said, kneeling over her body. "Are you okay?"

CHAPTER FIFTY

BAKER CUNNINGHAM SAT in a lounge chair on his private deck overlooking the crystal-blue Indian Ocean. Though the past week had been a roller coaster ride, with things changing rapidly and dramatically from day to day, his situation had turned out pretty darn good.

In the end, the chips fell in his favor.

A waiter had just brought him waffles, bacon, and a Mimosa with freshly squeezed papaya juice. As he worked on his breakfast, he waited on an important call. Once the call came through and he confirmed the next steps, he'd get right to work.

Life wouldn't be about politics and engaging in questionable jobs anymore. Life would be about building his dream resort. Islands for sale in the Maldives were plentiful. Since he'd been here many times, he already had a few in mind that he planned to visit later this morning.

Though he'd have to come clean and cut a deal with the feds, and likely never step foot in America again, Baker didn't mind that much.

Because he'd be staring out at this view for the rest of his life.

CHAPTER FIFTY-ONE

WE SAT AROUND Duke Tweed's expansive kitchen table. It was me, Ramona, Tweed, the man from Keating's porch—Tweed's lawyer—and a US attorney named Murkowitz. Ramona insisted on my presence since I'd been involved in everything from the very beginning and knew as much, if not more, than her. When the government attorney found out I was a former FBI agent, he agreed to let me stay.

Keating's place next door was a zoo. Just after we'd found Rachel Fornetti, the New York field office, along with ERT, descended on Keating's place. Three local cop cars showed up as well, but the officers didn't go inside. They were more than happy to control the perimeter of the crime scene.

Senator Fornetti had been drugged pretty heavily, so she couldn't remember or say very much. She'd been whisked to a hospital to be monitored and hooked up to some fluids.

I was anxious to hear what Tweed had to say, but I was equally anxious—if not more so—to hear back from either Slim or Hattie. I knew Slim would call right away once he found her, so as of now, Hattie Lattimer was still considered missing.

"Now's your chance, Mr. Tweed," Ramona said, "to explain everything."

Tweed glanced at his lawyer.

"Just like you told me," the lawyer said.

Tweed looked at the table for a moment, then began, "Edwin Keating made a mistake twenty-five years ago in this very house. A terrible mistake."

While he paused and swallowed, I felt like leaning across the table and smacking him. *A mistake?*

Tweed continued. "Edwin drugged Hallie Lattimer and lured her to his parents' place next door."

Ramona and I looked at each other with wide eyes. Edwin Keating had killed Hallie Lattimer, not Dan Rosenhip. *Was Dan involved at all?*

"Of course," Tweed said, "Edwin miscalculated and over-prescribed Ms. Lattimer, which caused her to stop breathing."

This time when I glanced at Ramona, I couldn't help but roll my eyes. Tweed's selection of words irked me. Now I wanted to punch him, not slap him. No doubt he'd been coached by his lawyer to avoid words like *dead* or *murdered* or *killed*, and to use words like *mistake* and *miscalculation* and *stopped breathing*.

Ramona held my stare. I could see the fury in her eyes, too.

"I take ownership for my part in Hallie's demise. I'm guilty of . . ." He shot his lawyer a look. The lawyer returned a subtle nod. "Tampering with a corpse," Tweed said. "In my youthful foolishness, I was terrified of what it meant for my future to have someone pass away at one of my parties, and more so what it meant for my good friend—at least he was at the time. Since Edwin's mistake was ultimately irreversible, I figured why not do what we ended up doing instead of forever jeopardizing our futures, especially Edwin's. Again, youthful foolishness and selfishness on my behalf."

Ramona leaned forward and glared at Tweed. "What did you end up doing? Say it. I want to hear you say it."

He took a deep breath. "We disposed of the corpse off the cliff between our properties."

Ramona's hands balled up. "And feigned ignorance of knowing anything else for more than two decades, isn't that right, you . . ." She stopped herself.

Tweed didn't respond. However, he did nod.

Murkowitz intervened. "Let's just get the story out, shall we? Let's proceed without further interruption. Go ahead, Mr. Tweed."

"Fast forward, I guess," Tweed said, "to twenty-five years later. Charlie, who was also involved in the unfortunate situation, received his medical death sentence. A few months after that, he had a crisis of conscience. He never was as strong as Edwin and me."

I saw Ramona leaning forward, about to let him have it. I tapped her on the knee, which settled her down.

Tweed continued. "Charlie approached me and said he couldn't harbor the secret any longer. That it ate away at his soul. That he needed to come clean before he died. He also told me he had video evidence from that night, which shocked me because I remember Edwin took the tape out of the camcorder. Charlie said that after Edwin took the original tape, and Edwin and I left the room to deal with the body, he set up the same camera again with a new tape and secretly recorded us when we returned to the bedroom. He couldn't show it to me because he stashed this new secret recording in a safe deposit box. He also made a copy of that secret recording and stored it in another box at a different bank. I'm not going to lie, I tried hard to convince Charlie to take the secret to his grave and destroy the tapes. For our sake, his family's sake, his legacy, all those sorts of things."

Ramona scoffed. "That the past was the past. Right? What's done is done. That there was nothing you could do to change it. I'm sure you used all the standard clichés on your supposed pal, someone you could always manipulate."

Tweed didn't respond to Ramona's comments. "My mistake," he said, "in retrospect, was letting Edwin know that Charlie was getting cold feet and had this secret video of us from the fateful night. Though I told Edwin that I could handle Charlie, and that—"

"Wait a minute," Ramona interrupted. "You're using such vague language, euphemisms in my opinion. When you say 'handle' Charlie, are you referring to killing him and making it look like an accident?"

"No," Tweed shot back. "No, I'm certainly not, Agent Sanchez. In retrospect, perhaps Edwin was involved in that, but I don't know for sure. Edwin hired a man by the name of Baker Cunningham to orchestrate the Byrd and Cooper murder-suicide. Perhaps Edwin also hired Cunningham to take out Charlie, but I don't think so since everything snowballed after Charlie's death, not before."

"We're getting ahead of ourselves," Murkowitz said. "Just stick to what you know for sure, Mr. Tweed. What happened after Charlie's death?"

Tweed nodded. "After Charlie passed away, and it appeared he told no one about that fateful night, and his secret video never went public, Edwin and I thought we'd dodged a bullet. But then..."

Tweed paused and ran his fingers through his gray hair.

Murkowitz prodded. "Then what?"

"Then his wife Gloria reached out to me and asked if Charlie and Hattie Lattimer were having an affair. I asked her why on earth she'd think that. She told me that Charlie had written Hattie a posthumous letter and that he'd secretly taken out two safe deposit boxes at different banks. She figured Charlie was maybe filtering money or jewelry or something like that to give to Hattie. She was super upset and paranoid about the situation and wanted to know if I knew anything."

"You knew better, though, didn't you?" Ramona said. "You knew you had to get your hands on those two incriminating videos before somebody else did." She shook her head. "You're so rich you decided to buy the banks to gain access to their safe deposit boxes and get the videos. Unbelievable."

Tweed turned and looked at Murkowitz. I think he was done speaking with or even looking at Ramona.

Murkowitz said, "So you illegally retrieved Charlie's videos then, Mr. Tweed? Is that safe to assume?"

"It is. After that, I told Edwin that everything was fine, that I had it handled, but he was insistent on seeing and possessing that secret recording. I told him no, that I would take care of them. He freaked out and cut off all communication with me. At the time, I had no idea why he was doing that, but now I do."

"And why's that?" Ramona asked.

Still looking at Murkowitz, he said, "Edwin spoke with Gloria, too.

He learned that Charlie had sent another letter to Cooper and the Ethics Committee. Which Edwin rightfully assumed was about him and his involvement in Hallie's demise. It certainly wasn't about me since I'm not a senator. Edwin then needed to deal with that letter and its implications. And so he did."

Ramona said, "To be clear, you're saying Edwin Keating hired Baker Cunningham to set up the murder-suicide of Byrd and Cooper. And Cunningham employed Sherman Adams to physically get that job done."

"I most certainly am. I'd introduced Edwin to Cunningham at a function years ago, but I had no part in the senators' murders or in the kidnapping of Rachel Fornetti."

I spoke my first words. "What about the men who went after Hattie? Who hired them?"

"Certainly not me." Tweed shook his head. "It was Edwin, obviously. No doubt he wanted every loose end tied up."

I eyed him. "It was all Edwin Keating. That's what you're saying?"

He held the stare. "It is. Listen, I didn't know that Edwin and Cunningham had planned what they'd planned. But as the story shifted from a murder-suicide to a double homicide, along with a third-party involvement, I suspected foul play. At the time, though, I didn't know what Edwin's angle was, didn't know what he was really up to. Not until I learned that Edwin didn't destroy the first video, the original one. Now it all makes sense."

"Okay," Murkowitz said. "Help it make sense to me, Mr. Tweed."

"Certainly," he said. "I didn't know the original video still existed; like I said, I thought Edwin had destroyed it. And I also didn't realize that Edwin's face didn't appear on the original tape, nor did we mention his name during that recording. Which, I guess, is why Edwin never destroyed it." Tweed gestured at Ramona and me. "These two can attest to Edwin's convincing story. He had this elaborate tale about how Dan Rosenhip played his part on the original tape. Dan, however, had nothing to do with Hallie's death. Edwin used his dead friend and business partner to take the fall for his actions. Dan wasn't a part of it at all, not even sure he was at the party that night. But Edwin needed me out of the picture for his version of the events to hang together so I couldn't refute his story."

He paused to let us process Edwin's motives. Seconds later, he kept going. "Everything went haywire after Mr. Chase told the feds of a third-party involvement, and then actually proved it by tracking the man down. If the story had stopped at the murder-suicide of Cooper and Byrd, and Edwin got Charlie's letter back, nothing else would've happened. But that's not what happened. And Edwin knew it wouldn't be long before Sherman Adams and Baker Cunningham were tied to him."

When Tweed paused to take a breath, Ramona filled in. "So Edwin needed you to be the fall guy, the man behind killing the senators, so the evidence didn't point to him. That's why he reached out to us, showed us the original video which he hadn't destroyed, gave us the story about how Dan played his part on that video, then told us you were responsible for letting Sherman Adams into the building."

Tweed nodded.

I was curious about the other two senators. "Was Edwin paranoid about the other senators on the Ethics Committee catching wind of Charlie's letter, so he hired Cunningham to take care of them as well?"

"Actually, no, Edwin wasn't part of that; that was all Baker Cunningham. Cunningham panicked when Sherman Adams was caught. He wanted the heat off him and his left-wing organization, so he devised the kidnapping of the two Democratic senators. He hired some men that had no affiliation with him or his organization. Apparently, they were to drive the senators to Florida and dump them in the Everglades somewhere, fully alive. But that plan went south, too."

Murkowitz eyed Tweed. "You know a lot, Mr. Tweed. Did Edwin Keating tell you all this before he was killed?"

"Fair question," Tweed responded. "I learned most things from Baker Cunningham, but also from Edwin, too. Keating brought me—and I guess Senator Fornetti as well—to his house this evening. A hired man did all the work, of course. Edwin didn't get his hands physically dirty. Since I'd been drugged, everything is pretty hazy from the past twenty-four hours or more. Anyway, I woke up next door tied to a chair."

Tweed briefly held up his raw wrists for Murkowitz to see. "I overheard Edwin and his man planning their next steps. Senator Fornetti was to be taken to my place, so it would look like I was responsible for kidnapping her. They were going to kill me, too, but make it look like suicide. Hattie Lattimer, however, thwarted their plans. I guess she snuck in through the office. Initially, she had the gun on me, but when she saw Edwin, she shifted her aim and took him down. Edwin's man returned fire, hitting Hattie on the hand, then he went after her. Not sure what happened since nobody came back. I worked my way out of the rope bindings"—again he held up his wrists—"then called the feds and my lawyer right away."

Murkowitz was busy writing. Less than a minute later, he looked up from his notepad. "You said Baker Cunningham told you some things, too."

"I did," Tweed responded. "He's key, Mr. Murkowitz."

"How so?" the lawyer asked.

"Before I was abducted, I'd contacted Cunningham because I suspected he was the mastermind behind Cooper's and Byrd's deaths. And he was; he admitted that because he was in dire straits and looking for an out. He'd fled the country after the murder-suicide job went wrong since he knew the feds would be coming for him. He admitted the kidnapping plan was a desperate attempt to throw law enforcement off his trail, to keep them confused and focused elsewhere and buy himself some time. He also told me that Edwin had offered him a lot of money to take me out, but Baker wanted no part in that. I appreciated his honesty and desire to not follow through. I told him that he and I could work together with my lawyer and a US attorney to maybe get a deal. We'd give up Edwin, turn over all our evidence, for leniency in our parts in this unfortunate situation."

I put my hands under the table and balled my fists. *Unfortunate situation?*

"What happened then?" Ramona asked. "Since you were abducted after all. Did Cunningham double-cross you?"

Tweed's lawyer answered. "No, ma'am. I spoke with Mr. Cunningham right after Mr. Tweed disappeared. He's my client as well.

He assured me he had nothing to do with it. Mr. Cunningham is still very much onboard with telling the truth to Mr. Murkowitz and handing over any evidence."

"Listen," Tweed said. "These guys Cunningham used for the kidnapping are guns for hire. There are plenty of men out there like them. When Cunningham said no to Edwin, I assume Edwin just got in touch with them directly. Or maybe he had other connections I don't know about."

"All right," Murkowitz said. "Let's talk proof here. What concrete evidence do you have of Edwin Keating's involvement? So far, it's just your word. There's no deal without concrete evidence, gentlemen." Murkowitz looked at Tweed, then his lawyer.

The lawyer responded, "I have contact info for Baker Cunningham. He's standing by and waiting to speak with you, Mr. Murkowitz."

"And I have the second video that Charlie secretly shot and kept in a security box," Tweed added. "You'll see it not only shows Edwin Keating's presence on the night in question, but that he was the person directly responsible for Hallie's demise. He never refutes it on video, not once. After you, Mr. Murkowitz, and my lawyer hash out a deal, it's all yours to watch. In fact, you can watch it in my den."

Murkowitz put both forearms on the table. "I'll let you know how this works, Mr. Tweed. You don't dictate the terms. I'll talk with your lawyer, get a preliminary agreement in place, then I'll watch the video myself and speak with Baker Cunningham. If it all checks out, then we'll make the preliminary agreement formal once I get approval from above. Got it?"

Tweed cleared his throat. "Absolutely."

I pushed back from the table and left without saying a word. Made my way outside onto Tweed's porch. Though I understood Murkowitz's position, and what he had to do to make a case against Edwin Keating, I fumed at the deal. While pacing, I hoped the frigid temperature would cool me down. After pacing a few lengths of the porch, Ramona joined me.

"What's going on in that head of yours?" she asked.

"A lot, mainly frustration." I took a deep breath. "I guess anger more than anything. I've seen deals like this cut before. Intellectually I get it, but emotionally I'm pissed. I mean, tampering with a corpse, what sort of prison time does that entail?"

Ramona shrugged. "I get it, and I don't know. Murkowitz could give us an idea."

"Surely Tweed will get some time for tampering with the safe deposit boxes, too, won't he?"

"You'd think," she said. "Not to change the subject, but any word on Hattie or Slim?"

My cell hadn't beeped or buzzed in a while, but I checked it again anyway. "Unfortunately, no. While they're working on their devil's deal, I think I'll sweep the properties and try to find Slim. Hopefully Hattie, too."

"I'll join," Ramona said. "That'll keep my mind off the deal as well."

We split up and scoured Tweed's backyard, as well as Keating's, using the flashlights on our cells to see. Honestly, I'd assumed I'd run into Slim back there at some point, so when I didn't after a half hour of searching, I called him again and also fired off a text.

No response.

Ramona found me standing in between the properties looking at my cell. She gestured behind me, toward the cliffs. "Think that's where it happened?"

I turned and headed toward the cliff's edge. "Think so." As I peered over the edge, I held my cell out, but the light only penetrated the darkness ten feet or so. Below you could hear the pounding waves.

"My worry," I said, "is that Hattie or maybe even Slim is down there. It's pretty dark and you could make a wrong step out here."

"Or," Ramona said, "Keating's man could've caught up with an injured Hattie and . . ."

"Thanks, thanks for going there."

"Sorry," she said. "You're right, that's pretty dark. Let's go check in with Murkowitz and see where things stand."

When we got back to the porch, Murkowitz was outside on his cell talking to someone. He pulled the cell away and covered the receiver. "If you want, head to the den and watch the second video. It's probably your only chance to see it before it's locked away in evidence." He was looking at me when he said it.

I wanted to ask him about the deal, but he put the cell back and started talking. It seemed clear he was working on the finer points of the agreement with his immediate superior.

"You want to watch it?" Ramona asked, opening the front door.

"Definitely," I said.

CHAPTER FIFTY-TWO

THE VIDEO'S GRAINY feed flickered on. The lens was still pointed at the beadboard on the bedroom wall. Charlie Milliken's face, flushed and sweaty, suddenly appeared in front of the camera. His shaky hand reached forward and nudged the camera a little to his left. Now you could see a bit more of the bed, along with Hallie Lattimer's feet.

He retreated backward, stopping at the foot of the bed and staring directly at the camera. I had no idea what he was doing. After about ten seconds, Charlie headed back and stood behind the camera.

Moments later, the lens inched a touch more to the right. Now you could see some of Hallie's legs but not her torso or head. Charlie walked back into the frame and stopped at the bed by Hallie's hips. He stared at the camera for a silent, long moment. Then he repeated the process once more, inching the camera a tad more to the right.

"What's he doing?" Ramona asked.

I now had an idea. "He's setting it up to secretly tape whatever happens next. That's my guess anyway. I bet he doesn't want the lens pointed right at the bed since it might draw attention and tip the others off, because that's not how the camera was left. But he also doesn't want it pointed mostly at the wall. He's going back and forth to see how it looks from the bed angle and from the camera's point of view."

"You're right," Ramona said. "That's exactly what he's doing."

Satisfied with the setup, Charlie sat on the edge of the bed facing the camera. He spoke quietly. "I didn't want any of this to happen. I had no part in her death. I want that on record. No part. I'm sorry, terribly sorry, for what happened. The other guys are scouting out a spot to dump the body and make sure no one is around to see. I don't know what to do. I—"

He stopped because voices could be heard outside.

Charlie hung his head as the sliding door opened.

"All right," Tweed said off screen, "party's winding down next door. Nobody's outside anymore. It's time to move the body. And you're doing it, that's for sure."

"Let's just get this over with," a voice said.

Sweeping in front of Charlie wasn't Dan Rosenhip. Clearly not. It was a young Edwin Keating. He stopped on the other side of the bed and slid his arms under Hallie's body.

Charlie looked over his shoulder at him. "What'd you give her anyway? How'd you screw this up so badly?"

Keating had begun to pick up Hallie, but suddenly dropped her onto the bed and stared at Charlie. "Not my fault," he snapped. "Get that into your head. Anyway, it doesn't matter at this point."

Charlie scoffed. "Doesn't matter? It certainly matters. You killed her." He pointed across the bed at Keating. "How's it not your fault?"

Edwin Keating batted the finger away, then threw the fastest punch I think I've ever seen. Charlie's head snapped back toward the camera as he slid off the edge of the bed. He sputtered and moaned and called Keating some colorful names.

Keating carried on. "It's not my fault because the drug must've been laced with something. Just ask—"

"Enough!" Tweed interrupted. "Enough, you two." His voice was still off camera. "We all have to work together on this."

Charlie sat up on the floor, pleading, "Guys, let's not do this. We don't have to do this. Please. Why don't we just leave her in the backyard somewhere?"

"Don't be stupid," Keating said. "If we do that, they'll assume extreme alcohol poisoning or a drug overdose."

"So," Charlie said. "So what?"

"So then they'll do a full toxicology report to determine how a perfectly healthy nineteen-year-old could just pass out and die on the lawn. Which will launch an investigation and could lead to us."

"Us?!" Charlie squealed. "What do you mean us? And what did you give her anyway?"

"Doesn't matter," Keating snapped. "We need to make this look like an accident."

"STOP saying that!" Charlie yelled. "It does matter. It does."

Duke Tweed came on screen, kneeling beside Charlie. "Listen, we can't bring her back. That's the takeaway here. We need to make this look like an accident, which it truly is. An accidental overdose."

Charlie was about to say something, but Tweed held up his hand. "I get it, Charlie. I do. I understand your concerns. But we might as well do this since we can't bring her back. Nobody gets prison time for an accident. Right? Nobody's reputation or future is ruined."

While Charlie buried his face in his arms, Tweed stood and addressed Keating. "What alcohol did she drink tonight?"

"Vodka," he said.

"Go get a bottle from your dad's stash."

About thirty seconds later, Keating returned with a bottle in hand.

"Sit her upright," Tweed said to Keating. "Hold her head up and prop her mouth open."

As Keating struggled to hold Hallie's body up, Tweed snapped an order at Charlie. "Don't just sit there, help him out. I've got to pour."

Charlie stood and backed away from the bed. "I may carry this to the grave with me, Duke, but I'm certainly not helping any longer. Not a chance."

He stormed off, sweeping the camera off the table in the process. While the lens faced the ground and the camcorder bounced from Charlie's steps, it kept recording.

Though you couldn't see Tweed and Keating, you could hear them.

Tweed said, "Hold her steady, will ya."

"I'm trying. Will this even work? If she's dead can she swallow the alcohol?"

"Maybe, maybe not. But if it gets all over her, that's okay. She'll reek like booze then."

The next sound was the slider. Following that, the camera really started bouncing as Charlie ran across the back lawn, breathing incredibly hard. He suddenly stopped and fumbled with the camera.

Immediately the screen went blank.

CHAPTER FIFTY-THREE

RAMONA AND I didn't speak to each other for close to a full minute. The television screen in the den went from black to snowy. The only sound in the room was the crackling of a spent video.

Ramona slowly turned toward me. "No point in letting Hattie see this, right?"

"Not a chance," I said. "Don't even think we should tell her about it."

"Probably wise."

I heard movement behind me. I turned to see Murkowitz entering the den.

"By the looks on your faces," he said, "I take it you watched the video."

"Tell me," I said, "please tell me Tweed's going to pay for his part. Tell me that."

"Listen," he said, "I can't tell you exactly what's going to happen, at least not the specifics. Exact sentencing is up to a federal judge. I can tell you he isn't getting what he hoped for." Murkowitz shook his head. "That smug bastard and his even smugger lawyer had the audacity to bargain for tampering with evidence as a misdemeanor. I couldn't believe it. I almost walked out on the whole deal after hearing that."

He expanded on what that meant when he saw our confused looks.

"Tampering with a corpse falls under the broader jurisdiction of tampering with evidence. And that charge can be a misdemeanor or felony depending on the severity of the cover-up. They shouldn't have even asked for me to consider a misdemeanor charge. Ridiculous."

"Okay," Ramona said, "so what kind of sentencing are we talking about for a felony tampering with evidence charge?"

"Max is twenty years when it comes to covering up a murder and obstructing justice." When he saw our excited faces, he held up his hands. "Don't hold your breath on twenty years. I bet a judge gives him ten."

"And what would he actually serve?" I asked.

Murkowitz shrugged. "Back in the day, most of it. With good behavior a year or two might've been shaved off. Nowadays, with the overcrowding in our federal penal system, I'd say he serves five years at most."

"Five years," Ramona spat. "You're kidding."

I walked out of the room.

While Ramona got heated with Murkowitz, I stewed outside the den and thought about Tweed in prison. With all his money, no doubt he'd pay off the guards and the warden and live in relative luxury. A tampering with evidence conviction wouldn't put him in some super max, uncomfortable prison. He'd be housed in some low threat comfortable facility.

I stormed back into the room and interrupted them. "What about him buying the banks and accessing the safe deposit boxes? What about that? He admitted to illegally tampering with them."

"Honestly," Murkowitz said, "we'll prosecute him for it, but it will amount to a slap on the wrist, in my opinion." He gestured at the TV. "He basically gave back what he took, so it won't add considerable time to his sentence."

"What about Cunningham?" Ramona asked. "Please don't tell us he gets some sweetheart deal, too."

"Hell no," Murkowitz shot back. "Baker Cunningham knew better. He knows if he ever sets foot on American soil, he'll go away for life. He didn't even ask about reduced prison time."

"What did he want then?" I asked.

"His assets. Didn't want us to go after him financially."

"Did you agree?" Ramona asked.

Murkowitz nodded. "We felt it was worth it, though he didn't have as much direct evidence as we would've liked. Apparently, all direct communication between him and Keating went through a super secure email server and Cunningham deleted all emails after reading them. But he did completely back up Duke Tweed's story."

"That's it?" I snapped. "That's all you got from him?"

"No, he also has direct proof of a huge sum paid to him from Keating."

I shook my head. "So Cunningham lives his life in the tropics with a small fortune to his name? Great. Sounds sweetheart to me."

"Maybe so," Murkowitz said. "But if he screws up and tries to come home or set foot in a different country that will work with us, we'll nab him."

I walked out again.

At the kitchen table, Duke Tweed and his lawyer were signing documents. Tweed had been fully prepared for this. There was a wireless printer right on the table spitting out official documents.

Ramona followed me outside. After some silent reflection, she said, "Not sure about this justice system of ours."

"Me neither," I quickly responded.

As we stood and watched the scene next door, an FBI agent in a blue jacket swept across the grass toward our direction.

"Agent Sanchez," the agent said once within speaking distance.

"Yes," Ramona replied.

"We found another woman in the house next door."

CHAPTER FIFTY-FOUR

"ANOTHER WOMAN?" I said. "Who?"

"Hattie Lattimer," the agent said.

"Where is she?" I jumped off the porch and hurried over to the agent. Ramona trailed behind. "How is she?"

"Pretty good. We found her in a closet on the main floor office. She'd been shot in the hand, but she wrapped it well, so she's stable."

I breathed a sigh of relief.

"In fact," the agent continued, "the paramedics wanted to bring her out in a stretcher and take her straight to the hospital. But Ms. Lattimer walked out on her own accord. And—"

I interrupted. "Where is she now?"

The agent thumbed over her shoulder. "Back of the ambulance being attended to. She's insisting on seeing you both before going to the hospital."

The ambulance was parked at the bottom of Keating's driveway. Ramona and I hustled in that direction. When we got close to the ambulance, we could hear Hattie speaking.

"I have to speak with them," she was saying.

A moment later she climbed out of the ambulance. When she saw me, she walked over and wrapped her arms around my waist.

With her face buried in the middle of my chest, she said, "It was Keating. Edwin Keating, not Dan Rosenhip. He killed my sister."

When she looked up, I nodded.

She swallowed. "I shot him."

"I know." I motioned toward Ramona. "We know. We were first on the scene. Saw the body, also saw the Springfield by the doorframe. What happened anyway? Where'd you go?"

She pulled back from the embrace. "The driver, or bodyguard or whoever he was, fired two shots at me after I took Keating down. One bullet hit me in the hand, which knocked the gun out. I slammed the door and locked it, then opened the sliding door. But I knew with my busted toe and gunshot wound I'd likely be caught if I ran outside. So I took my bleeding hand"—she held up her bandaged hand—"and whipped it out the door to leave a blood trail going outside."

She mimicked the flicking movement she'd made. "Just before he broke down the door, I wrapped up my hand with my shirt and hid in the closet. It wasn't hard staying quiet since I was in and out of consciousness."

"Smart," Ramona said. "Real smart, Hattie. That move probably saved your life."

I was about to agree, but Hattie's eyes went wide. I didn't look back to see what she was looking at because Slim suddenly stepped into view and distracted me. He was a little way past Keating's house, and he had a large man in a headlock. The police at the far end of the crime scene area were questioning him.

Seconds later, I turned and saw what Hattie was looking at. Duke Tweed, his lawyer, and Murkowitz had left the house and were walking across the front lawn, deep in conversation.

Hattie was frozen in place with her mouth agape.

To snap her out of it, I gestured behind her. "Looks like Slim captured Keating's man, the man who shot you."

Her eyes flicked up at me. She furrowed her brow. "You mean Duke Tweed's man. Speaking of Tweed, why's he not cuffed? What the hell's going on?"

Ramona stepped between us. "Hattie, you said Duke Tweed's man. Don't you mean Edwin Keating's man?"

Hattie jabbed her finger at Duke. "Why's his face all beat up and his wrists raw like that? That's not how I saw him last."

Just like that, things started dawning on me.

Hattie looked between Ramona and me. "He should be cuffed and in the back of a cruiser. Why's he walking free?" When we didn't respond, she snapped, "Why?! What's going on?"

Still in shock, I couldn't respond, so Ramona did.

"Tweed made a deal, Hattie. He gave up Edwin Keating."

"A deal?" she seethed. "What do you mean a deal?"

Ramona continued. "Tweed and Baker Cunningham, the leader of the left-wing militia, turned over evidence on Keating."

"And Tweed got a deal?" Hattie said incredulously. "What sort of deal?"

"He'll get between five and ten years for tampering with evidence, for covering up your sister's murder."

"What?" Hattie turned to me and grabbed my side with her good hand. "Tell me that's not true. Tell me there's no deal. Please. Keating killed Hallie and got what he deserved, but Duke also played a big part. And he's behind everything else."

She gestured at Tweed and the lawyers moving our direction. When Tweed saw Hattie, he immediately stopped. By the stunned look on his face, I knew without a doubt he was one hundred percent guilty, that the man had just fed us a smorgasbord of lies.

"Tell me it's not true," she said, shaking me with her good hand. "Tell me we can rip up any deal that was made."

I knew they'd already inked a deal. And I didn't know if it would be null and void now. I assumed so, but I hesitated to respond.

Since I stayed silent, Hattie shot a look at Ramona. "Tell me they'll rip it up."

Ramona hesitated, too.

The next few seconds were like a time warp. Everything seemed to happen in a blink of an eye, but also in super slow motion. I felt Hattie's left hand reach behind my back and slide the Walther out. She extended it toward Tweed, who stood stationary, about twenty feet away, still looking shocked.

Suddenly she blasted forward, screaming one word: "NEVER!"

Hattie seemed to cover fifteen feet in milliseconds. Stopping five feet from Tweed, she aimed at his head.

From the side, I could see the gnarled, twisted look on her face. Before I had a chance to yell out her name, Hattie Lattimer pulled the Walther's trigger.

And drove a bullet between Duke Tweed's eyes.

CHAPTER FIFTY-FIVE

TWEED CRUMPLED TO the pavement in a lifeless heap.

I ran toward Hattie, stopping a few feet away.

She had a wild look in her eye and was pivoting the gun between the lawyers. Both men cowered on the ground.

Two cops ran over, shouting, "Drop the gun! Drop it now."

Three nearby FBI agents had drawn their service weapons and cautiously approached.

"RIP IT UP," Hattie yelled at the lawyers. "Take back the deal," she seethed.

I tried to calm her down. "It's over, Hattie. Tweed's dead, so's the deal. Put down the gun. Please."

She didn't listen and yelled out the orders again, continuing to point and wave the Walther between the men, demanding them to rip up the paperwork.

I knew she likely wouldn't fire at them, but the cops didn't. They screamed another command to drop the gun. The younger male cop on the left was tightening his finger on the trigger.

"Don't shoot, Officers," I said calmly. "Hattie, drop the gun. Please. I know you're not going to shoot these men."

Unfortunately, she didn't drop the gun. And when the cops shouted another order to put down the weapon and Hattie didn't comply, I focused on the male cop and his tightening trigger finger. He wasn't about to let Hattie fire again.

Just as the cop squeezed the trigger, I jumped in front of Hattie with my left arm outstretched. A boom rang out, then a searing pain exploded into my forearm as I dropped to my knees.

"Garrison!" Ramona shouted from behind me.

When Hattie saw I'd been hit, she dropped the Walther and covered her mouth. But the cops and FBI agents descended on her quickly, so she turned and ran.

I got to my feet and staggered after her.

"STOP!" Ramona yelled after me.

"Please, Chase." It was Slim's voice. "You're bleeding everywhere."

I turned and kept walking backward. "Don't shoot. Nobody shoot. Let me talk to her. She has nowhere to go back there. Let me handle it. Please."

"I'm coming with," Ramona said, sweeping alongside me.

"Me too," Slim said, hustling behind her.

I eyed him. "Please, pal, just stay. I don't want a bunch of people back there freaking her out."

He reluctantly nodded.

I hustled after Hattie, who'd disappeared between the houses.

"Let me do it, Garrison," Ramona said. "I'll talk with her. You need to get your arm looked at."

But I steamed ahead, unfazed by my bloody, throbbing forearm. When I entered the backyard, I could see Hattie had stopped about ten feet from the cliff's edge. The same spot where they'd dumped her sister's body.

As I approached, Hattie turned. Her angry, red face was gone. Surprisingly, her demeanor was calm. A few tears rolled down her cheeks, but she wasn't sobbing.

"Stop, you two," she said. "No farther."

Ramona stopped, but I took two more steps until I was ten feet away.

"You shouldn't have done that," Hattie said, motioning at my bloody, dripping arm. "Are you okay?"

"I'll be fine, survived quite a few gunshots."

Hattie gestured behind me. "I was fine with being shot back there. I appreciate you trying to protect me, Chase. I appreciate everything you've done for me. Without you, we wouldn't have gotten Hallie's killers. Without your relentless pursuit, Duke and Edwin would still be free and breathing. But you shouldn't have taken a bullet for me. It's over for me."

I took a step. "Don't say that, Hattie."

"Don't take another step. I mean it."

I waved her toward me with my good hand. "Just come back from the edge, let's talk about this."

"You don't understand. I mean, you couldn't. It is over. For good. I'm not spending a second in a prison cell. Not one second."

"Help us understand," Ramona said from behind me. "Come back from the edge and let's talk about this."

Hattie shook her head. "You won't understand. I was at peace after killing Keating; haven't felt true peace like that for twenty-five years. I could've died in that closet and been okay with it. But I hung on because I wanted to make sure Tweed also got the justice he deserved."

I was about to say something, but Hattie held up her good hand and stopped me.

"I aimlessly wandered this earth since Hallie's death. Been alone, confused, and wondering what my purpose was. Why did I get to live and not my sister? Why did I get bronchitis that week and not her? Not a day in two decades went by that I haven't had those thoughts. Not a single day. Now I know why I lived."

"Hattie," I pleaded, "please just step toward me."

"You guys will need this." She pulled out her phone and tossed it onto the grass. "An audio recording of Duke and Edwin before I shot him. Password for the phone is 1970: the year Hallie and I were born."

"Let's listen to it together," Ramona offered.

Hattie didn't respond to that. "My destiny and purpose in life was to bring justice for Hallie. Now my purpose is complete."

As she turned, I shouted, "No, Hattie, don't, just stay right there."

She pivoted back, just a little. "You're a good man, Garrison Chase. You're the last good man that I'll ever have the pleasure of knowing."

With that, she turned and ran.

So did I.

"No, Hattie!" I jumped and tried to grasp her feet as she launched off the cliff.

I landed and skidded on my chest, swiping at empty air. Hattie's legs bicycled in midair for a few seconds, then she plummeted into the dark abyss.

With just my head protruding over the cliff's edge, I listened to her final scream.

At first, I thought it was a typical scream of terror. But right before it suddenly stopped, I deciphered what she was screaming.

Her sister's name.

CHAPTER FIFTY-SIX

I WOKE TO a foggy haze and the smell of a pleasant perfume in the air. To my right, I saw a woman's outline walking toward the bed I was currently lying in. My vision was cloudy so I couldn't tell who it was. *Maybe Karla? Had she flown in on a red-eye?*

The woman gently touched my right arm. I blinked a few times, until Ramona Sanchez came into focus. "How you feeling?" she asked.

I swallowed. "Like I just came out of emergency surgery."

"A dad joke right out of the gate." She smiled. "You must be doing okay."

I leaned on my good arm and struggled to a sitting position. Ramona handed me some ice water to sip on. I was shuttled to the hospital right after Hattie plunged off the cliff. The bullet hadn't exited my arm, so the ER doc wanted me in surgery right away. It wasn't a life-threatening situation; the doc just needed to quickly take out the bullet and repair the tendon damage.

After a few sips, I said, "What'd I miss last night?"

"A lot," she responded. "Mainly Search & Rescue getting Hattie's body off the shore before the tide swept it off the rocks."

I nodded. "That was intense."

"Very." Ramona collapsed into the hospital chair to my right. We were in a recovery room, so there was just a green sheet around my bed.

After a moment, I ran my good hand over my scalp. "I could've stopped her, Ramona. I totally could've."

She eyed me. "What do you mean?"

"I mean, all I could think about before going into surgery was Hattie reaching for my gun. I felt her do it; I knew what she was up to. And I could've stopped her. Could've grabbed her hand or knocked the gun away. But I stood there and let her shoot Tweed."

"Garrison, come on, I was there, it all happened so quickly. Within seconds."

"It did, you're right. Just being honest, though, I could've stopped her. I know that now. Not sure if a good man would let that happen, even if we are talking about a bastard like Duke Tweed. And if she hadn't shot Tweed, well, then Hattie would still—"

"Enough," Ramona interrupted. She grabbed her leather valise and pulled out an evidence bag. As she approached the bed, she extracted Hattie's cell phone and placed it on my lap.

"You listen to the recording Hattie took. Then don't waste another second thinking that thought. Not a single second. Duke Tweed was more involved in Hallie's death than we knew. Way more."

She took her purse and pulled out some earbuds, then motioned at the open room we were in. "Better use these, too."

As she turned to leave, I asked, "Where you going?"

"While you listen to that—which isn't too long—I'm going to check up on Senator Fornetti. She was taken here, too. I'll be back in a bit."

"Before you go," I said, "what happened with Baker Cunningham? That's been bothering me. Since Tweed and Cunningham lied about everything, is Murkowitz able to renege on the deal with Cunningham?"

"Murkowitz said yes, but it's complicated."

"How so?"

"Cunningham's lawyer, of course. He'll fight the reversal since there was an actual signed deal. In the end, Murkowitz said the government will rip up Cunningham's deal because it's predicated on lies. But that will take months to officially resolve. And by that time—"

"Cunningham will have spent or hidden all his money anyway, so it's moot."

"Exactly."

I shook my head and looked away.

"I know," she said, "that really bothers me, too."

"What bothers me more is Senator Logan Mills. His death, in particular his son watching his father die like that. If it wasn't for me intervening and killing Sherman Adams, then Cunningham—"

She pointed at me. "Again, don't go there; don't you dare. Listen to that tape. It's an order." With that, she left.

I couldn't help but think about it, however. For Hattie and Hallie Lattimer, justice was served. All three men involved in Hallie's death and cover-up were six feet under. But Cunningham hired men to kill and kidnap United States senators, solely for money. He left a wake of destruction behind, devastating multiple families. And that guy got to live the rest of his life in tropical luxury.

My mind wandered down a questionable path, so I refocused and slipped in the earbuds. Then I punched in the password and listened to the recording, which started in the middle of Tweed and Keating's conversation.

"Together," Duke Tweed was saying, "we were supposed to be together on this. We should've kept handling this as a team."

"Please," Keating scoffed. "It spiraled way out of control, Duke, you know that. What could you have done? Nothing."

"You didn't even give me a chance."

"You're full of it," Keating said. "Always were, Duke. I mean, you said Cunningham and Adams had a flawless plan to kill Cooper and Byrd and get the letter. Flawless, you said. How wrong were you there? And Charlie, don't get me going. The perfect murder. With his preexisting condition, nobody would be the wiser, you said. You had no clue he'd penned those letters. Plus, your men couldn't find and silence Hattie Lattimer. No, Duke, I absolutely had to intervene. I had to take control after your screw-ups ruined it for both of us."

"And trying to kill me was your genius plan? Just how foolish are you, Edwin? You can't double-cross someone like me. I'm the double-crosser. I know you had the original video and that story of yours, but killing me? You don't have the criminal mind or connections to pull off something like that. Except, of course, you knew Cunningham. And I bet you thought he'd do anything for you because of the huge sum you paid."

Tweed paused. When Keating didn't respond, he carried on. "You have a ton of money, Edwin, but nothing like what I have. Nothing. Cunningham didn't even contemplate killing me, just so you know. It was an incredibly naïve and stupid mistake. Cunningham's a savvy businessman and played you off of me. When he told me what you gave him to kill me, I gave him ten percent more to reverse the hit and grab you. Plus, he threw in the missing senator. She's upstairs, by the way. When the cops find your dead body here, you'll go down for all the senators' murders. Plus, the kidnapping. You clearly don't have the stomach or mind for this type of business."

"I guess you're right, Duke, I can't compete with someone like you. Somebody as deceptive and manipulative as you. Somebody who's spent his life—"

"You're going to take the moral high road here? Unbelievable. From the guy who planned to pin a murder on his dead best friend, not to mention hire someone to kill me. And, for the record, everything that's been done here is because of your screw-up with Hallie. Your horrible mistake, not mine. I've been trying to clean up your mess and protect you for twenty-five years."

"What!" Keating shouted. "You have amnesia, Duke? You gave me the drugs that killed her; you're as guilty in Hallie's death as I am. You've been protecting yourself all along, not just me."

"You gave her way more than I told you," Tweed shouted back. "Way more. You must've!"

"I didn't; I've told you that a hundred times. The drugs you provided were laced with something. Just shut the hell up and don't pretend you're any better than me."

Another voice suddenly piped in. "Both of you shut the hell up." It was Hattie.

A brief pause, then, "For Hallie."

A gunshot fired, followed by two more.

Then Hattie breathing heavily and moving about the office. I could tell what happened in the room played out the way Hattie had described it. I could hear her shallow breathing once she'd eased herself into the closet.

I could also hear the office door being kicked in, then Tweed shouting to his man, "Get her! Make sure she never sees the light of day. And don't bring her back here." After a brief pause: "Wait. Come back."

"What, sir?"

"Hit me hard, a few times. Quickly. I need my face messed up."

"Sir?"

"Just do it. Then grab the rope and saw away at my wrists."

"Seriously?"

Tweed sighed. "I have to pivot and change the entire story now."

A brief pause. "Got it, sir."

Seconds later I heard fist on face a few times.

Following that, silence, as Hattie must've stopped the recording.

I blew out a huge breath and looked up at the ceiling. For a while I stayed in that position, awash in thoughts about Duke Tweed and Edwin Keating and the things they did to cover their tracks. For twenty-five years. The lies, the guilt, the cover-up, which ultimately pitted the two against each other. I also wondered what other corruption Duke Tweed had been engaged in with other senators or congressmen.

Eventually, I picked up the cell and tried to shut it down. Since I wasn't familiar with iPhones, I swiped the screen. Instead of the phone turning off, however, Hattie's music player came on. It started playing the last song she'd listened to. I immediately recognized it as a famous one by the old British punk rock band The Kinks. The song was called "Money and Corruption." The lyrics referred to crooked politicians betraying people and pocketing profits.

Listening to that particular song wasn't coincidental for Hattie. Not a chance. She probably listened to it over and over, maybe to remind herself of exactly what she was up against.

After the song finished playing, I thought about Keating and Milliken and how those men were supposed leaders in our government. How they should've been above reproach, above corruption. And how Duke Tweed was a major influence in our democracy, simply because of the unholy amount of money he possessed.

I found myself squeezing the phone with my good hand, so I pulled out the earbuds and shifted to get more comfortable in the hospital bed before closing my eyes. To clear my mind, I thought about Simon. I missed my son and couldn't wait to get back to him. *How long would that be, though? How long would I be cooped up here?*

The sound of the curtain sliding back pulled me from my thoughts.

I opened my eyes to see Ramona at the foot of the bed.

"How's the senator?" I asked.

"Fine. She'll make a full recovery, though she doesn't remember anything about the abduction or what happened after." She motioned at Hattie's cell on my stomach. "How about that recording? What do you think?"

"I think you're absolutely right."

She tilted her head slightly to the right. "Right about what?"

"About Hattie shooting Tweed. I'm not going to spend another second thinking about how it all went down. About what I could've done to stop her."

Ramona walked over to the side of the bed and placed her warm hand on top of mine. "Good."

I eyed her and smiled. "Not one single second."

CHAPTER FIFTY-SEVEN

Eight months later
Maldives, Indian Ocean

BREATHING UNDERWATER WAS everything scuba diving fanatics said it was. It felt otherworldly to me as I drifted along the edge of the reef and listened to my own breaths reverberate in my ear. The real world above me seemed far off. As I floated through the depths of the Indian Ocean and marveled at its turquoise beauty, life above water seemed temporarily suspended.

But the feeling didn't last. I was brought back to reality when the dive guide waved me around the corner of the reef and motioned to follow him deeper. With the rest of the dive group far behind, the guide and I stopped our descent at ninety feet and hung motionless in the deep blue sea.

We were all alone.

The guide pointed upward, at the underside of the magnificent reef. It teemed with thousands of colorful fish. But I didn't focus on the beautiful sight.

Instead, I had a violent thought.

Over the past eight months, I'd completed beginner, intermediate, and advanced levels of scuba diving training, so I knew what I could do to this man. His backup regulator was clipped to his right shoulder. It was within my grasp. I could grab that with one hand, yank the other regulator out of his mouth, then pull off his mask. With my long reach, I could hold both regulators behind him. Meanwhile, as he struggled, I'd deflate my buoyancy compensator vest and drag him deeper. Since I far outweighed the man, fighting him off and holding him down wouldn't be a problem.

The dive guide waved his hand in front of my mask, snapping me out of my daydream. He gave me the okay sign. I smiled and gave it back.

Recently, I'd had an uptick of violent daydreams. Of course, I wouldn't act on any of them, but their frequency, if I was being honest, disturbed me a little.

Two minutes later, the rest of the group joined our little sea huddle. When the dive ended and we all surfaced together, the guide pulled off his mask and addressed me with a huge grin.

"How was that? Beautiful dive, don't you reckon?"

I winked. "I reckon so, Dennis."

I so wanted to call him Baker. All week I reminded myself to not call him by that name. In the Maldives, Baker Cunningham went by the alias Dennis Dwyer.

Slim was the only person who knew I was here to confront him. Everyone else thought I was on a surfing and scuba diving trip in Hawaii.

As we motored back to the Surf 'n Dive Resort, Dennis Dwyer stood at the front of the boat with a half dozen guests. He engaged in cheery conversation with his clients. Midway back, he pointed out some bottlenose dolphins and looked genuinely enthused about the sighting.

Though I knew it was unlikely, I'd hoped to arrive in the Maldives and witness a struggling Baker Cunningham. A man struggling with his business, and hopefully struggling personally as well. Unfortunately, I found the exact opposite. The man was thriving.

He'd bought a gorgeous white-sand island with two dozen over-the-water bungalows. He'd also purchased one large dive boat, a smaller one, and a hefty fishing/surfing vessel. Worse, the jerk was as happy as they come.

The captain pulled the boat into a tranquil, sheltered harbor. Once at the dock, three of Cunningham's workers helped the clients disembark, handing us Mai Tais as we stepped onto land. They were also there to promote the big night dive, encouraging every guest to be at the dock at eight p.m.

This was my last night in the Maldives, and I had no intention of going. I'd been planning the perfect setup for the past six nights. Tonight was my night to strike.

Around six p.m. I came down with a fake earache, which wasn't uncommon for new divers like me. I was the only guest to stay back, which was exactly what I'd hoped and planned for.

At nine p.m., everything on the island shut down for the night. Since it was a small island, Cunningham's employees didn't live here, so all the evening resort workers left on a boat at precisely nine-fifteen.

Once the island was desolate, I got to work. I pulled out my large surfboard bag from under the bed. Not only did it hold two of my boards, it also held the contraband I'd smuggled into the country.

It didn't take long for Slim and me to find Baker's exact whereabouts in the Maldives. What took time—aside from learning to scuba dive—was figuring out how to get Cunningham extradited. Most of my ideas revolved around narcotics. I wanted to plant drugs in his resort, then call in the authorities and frame him as a drug dealer. The problem with that was I had to actually get a hold of narcotics. And the last thing I wanted was to get caught red-handed with drugs in a foreign country. I had a son and other loved ones to think about.

As a result of the risks, Slim encouraged me to let everything go. But, of course, I couldn't. All I could think about was Logan Mills's son growing up without a father, and of the devastation that happened to Morse Cooper's and Felton Byrd's families. And of the nightmares that Rachel Fornetti was likely dealing with after being kidnapped and drugged for days.

No, I had to do something to bring the scales of justice back in alignment; I simply had to be smart about it.

Ironically, Slim provided my current idea for retribution. After telling him I had no intention of letting things go with Cunningham, he sent me a small New Testament pocket Bible in the mail. He'd stuck a bookmark in Romans, chapter twelve. In verse nineteen, he highlighted the phrase: *Vengeance is mine, I will repay.*

The entire verse read: *Do not avenge yourselves, but rather give place to wrath; for it is written, "Vengeance is Mine, I will repay," says the Lord.*

Naturally, Slim was encouraging me to leave it alone and allow God to bring the scales of justice back in alignment. However, I spent far too much time overthinking the verse. So much so, I eventually perverted it to my favor.

Perhaps, I thought, *I was the vessel God would use to mete out justice in this case.*

I pulled out two dozen New Testaments from my surfboard bag and laid them on my bed. Earlier in the day, I'd swung by the main office and swiped a resort stamp, which contained the name of the resort along with relevant contact information. It was perfect.

I opened the Bibles and stamped each one on the inside cover. Each New Testament also contained a bookmark that doubled as an evangelical tract. I loaded everything into a small backpack and left the bungalow.

During my research phase on the Maldives, I learned just how fanatical the country was when it came to religion. The island nation was one hundred percent Muslim. Not only was Islam the state religion, citizens were actually required by law to follow it. The government had zero tolerance for Christianity or proselytizing. I'd read about a few recent missionaries who were kicked out of the country for pedaling their faith.

From what I gathered, these missionaries weren't held in jail or tortured or anything like that. They were simply flown home and given persona non grata status. If I was caught red-handed with a bunch of Bibles, nothing bad would happen to me. The government would simply send me back to my family.

In my mind, it was a sure bet to get Baker Cunningham back on American soil to rot in prison.

I moved quickly down the elevated wharf, stopping at each bungalow and knocking. Nobody answered, of course, so I snuck in and placed a stamped New Testament in the drawer of each nightstand.

Only three of the doors were locked on the two dozen bungalows I visited. Which wasn't a problem. I ambled down the wraparound deck and entered the bungalow via the sliding door on the back veranda. Nobody kept that door locked.

My last stop of the evening was Baker Cunningham's residence, which was also a bungalow, except his was inland a little way. In a fitting tribute, I left the New Testament Slim had sent me in Cunningham's nightstand. And I conveniently left it open to Romans chapter twelve.

Then I had an amazing night of sleep.

In the morning, I used the phone in the main office to hail a water taxi to take me to the airport—and to also call the authorities.

I was soon on the dock with my luggage and surfboard bag, waiting for the taxi and thinking about home. I looked forward to getting back to normal with Simon, Karla, and Mom. I'd been distracted with Cunningham the past eight months, so I hadn't been fully present with the important people in my life. My son couldn't tell, but Karla and Mom certainly could.

I had some damage control to do back home.

To my surprise, the local police boat actually beat the water taxi to the resort. Five policemen jumped off the boat and stormed the island. Three of them went bungalow to bungalow while the other two headed to Cunningham's place.

From the dock, I could hear shouts and yelling from Cunningham's house, so I went to witness the scene. When I arrived at his bungalow, a number of other guests were there as well, wondering what was going on.

Cunningham was yelling, "You can't do this! What right do you have? What are you looking for anyway?"

Two other guests and I walked over to the bungalow's window, which was right by the front door. One policeman was holding

Cunningham back while the other tossed the place. Eventually, they opened the nightstand and proclaimed, "Ah-ha!"

Cunningham rushed over and peered into the nightstand, confused for a moment.

The officer beside him started berating him concerning the illegality of promoting a different faith.

Cunningham kept screeching, "That's not mine! It's not mine."

The other three cops descended on the bungalow. They rushed in and threw a bunch of New Testaments on Cunningham's bed.

One of them said, "Appears they're in every room, sir."

Cunningham was frothing and incredulous and shouting. Three cops dragged him kicking and screaming out of the bungalow. The two guests beside me cleared out of the way.

But I didn't. I stepped in behind the fracas and yelled, "Baker. Hey, Baker Cunningham."

Dennis Dwyer, AKA Baker Cunningham, suddenly stopped writhing and slowly looked backward.

The look on his face brought a huge smile to mine.

He managed, "What? What's going on? Who are you?"

I didn't answer. Instead, I quoted:

"Vengeance is mine, I will repay."

AUTHOR'S NOTE

Dear Reader,

Thank you for taking the time to read my book. I hope you enjoyed ALL THE GOOD MEN. If you did, I'd be grateful if you'd consider leaving a review on Amazon.com and/or Goodreads.com. Reviews are extremely helpful!

If you'd like to learn more about me, the Garrison Chase thriller series, or sign up for my newsletter, please visit my website at:

craignhooper.com

I'm also giving away a free ebook to all my fans! FALLOUT, the prequel to the Garrison Chase series, is FREE when you sign up for my newsletter. Please visit my website to get your free copy.

If you have any questions or comments, please don't hesitate to reach out at craig@craignhooper.com. I absolutely love hearing from fans!

Thanks for being a reader.

ALSO BY CRAIG N. HOOPER

Fallout (FREE!)

The Greatest Good

A Thin Line

All the Good Men

The Garrison Chase Series (Books 1-3)

Made in the USA
Las Vegas, NV
18 July 2021